Acclaim for KS Turner's Ch

Innovative and startlingly or
provoking. A triumph
BOOKTIME

Epic, tension-packed, loaded with mysteries and believable characters. A compelling read.
SPIRIT & DESTINY

Our reviewer was blown away by the book. Imaginative and speculative. Unique. More please.
BOOKBAG

Seamlessly unravels an irresistible narrative. . . wonderful.
DIVA

Refreshing and accomplished works of speculative fiction that are both thought-provoking and entertaining.
FANTASY BOOK REVIEW

A tantalising mix. . . no ordinary fiction.
THE LIST

Imaginative, quick moving, set above standard fantasy.
BOOKSELLER

Filled to the brim with an eloquent, seamless fusion of fantasy and science fiction.
***** Must Read Now
SCIFI NOW

Also by KS Turner

BEFORE THE GODS
TUMULTUS

time: the immortal divide

The Chronicles of Fate and Choice

Book Three

τime: τhe immϕrτal divide

K.S. TURNER

RUBY BLAZE PUBLISHING

Published in Great Britain in 2016 by Ruby Blaze Publishing

Copyright © 2016 by KS Turner

The moral right of the author has been asserted

All characters and events in this publication, other than those clearly in the public domain, are fictitious, and any resemblance to real persons, living or dead, is purely coincidental.

All rights reserved.

No part of this publication may be reproduced, stored in a retrieval system, or transmitted, in any form or by any means, without the prior permission in writing of the publisher, nor be otherwise circulated in any form of binding or cover other than that in which it is published and without a similar condition including this condition being imposed on the subsequent purchaser.

A CIP catalogue record for this book is available from the British Library.

ISBN 9780956224293

Cover art by KS Turner.

Typeset in 11/13.8 Adobe Garamond Pro by Blaze Typesetting.

Ruby Blaze Publishing is committed to working with planet-friendly sustainable resources.

Ruby Blaze Publishing.

www.rubyblaze.com

For you, who choose.

Acknowledgements

My very special thanks go to you, the readers, whose imaginations bring these stories to life.

My thanks and love to Paul, for making a space in life's chaos to give me time to write; for his love, support and patience, and for being the perfect blend of wild abandon and considered choice.

To Stefania, my mum and friend, for her strength of will, gentle empathy, intelligent opinions, and encouragement to follow dreams.

To my friend and genius of an editor, Jeremy, who has been with me on my literary journey since day one. Everyone should have a friend like Jeremy. Every author should have an editor like Jeremy. Lucky me.

To Zoe, for her humour, honesty, and most of all, friendship. To my wonderful and eclectic family: my step-dad, Ian, my brother, James, my sister, Jenny, and all my gorgeous nephews and nieces. To David, Elaine, and the book-army. To Leslie, and all those in the literary world who have been part of this path. The list is long, so I will simply thank you all.

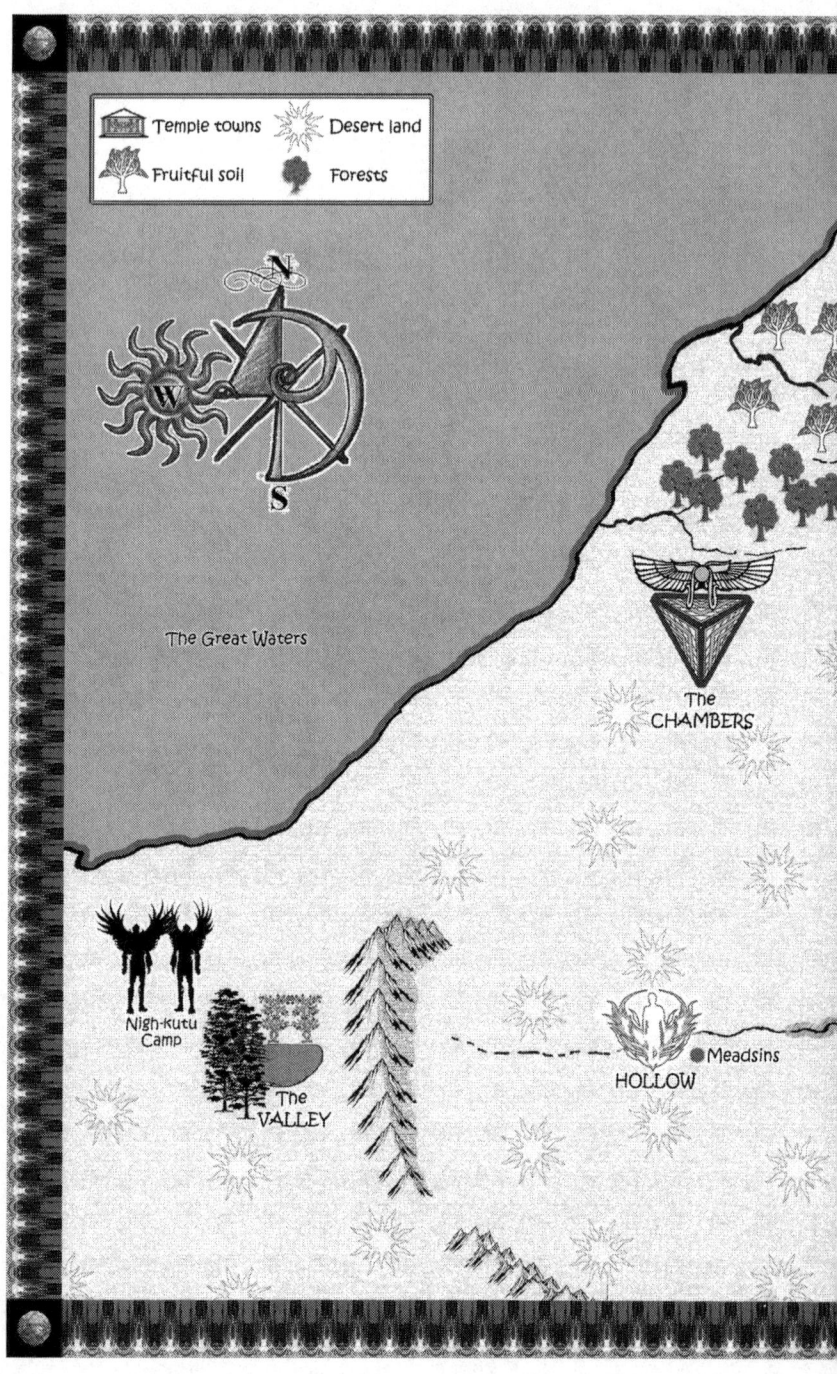

PROLOGUE

The Before

Before the Beginning...

In a time before time, when there was no such thing as time, and no such thing as right or wrong, everything was nothing and nothing was everything. All universes had a timeless consciousness. Consciousness naturally expanded, and universes enveloped each other; one rolling into another, one consciousness merging into the next. Growing and merging. Growing and merging. It was a natural fusion, until the last two universal consciousnesses remained.

The last two consciousnesses kept growing. Their destiny was that they would merge and become one.

At the moment the last two universal consciousnesses touched, realisation was born.

When realisation was born, time was formed.

When time and realisation came to be, choice was created.

The smaller of the consciousnesses realised that its end was close and did not want to lose its self-awareness. The larger consciousness realised that it did not want to envelop the smaller one, knowing that they were the last.

From that first realisation came the first choice.

The smaller consciousness chose not to merge with the other, and so fragmented, pulling itself into millions of pieces. The explosive fragmentation flung those pieces to distant galaxies. Some were pulled by the power of light and some by the strength of darkness. Each fragment was too incomplete for the larger one to merge with, yet was complete within itself, and no two pieces were the same. Those fragmented remains of the penultimate universal consciousness were many. Each piece was aware of time, realisation and choice. Each piece was conscious of itself. These pieces became a new race of beings. They became known as the kutu.

The Shaa-kutu were those drawn to the light. The Nigh-kutu were those drawn to the shadow. They inhabited opposite sides of existence, each unaware of the other.

The Shaa-kutu, as a whole, were beings of mind and thought. They enjoyed ascendancy by discovery. They found beauty in change, learning, sciences, the arts and engineering. They respected the differences in each other, accepting roles within their society that best suited who they were. As individuals, they worked as a whole for the best of the whole.

In contrast to the Shaa-kutu, the Nigh-kutu were beings of instinct and emotion. They enjoyed each moment for the moment. They found magnificence in vigour, craftsmanship, humour and brotherhood. They respected the strengths in each other and developed a hierarchical society where the strongest led, and those that followed did so willingly. Through the ages they divided into groups called clans, where those of similar makeup dwelled together.

All kutu, Nigh and Shaa, are ageless. They are strong, emotional, intelligent, driven and powerful. Their energy is visible to their kind; each a different hue, vibration, saturation and density. Through their energy they can see each other's thoughts, emotions and intentions, not just their form. All kutu exist in a state of energy and matter, and are able to live in any combination of the two.

Once the penultimate universal consciousness had fragmented

and become the kutu, the remaining universal consciousness realised that it was now the last and the most it could ever be. Knowing that it now filled all universes and touched all times, it centred its consciousness in a small planet, where it now sleeps. That planet has a name: Earth.

The last universal consciousness is neither a she nor a he. But for a word to have a word, I will call it a 'he'. He is everything and nothing, and all things in-between. He is all our yesterdays and tomorrows. He is past, present and future. He is all times and timeless. His consciousness is everywhere and he understands all things. He is both wonderful and terrible. He is the last.

The last universal consciousness has many names.

I simply call him the Old One.

My name is Tachra.

I was born second-generation human. My parents are both of the originals. The originals were created by the Shaa-kutu and placed here on Earth, along with other young human adults. They were prearranged in male-female pairs, designed to live and reproduce to sustain themselves and naturally fulfil their purpose. Their purpose was to harvest energies.

I was eighteen when I first discovered the kutu. At first, I was simply looking for my own answers. I had left my home in the idyllic village of Threetops and walked through wild-lands and villages, experiencing new lands and different cultures. I found people of all different types, and then I walked away from civilisation entirely. I walked through deserts and mountains, until my body was almost broken. Then, just when my flesh could endure no more, I found an isolated, bountiful valley. There, I made a heart-bond with a wildcat, Meah. I found the entirety of my link with the Old One. I found the ability to use his Voice and see with the true vision. And then I found the kutu.

I hadn't been looking for the kutu. At that time, I didn't know they existed. But the Shaa-kutu had been looking for me. They had thought that the Old One was a potent new energy to be harvested and that I was the human to harvest it for them. Those kutu soon learnt otherwise.

The Shaa-kutu had been shocked to learn the truth of what the Old One was, and of their own origins. They had thought that they were eternal beings. They discovered that they too had beginnings, albeit thousands of millennia ago. The small group of kutu who had travelled to Earth to discover a new energy, discovered instead that they had much to relearn.

At first I was apprehensive of these makers of humans, but once I came to know them, I came to love them. Those first few kutu that I met will always hold a special place in my heart.

Orion is the Shaa-kutu with raggedy red hair, wild red eyes, and an even wilder imagination. He is the embodiment of wonderment. He is the only red kutu. He has the perfect mix of theory and passion that creates artistic genius. He is highly respected as a kutu and is much loved.

Chia is the only Shaa-kutu I've met who has chosen to shave off all his hair. He is a sensitive, and has pure violet energy. He senses energy and intentions, but that does not make him a dreamer. He is proud, focused and thoughtful.

Kraniel has such an active mind. He can never hold fewer than a dozen thoughts at once, and each one could create a debate to last for millennia. He is the greatest analytical thinker and his humour is second to none. He is fast, singular and freethinking.

Stanze is one of the leaders of the Shaa-kutu Anumi warriors: tall, broad and rippling with strength. Stanze looks fearsome to those who do not know him. But he has the kindest heart, and his energy is as golden as his hair. He is honourable, brave and gentle.

And then there is Jychanumun. My black-eyed one.

Jychanumun is the one kutu for whom it says more about him to say nothing at all. He is not from the Shaa-kutu race. He is a Nigh-kutu. He chose to leave his own warring kind to exist with the Shaa-kutu. He is complex, silent, honest and resolute, with a rare combination of black and white energy. This precise meeting of opposites gives him unique skills. One such skill is that he can walk the paths between life and death. Another is that he can sense the Old One. Because of that, we can share thoughts.

Just as there are kutu who hold a special place in my heart, there are kutu whose choices I do not like. One is Shursa. Shursa wished to be more than he was. More powerful, beautiful, and respected. To attain that which he was not, he manipulated and deceived and took what was not his. His choices had terrible consequences. He facilitated an opening to the shadow. Through Shursa, the world was noticed by the warring Nigh-kutu.

The first time the shadow-dwelling Nigh-kutu came to Earth was short but terrible. As the Nigh-kutu attacked, the Shaa-kutu defended. It was potent aggression against protective might, each equal and opposite in strength, and both equally deadly. That kutu war could have finished all humanity, such was their ability.

I was almost killed in that short war. I was caught in the crossfire by a kutu weapon. The Old One healed me. He stopped time and made me whole again.

As the Old One stopped time and healed me, so the war between the kutu also stopped. I moved among them, awakening my friends, but most of the Nigh-kutu were too corrupt to awaken. So, instead, they had forgetfulness put in their minds and were sent back to their home-world. Those Nigh-kutu would not remember this place, or that fight, or any of us. When they awoke, they would have simply lost that memory.

After that first brief war, came peace. It was, to most, a beautiful and relaxed time. The Old One slept deeply, dreaming his endless dreams from infinity to eternity. The Shaa-kutu thrived with their new knowledge. My fellow humans flourished, expanding and progressing, living and loving in contentment. Humans existed in harmony with their kutu makers.

In that time of peace, the kutu built a temple in my beautiful valley. They built it from their finest ores: a stunning design, created to be a place where both humans and kutu could come to learn about their pasts. They called it the Temple of Learning.

To the kutu, the Temple was my home. To my human family, my home would always be with them in Threetops. To the Old One, I would never be at home until I joined him in eternal slumber. And as for me? I only ever felt at home in the forest, in my valley, sleeping outside, curled up with Meah. In the forest, we were free.

For five years, the world remained at peace.

But then the Tumultus came.

I had not realised that the first war with the Nigh-kutu had, to the Nigh-kutu, been no more than a slight skirmish, led by a small off-shoot of their warriors who had been attracted by Shursa's call. It had not even involved the formidable Nigh-kutu leader, Arrunn. When Arrunn became aware of the Shaa-kutu and the Old One, everything changed. Arrunn used the one connection to the light: Shursa. For the promise of rulership, power, and his heart's desire, Shursa readily betrayed his own kind.

All the Nigh-kutu came. Thousands of them. All had trained as warriors for millennia. They entered the light and attacked the Shaa-kutu home-world. The Shaa-kutu home-world fell. Most of the Shaa-kutu perished. Some managed to escape and hide.

As the Tumultus raged, I almost lost Jychanumun. He was saved by two defecting Nigh-kutu, Mardoch and Dragun. But there was no celebration for the reunited friends, because the Nigh-kutu warriors then came here, to Earth.

Here on Earth, we had just seventy-nine Shaa-kutu, three Nigh-kutu, a few humans, and myself, standing against Arrunn and his army. The odds were against us. We stayed underground, existing, surviving – even rescuing other Shaa-kutu where we could. But, not only were we outnumbered, Arrunn also had a type of energy that held more power than any weapon. That energy was held in small crystals, called life-crystals.

Life-crystals. Those potent little gems. Each one made from a murdered kutu's life. Each one filled with all the unfulfilled power and unlived life of a powerful, slaughtered being. Such potent gems could tip the balance of the kutu war. But we possessed none. Only one kutu had those precious crystals – Arrunn.

Most of Arrunn's life-crystals were stored in a vast kutu vault. When Arrunn came to Earth, that vault was kept in the middle of his warriors' camp. Also contained in that vault was a Nar beast: a fierce creature that would defend and kill. None of my kutu friends could get close to the vault in order to steal any life-crystals. But a human would go unnoticed. A human disguised as a slave; a human with Earth skills could do it. I volunteered.

But our plan did not go as planned.

It was not because of the Nigh-kutu warriors that our plan failed, for I played the part of unnoticeable slave well. Nor was it because of the Nar beast, for he turned out to be an intelligent creature. It was nothing more than the defensive anger of a fellow human, inadvertently revealing my stolen stash of crystals, which negated our war-winning scheme. I was captured and taken to Arrunn.

Arrunn knew exactly who and what I was. He wanted my link to the Old One. To make me give him what he wanted, he threatened everything I loved, cut out my tongue to stop me using the Voice, and then murdered my wildcat, Meah.

When Arrunn murdered Meah, my heart fractured. I left my body and took her spirit to a place of beauty that I created for us: Elysium. Elysium was a world between worlds, created by memory and love. We were happy there, eternally living as girl and cub, and I did not want to leave. But, Jychanumun risked his life in coming to Elysium, to make me realise that my being there would have consequences. Those consequences would affect all futures.

When I returned to my flesh body, I was changed. I had discovered grief. I had discovered hate. And I was no longer free. I was Arrunn's prisoner. There was something different about Arrunn. Something hidden. Within his shadow was something I did not understand. He – that – it terrified me.

Arrunn kept me imprisoned, deep inside the drained well, and was persistent in trying to break my will. Time passed, but I wasn't sure how long. It was hard to tell, when day and night rolled together. In that time, while the war raged, my body weakened. Time and injuries had taken their toll. Too weak to move and too exhausted to think, I had finally run out of options.

My body was maimed and emaciated beyond my abilities of repair. My flesh was useless, barely functioning, nothing more than a broken mess, laying inert in its own grime and stink. Yet I could cope with a broken body. I could distance my thoughts and block any pain. But I could not distance myself from the signs that my mind was beginning to break too. I knew I must keep my wits. Without my wits, I would be malleable to Arrunn. I would be his tool. I did not know if that would have any consequences, but I could not take the chance. Too much was at stake.

I fought against myself to hold my thoughts together: Don't listen to Arrunn's subtle suggestions. Don't sleep, lest he send his kutu to do something to my body. Don't drift, lest I open my mind to his manipulative skills. Don't daydream. Focus on anything.

But, as much as I tried to stay focused, my mind drifted more and more often. I was simply too damaged. My lucid moments became increasingly scattered and harder to hold onto. And when I did manage to hold onto solid thoughts, they tormented me with the lingering images of the horrific things I had seen. I tried to focus on memories of happiness, but every positive recollection became marred. My beautiful bonded wildcat, Meah, tortured. My dependable father, murdered. My fellow humans, each and every one in jeopardy. My kutu friends, so many valiant yet brutal deaths. Every memory of joy now had an equal picture of sorrow. Or slaughter. Or torture. Fear. Violence. Suffering. Heartbreaks. These were the things that I did not want to remember. But these were things I could not forget. In response, my mind seemed unwilling to hold onto any thoughts. And, as much as I fought, I knew that I could not hold onto life, or clarity, for much longer.

I had begun to wonder if Arrunn was right after all: that he would eventually break me. He said it was inevitable. He said that I *would* give up. Sometimes, for a fleeting moment, when the haunting memories surfaced again, I wanted to agree with him.

But I would not give up! Something within me, some inner strength, like an eon-aged rock, would not let me. That something made me determined to fight, however I could. And if all I could do to fight was through the simplicity of taking another breath, and then another, I would do just that until I could breathe no more.

And my kutu friends would never give up! No matter the odds, they would stand for freedom and life and all things that were right. They would fight with wits and weapons until the end, they said. They would stand united until none were left. They were, in every respect, brave and brilliant.

How I wished that greatness such as courage and honour could win such a war. But it didn't seem to work like that. Courage and honour did not ensure victory. In this war we were not winning. We were losing.

We were in critical, final times. When it seemed that all was lost, that we would lose this war and all life would end with it, my kutu friends formed a new plan. It was a desperate plan of last measures. It was unquestionably dangerous, and it did not guarantee victory, but it did offer what we needed: hope.

Through my link with Jychanumun, I learnt that Kraniel had discovered how to separate the shadow and light energies. He called it the result of polarity. Once Kraniel's invention had been activated, all kutu would be forced to polar opposites of existence. The Nigh-kutu would be drawn to the shadow. The Shaa-kutu would be drawn to the light. The two kutu races would be forced so far apart that they could not interact. The pull would last for millennia. Meanwhile, humanity would be left in peace. And hopefully, just hopefully, during that time, the Shaa-kutu would discover how to conquer Arrunn and his armies.

Kraniel's theory could only be tested once, and tested with all kutu lives. And he could not guarantee that humans would be unaffected either. There were many risks. Still, even the smallest chance of victory was better than certain defeat.

A complication to this plan came from Jychanumun, Mardoch and Dragun. As defecting Nigh-kutu, if they returned to the shadow they would be destroyed. So instead, Jychanumun agreed to take Mardoch and Dragun into the kutu death-paths. There they would wait, neither dead nor alive, in oblivion, until the time was right to return.

I too agreed to wait in the death-paths with Jychanumun. I understood the potential dangers. The death-paths were a perilous place where a being could get lost forever, and I was human, not kutu. Plus, Jychanumun had never held more than one being in the paths at any one time. He assured me that he could do it, but it would be difficult. To succeed, he would need to guide us all at the same time. For that, timing would be critical.

To walk a kutu death-path, I would have to embrace a physical death. I would have to leave my body and let the entirety of my energy walk away from my human flesh. And, as timing was critical, my flesh would have to die at a specific time. I would need to end my flesh-life at a precise moment. I had to struggle to survive, and then to choose to die.

All I had to do was stay alive just a short while longer.

ONE

The Instruction

"Do you understand?"

Jychanumun towered above her. His huge black wings undulated as if breathing deeply from his hasty flight. It felt as if he was staring at her; but that was impossible as his eyes were bandaged. He was clearly injured. Dark smears of iridescent, black kutu blood were smeared down his cheeks. His torso was a mesh of lesions and cuts. A gaping wound in his side still pulsed with kutu energy and blood.

"Do you understand?" he asked again.

Soul had so many questions. None of them seemed appropriate anymore.

"I understand," she nodded.

Jychanumun turned to leave.

Soul's feet automatically took a tentative step forward. Although she bit her lip, she couldn't stop the words spilling from her mouth.

"Will Tachra be alright?" she asked.

Jychanumun paused. He didn't look back.

"Always," he replied. "Soon she will be free."

And then he was gone. In three swift strides, the black-winged kutu had re-launched into the night sky and flown from sight.

TWO

The Path

A faint whisper. *Tachra...*

Iastha Tachra.

My ears heard nothing, yet the voice reverberated around my mind like a distant echo. It was as if someone was whispering into my thoughts. Were the words supposed to mean something to me? Were they a place I had known? Someone I had loved?

My mind floated aimlessly, unable to focus. Words didn't matter. I didn't know their meaning. I couldn't remember anything. And even if I could, I didn't care to remember.

I ignored the silent calling. I kept my eyes shut and didn't move from my inert numbness on the ground. My muddied thoughts tumbled around, telling me that it was nothing more than my imagination playing tricks yet again. Or maybe I was asleep and this was another nightmare that I couldn't wake from. Whatever, dream or imagination, it didn't make any difference. In this lightless place, in my delirious stupor, I couldn't tell if I was awake or asleep anyway.

Iastha Tachra, beloved.

Those words again. That voice. It disturbs my weary thoughts. Let me be. I don't want any more hallucinations. I want them silenced. All of them. Just let me sleep in peace. Let me sleep without dreams or feelings or thoughts. Go away. Be quiet. Let it all be silent.

Silence. . .

That's better.

The emptiness began its welcome return. Blankness crept through my body and mind like a soothing balm.

I drifted back into a vacant void. No feelings. No thoughts.

Nothingness. . .

Nothing. . .

No thing. . .

. . .

. .

.

Tachra. . .

Tachra. . .

Tachra. . .

Iastha Tachra. . .

TACHRA! COME BACK! The words exploded through my head.

It was like the roar of thunder on a quiet night. It wrenched me from my murky daze, my every sense shuddering with an intense, torrential sense of urgency. My body flinched involuntarily, making pain soar through my flesh. It was as if I had been thrown into freezing water from a deep, dream-filled sleep. Clarity and awareness flooded through me, stripping away the layers of fog that shrouded my perception. Tachra? I knew that word. It was a name.

It was *my* name!

Countless images, sounds, and thoughts that were memories, my memories, flooded back to my consciousness, bombarding me with knowledge I had almost forgotten: My village, Threetops. My strong father. My caring mother. My siblings; their children. Golden crops. Luscious berry groves. The deep ravine. The choosing. The long walk. The Hollow town. Soul. The Old One. The waterless mountains. My beautiful valley. Meah. The Old One's dreams. Finding the kutu. Kutu friends. The Temple. Treachery. Nigh-kutu warriors. Arrunn. War. Fear. Severance. Imprisonment. Darkness. Desolation.

Yes, I remembered it all.

I remembered now: not only who I was, but also where I was, what I was, and why I was. The reality was dire, but I didn't linger on despair, because my insides lurched with hope. Such a compelling call, direct to my mind, could only come from one being – Jychanumun. Only the kutu Jychanumun had the ability to speak directly into my thoughts. Only he could pull me back from near insanity. Jychanumun must still be alive. All hope was not yet lost.

Concentrating on the memory of Jychanumun's face, I imagined he was in front of me. I imagined he stood with his black wings outstretched, his shadow gaze intense yet distant. I pictured something beautiful, as if we were standing in the valley, doing nothing more than watching the movement of the world through shared eyes. Holding onto that image, I opened my mind, searching for any trace of my connection to him.

There it was.

It had never gone.

Jychanumun's presence intensified. I sensed his composure and focus. I also sensed his concern. Through our link, I now felt many things from him as if they were my own.

Is that truly you? I silently spoke with my mind, hardly daring to trust my senses.

Yes, Jychanumun replied.

My nightmares taunted me that you had been slain.

You have been blocking me, he said. *I thought I was losing you.*

I almost told him that I feared I was losing myself.

The darkness and isolation here penetrate to the core of me, I said. *And I think my body is badly damaged.*

You must hold on. Just a while longer. Jychanumun's words were filled with gravity. *The arrangements are in place. Do you remember?*

I told him that yes, I remembered.

And you still choose it?

I told him that yes, I still chose it.

I will remain with you, he added. *It is almost your time.*

My time? My time for what?

Oh yes. My time.

Thank the skies, I sighed.

This was what I had been waiting for. This is what I had been struggling to hold onto life for. It was, at last, my time to die.

I felt Jychanumun's focus change. I sensed that he was talking to Mardoch and Dragun. I silenced my thoughts from him, knowing he needed to concentrate. He would be initiating a death-path for them. Soon, it would be my turn.

I thought of my kutu friends. I hoped they would survive what was about to happen. I hoped Kraniel's device worked. I wondered if Arrunn was watching me from the top of the pit, gloating at my broken state. I didn't care. I had managed to do what I needed. I had managed to stay alive. I had survived to choose death. I had lived to die. In the darkness of the pit, I think I smiled to myself. My friend Orion would have called that a paradox.

Tachra.

Jychanumun's call interrupted my thoughts.

I am still here, I replied.

It is time.

Now?

Yes.

I forced my tumbling thoughts to still.

A new nervousness danced unwelcome over my calm.

I sensed the intensity of Jychanumun's connection. He would stay with me through this. But this, what I had to do, he could not help with. For this physical task, I had no hands except my own.

From my curled position on the floor of the well, I mustered my strength to sit. My body gave no response. I strained again to move, but my flesh had been motionless for so long that it had become unresponsive. I tried to shift my arms. They didn't want to work. I couldn't get my fingers to move. I couldn't feel my fingers.

A sense of panic started to consume me. If I couldn't move, I wouldn't be capable of doing this. But I couldn't be beaten now. Surely, having fought to stay alive for this moment, I couldn't fail at the very last.

Dread raced through me. It made my stomach lurch and the beating pace of my heart grow stronger, thumping through my chest. Within my fretting, racing thoughts, a clear awareness grew. Panic is good, I realised, conscious of the changes in my body. Panic has a strong energy. If I have nothing else, then I can use this panic.

I concentrated on the feel of my flesh, on anything that I could still sense. Blood still moved through me, pulsing. My heart beat a strong, racing rhythm. I was still breathing.

I pushed the energy surges through me, awakening the dormant parts of my flesh: my fingers, hands, arms, legs. My nerves tingled in response, like a thousand thorns penetrating my skin. Eventually, despite the frustration of clumsy, weakened flesh, I pushed to sit, slumping against the wall of the pit.

I traced my fingers in the dirt, using my true vision to see the different energies of any substance on the ground. There it was; the small shard of metal. It was invisible in the darkness to my physical eyes, yet luminous and silver to my true vision.

Without a pause to allow doubt or fear to enter my mind and

stop me, I wrapped my fingers around the shard of broken metal, picked it up, pressed the cold point against my arm and pushed the blade deep. It didn't hurt.

I watched my hand, as if it was not my own, forcing the blade upwards through my pallid flesh. I watched the cut grow with a remote curiosity as the life blood welled. The blood dripped from my arm, trickling down my legs and pooling onto the ground. I didn't feel sorrow. I didn't feel anything.

Tachra, Jychanumun spoke softly, *remember: you must not walk to the Old One. In death, he will embrace you. Remember, walk towards my voice, towards the death-paths.*

I closed my eyes. I knew I must not, but now, with death so close, I wanted to walk to the Old One. With the Old One I would be at peace. *We* would be at peace. We would dream eternal dreams forever.

As death overtook my flesh, the Old One's consciousness reached out, beckoning to me. His colours of everything flowed through me, embracing all that I was. Within his timelessness, I also felt the essence of what I would become, and of all things beyond my mortal life. It was a moment of true peace, a moment of wholeness. But he felt my choices. One day we would exist in harmony as one; it was my destiny. But not yet. For now, I made a different choice.

As my body weakened, my mind grew more focused. The spirit of my beloved wildcat, Meah, now sat poised calmly beside me. She looked beautiful. Even though Arrunn had killed her flesh, death had not broken our bond. Now she was as clear to me again as if we were merely sitting in our forest together, cub and girl, just as we use to be.

It was too late for my Nigh-kutu guard to stop my wilful demise. I watched, as if in a dream, as he rushed into my prison, shielding his eyes from the curses I had scratched onto the wall. I knew his name was Shemya. I knew all hope was not lost for him. I told him so with my mind. I told him to remember who he once was, Shemya of the Gathering Clan, and that once he had been a great kutu; a kutu of honour. I told him that he would not stop me. Even if he could, he wouldn't. He heard every word.

Arrunn, too, tried to stop me. Perhaps he would have succeeded, but Jychanumun's timing was perfect. I saw the effects of Kraniel's kutu-divide begin to take place.

As Arrunn barged into my prison, intent on stopping my action, I witnessed his energy being drawn from his body like smoke from a fire. His energy was being compelled to a place far beyond these realms. His body could no longer move. He was rooted to the spot, frozen mid-stride, a curious expression on his face. He was trying to say something. I didn't listen. It didn't matter. He couldn't stop what was happening to him. He couldn't stop what was happening to me.

I think I had almost forgotten my hatred of Arrunn. Almost. He had succeeded in controlling so many choices in life, but he could not take away this choice for death. That choice was mine and mine alone. I could leave in peace knowing that Arrunn would be unable to harm any more of my loved ones. He had not won every battle.

With the spirit of Meah by my side, my awareness of the Old One acutely heightened, and my connection with Jychanumun stronger than ever, I stood. My movements were fluid. There was no pain.

I looked down. By my feet was the naked, injured body that had been my own. I barely recognised it. Its filthy, bruised, cut, pallid flesh was pulled taut over bones. It looked wretched, yet I felt only acceptance. Everything seemed so clear now. Everything mattered. Nothing mattered.

I glanced around for one last time at the place that had been my prison. The etchings on the walls were luminous. Arrunn was still focused on my body. And then, with Jychanumun's voice beckoning, a dark path began to form. It was a kutu death-path. For now, it was my path.

I stepped forward into that death-path and, with that step, left all remnants of my bleeding, dying flesh behind.

THREE

The Emptiness

Meanwhile, in Threetops...

It was a half-moon night and Soul's turn to prepare supper for the village mothers. The work surfaces were littered with the remnants of freshly dug vegetables. The hearth space was crammed with simmering pots. The cooking fire had been burning strong since high sun and the hut was far too hot.

Condensation rolled down the bare wooden walls, sweat trickled down Soul's face, and her damp dress stuck to her clammy body. She didn't notice. She needed to keep busy. She needed to throw herself into whatever chores she could until she fell down with fatigue. Sheer exhaustion was the only thing that masked her overwhelming sense of unease.

Jychanumun's unexpected visit earlier had not alleviated her fears. "Soon she will be free," he had said. At first she had felt better. Subsequently, she had thought about it. 'Free' to Jychanumun was not the same as 'free' to her. To her it meant that Tachra would be healthy and home and that this war would be over. But the kutu had a different way of talking and Jychanumun could have meant many things. She now didn't feel better at all.

Soul had been waiting earnestly for news of Tachra's escape or rescue. Tachra was her friend. And, with so much at stake in this kutu war, surely it would be Tachra's link to the Old One that would save them all. So why hadn't Tachra used her abilities to free herself? Too much time had passed and too many people had been hurt. Tachra would have stopped it, if she could. She would have escaped by now, if she could. That had to mean that she couldn't. And, if Tachra couldn't save herself, how could she be expected to save them all? She couldn't. Then surely they were all damned.

The dreadful notion made another flip in Soul's stomach.

Tomorrow, she deliberated, forcing her fretful thoughts to quieten, *I'll plant the field next to the apple orchard. I'll work through high-sun to avoid the black-winged ones. Then I'll finish harvesting the junir. We've blankets that need darning. Iris needs a new apron. And somehow,* she glanced at Tachra's mother, *I have to make Ellen rest.*

Tachra's mother, Ellen, was scrubbing the eating table again. Her usually neat, greying hair fell scraggily from its ties, clinging to her damp, frail face.

"Ellen," Soul indicated towards the bench. "Take some food. Please rest."

Ellen either didn't hear or chose not to listen, continuing to scrub the table in silence.

"Iris?" Soul called out, concerned that she hadn't seen her daughter for a short while.

"I'm here," a little voice replied.

Soul turned to see her daughter, freshly washed and clean from her afternoon chores, just as instructed.

"Can I go now?" Iris asked.

"And where exactly are you going?"

"To collect berries," Iris replied with careful deliberation. Her eyes widened as she made sure she answered correctly. "Only around here. No further than being able to see our hut," she added.

"Very good," Soul nodded. "Do not let the hut out of your sight. And it's not long until dusk, so return before then."

Iris skipped away with a smile, clutching her little berry bag with the promise of filling it to the brim. As she closed the door behind her, Ellen glanced up, shaking her head, frowning. Her disapproval was almost tangible.

"You think I should keep Iris indoors?" Soul asked.

Ellen did not reply. Instead, she scrubbed the table even harder. Her frustrated vigour made shards of bristle break from the cleaning brush and recoil from the wood.

"She knows not to stray again," Soul said in justification. "She has learnt her lesson."

Soul then fell into a doubt-ridden silence. She hoped, by the skies, that Iris *had* learnt her lesson. But perhaps it was too soon. After all, it was only yesterday that Iris had stolen away without telling anyone. She had climbed on board a Nigh-kutu pod, with a woman from Longsdale, in order to get to the Temple. She had wanted see if she could rescue Tachra, she had explained. And no, she didn't think that she'd done anything wrong.

Soul's initial shock at hearing Iris' tale had quickly turned to horror, then anger, and then fear. She'd tried to explain about the potential jeopardy Iris had put herself into. And, even though Iris had returned unharmed, she was not to go anywhere, ever, without telling her mamma, especially anywhere close to those Nigh-kutu. Arrunn was bad. The Nigh-kutu were bad. And yes, Jychanumun was a Nigh-kutu and he was a good kutu, but he was an exception and Iris must be wary of them all.

Soul hoped that her daughter had understood the scolding. Iris had promised she would never do such a thing again. She had even looked suitably remorseful. Nevertheless, Soul knew that the remorse was only from making her mamma worry. For the act of trying to rescue Tachra, her daughter clearly didn't feel remorse at all. For that, Iris' childish expression had turned to one of stern determination, telling her mamma that if she had wings like a kutu, and was as strong as a kutu, then Tachra would most certainly be free by now. Soul's scolding had needed to be harsh, for Iris' safety. But secretly, she had felt full of pride.

"You should guard your child," Ellen suddenly spoke. "Protect her better than I have protected mine."

It was the first time Ellen had spoken in days.

Soul stopped cutting roots, looking at the old woman.

"Oh Ellen," Soul spoke, instinctively putting her hand to her heart. "I grieve for all your losses more than words can say. I truly do."

Ellen looked at Soul beseechingly. The pain and hurt she had suffered was etched into her face.

"I have born sixteen healthy babes and seen them grow to make young of their own. But now," Ellen's voice was shaking. "They have all, bar one, had the breath of life taken from them. Fifteen children taken from me and ten times as many grand-children. And the babies too; even the new born. . ." Her voice trailed away as if even the words were too much to bear. She hung her head. "I have only one child left. And for her there is no hope."

"There must be hope," Soul implored, banishing her own doubts. "Tachra is not just my friend and your daughter, she is needed. She'll rid this world of the black-winged ones. She *has* to be freed."

"But she is still just a girl," Ellen shook her head. "My last child."

Ellen looked ready to crumple. Soul moved to her side, guiding her to sit on the long-bench, sitting with her, holding her tightly because no words seemed enough.

"We are done cooking," Soul soothed. "And the table is the cleanest it has ever been. I'll deliver the food. You rest. Have some stew. You've not eaten for days."

Ellen shook her head at the offer of food. Nevertheless, Soul spooned a generous helping of stew into an earthenware mug. As she held out the steaming broth encouragingly, suddenly her insides churned with a deep sense of loss.

Something had changed. It was as if the world had stopped.

The heat seemed to dissipate from the hut, as if sucked away by an engulfing breath. The bubbling noise from the simmering pots hushed. Even the fires paused, their soundless flames seemingly held motionless in their dance.

Soul didn't feel the mug in her hands slip from her grasp. She didn't see it drop in slow motion, a mere drip trickling over the edge as the container tilted, falling slower than the lightest feather. She didn't hear the shattering of the heavy earthenware as it hit the floor; its hot contents splaying like a blossoming flower, the clay splintering outwards like slow moving stars. It went unnoticed.

Soul could see Ellen moving towards her. She could feel her trembling, concerned grasp on her shoulders. She could sense the alarm in the old woman's voice as she said something. But she couldn't hear the words. It was as if her heart had disconnected her from everything around her. All she could sense was loss.

"Tachra," Soul's mouth instinctively spoke aloud. Her mind searched. Her heart searched. She looked into the deepest parts of her essence, searching for the connection that she shared with her friend. But it wasn't anywhere. It wasn't anywhere because it wasn't a thing to be found, and its absence now shouted louder than all else. Where once had dwelled an intuitive link, only emptiness remained.

No, Soul thought.

But she knew.

"Tachra has ceased," she whispered.

FOUR

The Pull

In the Temple. . .

"What have you done?" Arrunn demanded.

Tachra did not reply. Her dying breath eased from her lips like a shallow, contented sigh. She had wilfully left her flesh.

Arrunn went to step forward to reanimate her human body. But he couldn't move; not his legs, arms, nor any part of his flesh. He tried to speak again, to command his guards, but now his mouth wouldn't function either. Something was happening. Something that he had not prepared for.

From his static eyes, he could see tendrils of his life-energy discharging from his skin. It flowed away from his body in long, shadowy lines, weakening him with every passing moment. He fought against it, willing his essence to retract into his body, but it made no difference. His presence here was reducing. It was as if his energy, he, was being pulled to a place far away.

Despite Tachra's lifeless body, Arrunn now had one primary objective; regain control. For that, *he* required an alternative body.

Before he was too weakened to act, Arrunn pushed what remained of his life-force out from his body and propelled upwards, leaving his physical matter poised like a statue at the bottom of the well. He ascended the deep pit and soared over the walled edge, into the main chamber above. There, one of his clone-guards stood close by.

Arrunn eased his essence into the empty flesh of his clone guard, and then pushed forward to move once again.

Nothing. This new body was just as immobile as his old flesh.

Arrunn re-evaluated. His clone guards were clearly of no use. He would have to utilise the body of a common Nigh-kutu instead.

Nevertheless, from his position, it was clear that utilising a common Nigh-kutu was no solution either. At the far end of the chamber, High-warrior Deimom stood paralysed as his shadow energy also slipped from his flesh. Beyond Deimom, another Nigh-kutu had slumped to his knees, his expression frozen into one of uncertainty, while his life-force flowed from his body. Two more Nigh-kutu stood by the chamber's entrance with the latest group of human captives. They too were immobilised by the same unknown phenomenon.

But, Arrunn observed, the humans appeared impervious. Some of them were already edging away from their guards, their mobility unaffected.

Arrunn propelled his energy forward, out of the body of his clone-guard and towards the humans, driving his essence into the core of the closest human. The young woman did not have enough strength for what he needed, but it would be enough to momentarily nourish him.

First in the queue, the human woman Shansal knew nothing of what happened to her. In less than a moment, Arrunn had entered her body, consumed her life-energy, and left her human flesh degrading into fine, grey, depleted dust.

Before Shansal's lifeless dust had fallen to the floor, Arrunn had propelled his essence into the next human. Again, he absorbed what paltry energy the human had left of life. He then moved onto the third. Then the fourth. Fifth. Sixth. Seventh. Arrunn coursed through the group of humans so swiftly that none had any perception of what was happening. Eight. Nine. Ten. Eleven. Twelve. Thirteen. . . This one.

Human bios thirteen was strong enough to hold his energy for more than a fraction of a moment. This one would suffice.

Cautiously, so as not to immediately destroy its fragile flesh, Arrunn eased his energy into human number thirteen. The sensation was unpleasant, as its organs began disintegrating at an increasingly faster rate, but he only needed seconds. He only needed the ability to move physically to the far end of the chamber.

Leaving the remainder of the humans to scatter, Arrunn directed his temporary host-body to the back of the chamber. There, between two collapsed stone columns, was where he kept his twelve favoured life-crystals in a secure shadow-box. Each one of those crystals had once been a Nigh-kutu from the old council. Once they had been considered great beings. Now, they were nothing more than a bank of energy to be utilised. Their time had come to be of use.

He guided the clumsy human hands to open the shadow box. As soon as the human's flesh moved closer to the powerful gems inside, its skin singed and withered, its flesh burning pungently. With time running out, Arrunn swiftly removed the crystals from their box, placed them on the floor, knelt over them, and then crushed them with his fist.

Their confines shattered, the energy from inside the crystals sprang loose and began whirling around each other. Hues of green, orange, blue and silver lit up the darkened chamber like a coloured light-storm.

Arrunn leant over the aurora and exhaled his essence from his host, surrounding the energy from the crystals, holding them together. And then he pushed inwards, consuming every morsel of potent kutu life-power that those little crystals had held.

Arrunn's strength increased. His senses heightened. The potent life-energy from the twelve crystals was now his, coursing through him. He now had the power he required, yet would still need to act fast. His energy was still dissipating.

As the human flesh of number thirteen turned to dust, Arrunn pushed his will forward, directing his bodiless essence out of the chamber. He flew through the golden building and beyond the entrance. He accelerated ahead, travelling across the valley, through trees, over sandland, above mountains and through the wasteland beyond. He travelled at an almost instant speed, fuelled by the life-energy he had just consumed. He knew exactly where he was heading.

The kutu were of no use to him at this time, and most humans were too weak to sustain his energy. A few might last just a short time, eventually becoming dust, burnt to ash by his power. But he had known one human to survive after hosting his energy. That human had an inner core of fire and will, strong enough to hold a kutu's life-force for longer than a short while. Yes, she would eventually degrade, but she would facilitate his needs for some time: time enough for him to reverse whatever affliction had been cast upon him and his warriors.

Her inner core would shield him.

She would become his host.

It was time to utilise Soul.

FIVE

The Host

Soul's head hurt. Everything hurt. The pain made her so giddy that she couldn't think straight. She could feel herself laying on a hard floor. She couldn't remember how she got there.

Concentrate, she willed the thought to form. *I must have fallen.*

Soul forced her eyes open. At first she couldn't focus. The sunlight looked strange, and even though the window indicated that it was almost dusk, the vividness hurt her eyes. Slowly, the uncomfortable brightness subsided and her surroundings became familiar. She was still in her hut: Tachra's old hut. She was sprawled out on the worn, wooden floor of the eating room.

Immediately in front of her, the large table was turned on its side, one half shattered, the jagged edge of a broken leg now pointing precariously close to her face. All around, furniture had been upturned and utensils littered the floor, with the remains of vegetables trodden into the broken pieces. The hut looked ravaged, but it smelt even worse. It wasn't just the burnt food smoking on the dying embers of the fire: another, unfamiliar, acrid smell tinged her nostrils.

Soul had no recollection of how she came to be unconscious on the floor, or how the hut had sustained such damage. The last she remembered she had been giving Ellen some stew. And then... oh yes. Her heart sunk at the thought. She had felt Tachra's passing.

A part of her wanted to stay where she was, laying on the floor, feeling the sorrow of the loss of her friend. But her stomach lurched. Had no one seen her fall? Where was Iris? Where was Ellen? Neither were in sight.

Pushing herself to sit and ignoring the thumping rhythm that spun havoc in her head, she glanced down. Her hands! They were covered in blood!

Congealing lumps of red stuck between her fingers. One hand rigidly clasped a short chopping knife. That too was covered with blood. She dropped the knife in horror, her vision drawn to her attire. Her gown was ripped and splattered red, its hem sodden. There was so much blood.

In a state of shock, Soul's eyes rapidly scanned her exposed flesh while her hands brushed her torso. She couldn't find any injuries. The blood didn't seem to be hers. Her eyes skimmed her surroundings. To one side, a thick, drying smear of darkest red ran from the kitchen towards the open door of the hut.

Iris? Ellen? Soul's mind raced, her heart beating a frantic rhythm.

"Iris!" Soul tried to call. Her words came out spluttering, her voice hoarse; her mouth was filled with something congealing. She spat it out as she scrambled to her feet. What looked like red-raw flesh and blood splattered from her lips.

Dread consumed her. With her entire body feeling weak with worry and shock, Soul half-ran, half-stumbled towards the door. Her thoughts were so full of trepidation that her legs would barely function, tripping over their own feet with each determined yet shaky stride. Her mind feared terrible things, but it was as if it couldn't contemplate anything; frozen instead on the singular thought of needing to find her loved ones.

Soul burst out of the hut and into the dusky view of green land

and trees. There, just beyond the hut's entrance, face down in the thick grass, the trail from the hut stopped at a blood-covered body.

Soul instantly knew that it was Tachra's mother.

She rushed forward, crouching beside her.

Ellen's exposed back was a mess of ripped, jagged flesh and visible stab holes. The wounds were bad – worse than anything Soul had seen before. Her dress hung from her shoulders in bloodied tatters. She was not moving.

Soul carefully turned Ellen around.

"Iris!" she shouted.

She had found Ellen, but where was her daughter?

Tachra's mother looked dead. The wounds to her face were horrifying. The lacerations down her cheeks were so deep that they exposed her teeth. Large chunks of hair and flesh had been ripped from her head. Her eyes bulged wide and she had a look of horror set on her cold, mutilated face. Soul noticed Ellen's blood-covered arms where gaping cuts ran from her wrists to her elbows. The blood would have flowed fast from such wounds.

"**Iris!**" Soul shouted louder, her voice coming out shrill and panicked.

Soul put a hand to the old woman's mouth. She wasn't breathing. She pressed the points at the side of Ellen's neck to feel for the beat of life, just as she had been shown how to do. Still nothing.

"Please, Ellen, wake up," Soul whispered, anxiously lifting the old woman's upper body and shaking her gently, as if she could wake her from mere sleep. "Please."

Soul may have wanted Ellen to wake up, to speak, to move and be alright. But she knew that Tachra's mother wasn't going to speak, or move, or be alright ever again. Ellen had clearly ceased.

Soul battled against the shock that tried to freeze her thoughts. Ellen's dead. Ellen's dead! She let the old woman's corpse drop to the grass.

"*Iris!*" Soul shouted louder this time, standing up, scanning the surroundings for any signs of her daughter. "Come here now! I'm not playing."

There was no reply.

Right now, nothing else mattered other than the safety of her daughter.

Soul ran back into the hut, looking for any signs of Iris. Her body found a heightened strength, turning over furniture as if it weighed nothing, lifting beds, searching every storage space where a child might hide at a speed that seemed almost kutu-like. The hut appeared empty. She ran to the centre of the space and stood motionless, covering her mouth to muffle her panicked breaths, and listened. Only the crackles of dying fire embers and the gentle creaks of settling wood in the early evening cool were to be heard. The hut not only looked empty, it sounded empty too.

As her eyes and ears scanned, her mind raced. The last she remembered, Iris was heading out to collect berries. But when was that? It seemed only a moment ago, but somehow, in that moment, terrible things had happened to Ellen, she herself was covered in blood, and Iris wasn't here. Time had passed, events had occurred, and she remembered nothing of it.

Suddenly, a shrill scream from outside made Soul feel like her heart had stopped, but her legs were already moving. She started running towards the scream. She recognised that voice. The scream had come from her daughter.

Outside, Iris was standing, rooted to the spot, in view of Ellen's bloodied corpse. Her arms were rigid by her sides, her hands clasped into desperate fists, her little berry bag dropped to the grass with berries littering the ground around her feet. While Iris' wide, terrified eyes were fixed on Ellen's motionless body, her mouth was letting out scream after scream.

Soul dashed towards Iris, scooping her up into her arms.

"It's alright. It'll be alright," Soul reassured, clasping her daughter to her. *Where's safe?* She thought. *Where can we hide?*

The hut was the only place where Soul could think of to go to. She had checked it herself. It was empty. Right now, it seemed like the safest place to be.

Iris continued screaming, unable to pull her gaze away from Ellen's body, as Soul ran back towards the hut.

Once in the confines of the hut, Soul brushed aside the chopped roots on the food preparation area and sat Iris down.

Be safe, Soul's mind raced. *I can work out what to do, but first I have to make sure we are safe.*

Soul quickly closed the hut door while her mind calculated the options. The latch on the door was old and would easily break. She needed something better to secure it. The table. That would do.

With all her might, Soul pushed as forcefully as she could to get the large eating table flat against the door, while her eyes constantly returned to her daughter, ensuring she was not in danger. The broken table scraped noisily on the floor, smearing the near-dried blood stains even more. It kept catching on the irregularities in the planks. It was very heavy. Good. The heavier the better.

With the table good and wedged against the only door into their abode, Soul glanced around, looking for any further entrance points.

The lone window on the ground floor had a storm shutter. She ran towards it, slamming the wooden covering against the opening and threading the thick wooden stick through the catch to secure it. The only other window was on the upper floor, in Tachra's old room. That was safe. That one always had its storm shutter closed now, and Soul had fashioned a strong new bolt for it the morning after Dannel had ceased. But the cooking hearth in front of her was a possible access point, albeit a difficult one. The hearth was under a small funnel opening from the roof. It was too small for anyone to get through. Nevertheless, she wasn't going to take any chances. She removed the burnt cooking pots and threw more wood onto the embers to build up the flames and make their reach even higher. Such heat should surely bar anyone's path.

Once satisfied that the hut had been secured, Soul glanced around, making note of every hiding place. She hoped that none of them would be necessary. She hoped that some of the villagers would soon realise she hadn't delivered food that evening and would come looking for her. If she could just keep Iris safe for now, help would surely be along soon.

Iris had quietened. Her screams had reduced to exhausted whimpers. She had pulled herself to the back of the ledge and now sat against the wall, cradling her knees. She kept rocking back and forth as if to console herself, while watching her mother's every move.

"Are you hurt?" Soul asked with concern, brushing the hair away from her daughter's face, looking for cuts or bruises, inspecting her arms, examining her little body for any damage.

Iris shook her head to indicate no, she wasn't hurt, her eyes fixed firmly on Soul, her face set into an expression of wariness and shock.

"You're alright," Soul said, consoling her daughter, checking her once more for any signs of damage.

Iris flinched away from her mother's touch.

"We're safe. It's alright," Soul repeated reassuringly.

Iris shook her head. "It's not alright," she suddenly spurted. She burst into tears, her sobs ragged, barely able to catch her breath.

"What is it?" Soul asked, suddenly aware of her own blood-covered body and dress. She quickly wiped her face with the back of her sleeve, aware that her appearance must look frightening.

"Is it the blood?" she asked. "It's alright. Look," she wiped herself again. "Mamma is not hurt."

Iris shook her head as if not wanting to speak.

"Iris," Soul spoke firmly and gently. "Tell mamma. Are you injured?"

Iris shook her head again. And then, hesitantly, her little hand slowly raised, her index finger held in a reluctant point. She was pointing directly at Soul's face.

"You're scaring me," Iris wept. "He's in you. He's in your eyes."

Iris' own eyes were full of fear. Soul had never seen her daughter look at her with fear before. The look alarmed her even more than the blood in the hut or the discovery of Ellen's mutilated dead body.

He's in me. . . he's in my eyes, Soul repeated to herself.

Her insides lurched with dread. Suddenly, everything added up. She knew what Iris was saying. She had felt something was amiss. She knew that the hut couldn't have damaged itself. She knew that the pain in her head was not a normal pain. She knew that the light now looked different to her, as if her eyes could now see things in a different way. And she felt different. She had felt this way once before. Arrunn had used her once before. And undeniably, the very same dark taste now filled her awareness. She didn't know how and she didn't know why, but she did know that her daughter was telling the truth. Somehow, the Nigh-kutu Arrunn was inside her.

Soul nodded slowly at her daughter, trying to indicate that she understood.

"Iris, my flower, my love," Soul slowly whispered through gritted teeth. "Run. Mamma loves you. Mamma will be alright. Run. Hide."

Soul took a cautious step backwards, giving Iris room to get down and get out. "I will come and find you. But for now, run, get away, hide. Run. . ."

Soul's words stopped abruptly. It was as if something, someone, had seized the tongue in her head with the coldest, numbing hold. She couldn't speak another word.

Soul watched her hand move. It was not her will guiding her hand and she could do nothing to stop it. The hand, her hand, clasped Iris' leg, holding her daughter fast.

She felt her head move forward, stooping close to her daughter's face. She tried to pull her head back, but she had no control. It was her own eyes focusing on her child, yet the gaze was not her own.

Soul could only observe as something powerful, someone formidable, watched her daughter through her eyes.

SIX

The Wills

Humans were so pliable. Their energy was like Earth's water, their bodies like Earth's clay. Together, the combination was yielding and malleable. In that respect, Soul was no different. She had not resisted his energy. Arrunn had possessed her without complication.

Soul's inner core now shielded Arrunn's essence from the energy pull. Whatever the phenomenon was, it had almost dissipated him. Now established in his new host, he was not only shielded, he could absorb additional energy from her. The life-source was diminutive, but sufficient.

Despite Soul's inner core now protecting his energy, Arrunn discovered that he could only fully control her for a limited time before the energy pull affected him once again. This was a hindrance, but not insurmountable. He would simply need to work to a rhythm: control and manipulate, and then retract and recuperate.

Arrunn had already scanned Soul's mind. She had no knowledge of the event that was afflicting the Nigh-kutu. Nor did Tachra's mother know, although it had required a more physical approach to make her talk. Before him now was Soul's offspring. From Soul's mind he had found her identifier, Iris.

Arrunn began scanning Iris for information or resources.

Iris' response indicated that she had some perception of what he was doing. She even tried to block him. The response initially seemed automatic, no more than a reflex of human programming, but not only did she try to block him; she could sense him. It appeared that this creature, Iris, could see him within Soul's body. She even seemed to recognise who he was. And, although she was clearly frightened, she did not submit.

Arrunn studied the child further. For a kutu-made bios, she had a markedly strong essence. Within Iris' core was an energy that resembled a fire. The fire danced like an unexploited, underdeveloped vehemence. Such energy would prove useful. It might even be enough. Could he develop the potency of her inner fire so as to be useful? Almost certainly: humans were constructed to produce and exude emotional responses. Emotional responses had always proved to be the best influencers.

Testing what emotional responses would increase Iris' life energy, Arrunn pushed his essence forward, making Soul's eyes darken and flash, knowing that lesser beings often found such a thing fearful. He then moulded the flesh of his host's face, contorting it, making it bare teeth like a Nar beast.

In response to his attempt to induce fear, although the child did not look away, its terror was great. As expected, fear was one of the most effective ways to enhance the power of life. Better still, Iris' inner core visibly increased, the fire within her churning chaotically.

Here, Arrunn thought, in this seemingly insignificant, paltry human child, was a life-energy that was worth taking. This was an advantage he had not foreseen.

"Make him go away, mamma," Iris spoke, her voice shrill. "Push him away."

His host seemed to hear the words of her offspring. As a result, he could feel Soul's heartbeat increase as her sense of urgency intensified. A pressing sensation pushed at his perception. Soul was trying to override him. Stupid creature.

He had not intended on coming forward from Soul's subconscious so soon. He had merely intended on guiding her as his own body until no longer required. But the child had made Soul aware of his presence, and now Soul battled against him. As a result, he would have to control her again.

"She cannot push me away," Arrunn spoke through Soul's mouth.

Soul was unable to stop his words. Nevertheless, he could feel her pushing harder with her mind, straining to resist his control.

"You can, mamma," the child cried in earnest. "Push him away!"

Iris lurched from the work-surface, sliding to the floor.

Arrunn let the child escape his grasp. These humans were not so different to the creatures he had made on Immorah. Just as they had been contained until useful, Iris could not escape this small abode, but her distressed efforts would increase her desire to live. The more she desired to live, the more her life energy would increase. He would let her run and seek refuge. He would let her fight or flee for her life until her energy was at its peak.

As the child hid behind the stairs, Arrunn scanned the surrounds for any matter that could store Iris' life energy. The wood, clay and fabrics that these humans used were of little use to him. But Soul's memories were open, and he knew she had been given a kutu communication device. Such a device would contain storage crystals. Any crystal could be modified to hold life energy.

Secure the child. Find the device. Obtain a crystal. Drain the child.

Arrunn took a step towards Iris.

"No you don't!"

It was Soul. She had sensed his intention to incapacitate her daughter. She was aware of him, aware of his control, and battled to halter his step. Her adrenaline and will were fighting with all their desperate might against him.

Be calm, Arrunn thought smoothly, sending his thoughts into Soul's mind. ***Do not prolong the child's suffering by trying to stop me. You cannot stop me.***

"I will!" he felt Soul's retaliation burst from her mouth. "You'll not have her. Run, Iris, run!"

It was as if a small light within his host had exploded with luminous energy. It was an energy driven by emotion. Soul's will was prepared to fight him to her inevitable end.

* * *

"Run, Iris, run!" Soul pressed.

Despite the bitter, gnawing pain that crawled through her flesh, as if stabbed by a thousand icicles that made her want to retreat into safe numbness, Soul would not back down. But Arrunn was strong; so very strong. She didn't know how much longer she could hold out against him. She felt his dark, insidious thoughts trying to convince her to relax, to accept that this was best for them all. But Arrunn intended on harming Iris! He intended on using her very hands to harm her own daughter! No! It would not happen. Not while she could do anything about it. She would fight in any way that she could.

Right now, the only thing Soul could think of to slow Arrunn down and give Iris time to escape, was to injure her own flesh.

Soul pushed her will forward, battling through her sense of confinement to try and regain any use of her body. Her hands – if she could just get control of her hands, then she could chop them off, injure them – anything to make them useless. But most parts of her body were blocked from her will, as if she were no more than a tiny, observing insect.

Most parts.

Arrunn was focused on utilising her arms, hands and eyes, but right now, he was not aware of her legs or feet.

Soul gathered all the might she could muster and made her legs launch into a run. They felt as if they were no longer her legs, as if she were holding onto the joints of a puppet, forcing them to move. She lurched forward, increasing her momentum, and charged with pace. Using all her available strength, she flung herself against the wall of the hut.

Soul's body hit the wall violently hard. A loud crunch sounded as her face thumped against the wood. Her head rebounded backwards with a sharp snap. Blood splattered from her nose and her lips. Her flesh recoiled from the impact and she fell, crumpled, to the floor.

Despite Soul's best attempt, the impact with the wall had not made her cease. It hadn't even rendered her unconscious. As her flesh lay dazed, Soul felt Arrunn push against her will, taking control of her limbs, making her legs move once again. Soul fought against him, but could not stop him. Slowly he made her body stand, and then turn to face Iris.

Iris had run to the hut's lone doorway and was desperately pushing at the table that blocked her exit.

Panic consumed Soul, yet somehow within that panic her thoughts for her daughter remained clear. She knew her daughter had no chance of moving the table. It was far too heavy for one so small. There was no time to curse the fact that she herself had securely blocked every available exit and consequently trapped her own daughter in this place. Arrunn had control of her entire body now. She had to break that control. If she focused, if she really focused, she could maybe push her will into a piece of her body again, even just one piece. If she could, then this time she would have to make it enough. With every passing moment Arrunn grew more dexterous at utilising her.

Soul was unable to control her eyes to move them, but in her peripheral vision she could make out the broken table leg on the floor by her feet. That might do it. It was certainly heavy enough. She'd probably only get one more chance. She would have to be fast.

Arrunn's focus was directly ahead. As he concentrated on animating her body, moving it towards Iris, Soul pushed her torso down, picked up the broken table leg and, using the strength of sheer desperation, lifted the wood above her head. She swung it down with force. The jagged broken end smashed down hard against her ankle. The ankle cracked, bending instantly. Her leg knocked out from below her. She buckled, slumping sideways, falling clumsily to the floor.

From her awkward position on the floor, Soul tried again to lift the table leg, intent on doing as much damage to her body as she could. But the burst of previous energy had taken most of her resources and she could not even lift the heavy item. She mustered her waning strength, but Arrunn would not let her move.

"You will not have her," Soul whispered with determination.

That was the last thing she could say. The last thing she could do.

Arrunn muted her.

* * *

I do not wish you damaged or harmed, Arrunn told his host. *Yet you willingly break the only flesh you will ever have. I promise that your child will not know pain by my hand. Feel the truth of my promise.*

Arrunn felt Soul's response. It was not rational, nor did it give her any advantage. She felt the truth in his words, yet still she did not believe him. She understood that she did not have the ability to repel him, yet still she tried. She knew she could not defeat him, yet was prepared to die trying nonetheless. It was an irrational set of juxtapositions. Even now her suppressed thoughts struggled to find new ways to conquer him. Could she make herself stop breathing? Could she successfully smother him? And, quite cleverly yet unwisely, she was even calculating if she had the strength to pull him deeper into her own inner core, to render him incapacitated. Could she, a mere human, do that to him? The beautiful, naive audacity almost made him smile.

Just as Soul's thoughts had betrayed, Arrunn could already feel her pulling at his energy. She wrenched with all the enervated power that she had left, trying to drag his energy deeper into her own, trying to contain him, trying to stop him.

Enough!

Soul had no choice but to stop.

He grew tired of her. This human had once interested him with her obstinate strength; now her will was irritating. He required her as a host, nothing more. If he hadn't needed the use of her body, he would have finished her already.

Arrunn pushed his energy against Soul's, taking full control of her body, linking into the entirety of her nervous system and pushing her consciousness into the smallest recess at the back of her mind. Soul would not cause him trouble again. She was now nothing more than a body to animate.

By the hut door, Iris had stopped her futile attempts to move the table and unblock her exit. She paused a moment, watching him, her focus on his eyes. And then, clearly aware that it was he who watched back and not her mamma, she ran past him in a wide arc. Once past Arrunn, she sprinted up the stairs with agile speed.

Arrunn relaxed, easing his energy through Soul's body and mind, knitting together any flesh damage that could hinder him. And then, ignoring Soul's futile protests, which rang through the back of her mind like a baby rag-beast at the far end of the great tunnels, he turned towards the central stairs and headed towards Iris' position.

* * *

Upstairs, in the far recess of Tachra's old room, Iris huddled into the corner behind the large storage chest. She had managed to unlatch and open the storm shutter on the window. It had been heavy, and the bolt had snapped against her hand, crushing her fingers, but she had done it. Her fingers now throbbed with a hurt so bad that she wanted to cry. But she would not cry. She knew she had to be grown up.

Iris still wasn't sure if she should leave. She had very nearly climbed out of the window and run away. Mamma had told her to run. She really did want to run away and be safe; to run as far away from the bad kutu ghost as possible. But she had decided that she wasn't going anywhere without her mamma. But mamma had the bad kutu ghost in her, right inside her. Iris had no idea how to get a kutu ghost out of her mamma, especially one who clearly wanted to hurt them both. How she wished she still had a papa. She'd been told stories of how strong he was. He wouldn't have let that bad kutu hurt them.

I could get out and run to Mele's hut for help, Iris thought. *Mele's hut is close and she has lots of children who are big. They're all nice. They would help.*

Iris wanted that idea to be a good one. Mele's hut was indeed close and she could get there quickly if she ran through the fields. But, as much as she wished otherwise, Iris knew that the idea wouldn't work. The bad kutu ghost was too strong for them. Mele and even her grown up children would just end up hurt or ceased. And anyway, even if Iris did go to them and try to explain what had happened, they probably wouldn't believe her.

What Iris needed was help from one of the kind kutu or Tachra.

Tachra would know how to get rid of the bad kutu ghost, Iris thought. Tachra knew lots about the kutu. But the last Iris knew, Tachra was trapped at the bottom of that deep well, and it didn't look like she could get out. Iris was sure that Tachra wasn't at the bottom of that well anymore, but she didn't know where she was. She must have gotten out, because now she felt very, very far away.

But surely, even if she was too far away to help, Tachra would ask one of the nice kutu to help instead. Yes, that would work. The last time Iris needed Tachra's help she called for her with her head, just like Tachra had told her to do. She had called for Tachra with her head and she knew that Tachra had heard as she had sent Stanze to rescue them and Stanze had said that Tachra had sent him. Perhaps Tachra could do that again. Perhaps she could ask Stanze to come and get that bad kutu ghost out of her mamma.

The loud noises from downstairs in the hut had stopped. It was much quieter now. The silence was scarier than the noises.

Iris stayed as quiet as she could and took the bead pendant from around her neck. Tachra had made that bead and given it to mamma and mamma had given it to her. Tachra had said that the bead was special and Iris knew that it was. It was her special talking bead. She had used that bead to call for Tachra before. She hoped it would work again.

Talk with your head, Iris told herself. *Remember how Tachra told you to do it; you have to think loudly.*

Tachra. Tachra. Tachra, Iris began calling with her head. *Please help.*

She tried to think clearly, but then her thoughts began tumbling together like a pleading dialogue, trying to explain what she had seen in her mamma's eyes, trying to explain how her mamma had tried to fight it, how the table across the door was too heavy to move, how it was all quiet downstairs and that scared her. The words stammered through her head, each time with the lingering images of the chaos in the hut and of old lady Ellen's blood-covered body.

My head's muddled, Iris chastised herself, rubbing her eyes with desperation. She knew she had to think loudly and clearly.

A quiet shuffling noise downstairs was followed by the sound of slow footsteps. The footsteps were her mamma's, but Iris didn't know if the bad kutu was still in her or not. She had a horrible feeling that he was. The footsteps were moving in her direction. They were on the stairs. She had never felt so scared before.

Tachra. Tachra. Tachra. Iris thought in earnest, clutching the bead pendant between her hands.

Tachra! Tachra! Help me. He's here!

SEVEN

The Return

There was only darkness all around, yet the kutu death-path felt velvety underfoot. It was a soft, dark, inviting path that smelt of nothing.

Meah walked by my side. I rested my hand gently on her head as we moved, embracing her closeness, the feel of her fur so real. She seemed aglow in his place. Her tones of gold and brown were luminous with her spirit. The lines of energy that connected us shone brighter than ever.

I watched my bare feet take footsteps and my hand rest on Meah's head as it caressed her fur. It looked just like my hand. They looked just like my feet. But I knew that I no longer had a physical body. The skin and bones that had once been mine were now left behind in that pit. The form I now held was merely the memory of my flesh. But it felt right. I was still me.

I glanced ahead. In the distant darkness, I could see Jychanumun.

Jychanumun stood at the end of the death-path, his hand outstretched towards me. He appeared just like my first memory of him. His long black energy wings spanned out behind him, moving as if swaying in an invisible breeze. Their darkness was edged in shadow-light. His pale skin glowed. His all-black eyes were healed, restored, casting shadows across his composed expression. He was the pure black and white kutu. Jychanumun looked beautiful and magnificent, radiant and serene in this place. These paths were his, the Death-Path-Walker. He was home.

Beside Jychanumun stood the spirits of his Nigh-kutu brothers, Dragun and Mardoch. They were watching me, their wings held straight to a point as a mark of respect. Their honour humbled me. Both still wore the memory of their matte-black Nigh-kutu war-wear, yet now it contrasted with pieces of golden Shaa-kutu armour. The energy from the golden armour shimmered through their darkness, making the tips of their shadow wings luminous with flecks of gold. They stood tall and strong, with an aura of calm, sombre readiness that reflected the warriors they had become and the noble kutu they had always been. I was honoured that my wait in the death-paths would be with such fine beings.

As I travelled towards the three kutu, I glanced around at the path that I walked. At first, it had seemed nothing more than an empty, dark place; a tunnel of nothingness between my flesh and my destiny. But the more that I opened my awareness, the more depths I perceived. This surrounding darkness was not emptiness, but filled with possibilities. Every shadow, every absence of anything, had meaning, hope, discovery and the potential of everything. This was not the place of oblivion that I had expected, but one of harmony.

This may not be my home, I decided, but I could find peace here. And, as much as I hadn't wanted to leave the world behind, I was grateful for the prevailing sense of safety. Here were some of my friends in front of me and Meah beside me, in a place of serenity.

I caressed the fur on Meah's neck, breathing a sigh of content that I thought I had forgotten.

Yes, we can wait here, I thought. *Here we will be at peace.*

Jychanumun called me towards him.

His voice was melodic, enticing, guiding me.

Tachra, come to me. Let my voice guide your way. His song flowed. His words created a place for each silent footstep to fall as I walked.

With every step, I moved ever-closer to the innermost place in the death-paths where Jychanumun called from and all the doors converged. The doors were made of darkness and surrounded by darkness. Only the faint glow around their forms gave any indication that they were there. I knew that place and those doors. I had seen them in my dreams. They were access points in Jychanumun's mind, gateways that led to other places, other realms to which he was the only guide.

As I travelled my dark, inviting path, moving closer to the central place, the nothingness around me began reflecting my own essence, adapting to who I was. The blank darkness began shimmering with subtle glimpses of my colours. With each inbound step, more colours were added, and within the darkness those colours began to move and merge, forming indistinct pictures. The pictures grew in clarity, becoming reflections from my mind, hints from my imaginings, and stories from my dreams. Some images had sounds. They were like whispers of a gentle wind echoing through a forest of leaves. It was as if this place was coming alive. My death-path was being brought to life by my presence, my life and death. I understood, now. Here, in this place, Jychanumun's place, life and death held equal value and meaning.

A whisper seemed to take precedence of form. It grew louder than all others until its sound was distinct.

Tachra, Tachra, Tachra. . .

The words were a calling. It sounded small and shrill and scared. The tone of desperation was clear. It sounded like Iris.

Meah had heard it too, her ears rising to a point as she glanced behind us.

I half turned. Behind me was my path, whose beginning was my entrance to this place. The entrance was still open. Beyond the entrance a colourless light was shining with the brightness of the world. Inside the luminous opening was the small silhouette of a girl. From her proportions and energy colours, it could only be Iris.

Is this real? I asked Jychanumun with uncertainty. *Should the entrance to my death-path show another?*

Stay on your path, Jychanumun instructed. *Continue walking towards me.*

But I could not disregard what I could see. My logic told me that this was no more than Iris sensing my death and she was now calling out to me, searching with her mind. But my heart told me that she would only call if something was wrong. I *knew* that something was wrong.

And then, in the distant, bright entrance to my path, something else came into view behind Iris. It looked like another silhouette, one made of dark moving lines that wound around each other. The shapes seemed to struggle to hold form, snakelike, rippling, trying to merge to form wings.

The image behind Iris unsettled me, vibrated at the very core of me, creating an anxious twist in my belly. This could not be right. I must be mistaken. But, I knew I was not mistaken. I recognised that energy too well: the tendrils of shadow that moved and undulated, flickering out as if sensing the space around them. Only one kutu had energy like that – Arrunn.

Please help. Iris' new words formed in my path. *He's here!*

He's here?

He's here!

It *was* Arrunn.

"Is this not finished?" I whispered in horror.

It's not finished, I realised with dread.

Jychanumun. . . I tried to ask, but the thoughts would barely form.

Jychanumun had seen what I had seen and was already thinking at a speed that was almost too quick for me to absorb. He didn't know. This didn't make sense. He had seen the kutu-divide activate and be effective. The Nigh-kutu had been pulled back into the shadow. The Shaa-kutu had returned to the light. Arrunn should not be on Earth. Arrunn, by now, should be in the shadow realms. What Iris' thoughts called out should not be correct, *could* not be correct. But Jychanumun also knew that this small human child had no ability to project falsehood into these paths of actuality. Iris was telling the truth.

Come quickly, Jychanumun directed. *I cannot protect you until you are in this central place and I can close your path. Get here, then I can determine what to do.*

I knew Jychanumun was right. He understood Arrunn better than anyone. Jychanumun would find a way to resolve this.

But my own racing thoughts stopped my legs from walking. Arrunn, the primary kutu that we had wanted removed to the shadow realms was still on Earth. If all the other kutu had gone, and Jychanumun had to remain in the death-paths, left alone and unchallenged, without anyone to stand against him, Arrunn could destroy every living thing on my beloved planet. And if Iris could see him, was he coming for her? Had she gone to the Temple again? Iris was special. She was born from the very first love between humans; that made her unique, and would never exist again. Could I turn my back on one loved one? Even for the greater good of everything? I knew that I should. My head reeled with the facts that everything was at stake, not just the life of any one single being. But every life had value. Without that, soul, hope, trust, integrity and honour, and all those things that connected us and which made life precious, would not exist at all.

Tachra, Jychanumun urgently called, *we must close your path lest Arrunn finds his way in through Iris. You must get here **now.***

I heard the urgency. I sensed the danger. Jychanumun had tried for millennia to conceal himself from Arrunn; not for himself, but to protect and obscure these death-paths. Nothing would be safe if Arrunn found access to this place. I knew my entrance needed to be closed.

I had a choice. To one side was the opening to my path and the silhouette of Iris asking for help within the brightness of the physical world I'd left behind. To my other side was Jychanumun, with Mardoch and Dragun, calling me to where I needed to be for all our futures.

My conscious and sub-conscious seemed to work in perfect synchronicity. I didn't have to think. I knew what I must do.

It was as if time slowed. Time did slow, for my heart and mind were now working with the unity I had learnt from the Old One. I put my hand against the dark rippling wall. Where my fingers touched, I projected my thoughts. From my thoughts, I made a picture. The picture grew in definition, blossoming with detail, finding depth, texture and movement until it became the image of Elysium. The image sprung to life. I could smell the breeze and blossom. I could see the movement of the leaves and the long grasses, close enough to touch. This was no longer a picture but a window, a doorway. Here in the death-paths, I had created an entrance to Elysium, the untouchable haven for the ceased.

I gently put my mouth against the side of Meah's head. "Be safe," I whispered to her. "I'll be but a moment." I closed my eyes, breathing against the soft warmth of her fur, letting her sense my intent.

Meah didn't need to understand my words. She felt my meaning. Without hesitation, she leapt through the doorway and into Elysium.

Knowing Meah was out of harm's way, I brushed my hand over the entrance to Elysium and closed the access, leaving only the same dark path that had shimmered before.

I glanced up towards Jychanumun and shook my head. He had stopped calling to me, his expression now set into one of realisation.

He could see it in my eyes. I was scared and sorry for what I was about to do.

Jychanumun was already asking me not to do it, but he knew I was going to anyway. I felt him talking to Mardoch and Dragun. He was talking fast, telling them things, giving them instructions. He was talking with words, thoughts and energy on every level. I didn't listen. I didn't need to. Right now, all I needed to do was to trust myself. He knew. I knew he knew. My decision was made before I'd even made it.

I felt as if I was watching myself from beyond myself. I turned towards the entrance to my path where Iris' silhouette still pleaded for help. That. . . that place was my focus. Everything else seemed to melt into the distance.

And then I ran.

I ran and I ran.

I ran with the lightness of the clouds and the freedom of the winds. I ran as fast as I could, undoing the very path that I had just walked. I ran away from Jychanumun, to keep him safe. I ran to close the paths and keep Jychanumun's abilities away from Arrunn. I ran in the hope that I could help Iris. I ran for all the things I loved and would never lose hope for. I ran back towards that entrance. I ran back towards the world. I ran back towards the flesh body that I had left behind.

I didn't glance back.

I didn't look to see if Mardoch and Dragun headed through one of the doorways that Jychanumun opened for them.

My path was almost undone.

My entrance back to the physical world loomed before me.

Without hesitation, and with all the will and determination that I could muster, I leapt through that opening and back into the world that I thought I had left behind.

I had no idea if what I was doing was right.

I only hoped that I didn't end up in the emptiness of nothingness.

I didn't contemplate the consequences of entering a dead body.

I hoped my body could still hold me.

I hoped I could find it.

I hoped. . .

I. . .

Suddenly, my thoughts tumbled around in a whirl of darkness, dislocated from me, yet drawn towards something I didn't want to go towards. Something felt unnatural. I saw words and sounds break into pieces, their meaning falling apart and re-building into monstrosities. I heard images shatter into splinters of shadow noise and nothingness, only to grow again into a swarm of terrible moving darkness. And the sensations were the worst. They were unfamiliar; each tinged with an abstract disorder that I felt I was falling into, yet falling away from. This was worse than when I had dislocated my mind from my flesh, worse than grief or fear or any despairing emotion. This was wrong, wrong in every sense. But there was no point in screaming, no point flailing. I was caught in a void of knowing that I should not enter this body, my body, but knowing that my decision was already made. I was there.

And suddenly.

So dark.

So. . . nothing.

My thoughts were straight and true, but I had an overwhelming physical numbness. There was only darkness and stagnation. No senses. No warmth. No light. No sound. No colour. No movement.

What have I done? My thoughts reeled. *I am trapped inside a dead body.*

You are not trapped, Jychanumun calmly spoke into my thoughts. *Remember your lessons. Your body is merely a vessel.*

But I need my body and I can't move it, I thought with desperation. *It is too long ceased.*

Trust me. Trust Dragun and Mardoch. Jychanumun's tone was firm. *Tachra, I must concentrate. . .*

I muted my connection.

I had made my choice. I was responsible for the consequences. I was in a dead body and I could not move.

Iris? I called out.

Iris heard straight away. *Please, Tachra, help,* she immediately responded. *The bad kutu ghost is here. Papa is keeping him away, but mamma is hurt and she can't hear me anymore. I can't get to her.*

Iris' dialogue continued. It was the frantic, terrified thinking of a child. Much of it didn't make sense. I reassured her that help was on its way. I managed to conceal my doubts and fears; I knew that those things would only frighten her further. She was only five summers old. If she could just stay alive it would be a miracle.

So Soul was there too? And was hurt. This was getting worse. And who was this 'papa' who was keeping Arrunn away? I only hoped it was a kind, strong villager who perhaps had been taught some of the kutu ways, although I couldn't imagine any human successfully keeping Arrunn at bay. I was desperate to help. I had to do something. But what? I was stuck inside a ceased body. And if that was not hindrance enough, my own lack of caution had not taken into consideration the fact that my body was down a well so deep that it would be impossible to climb out. Even so, I had to try. I somehow had to make this body work, even if it just meant animating a pair of lifeless legs. But right now, nothing would move. All I could feel was cold.

I was so cold.

Cold? How could my stagnant flesh feel anything at all? It should not. But I certainly felt a chilling ache.

Was that cold wind against my skin?

My eyes bolted open.

At first I thought that I was blind, as only darkness welcomed me. But then I realised I had something covering my face. I tried to shout, the noise coming out of my mouth more like an animal huff. Something was in my mouth. I tried to move, but I felt as stiff as a stone.

"It's alright, I have you."

Although I could not see him, I recognised Mardoch's voice.

I must be alive. I really must be alive!

Light came into my eyes as the covering over my face was pulled down. The light was not bright – it was only the last rays of sunlight – but still, after the death-paths and the darkness of the well, it seemed overwhelmingly luminous. The cold wind against my skin made my eyes water. The smell of sharp metal indicated that I was high above ground. The gently rhythmic sensation was familiar. I was flying. I was held firm by Mardoch and moving through the high-air at an incredible speed. My skin tingled. I had been wrapped tightly in a healing sheet, and in my mouth was something which made it prickle as if filled with a thousand crawling insects.

I tried to spit out the object in my mouth, but it would not move.

"Do not remove the healing disc, not yet. I am no physician, but I have done as Jychanumun instructed," Mardoch told me.

I wondered where we were flying to. Mardoch must have retrieved me from the well in the Temple, but where were we going? I went to ask Mardoch the question, but the object in my mouth would not allow it and Mardoch kept talking anyway.

"I have to be quick," Mardoch continued. "The kutu pull is

in place and I have only six-hundred kutu core-beats until I am pulled back to the shadow realms. Until then, Jychanumun has remained in the paths to reopen the doorways for us."

Six hundred kutu core-beats? That was all the time that Mardoch could survive here before being pulled to the shadow? Six hundred core-beats did not sound long at all. I hoped that a kutu core-beat was much slower than my human heartbeat. My own heart was racing.

"You cannot fully heal," Mardoch warned. "I do not have the skills. But the healing sheets will repair much and the disc in your mouth has implanted nanos that should restore your tongue. . ."

Restore my tongue; so that was the strange crawling sensation in my mouth.

"You will feel weak, as I used a synthesis to replace your lost blood. It was all I could find in a hurry. It will suffice. I've wrapped healers around your arms, but do not know how well your hands will function. Your muscles are depleted and many other functions will take more time to complete than we have available. Tachra Iastha, your human body is what I would call a *cathunali:* a complete mess. I do not know if I admire you or think you a fool." He laughed, more to himself. "In this, I do believe you have been even more reckless than me."

Mardoch paused. He needed to take a deep breath. I saw that the flight was strenuous for him, and that talking was strenuous too. His pale skin had flecks of deep, vivid green, the colour of his energy, moving across it, over it, and then away from it. He was visibly waning. This was the result of the polarity pull. His energy had already started to disperse.

I felt a sharp descent as Mardoch swooped downwards. I could see his expression, his brow furrowed, intense with concentration. His black braided hair, still embedded with the little green crystals, moved wildly in the current of his hurried flight. Now I could see his energy around him, swirling vivid green, remaining in the air as he descended, ebbing away with every passing moment.

As we descended, from the corner of my eye, I glanced a different type of green. It was the dark green of rolling hills at sunset. My stomach lurched with the vision of such a familiar sight. I had thought I would never see this place again. Those hills were unmistakable. They were the luscious, tree-topped mounds around Threetops, my home village.

But of course, it made complete sense now: Soul and Iris would have returned to my old hut in Threetops. Of course Iris would be here. But Arrunn too? Only moments ago he had been directly before me in the pit at the Temple. How had he gotten here?

I felt Mardoch land, running as he hit the ground. I smelt burning. From my tightly swaddled position I could see thick black smoke bellowing into the air.

"Do not put Tachra there!" I heard a voice shout. It was Dragun. "Go around the other side."

"Eskah!" Mardoch muttered under his breath. I felt him leap sideways and mutter another word, a word from a Nigh-kutu that I had not heard before.

"Where is he?" Mardoch shouted.

"In the hut," Dragun replied. "So are the female and child."

The female? Which female? Who was with Iris? My mother or Soul? I wanted to ask. I needed to speak. I wanted to be out of this healing sheet and running to help.

Help is coming, I told Iris. *They are Nigh-kutu, but good Nigh-kutu.*

Iris did not reply. That heightened my concerns even more.

Mardoch put me on the ground.

"We may need your Earth skills," he said. "But wait here until I say it is safe." He then turned and sprinted away.

Mardoch had leant me against one of the large natural boulders behind my old hut. I tried to move the tightly swaddled healing sheet, contorting my body until it fell from my shoulders. Mardoch was right: my hands weren't functioning properly. My arms, however, would move, although their skeleton-like appearance felt as heavy as a tree. I twisted around so that I faced the hut.

My hut! It was on fire!

Smoke oozed out, thick and black, from every crack and hole in the hut's walls and roof. The storm shutters appeared closed, with even more smoke pouring out from around them. And it bellowed out from the smokestack, so thick that it created blackness in the darkening sky. I could hear the loud crackles of fire from inside. It was a horrible sound.

I crawled towards the hut, clutching the healing sheet as best as my malformed hands would allow. By the skies, my body was frustratingly feeble!

"I've retrieved enough force-field blocks," I heard Dragun tell Mardoch. "We'll barrier the entire hut and stop the fire. It won't stop Arrunn fully, but it will slow him down long enough."

Mardoch had already run to Dragun and collected a small, smooth, silver cube. He moved a few strides to one side of the hut, crouched, and thumped the small box hard into the ground as Dragun did the same.

"What beat are you up to?" Dragun asked.

"Over four hundred," Mardoch replied. "We will have to cut this fine."

"Get Iris out," I tried to speak. My restored tongue felt strange. It seemed to function, yet the words came out merely a whisper.

Mardoch and Dragun didn't hear me. They were too busy producing more silver cubes, positioning them on the other side of the hut.

"Ready," Mardoch shouted to Dragun.

Dragun moved from view. Almost immediately, a sharp snap

sounded. A pale luminosity began shimmering from all the small silver boxes, rising up and joining into one large sheet that curved until it encompassed the entire hut. It was a kutu force-field, dome-shaped, protecting or containing what was in the hut.

"It's not reducing the fire," Dragun shouted as he raced back towards Mardoch.

"It should have absorbed the flames," Mardoch replied. "Fire or not, we will have to go in."

Dragun pulled a long, carved knife from his armour, looked at Mardoch, and then nodded.

Side by side, Dragun and Mardoch ran towards the hut with their heads low and a speed that was barely visible. The force field rippled as they passed through, their momentum not faltering. And then, with one leap, they flew straight towards the hut.

In perfect synchronicity the two kutu struck the wall of the hut with their right arms raised, pounding their fists against the wood. They let out a unified guttural yell that made the air pulsate. Suddenly, a large section of the hut, almost half its entire width, shattered beneath their blows.

Flames bellowed out from my old broken, burning home, but the two Nigh-kutu did not pause. They resumed their momentum, vanishing into the burning hut, obscured by smoke and fire.

Iris, if you can hear me, keep away from the fire, keep away from Arrunn. I'm outside. Good kutu are coming, I thought. I hoped Iris could hear me. I hoped she was still alive.

From inside, I heard a load roar. It didn't sound like the kutu. It sounded more like an angry animal. Then, from deep within the earth, I felt movement. The ground tremored. A rumbling echoed.

Suddenly, a vast flame exploded through the hut's roof, its blast so great that I was almost thrown tumbling back. There, from my old hut, a huge fire now propelled upwards, like a violent blizzard of red and yellow. The flames were immense.

From within the flames Mardoch sped out, half flying, half running. Smoke and energy swirled off him. Under his arm was Iris, clearly alive and surprisingly undamaged.

Close behind Mardoch followed Dragun, cradling a badly injured Soul. Soul looked barely conscious and was black with soot, her dress singed to blackened rags. Her eyes were shut and she weakly held onto Dragun. But she was alive. Soul and Iris were both alive.

Mardoch headed towards me, panting heavily as he carefully placed Iris on the ground. Iris fell to her knees, clutching on to me as if I was life itself.

"My mother," I urged Mardoch and Dragun.

Dragun shook his head at me. He looked sombre. I didn't like that look.

"Tachra, she is not in there. . ." he began to speak.

"That should wait," Mardoch purposely interrupted. "I couldn't find Arrunn and we are running out of time."

Dragun nodded his acknowledgement. It was true; I could see that they were running out of time. Their energies were drifting from their bodies even faster now. Their exertion had only hastened their depletion. They were both clearly exhausted from their energy waning so much.

"Tachra," Dragun indicated towards Soul, "This one needs your Earth healing. Do what you must. We will have to return for you. We will be quick. We will deal with Arrunn when we return. The force-field will contain him until then, and we will also address the situation with your mother. Meanwhile, do not move from here and do not enter the hut. Yes?" He looked at me questioningly.

I nodded, indicating that I understood.

Dragun gently put Soul on the ground by his feet.

"Mardoch," Dragun was talking fast. "I'm at five-hundred and twenty. We will come back as soon as we're rebalanced." He indicated towards the hut. "Something else is in the fire. We will need full strength to tackle both that and Arrunn."

As the two kutu conversed, I looked over Soul's body for injuries. As I did so, Soul opened her eyes. I went to smile at her, joyous to see my friend alive.

My smile halted. My joy was replaced with uncertainty.

Soul's face was set into an expression of alarm. Her eyes were full of fear and warning. She was staring at me, as if trying to tell me something without words.

Something was wrong.

And then I was sure that I saw her eyes change. Just for the shortest moment. Soul's eyes looked as if they darkened.

Soul's gaze moved from me, to Dragun, and then to Mardoch. The two kutu were too engrossed in conversation to notice. Soul's stare lingered on Mardoch, moving from his face to his hair, scanning over the glowing green crystals embedded in his braids. Soul's expression now had a calm, cold poise. Something wasn't right. I could almost taste bad intent. Her expression had changed from one of absolute fear to one of calculated consideration. It was like two completely different people.

The eyes. . . Two different people. . .

Oh no.

Oh no. No, no, no.

Show no fear. By the skies, keep calm. I must not change my facial expression. I must not show panic. I must smile with all the genuine gladness to see my friend alive.

Soul hadn't just been trying to tell me something; she had, with her expression, been trying to warn me. Now that I saw with my true vision and not just my eyes, I could see that this wasn't just Soul. Somehow, it was Arrunn too.

The person in front of me still looked like Soul, but now it felt like Arrunn. And whatever part of Arrunn I could sense, he seemed very interested in Dragun and Mardoch, especially the crystals embedded in Mardoch's braids.

Jychanumun, I pushed out urgently with my mind. *Do you see this? Arrunn is within Soul. Tell Mardoch and Dragun. Make them hear you with your thoughts, with anything. Warn them.* My thoughts came out frantically. I could barely think straight. Somehow, I had to make Mardoch and Dragun aware without Arrunn sensing my awareness.

"Mardoch," I said slowly, "Take Iris to a safe place, away from the danger of the flames." I had to make sure the words formed in my still-numb mouth so that I didn't have to repeat them. I couldn't raise Arrunn's suspicion that I could sense him, lest he strike. "Make distance from the hut, from Arrunn in the hut," I added.

Mardoch looked at me questioningly. He frowned slightly, glancing at the burning hut and then Iris. I knew he was about to query my instruction. Rightly so; he and Dragun were almost depleted and had no time for non-necessities. I held my stare, hoping, and biting down the words that I wanted to shout.

Then I also saw a change in Dragun's stance. Although Dragun never moved, he stiffened. Had he seen something? Or had he just noticed my own expression? Mercifully, I think he understood.

"Go!" Dragun suddenly yelled to Mardoch.

As Mardoch picked up Iris, immediately launching into the sky, Dragun twisted around, grabbed Soul, wrenching her from the ground with his hand under her chin. He drew his knife, moving it towards her throat.

"No!" I launched towards Dragun, "Don't kill her!"

Dragun looked at me, his blade poised against Soul's skin.

"I must," Dragun replied. "It is the only way to be sure that Arrunn leaves this place."

"No!" I protested, holding onto Dragun's arm. "Not my friend, not Soul. Anyway, Arrunn could simply find another human body to use. Or worse: he might try to enter you."

Soul looked up, not seeming to notice that the skin on her neck was pressed against the edge of the knife, making small droplets of blood spill across the surface.

"High Warrior Dragun." Soul's mouth spoke with a voice that was not her own.

It was Arrunn. Soul and Arrunn. Soul's face and body, but Arrunn's mind and essence.

From the centre of Soul's torso, a fine tendril of dark-brown energy emerged like an uncoiling snake. It eased forward, staying connected to Soul, moving up towards Dragun. It was Arrunn's energy.

"Dragun, move away," I warned.

Dragun released Soul and quickly stepped sideways. With a swift movement, he slashed at Arrunn's tendril of energy with his blade. The tendril severed in two.

Arrunn's energy recoiled, as if in shock, but then the two severed parts moved together, rejoining to become whole once again. The renewed energy tendril hung poised in the air for a short moment, and then lashed viciously towards Dragun. Dragun had to move fast to avoid the strike, and the two began aggressively sparring, energy against blade. At first it seemed that Dragun was faster with his knife and could overcome Arrunn's attacking energy. But then, just as Dragun was becoming adept at severing the energy tendril faster than it could reform, a second tendril of Arrunn's energy emerged from Soul's body. And then a third. Then another. Within moments there were dozens of lashing tendrils assailing Dragun.

The assault on Dragun grew more concentrated. Arrunn's energy drove towards him, forcing him to retreat. Dragun cut and lacerated with speed and precision, his knife dancing from one hand to another in a blur of speed, but it didn't seem to stop them, only encourage more. No matter how quickly Dragun responded, Arrunn's energy continued to reattach itself and intensify its relentless attack.

Despite Dragun's speed, the faster he moved, the quicker his own energy was depleting. He was almost diminished.

"Dragun, you must return to the paths!" I shouted.

"Cannot," Dragun panted. "Cannot chance giving him access."

But of course! This was terrible. Dragun was almost spent. He couldn't open his entrance to the death-paths or it would let Arrunn in too. And now, when I looked, it was as if Arrunn was merely playing with Dragun, waiting for his opportunity to enter the paths too.

I had to help. I dug my fingers into the ground, feeling the energy of the soil. I drew in that energy, pushing it out against Arrunn, trying to aid Dragun. The Earth energy gave Dragun more speed, and even healed the wounds that bled energy from his kutu skin, but it could not restore his unique, depleting core.

Dragun was fighting for his life. He glanced around, looking for any vantage point, his ornately carved knife still moving in a blur of speed to keep Arrunn from overpowering him. He slowly gave ground until he was backed up against the largest boulder. I desperately pushed more Earth energy towards him.

"I'll come back for you, Tachra." Dragun rasped, throwing something as he fought. "I have just thirty beats left."

A small silver cube landed directly before me. It was one of the kutu force fields.

Momentarily I wasn't sure what to do with that little cube; instinctively, I just placed it right in front of me. I didn't do anything to make it work. It just tingled in my hand and then activated, sending a pale blue light all around that extended to encompass Soul.

As the kutu force-field grew around Arrunn's host body, Arrunn's attacking tendrils faltered for the shortest moment, but they did not stop. They continued emanating from Soul, working through the barrier. If anything, Arrunn's efforts grew more vehement. I had expected Arrunn's energy to be contained, but it didn't seem to make any difference.

Dragun was backed up against the boulder. He had nowhere else to go, but it was the wry smile on his face that told me he was not about to cease. Still sparring, he began moving backwards. As he moved, the solid grey rock gave way for him. It looked like nothing more than Dragun leaning into the softest bed. Within a moment, Dragun's back had entirely vanished into the boulder. He glanced at me and nodded, the half-smile still on his lips. And then, with one final step, every part of him bar his knife-wielding hand disappeared from sight. With a final flurry of slashes his remaining hand severed more of Arrunn's tendrils, and then that too disappeared, melting into the rock.

Dragun, Rock Weaver, the last surviving kutu of the Weaver clan, whose skill was bending stone and moving matter, had absorbed himself into the boulder.

Only Dragun's long, carved knife remained. Its hilt was embedded in the rock. The serrated blade protruded, glistening, pointing upwards like a final salute.

EIGHT

The Opportunity

Just as anticipated, Arrunn could sense a death-path opening. He almost reached it. But just before he could, High-warrior Dragun had absorbed into the stone. Arrunn had not been able to pass through.

No Rock Weaver should exist. No Weavers of any type should exist. Arrunn thought he had destroyed them all.

Arrunn retracted his energy back into his host. Soul's inner core had diminished considerably. Much more and she would become useless dust like the other humans. He would need to work with consideration for a short while until he was finished with her.

Despite not accessing the death-path, Arrunn still wanted to smile – every time fate tried to change his course a new opportunity would arise. Tachra was here, alone with him. Jychanumun was in the death-paths. The connection between Jychanumun and Tachra was open. All options now had conclusions that were positive. It was almost beautiful.

He glanced around, evaluating, extending Soul's hand to feel the rippling blue energy of the barrier. His host's flesh would not pass through, but it was no more than a standard resonating light-kutu barrier. There would be means to overcome it.

The human, Tachra, the link to the heart-of-all-things, now sat before him. Make her converse. Make her anxious. Speaking reduces her inner peace. Anxiety makes her vulnerable to suggestions. Eventually, it will make her reach out to the Death-Path-Walker.

"It appears," Arrunn nodded towards Tachra, "that once again, it is just you and me."

Tachra did not reply, but she was listening.

"I know you can speak," Arrunn continued. "I am assuming you have a reformed tongue, credit to kutu healing."

Tachra hesitated. She seemed unsure. "Yes," she eventually replied. "I can speak."

He opened his arms, Soul's arms, wide, lifting his face to the sky.

"Then come, Iastha Tachra, use the Voice," he calmly goaded. "Use the Voice of the Old One and banish me. Command me gone. Save your friend from a painful, inevitable death. Just one word through the Old One and banish me."

He lingered, unmoving, sensing her reaction.

"No? Nothing? No Voice?" he provoked. "You are not going to command me gone? Order me diminished? Nothing at all?"

He lowered his arms, his gaze settling upon her once again.

"Has Iastha Tachra lost all her powers?" he asked.

Her uncertainty increased. She remained silent as he stood watching her.

"If you could use the Voice, you would have done so already," he noted. "It seems that you were telling the truth, and that removing your tongue was not necessary." He made sure he paused. "For that," he inclined his head, making a small bow, "I apologise. I ask for your forgiveness."

NINE

The Severance

Apologise? Forgiveness?

I knew that Arrunn was trying to provoke me. I knew that I must ignore him and think straight. But, having the familiar figure of my friend wearing Arrunn's contemptuous expression was both disturbing and chilling. I forced my gaze away, barely able to concentrate with his steady stare fixed on me through Soul's eyes.

I wanted to destroy Arrunn, or at the very least dispatch him to the shadow realms. I had to do something and my mind spun with possibilities, but every idea was either foolish or impossible. Arrunn was still so strong. I was disadvantaged. My body was too damaged to fully stand, let alone fight. I had no weapons. I only hoped the kutu barrier would hold until Dragun and Mardoch returned. This situation was something the kutu had not predicted, nor made any contingency for.

Jychanumun, I called with my thoughts. *Can you still hear me?*

Yes, Jychanumun answered straight away. *Once Dragun has regenerated, he will return to collect you.*

What about Arrunn? I asked. I was not going to leave while he was still here and in my friend.

Dragun will attend to that, Jychanumun replied.

I couldn't see how. Dragun was clearly overwhelmed before. I couldn't see what had changed to give him the advantage. I told Jychanumun as much, allowing him to sense my unsureness.

Arrunn will retract for short periods, to stop Soul's flesh from disintegrating, Jychanumun told me. *When he is retracted, Dragun will end his host body. Without a host body, Arrunn will be drawn to the shadow realms. You must not stop Dragun this time.*

But Dragun wanted to kill Soul, I protested.

It is not Soul anymore, Jychanumun explained, *but only empty flesh that looks like Soul. No human could withstand a kutu's energy for so long. Soul's essence will already be diminished.*

Diminished? Already? Diminished meant gone, ceased, the forever death. Diminished meant no existence anywhere.

My alarm made me open my true vision again, this time to look deeper at the merged being that was Arrunn and Soul. Instantly, I was bombarded with the brightness of the kutu force-field. Layers upon layers of every colour, tightly woven with threads of brightest white, surrounded them. Beyond that, Soul's body appeared like a contained mass of darkness in the vague semblance of a person. Arrunn's energy sickened my true vision, but I pushed further, deeper. There. It was almost invisible. But it was there.

Within the darkness of Arrunn's energy was the tiniest remnant of Soul's essence, clinging to her very core. It was weak, exhausted, and completely dominated. Arrunn's energy pierced through her core, rooting him to her flesh. Soul was very weak, but she was still alive. She had not diminished.

I could feel Jychanumun re-evaluate.

We are fortunate. Jychanumun's voice was now more urgent. *We can save Soul's essence. Do not prevent Dragun from ending her flesh. You will be able to take her spirit to Elysium.*

Is there no other way? I asked.

None that I know.

Jychanumun felt my reserve. *Soul has already lasted longer than most,* he added. *Dragun will recuperate soon. He will return for you and do what must be done. Until then, withdraw from. . .*

I stopped listening. I perceived movement. I felt intent.

A single tendril of Arrunn's energy began emerging from Soul's torso again. It eased through the kutu barrier, and then suddenly bolted forward. It stopped directly in front of my face.

I recoiled, guardedly moving backwards. The tendril followed, curving around until I was surrounded. I stopped moving. It now lingered poised in front of my face, swaying.

Keep still, Jychanumun warned. *Arrunn cannot overtake your body like a mortal human, but touching his energy would be painful.*

I kept perfectly still. I had experienced Arrunn's energy assailing me when I was in the pit; painful was an understatement.

"I see you, Death-Path-Walker," Arrunn's words spoke through Soul.

How could Arrunn sense Jychanumun? Jychanumun was in another realm. Arrunn should not be able to sense any part of him.

"Your connection remains," Arrunn stated, as if he could hear my thoughts. "You can neither be invisible nor silent to me. Iastha Tachra and Death-Path-Walker, through all realms I can see the line that binds you."

Can he hear us? I quickly asked Jychanumun.

No, Jychanumun replied. *Impossible.*

Then how. . . I stopped the question. It was as if my mind was holding too many thoughts at once. Arrunn's energy was looking through me, not at me. Arrunn was searching for my connection to Jychanumun.

*I think he senses **you** through me,* I quickly told Jychanumun. *As you are in the death-paths, our mind-link means there is still an opening. Arrunn could find a way in.*

I do not think that possible, Jychanumun replied.

But what if he can? We cannot take the chance. Jychanumun, I stated, *you must sever your connection to me.*

Never, Jychanumun firmly replied.

"You think loudly," Arrunn stated.

Tachra, Jychanumun growled, *Arrunn cannot hear our thoughts. Do not listen to him. He is trying to manipulate you. Do not listen.*

Even if he is, he does sense the paths. Jychanumun, I pleaded. *You must break our connection. Our connection opens a doorway from this world to that. You **must** sever our link.*

I felt my head pleading: please, just do it. Stop the link between us. You made me see how perilous it would be for Arrunn to have access to the death-paths. And you're there, in the paths. Our connection could become that open door for him. Our connection is the last vulnerable link. Arrunn can sense it. If he got into the death-paths, you would not be safe, your skills would not be safe, and Arrunn would be able to bring death at will. We have to prevent that. We must break our link, for all our futures, before it is too late.

Jychanumun understood. I felt his understanding. I also felt that he was torn between what he wanted to do and what he knew he had to do.

Arrunn's gently swaying tendril suddenly stilled entirely. It was as if all around grew thick with intent. Arrunn was about to strike.

Jychanumun, I urged. ***Now!***

Severance.

Silence.

A dullness washed through my thoughts. An emptiness. It was unfamiliar; something I had never felt before.

I did not know who had done it, Jychanumun or me, but I did know, without doubt, that we had broken our connection.

TEN

The Closing

Jychanumun stood so still, so soundless, that Mardoch thought he might actually be no more than an apparition. He was clearly troubled. Something had changed. Whatever it was, it was not good.

"What has happened?" Mardoch asked.

Jychanumun did not reply, or move. The atmosphere around him had grown thick, almost tangible, its intensity escalating until Mardoch could feel every particle of his being pulsate with the pressure.

The sensation intensified. Beneath Mardoch's feet, the shadow began rippling. The image of doors seemed to shift, blurring with movement. The energy of the paths, previously so calm, now seemed affected by a strong undercurrent. It was as if Jychanumun was so withdrawn that the energy around him, and everything within it, was being affected.

Mardoch had not seen his brother this way before. Although Jychanumun appeared tranquil, his silent agitation and troubled energy was creating this turbulence. It was like a dying sun collapsing to a white star. And with the collapse and reversion, the death-paths and this central place were fragmenting, undoing.

The movement within the paths continued to escalate. Whatever

Jychanumun was doing had to be stopped before the paths collapsed entirely. None of them, no being, could survive such an event.

Mardoch touched his brother's shoulder to make a connection. "Brother," he warily spoke.

Jychanumun's head slowly turned. His eyes were now so black that they absorbed their own shadow. His gaze moved from Mardoch down to Iris.

"Why bring her here?" The tone in Jychanumun's voice was distant, detached. "This is no place for her."

Iris had not said a word since Mardoch had brought her into the paths. She had just stood, staring wide-eyed at her surroundings, and now clung tightly to Mardoch's leg to steady herself.

"It was the safest place, and I had no time to do otherwise," Mardoch quickly defended himself.

"This place is not safe," Jychanumun replied. "I warned you of the dangers."

"I will return her when my energy permits."

Jychanumun slowly shook his head. "No, brother. She cannot be returned. There is no returning. Not for any of us. Nor can Tachra join us. My link to her is broken. All paths to the physical world are closed."

"But Arrunn. . ."

Jychanumun shook his head. "We are fixed here for millennia. He has manipulated this. I should not leave Tachra with him again, but now I have no choice. It may already be too late."

Mardoch heard the gravity in Jychanumun's voice. Worse still, the severity and consequences of the situation were visible all around. While Jychanumun stood unmoving, unaffected, like a death statue in a sand storm, the movement within the death-paths intensified. The turbulence blew all around them. Even the vision of closed doors in this central place now rumbled and undulated like a craft caught in a vortex. The situation was reaching critical.

Mardoch had to think fast. "There are preferable ways to embrace the forever death," he tried to intervene.

"This is not a choice," Jychanumun flatly replied. "I cannot stop my will. My will to rejoin Tachra clashes with the possibilities. My will makes the paths disintegrate."

"But I thought the paths were in your mind?"

"It is my mind that fractures."

"Then we shall return," Mardoch determined. "So, we might die if there are no doorways, but at least we will die trying."

"I cannot create new paths. All would lead back here. I can do nothing."

Jychanumun looked away, his gaze growing distant once again.

Mardoch knew that he had lost his brother's attention. He had not been able to make him hear. Mardoch had always been able to make him hear, but not this time. It seemed that there truly was no way out.

Mardoch looked around at the turbulence, feeling a peaceful acceptance. So, today was the day he really would meet the forever death. Today. Well, why not today? He shrugged to himself. It was just a shame it could not be more glorious.

Within the chaotic movement of the paths, the child Iris stumbled away from Mardoch and towards Jychanumun. She half lurched, half fell against Jychanumun's leg, tugging at his skirt, calling his name.

Jychanumun's gaze looked down at the small human child, his face impassive, detached.

"Are you giving up?" Iris asked.

There was no recrimination in her words. It was just a simple question.

"I won't give up," she added, her tone one of determination.

She held up her cupped hand to Jychanumun, showing him something, ignoring the unsteadiness that she felt.

"I still have this," she said. "It's special. It's Tachra's talking bead. I give it to you. You can use that."

At that moment, the atmosphere switched.

Mardoch saw a change come over Jychanumun's expression. He had heard. And, with Jychanumun hearing, it was as if something broke. His withdrawn expression softened.

Jychanumun closed his eyes for a moment as if to collect his thoughts, breathing a long, steady breath. And, as he calmed, the paths calmed, the motion and turbulence starting to reduce.

Jychanumun knelt down to Iris. He took her little hand in his, closing her fingers around her prized bead.

"That is yours alone," he told her. "And no, young Soul-child, I will never give up."

He stood, looking at Mardoch.

"All may be lost, but I will find a way," he said.

"You always do," Mardoch replied. He wanted to laugh. He wanted to laugh and take a long drink of that sweet earth mead they stored at the Temple. Or, if he was back on Assendia, he would fly with the twin winds, blindfolded, just because he could. He really had thought that he was finished; that all of them were finished. It had been so close. This time, it had not been him who had connected to his brother to stop the devastation, but a human, and an infant one at that.

"Do we have a plan?" Mardoch dared to enquire.

"Only that I must find a way to Tachra," Jychanumun replied. "It is not just for myself that I say this; all fates depend upon it."

ELEVEN

The Test

I could no longer feel Jychanumun's thoughts. More than that, his presence had gone. It left a silent void where I did not realise there had been fullness. It felt strange. All my thoughts were still there, but they felt flat. I felt alone.

With Arrunn's energy still entwined around me, poised like a tensed snake, I looked at my hands as if seeing them for the first time. Everything felt different. Everything *was* different. I looked at Soul's body, Arrunn's host. Arrunn. On Soul's face, Arrunn wore an expression of satisfaction. It was not the expression I had expected to see. I had expected to see defeat.

I realised now that Jychanumun was right. Arrunn had wanted me to break my connection with him. He had manipulated my choice. Although that choice had made me realise something that Arrunn could never know or manipulate – that I had always been connected to Jychanumun. Even before we met, somehow our thoughts were intertwined. I did not know how that was possible, but it was. I had only known Jychanumun six summers, yet I had always shared a link with him. I knew it because I had never felt this type of emptiness before.

I closed my eyes, forcing my thoughts to focus.

"Why don't you just leave," I said aloud for Arrunn's ears. "If you leave, you will not perish, but just be pulled to the shadow realms like the other Nigh-kutu. Your time here is pointless. Your warriors are gone. All the kutu are gone. Accept that you cannot kill me or control me. See that your remaining here serves no purpose, and leave."

I didn't feel as if I was being brave, or clever. I felt no objective at all. I was merely stating the truth. He should just leave.

"And Arrunn," I added, "You are hurting my friend. Hiding inside Soul, like a rabbit seeking refuge from a hunting bird, is not honourable."

The tendril of Arrunn's energy arched angrily. I expected retaliation. Instead, it uncoiled from around me and retracted into Soul's flesh.

Soul suddenly began screaming. The screams were screams of agony. Her body twitched and tensed as if overcome with severe pain. Her feet lifted from the ground until she hovered mid-air. Her back arched into impossible shapes that should snap her in two. Her head was flung around on her shoulders as if it would break from her neck. Her eyes bulged; her own hands clawing at her head, pulling chunks of hair from her scalp. Then suddenly she stopped screaming, poised mid-air in a contorted, disturbing pose.

"This is what I could do." Arrunn's words came from Soul's mouth. "I choose not to give her more pain than necessary. This is the suffering she could feel, if I so desired."

I watched in horror as Soul's body began twisting and contorting, writhing in agony once again. Her arms flailed wildly, beating at herself. Her mouth was open, as if held in a silent scream. Soul could not endure this. I could not endure it. It was unbearable.

"Stop," I pleaded. "Please. You are breaking her."

Almost immediately, Soul's body slumped to the ground.

Soul had sprawled awkwardly on the thick grass. Her silent

screaming had stopped. Her writhing had stopped. In fact, it didn't look like she was moving at all. She looked as if she was dead.

I wanted to rush towards Soul, but held back, moving cautiously closer. In the gloom of the oncoming evening, her body was lit by the force field barrier. I could see her chest moving in small, shallow breaths. Thank the skies. She wasn't dead.

I was so intent in watching for signs of life that I didn't notice that Soul had opened her eyes and was staring at me. I caught her gaze. She looked unsure, guarded. I think that my own gaze was exactly the same.

"Have I ceased?" Soul whispered.

"Is that you, Soul?" I cautiously asked.

"I'll tell you if you tell me," Soul tried to smile.

I wanted to rejoice. It did sound like Soul. It was just the sort of thing she would say.

Barely trusting my own ears, I opened my true vision to see whether Soul's or Arrunn's energy now controlled her. Immediately, I could see Soul's form shining further than her physical body, in tones of blue and gold. My heart was comforted; this was indeed her, but I could not rejoice – Arrunn was not gone. Within Soul's colours there was also a darkness. Arrunn's darkness. He had merely withdrawn into her inner core.

"You have not ceased," I assured my friend. "Although your body is not in good shape."

Soul closed her eyes, the relief clear on her face. "I feel like I'm dead," she stated. "I am seeing the dead. First Wirrel, now you. If I'm not dead, I must be dreaming. I felt you cease."

"I am here," I held out my hands. "Iris called me."

"Iris?" Soul alarmed, trying to coordinate her body to move. "Where is she?"

"Safe," I comforted her. "I don't know where. It's probably best for us not to know right now."

Soul thought for a moment, looking around at the kutu barrier that surrounded her, her expression of relief turning to one of desperation. "Oh no. Tachra." Her eyes widened. "He's still in me. I can feel him. That kutu Arrunn. I thought he had gone."

"I know," I nodded gravely. "He has withdrawn to recuperate."

"You mean he's coming back?"

"In truth, I do not know. But probably, yes."

Soul tried to strengthen herself. "The kutu will come to help," she said. "They'll know how to get him out of me."

I realised that Soul knew none of what had happened over the last day. There was far too much to explain.

"I must resolve this on my own. There are no kutu," I simply told her. "They're all gone, except Arrunn, and he should not be here, either."

I didn't want to tell Soul what Jychanumun had told me, but my mouth was saying it anyway. I told her that if Arrunn wasn't in her, he'd have to return to the shadow realms. I told her that he would only leave by her ceasing. And I also told her that if she didn't cease soon, then things would become worse, because her essence would degrade and die. My own bluntness surprised me. "Apparently," I concluded, "you've already lasted longer than most."

"Oh."

"I know," I rubbed my brow, as if I could force a solution from my mind. "I have to find another way. You just have to stay strong. I will find a solution, but I don't know how much time we have."

"No?" Soul's brow furrowed. "Then what are we waiting for? For Arrunn to take control again? I can't stop him and I've tried really hard." Her alarm grew. "What if this kutu barrier fails? We cant take the chance. We must do something while we can! Truss me! Tie me up in case he overtakes me before we manage to get rid of him."

I knew that such basic physical confines wouldn't stop Arrunn.

But perhaps it would hinder him from inflicting more damage to Soul's body again. It was an idea that was better than doing nothing.

Despite her injuries, Soul had already pulled off her soot-covered tunic and began tearing it with her teeth, shredding the blackened fabric into lengths. She secured a piece around her ankles, wincing with the pain of her damaged foot, knotting more pieces together, binding it around one wrist. She put both her hands behind her back.

"Make sure it's tight," she indicated. "I know you can push through these barriers. I won't move. If I do move, pull out, because it won't be me."

The force-field energy tried to repel my flesh as I touched it, but I understood the light-energy and eased my hands through the barrier. It took a frustratingly long time to tie the knots as many of my fingers would not move, staying clenched into an awkward fist. As I worked, Soul told me about the unusual visit from Jychanumun earlier that day, how he had given her the instruction to make way to my old place in the ravine at first light. He had told her little more than that, and hadn't specified why.

"I know nothing of it," I replied, as I finished the last knot.

"If I do not survive," Soul spoke matter-of-factly, "you must do what Jychanumun asked of me."

"It won't come to that," I determined. "You and I have been through too many difficulties for it to end here."

I withdrew from the barrier, looking at the ties around Soul's hands, unconvinced that such flimsy work would hold. "Trussing a friend does not feel right." I said unhappily.

Soul shuffled to face me. "At least he cannot use my arms or legs now. Now, how are you going to do it?"

Do it? What?

Oh.

"I cannot," I replied. "I must find another way."

"But please, you must," Soul protested. "I can't have Arrunn overtaking my mind again. My memory can see it. My own hands, Tachra. Me..."

"That's not you," I interrupted. "It's Arrunn."

Soul closed her eyes, shaking her head.

"Even now, I can still feel his thoughts," she said. "He tells me to do things with hints so quiet that I would think they were my own. I know how much I care for you, yet I see images of hurting you. I fear what he may make me do next. Don't let my body allow him to hurt anyone else. Please, Tachra."

"I have to find another way. This," I held my hands out to her, "this is you, who I care for. How can I end that which I treasure?"

Soul bowed her head. I could see she was exhausted. I could see her anguish. I could see her hurt. Worse still, I could see that she was almost on the point of giving up.

"If I am going to cease anyway, please let me go in painless peace by your gentle hand, not by his terrible means," she spoke quietly.

My heart ached. I knew the truth of her words. I saw the truth of our situation. It was dire, but I still had choice. If I could do this, I could take Soul's essence to Elysium. I could still save her spirit.

It was a dreadful, terrible choice. One made purely from love.

I would have to kill my friend.

Without a word, and with a heavy heart, I stood and limped towards the rock into which Dragun had dispersed. There, set deep into the stone, as if made from stone itself, was Dragun's Weaver's knife. Its blade protruded, glistening like shadow crystal. Even just by sight, I could see that the kutu blade was good and sharp. Such a knife would not give any pain in death.

Dragun's knife was set high into the rock, an arm's length above my head. Standing tall, I carefully grasped the blade and pulled. The knife did not move. Its hilt was fused into the stone. It would not be released with strength alone. When I looked at

Dragun's blade with my true vision, its energy looked exactly the same as Dragun's, unlike any other: absolutely still, yet radiant. I touched it again. Yes, I could feel the energy surging through it. It *felt* like Dragun.

Remembering what Dragun had told me about his stone weaving, I pushed energy into his blade. I imagined energy around the hilt, separating it from the stone. Immediately, something hit my hand. The knife had spun around, its haft now in my palm.

I had it, Dragun's blade: the tool to both kill and save my friend.

I clutched Dragun's long, heavy knife as my cumbersome feet stumbled back towards Soul. My heart felt deeply troubled with the burden of what I had to do. Soul was my friend. I loved my friend. As much as I didn't want to, I was going to take her mortal life. Killing her was the only chance to save her.

Concealing the knife, so as not to scare her any more than she already was, I called to Soul as I approached. She did not respond.

I stopped.

Within the kutu force-field, Soul was still sitting. My eyes saw her in the same position, but the energy around her had altered. Arrunn's dark shadow now overpowered her once again like a dense swarm of flies. He was back.

But that was such a short time! I thought he would need to retract for much longer. Surely Arrunn couldn't recuperate that quickly. I should have acted while I could. I shouldn't have spent so long coming to the conclusion that ending Soul's life was best for her too. I only hoped that Soul could hold on until he retracted again. Next time, I would not hesitate to end her life and take her spirit to Elysium.

Right now there was only one thing I could do – wait.

I chose a position a safe enough distance away and sat down, putting Dragun's knife on my lap. I kept my eyes fixed ahead, not wanting to blink for fear of missing the instant Arrunn retracted.

The moments passed. They seemed to drag. My anxiety beat through my chest as if trying to break out. Why wasn't Arrunn trying to do anything? Every moment he remained in Soul, his presence damaged her a little bit more.

Just as the silence and stillness became unbearable, suddenly, a movement.

A glimmer of a darkness flickered across Soul's face. I tensed as Arrunn's shadowy essence continued moving, drifting away from her flesh. As it left her body, it began drawing together, more and more, until it stood as a figure of a kutu. It was Arrunn – Arrunn in pure energy. A fine line of shadow connected him to Soul, running from the centre of her torso into the middle of his back.

Arrunn stood, watching me. I wanted to look away.

"Fate brings us together once again," Arrunn eventually said.

As Arrunn spoke, I noticed tiny threads of smoky brown energy ebb away from his form and dissipate into the air.

Perhaps, I realised, if Arrunn kept in this state and talking, he would wane quicker. I did not like the thought of having Arrunn so close and able to be seen, yet alone talking to him. But I knew that the quicker he waned, the sooner he would have to retract. For Soul, time was now critical.

"I do not want you to be here in front of me." I forced the words.

Arrunn shrugged, just a small incline of the head and shoulders, barely noticeable. "Are you sure?" he asked. "You chose to come, knowing I was here. *You* came to *me*."

I went to object, but stopped. His words were right. I did make that choice.

"Perhaps," Arrunn continued, "as you came to me, you should consider what *you* want from *me*. I could give you anything you wanted." He paused, watching my reaction. "How about the Shaa-kutu? Tell me who you would like saved and I will give them to you. Or perhaps my warriors; I could give you the fiercest army to command. Or perhaps you prefer quiet solace and would like eternal harmony with your black-eyed Jychanumun." He held out his hand as if offering me something. "I am not your enemy. I offer you your heart's desires. Just ask and I will give."

Arrunn's words took me aback. Give me Jychanumun? His warriors? The Shaa-kutu? That was terrible, as if their lives were at his disposal. Arrunn did not own them. Not any of them.

"No one," I forced words of strength, "has that right."

"I do," Arrunn coolly replied. "Their lives are fated. As is yours. All fates are set."

"I don't believe that," I shook my head, trying to block the insinuations that Arrunn was trying to put into my mind.

"Tachra," Arrunn's gaze did not leave me. "Your beliefs are set because you are naïve. I have seen a thousand fates unfold to be exactly as they should. This particular fate is no different. Your fate, my fate, these things are set."

Arrunn stopped talking, holding his calm stare. I felt his sincerity. I think I even felt truth. That perplexed me.

"Or perhaps you wish me to explain," Arrunn spoke again. "It was fated that you would exist; a being that shared a link with the last Old One. It was fated that you would bond with a kutu, and that kutu would have access to the Old One. Jychanumun ensured that he bonded with you before any other, because he knew that connection was fated to be with me. That fate will still come to be."

I recoiled at the thought. Connect with Arrunn? I would never, by any choice, bond with him. Never in a thousand turns of the seasons. Never for all eternities.

Arrunn sensed my disbelief. He looked around, as if making note of the scene that surrounded us.

"Even if I choose to leave this place," he stated, "one day, you will call me back. When you understand your fate, you will willingly call me to you. Then," he paused, "we will be as one."

My head was screaming as I felt a terrifying truth in his words. No. Please no. Please don't let me think I might fall to Arrunn's will and give him everything. Please don't let me feel any truth to his words that I would ever call him willingly. It couldn't be true. No, it couldn't. Surely it couldn't.

"You lie," my words came out as barely a whisper.

"You want truth?" Arrunn scorned. "Truth: Jychanumun found the Shaa-kutu to change events. Truth: if Jychanumun had not manipulated fate, you would have lived a peaceful life without knowing him. Truth: you would have gladly opened the doorway between the Old One and me. Truth: it is Jychanumun who has tried to change fate, not me, and because of this you have suffered. It is not me, Tachra, who has ruined your short life. It is Jychanumun."

I did feel a truth in Arrunn's words and was shocked into silence. It can't be right, I thought. I have trusted Jychanumun with my life, and death. I have trusted him with everything I hold dear.

Arrunn's insidious voice did not stop its flow. "It is paradoxical for you, is it not? You have bonded with the Death-Path-Walker, one who values life and death on equal merit. And you wonder why your short life is tinged so strongly by death? The answer is obvious: Jychanumun."

I felt sick.

"You yearn for life, yet you are so often confronted with death? Your link with Jychanumun brings death to you."

My head spun, consumed by dizziness. I closed my eyes to stop myself reeling.

"Ask the Death-Path-Walker. You seem to believe his words, even though he is the very kutu who stains your life. He will confirm these truths."

Arrunn's words had to be wrong, but they felt like the truth. Had I trusted Jychanumun with everything when he was least trustworthy? Had I merely been a tool for Jychanumun to preserve his own kind, or even worse, himself? Arrunn's words felt so truthful, but, but...

I desperately twisted my hands into the grass, looking for solace. I sensed the essence of the grass, their roots low in the soil, all interlinked like a shallow, calm sea. Their calm gave me calm. I felt the soil beneath the plants and the cool honesty of the earth humming with peace and simplicity. Here in the earth was nothing more than the way things were meant to be. Here I felt the absolute truth with clarity.

Holding on to the peace and simplicity of the earth, the complications of Arrunn's words unravelled in my mind. I saw it now; Arrunn was trying to bend my understanding to his will. His words held a certain truth, just enough to twist with a dishonestly honest conviction. Jychanumun was true and always had been.

Arrunn was trying to manipulate me.

I held my hands in the soil, rooting to clarity and strength, and looked towards Arrunn. My heart had calmed. My thoughts now sang true.

"Your deceit is the worst of all," I said, "for you give me many truths, yet within them are twisted threads so that I will hear with ears of your choosing. And even my logic finds flaws in your words, if logic is the standard you prefer to understand by. For if your words were true, why would you try to offer me things to convince me to change my choices? If you knew this fate was no different to the ones you have already seen, you would not be trying to guide my choices."

I knew I had it. My words felt as true as the soil beneath me and the air that filled my lungs.

Arrunn's form crouched until his gaze was level with mine. His smoke-like wings undulated slowly in tones of the deepest multi-colours that blended together to appear like the darkest brown. His long, straight hair didn't move. Unlike most kutu hair, it stayed motionless. Like his expression, Arrunn was in full control of his energy.

As Arrunn watched me, I silently repeated to myself that I was not to allow fear to override my clarity.

"We are not so different," Arrunn said. His voice had softened. "We both see more than most. Perhaps we are more alike than either of us realise."

I could feel Arrunn's probing thoughts. He continued talking, finding similarities in our existences, his tone now calm.

I was not fooled by Arrunn's soft voice; I knew that he was still trying to manipulate me. Nevertheless, I could feel his words trying to fester in my mind. I battled against them, hating how his words so easily felt like my own.

"I despise you." The words fell from my lips.

Arrunn was silenced. Suddenly, his composure broke. He flicked his head back and roared with laughter.

"You despise me," Arrunn continued laughing. "You stupid, ignorant creature; you have not experienced things to be capable of it."

Arrunn pointed at me. His gesture felt incriminating. "Your heart knows peace. How can a being with a core of peace harbour hatred? It cannot. Only in chaos and suffering can pure hatred exist. I, on the other hand, remember peace, but cannot attain it. I remember perfection, yet am aware of every flaw that now exists. I should have perfection, completeness, peace, yet I cannot attain it. Why? Because of you. You have what is mine and fight me at every step in this fate. You, you stupid human, could never despise me. But I have every reason to despise you."

"One day I will kill you," I stated boldly.

"Your hate isn't enough to kill me," Arrunn calmly replied.

"Then one day I will kill you with love."

There was a pause.

Arrunn then smiled a derisive smile.

"Tachra. Human. Love is no more than a worthless word. Your love is programmed into you and nothing more than a series of reactions built into your programming. And the kutu? None of them love you. You are their tool. You are just too blind in your own conviction to see it."

Arrunn continued talking, his words taunting me with more insinuations. I fought with myself to remain staunch, refusing to be pulled into his games and persuasions. He told me that humans could not love. He said that humans corrupted all emotions. He tried to pull me into his conversation, reminding me of when people threw stones at me in the well. He insisted that, given time, humans would destroy each other and everything else around them.

"I am the only being who is prepared to see the truth of this imperfect existence," Arrunn said. "Life is imperfect, and imperfection suffers. I am not cruel. I am showing empathy in ending the suffering of life. If you saw an injured creature, in pain, would you not want to end its suffering? Yes, you would. You have already shown that you would. You removed your wildcat from this world to prevent her suffering. You saw her in pain and chose to end her life."

My defensiveness instantly rose. "You were torturing her!" I snapped.

"I needed to make you see that you would make the same choice and end suffering," Arrunn replied. "And you did."

Arrunn's insinuations were cruel. I was angry at him, and I was even more at myself for getting angry. Arrunn was twisting the meaning of all my choices. I had tried everything to save Meah. My heart had only ever wanted to protect her. One hand instinctively moved to Dragun's knife and I felt my grasp tighten around its haft. I wanted to plunge it into Arrunn. I wanted to plunge it right into the middle of his self-assured kutu face.

Remember Soul, I disciplined myself. *This is about saving your friend. Concentrate on breathing. Stay focused.*

"This world is destined to suffer," Arrunn continued. "Not by my hand, but by humans; by their own nature they will suffer and create suffering. I can prevent that. Do you defend a world that will allow pain and suffering to flourish? Is that your choice?"

"I defend the right for all to choose," I stated.

"So, let us say that I give you all the time humanity needs. If you are right, this world flourishes and humanity can change fate, then I would bow to that fate. But if I am right and love is worthless and changes nothing, would you step aside?"

"Of course I would. But it would never happen," I answered him heatedly.

"Then that is our agreement," Arrunn bowed. "And for that, I will consider leaving."

As Arrunn bowed, his energy moved backwards, recoiling into Soul's flesh. It moved so fast that it looked like Soul was inhaling smoke.

For a short moment, my mind was in turmoil. I felt violated. I felt drained and frustrated. Arrunn had twisted everything I'd tried to say. I would never agree to anything with him.

But then I felt a change. Arrunn's energy had sunk deep into Soul's inner core.

Arrunn had retracted.

All the turmoil in my mind cleared. This was the moment I had been waiting for.

I rose to my knees, Dragun's knife in my hands, pausing as Soul opened her eyes. It was Soul, not Arrunn.

Soul looked at me imploringly.

"I can't do this," she whispered. "I am sorry. . ."

She then let out a long breath, like a gentle sigh.

As Soul exhaled, every muscle in her relaxed. Her head slumped forward. Small drips of red began trickling from her nostrils and eyes. It looked like she was weeping blood. She had stopped breathing.

Soul was dying; not just in body, but in essence too.

I crawled forward, quickly pushing through the kutu barrier, cutting Soul's bonds using Dragun's blade. Her body slumped. I caught her, gently laying her on her back.

You cannot kill. It is not within you, Arrunn's voice echoed in my mind.

Don't listen to him.

Don't think.

Just do.

TWELVE

The Weaving

"Jychanumun," Dragun called. The word came out as barely a murmur.

Dragun had barely moved since his return to the paths. He was still so spent that he'd scarcely registered any acknowledgement when the paths had almost collapsed. He'd remained silently hunched over, with his hands on his knees and his eyes closed. His frayed wings trailed loosely behind him. His arms bore deep, fresh lacerations that bled energy, and even more that were recently healed from his sparring with Arrunn. He was still desperately trying to rebalance. His recovery was taking far longer than it should.

"Jychanumun, Death-Path-Walker," Dragun called again under his breath. "A connection – Tachra."

This time, the whisper carried through the dense air. Jychanumun heard him, turning his attention from Iris to his fellow Nigh-kutu.

"Speak," Jychanumun encouraged, "for time is not with us."

Dragun looked up. Kutu energy beaded on his forehead and ran down his face like human sweat. His expression was one of distant concentration. "Paths closed," he laboured. "But not all links." His breaths were ragged and shallow between each word. "I sense her," he added.

Jychanumun knew that all the paths were closed. There were no bonds between Dragun and Tachra. No connection should be possible now. Still, the truth of Dragun's words rang true.

"How can you sense Tachra?" Jychanumun simply asked. He could see that Dragun's exhaustion was making it difficult for him to talk. "Feel the energy of these paths. It will help you speak."

Dragun's eyes grew distant. He took a long breath, as if trying to stabilise.

"I am my blade. My blade is I. Weaving our matter for sight of no eyes. I am my blade. My blade is I. United as one, through matter we fly," Dragun recited.

Jychanumun paused a moment, watching Dragun, ascertaining, understanding. He noticed that the concealed holster in Dragun's armour no longer had the haft of his knife protruding from it.

"Where is your Weaver's blade?" Jychanumun asked. "Did you leave it in the physical world?"

"Yes," Dragun nodded. "I left it in the rock. Through it, I sense."

"Can you communicate with it?" Jychanumun pressed.

"No. Just sense. At this moment, I sense Tachra."

Mardoch walked forward, unconvinced, feeling protective of his brother. After all, he had known Jychanumun for millennia upon millennia. They had even chosen their original clans together. They were clan-brothers and friends. But Dragun? They had only been acquainted since this kutu war. Mardoch had trusted him with his life, yes, more than once. Still, any warrior knew that new-found trust was only as good as the moment in which it existed. Mardoch reserved the right to question, especially when so much was at stake.

"It should not be possible for you to have any link to Tachra," Mardoch intervened. "Jychanumun has said all paths are closed. If he cannot make a connection, no one can."

Dragun smiled a faint, wry smile and shook his head. "I respect your uncertainty, but save the sceptical face for Arrunn. You Walkers; do you still not think me different? My weaving always made me so. I do not weave just with mineral and metal. My blade is made from my own flesh, my own matter. My blade and I are one."

"You left a part of you behind?" Mardoch asked.

"Yes," Dragun replied. "I could not leave little Tachra defenceless."

Mardoch felt the truth of Dragun's words. So the Weaver's knife was not just attuned to Dragun, it *was* Dragun, or at least part of him. It sounded feasible. It explained why only Dragun could wield his blade. And, separated from his blade, no wonder Dragun was not rebalancing as quickly as he should. But, as much as this caused complications for Dragun, this was good news. If Dragun could sense Tachra's energy, that meant Tachra was still alive. If Tachra was still alive, then a reconnection was possible for Jychanumun. She may even have released Arrunn's energy back to the shadow.

"Arrunn?" Mardoch quickly asked. "Do you sense him too?"

"I do not know," Dragun shrugged. "I am not a sensitive, just a humble Weaver. I do not know how to sense beyond my matter. Tachra has released my knife. She has it with her. I feel her energy through it."

Jychanumun moved to place a hand on Dragun's shoulder. "Do not block me," he requested. "I will sense through you, through your blade. I will give you my energy. This may be my only way to help her."

Jychanumun indicated to Mardoch. Mardoch moved forward, placing a hand on Dragun's shoulder too. He and Jychanumun now stood side by side, feeding their energy to their fellow Nigh-kutu.

"You have my energy," Mardoch assured Dragun. "I, we, will not let this finish you."

Dragun merely nodded. Mardoch could see that this was taking all Dragun's concentration; his already low energy was still ebbing away. His connection with his blade in the physical world was gradually reducing him. His brother, Jychanumun, would try to guide this. The actual act would be down to little Tachra. Mardoch himself had the easy part. He just had to be prepared to give his all.

"I am going to my blade now," Dragun whispered. "It is time."

THIRTEEN

The Connection

I imagined it was Dragun's hand around his knife, not mine. I could feel his strong fingers wrapped around it: the calluses on his palms; the connection with his blade.

Instinctively, I moved. I could not see where I was aiming for, but I felt Arrunn's darkness at Soul's core, in the centre of her torso. It was like a disease to her, feeding from her. To save her, that darkness had to be severed.

My arm came up. I tilted the blade and thrust down with all the strength that I could muster.

I thrust the blade right into Soul's torso.

The blade passed through Soul's skin, her flesh, slicing deep between her ribs, aiming for her core. I twisted the blade and pushed down so hard that my knuckles touched the soil below her body. I could feel the strength of Dragun's hand around mine, as if all his kutu power ran through me, focusing his blade and will on that one shadowy point: Arrunn's connection to Soul.

As Dragun's blade touched Arrunn's freezing coldness, the knife seemed to freeze too, paralysing my grip. Despite my instinct to let go, I firmly drew the knife back up through Soul's flesh, through her inner core, severing the line that connected Arrunn to her.

As I cut through Arrunn's connection to Soul, something released. A tension snapped like a taught vine, whipping past my face, making ice crystals crackle on my skin. No longer connected to Soul, Arrunn's energy spiralled above.

Suddenly, a force with the strength of a thousand winds bore down on me, throwing me aside and onto my back, knocking the air from my lungs and the knife from my hands. I couldn't move, pinned to the ground by a power stronger than my flesh.

Above me, Arrunn's dark energy gathered, spinning in multiple directions to contain itself. I could not move.

I have broken her will, Arrunn's shadow formed the words. ***You cannot save her. You cannot save any of them. When you understand that, that is when you will call me. Know now – I choose to leave.***

And then Arrunn's energy was gone, ascending into the night sky like a ball of darkness against darkness.

I had no time to rejoice that Arrunn had gone. I scrabbled back towards Soul and flung my true vision open. Arrunn's energy had indeed gone, but Soul's spirit was nowhere. Her essence did not stand beside her empty flesh, waiting for me to take her to Elysium. Neither was any part of her aglow in her flesh. Soul had no essence. She really had diminished.

"Oh no, my friend, no," I stammered. My hands quickly examined her torso, scrutinising every part for blood upon her skin, lifting her tunic to inspect for damage where Dragun's knife had pierced. Soul's body was bruised and dirty, but there was no sign of any knife wound for me to heal. Dragun's blade had done it. Somehow, Dragun had done it; his blade had left no mark upon her flesh. But it was too late. I was too late. Arrunn had broken Soul's will and diminished her.

"My friend," I softly called, moving to cradle Soul's head in my lap, wrapping the healing sheet around her.

"Come on," I whispered. "Don't give up. You can't give up."

But all signs looked like Soul had indeed given up.

I looked to the skies, my heart wanting to scream. There, between the stars that were shaped like a kutu time-glass, the shadow energy that was Arrunn rapidly grew smaller into the distance. Arrunn was gone, but he had destroyed Soul's will. Without a will, Soul had no essence. Soul had ceased – the forever death.

I was too late.

I didn't know what to do. Soul was dead. Should I sit here with her empty flesh until the morrow's sun started to bring its decay? Should I just walk away? Should I bury her? No. It did not seem right. I would not give up this easily. I would not let Soul give up either.

"You can't go," I told Soul's empty body. "You don't give up."

I flung open my inner vision and frantically pushed my own depleted energy into Soul. I roamed through her static flesh, searching for any sign of life that I could ignite and grow.

There was no spark, no fire of life. Soul was ceased. She was not breathing. Her heart had stopped. Her inner core was an empty void. There were only the last fading embers, the final memories, sparking in her mind. They were the last dreams of the dying. They were nothing more than the final reflexes of a brain closing down.

But surely those last embers of memory in her dying mind must count for something! Even now, they dwindled to almost nothing, like the final glow of a candle wick just after it had been snuffed out. But it was something. Surely there was hope while the tiniest ember remained.

If I could give her a spark of life, if I could make her body work, she might remember her will. I knew that it should not be possible, but I didn't care. I was going to try anything.

"Live," I urged. "Soul, this is not your end. Remember the fire of life, and live."

I flung my true vision wider. I saw and felt the life in everything: the plants, the air, the moisture, the earth. I embraced life even where my eyes had never seen and life that had not yet sprung into life, and was still only potential. I drew in that energy, pulling it from all around and then pushing it into Soul's mind and body. Nurture her; give her the spark of life. Caress the embers with the strength from the land. Bring Soul the fire of life.

Soul's dying embers responded to the saturation of life energy. They sparked, reaching out like a thirsty plant welcoming water. The spark became the tiniest flame. Good. Give the flame more energy. Breathe energy into that flame and make it a strong fire. Push the flame and the energy through her body. Give Soul the fire of life. Give her the will.

I could do this. I knew I could. I just had to bring together her diminished essence, her spirit, her soul, and her will. For that I needed the greatest fires of all.

I drew deeper from the land, pulling energy from the soil, from the rock below the soil. Here the energy was raw and powerful. My instincts raced even further, throughout the world, looking for the potency that she needed. I raced through hot springs, molten rock, the hot gasses that rumbled below the rock, and through the thick molten metals of Earth's very core, searching for an energy strong enough.

"Do not give up," I told Soul. "You will not die."

I felt the distant presence of a furnace, a fire for life so great that it would surely rekindle Soul. I called that fire to me. Through air and rock, I called. Through worlds and space, I called. I called that fire to me with the strength of love and the clarity of intent.

I then I felt it. It was a fire like no other. It did not just draw towards me. It heard.

This fire came by choice.

FOURTEEN

The Father

Dragun slumped, collapsing from the exertion. He was almost spent.

Jychanumun laid Dragun in a more comfortable position and wiped the energy that bled from his eyes. Dragun was indeed depleted, but he would rebalance, given time.

"You have done it," Jychanumun reassured him. "Rest."

"I just need to lie here, just for a little while," Dragun quietly responded. "I'll regain my strength in a moment."

"We have time," Jychanumun affirmed. "Millennia."

He turned to Mardoch. "It could not have been done without your help. Thank you, brother."

Mardoch waved a hand as if it had been no effort at all. In truth, he too was spent. He had never felt so exhausted. Not even the time he had first become a warrior, or when he had become lost in the trailing mists. He had given this the very utmost of his energy. They all had. Even so, the three of them, even along with Tachra's ability, had not managed to save the human, Soul, nor destroy Arrunn. They had merely helped to despatch Arrunn to the shadow realms.

Maybe, Arrunn really is invincible, Mardoch considered. *Would it matter if he is? No. Mardoch would fight him to the end nonetheless. Victory was not so important anymore. He would fight for principle.*

Jychanumun looked at him.

"Am I thinking too loudly again?" Mardoch asked.

"That has never changed," Jychanumun nodded. "Nor would I change it."

Jychanumun was also clearly exhausted, but remained standing, staring wistfully into the darkness. It was as if he could see something that they could not.

"Death-Path-Walker," Dragun suddenly called, trying to stand.

Jychanumun moved back to Dragun.

"Something else occurs," Dragun said. "I feel Tachra calling. But not to me, not to you, not to any of us."

"To whom?" Jychanumun asked.

"I don't know. She calls things that are beyond kutu. I sense flames. A fire. . ."

"A kutu fire?"

"No. This is something else."

As Jychanumun placed his hand on Dragun's shoulder once again, Mardoch beckoned to the young human, Iris.

The child had been watching Jychanumun with concern, not speaking, not moving. Mardoch knew that someone was going to have to tell her that her birth mother had diminished, and also that this place would now be her home for a long time. It would not be a pleasant task. Dragun was too spent to do it. Jychanumun did not have a good way with words. Both of them were now preoccupied. That, Mardoch realised, left him.

"Little human." Mardoch beckoned to the child again, trying to put on his best friendly face.

Iris shook her head, as if to say no. Instead, she followed Jychanumun, tugging on his skirt and calling his name.

"One moment," Jychanumun told the child.

"No, now," Iris insisted. "It's important. You must take me back."

Jychanumun glanced down at Iris, not letting his meditation with Dragun slip. "I cannot take you back yet," he told her.

"You have to," Iris determined. "I hear Tachra. Papa hears her." She continued tugging frantically at Jychanumun's robe. "Papa is going to help. He tells me his fire is being pulled there."

Jychanumun's attention immediately flicked to Iris. "Your papa?"

"Yes," Iris nodded. "You need to let him out. Tachra is calling him. He's going to go whether you like it or not."

Jychanumun looked at Iris, looked at Dragun and then at Mardoch, his thoughts piecing together all he knew of yesterdays and tomorrows.

"Your papa? As in, your father?"

"Yes," Iris nodded frantically. "He came to me in the hut. He saved me with his fire. You have to take me back."

Jychanumun removed his hand from Dragun's shoulder. Her papa, her biological father. Wirrel. Jychanumun knew of Wirrel from Tachra's stories. Wirrel was the human killed by burning. He was the man Tachra had tried to save from the flames. Wirrel was dead. He had died in the fire.

"Where is your papa now?" Jychanumun asked.

"Within me," Iris replied. "He stayed with me to make sure the bad kutu ghost couldn't get me. But he tells me that he needs to leave now. He has to get out."

Jychanumun placed a hand on Iris' forehead, reading her thoughts and looking into her energy. Iris had indeed seen her papa. But he was no longer human, not entirely. He was both man and fire; a new entity. And this new entity, man and fire, was inside Iris' mind. Wirrel looked like a tiny, potent, whirling fire pushing to get out.

Jychanumun had seen this entity in his visions, yet he had not known what it was. He had just known it was both unique and powerful. He had thought it a kutu. What he had seen of the flame-dweller was a being both vengeful and just, always unstoppable. Such a being could bring destruction. Such a being let loose could even fracture the death-paths if there was no exit.

The flame-dweller needed a way out. But Jychanumun could no longer create any new doorways to the physical world. There was one chance. One slim chance. But even now, that chance may be too late.

Jychanumun was already instinctively acting. He picked up Iris, tucking her under one arm.

"Do not move," he shouted towards Dragun and Mardoch as he began running.

"Hold on to me tightly," Jychanumun quickly instructed the child. "Contain your papa a moment more. I will place you exactly where Mardoch took you from. Close your eyes. Do not look at me."

And Iris did as he asked; she closed her eyes so tightly that it hurt her face. Even though she wanted to peek, she didn't. She wrapped her arms around Jychanumun's shoulder. Her hands wouldn't meet, so it was difficult to hold on firmly. She hoped Jychanumun wouldn't let her go. She could feel him running fast. She hoped he was running fast enough. She had to keep telling her papa to please wait a moment more, and that took all her concentration. Her papa didn't want to wait at all.

Jychanumun connected to Iris as he ran, aware that every moment was a moment borrowed. This was not the time for him to think. This time he could only act on intuition.

All paths were closed. No new paths could be made. The path that Mardoch had traversed with Iris such a short while ago was almost degraded to nothingness. Fractures of grey time energy splintered the blackness of the collapsing path like lightning in the night sky. The fragments drifted, reducing, as if melting into nothingness. This was all that was left of Iris and Mardoch's path. It had almost gone.

No other kutu could have travelled such a degraded, disintegrating path, yet alone run it. But Jychanumun deftly placed his feet on the few partial fragments that remained, pushing forward, half running, half flying. His form changed as he ran; more legs, more power . This would take every skill that he had. As the path became lesser, he had to use remnants of the walls, the ceilings, and whatever part still lingered to move along.

Fragments of the path continued to dissolve as Jychanumun ran with incredible speed. Time was against him. There was no longer any doorway at the end of the path. All access points were closed. Jychanumun would have to use his sensing. He could not pass through, but hopefully some resonant energy of Iris would remain as long as he found the exact place she had entered from. If any resonant energy did remain, then perhaps Iris would be able to pass through. It was a slim, ever-diminishing, chance. It could be the end of the child. But Jychanumun knew that if he did nothing, from what he had foreseen of the flame-dweller, it would be the end of them all anyway.

"I can't hold papa back," Iris said apologetically. "He's coming. I'm sorry. It's too late. . ."

With those words, Jychanumun thrust the child forward, half throwing her through the empty space where his instincts told him that a door had once stood. He had no time to pause. He had to return to the central place while he could. He hoped there were still enough fragments of the path to traverse along. He hoped Mardoch and Dragun had not moved. He hoped that time had stayed consistent for them all.

Jychanumun turned in the paths without stopping, running along a section of fragmented black that he no longer could tell if it was wall, ceiling or floor. As he turned, he glanced back.

Behind him, the energy rippled, dispersing entirely as Iris passed through. And, as Iris disappeared from sight, the brightest light began emanating from her little body. It was like a thousand suns trying to erupt.

FIFTEEN

The Flame-dweller

I called the fire to me, to Soul, with the strength of love and the clarity of intent. I would not let this be Soul's end.

"I heard your call," a strange voice suddenly spoke.

My concentration jolted. The voice was unfamiliar. It sounded close, too close. I had not sensed anyone approaching.

I quickly looked up, relinquishing my true vision, allowing my eyes to see. To my shock, all I could see was fire: real burning, flickering, scorching flames. The fire was all around me. This was not my inner vision. These flames were real. For the shortest moment, all I could think was that the fire should be burning my flesh. But somehow, I was not touched by their destruction. Neither was Soul. We were both intact, unburnt, enveloped by a tremendous inferno, ablaze with condensed red and yellow flames.

I looked for the source of the voice. There, within the fire, I distinguished what looked like a human-sized form made by the flames. It looked like a being made of fire, inside the fire.

The being made of fire sensed that I had noticed it. It moved towards me. As it drew closer, I could see that it was in the shape of a man. But though made of flames, his face had human definition and features. Deep amber tongues arched around his head like unruly curly hair. His tense, furrowed brow framed his deep-set tawny eyes, which flickered with life, watching me. His high cheekbones and strong jaw were alight with moving fire.

I knew that face!

I knew that man!

But he should be dead. I had seen him die. I had seen him burnt to death.

"Wirrel?" I spoke aloud.

I knew that it was. Although I had only glanced him once, his image had been etched in my mind forever. Soul had loved this man, when he was a man, for I had previously seen Wirrel as a normal human. Wirrel had stood firm against Huru, just before Huru had burnt him to death. Now he was something different. He was made of these flames. His intentions felt like a man's, but now he also felt like potently, chaotically focused fire. I had no idea that such a thing was possible.

I felt no fear towards this man made of flames, only compassion, knowing how he and Soul had loved each other, respect for the courage he had shown before his death, and sadness that such a beautiful life had been cut short. From what I had learnt about Wirrel, he had been both brave and honourable.

The fire image of Wirrel tilted his head to one side, as if analysing who I was.

"You." His flames crackled, forming words. "I remember you, choice-bringer. You tried to save me. You brought the light. The light gave me choice."

"And I remember you," I replied. "You are Wirrel of Hollow. Soul's love. Iris' father. But you are not as I remember. I remember the man."

Wirrel looked at his hands, at the flames licking from his fingers.

"I chose to join the flames," he stated.

I hesitated. It made sense, yet it didn't make any sense. I had not wanted the townsfolk to burn Wirrel. I had tried to stop them by using the voice of the Old One to stop the fire. But Wirrel's wounds were to great and he had chosen for the fire to finish him. His flesh had been finished, yes, but not his will or his essence. It was the power of the Old One that had made this possible. It had given Wirrel choice. Wirrel had chosen to join the flames.

"Then you didn't cease," I thought aloud. "You became one with the fire?"

"I *am* the fire," Wirrel bristled. His brow tensed as he frowned. "I was shaped by flames and injustice. Now I burn for all injustices."

Wirrel sounded vehement, almost angry. The flames flickered wildly as if in response to his words. But then he looked down at Soul and his expression changed. His face softened.

"My heart," he smiled a smile that looked sad.

"She has lost her will to live," I said. "My energy keeps her body alive, but without a will it is nothing more than empty flesh. Can you help me to save her?"

"Is that not why you called me?" Wirrel replied.

"Yes," I nodded, "But I did not know that it was you that I called."

Wirrel moved towards Soul, leaning over her. "You called what was needed. . ." his voice trailed away, his concentration on Soul's motionless body. His gaze was serene and full of love.

Wirrel knelt down by Soul's side. As he knelt, his flames grew in intensity. He put one hand on Soul's forehead, the other on the centre of her torso. Tiny flames began dancing upon Soul's body, as if she too was now made of fire. Within the flames, it looked as if the two were one being and nothing else existed.

As Soul's motionless body flickered with flames, Wirrel bent until their faces almost touched. And then, with his lips poised above hers, he began breathing fire into her open mouth.

It poured forth; Wirrel's potent fire entered Soul's body in a stream of luminous flames, flowing like condensed pure power. And, as Wirrel breathed his fire into Soul, the flames around them reduced, shrinking inwards. In the evening gloom, their fire-forms were aglow against the dark surroundings, illuminating the land in hues of golden light. As the last of the flames poured into Soul's open mouth, only Wirrel remained alight, leaning over Soul, now fire-being and human. He paused, and then bent down and kissed her.

"Remember," Wirrel whispered to his love.

The word was so quiet that I barely heard it. And, as he spoke, his fire form changed from condensed flames to a myriad of tiny, bright firelights. It was like all the stars in the skies now poised above Soul, held in the shape of Wirrel, the man.

The tiny firelights remained poised in mid-air for a moment, and then began slowly drifting down. Some seemed to absorb into Soul's body, others merged into the soil around her. It looked quite beautiful, serene, like radiant snow melting.

The last firelights were gone.

All became still.

Soul suddenly took a long, deep breath.

I didn't need to concentrate to see it. There, in Soul's inner core, her life now shone bright once again. Her mind was awash with colour and light. Her colours were true in vibrant gold and pale blue. Not even a speck of Arrunn's shadow remained to taint her.

Soul lived! She was alive! She was complete and whole.

I moved to Soul's side, joyous, in wonder at what I had just witnessed.

Soul's body was healed. Even so, I wrapped the healing sheet around her and sat watching her breathe. Her long, steady breaths were like a soothing balm.

Although Wirrel had gone, I still felt his presence. By Soul's resting flesh, the charred remains of blackened grass and soil still smouldered from burning. Wirrel had almost given his all. I didn't doubt that he would have given everything to save her.

My heart felt at peace; this is what Arrunn could not predict. Yes, we humans were made. Yes, we humans were capable of being swayed. Yes, some were even born with a need to have power over others and all the terrible connotations that lead from that. But we are also capable of greatness, true greatness, in the face of adversity. That is choice. We all have plain and simple choice.

I scooped up a handful of the smouldering ash.

"Wirrel," I spoke aloud.

A small flame reignited. It did not burn my hand.

"Man and flame," I quietly spoke, "thank you. Who you are, your acts, these things have given me hope beyond words. And I pledge that I will show Soul and your daughter how to knowingly call you."

The flame moved in the palm of my hand, responding without words. I placed it back on the ground. It flickered, sinking into the soil and away from sight. I felt that Wirrel would withdraw to the earth's core where the natural fires would be a balm to him. He would soon recuperate. It would not take him long. I did not doubt that our paths would cross again.

On the ground, the deep grey of Dragun's knife was iridescent in the night's gloom. It caught my eye. It was neither charred nor marked by the fire. Just as Dragun, the Rock-Weaver, could not be marred by fire, neither could his blade. What had been done would not have succeeded without Dragun's knife, without Dragun; for I now saw that they were one and the same.

Knowing Soul was safe, I picked up Dragun's knife and went to the rock from whence it came. It took no effort to return it. I pushed that blade against the stone and it was drawn in as if absorbed by it. Whatever part of Dragun was still connected to his weapon, at least he would now be at peace.

From my position by the boulder I could feel the presence of another, and my heart lifted even more. Across the landscape, beyond the charred remains of the hut where the luscious greenery remained untouched, and although it was too gloomy to see, I felt Iris. She was hiding, concealed by the trees. She was watching.

"Iris," I called, "you can come out."

Beyond the first crop field where the trees grew thick and untamed, the small silhouette of Iris came cautiously in to view. She stood still for a moment, watching, ensuring that all was well and I was me. Seeing that it was truly me, she ran towards me. I felt a wave of calm. She was unharmed.

Having greeted Iris, we both returned to Soul, kneeling by her side. The healing sheet had helped her reach a deep, restful sleep. Iris carefully wiped her mother's soot-covered face with her apron, telling her stories of what she had seen and experienced in the death-paths. It sounded as if Iris had gone through adventures of her own. Yet she seemed unfazed. She had a new confidence about her, as if she knew everything would turn out right.

Soul began stirring. She looked tranquil as she opened her eyes.

"We've done it," I said.

Soul cautiously moved her hands to her torso.

"Arrunn has gone; completely gone. You're safe," I said. "And," I put Iris' hand over hers, "Iris is here."

I could see the relief on Soul's face.

"How. . .?" she began to ask.

"When you are rested enough," I replied, "I have much to tell you."

SIXTEEN

The Windows

When Jychanumun returned to the central place of doors, his energy looked frayed, but undamaged. His shredded wings had almost gone entirely. His skin looked matte in consistency, bar the lines of energy-sweat down his back. He no longer had the human child with him, but he did not seem perturbed. He hadn't uttered a word. He had just indicated with a nod of his head towards Mardoch, and that had been enough. It was confirmation. Whatever he had tried, had succeeded.

Dragun had at last begun to recuperate. He still appeared spent, but now his breathing was consistent and his energy had stopped fluctuating. While Dragun began to strengthen, and with Mardoch almost back to full strength, Jychanumun now stood, silently staring into the empty darkness that surrounded them.

Mardoch glanced around. From his perspective, there was very little to look at here in the death-paths. It was impossible to see what held his brother's gaze. All the doors in this central place were closed. The only thing that had changed about them was that, whereas before they had appeared only an arm's reach away, now they looked small, as if in the far distance. And they offered nothing to feast the eyes or mind upon. They were just more darkness within the darkness. This was indeed a place of nothingness.

There was nothing to see. Nothing to do.

This, Mardoch decided, was going to be a very, very, long wait.

"Will you be able to reconnect to Tachra now?" Mardoch asked his brother, already feeling restless as the prospect of so much emptiness.

Jychanumun did not turn from his fixed gaze into the darkness.

"No," he replied. "That was never my doing, but hers. Thousands of clicks ago, long before she existed, she came to me. Although our bond is eternal, our mind-link will only be reinstated when she remakes it."

Mardoch shook his head. "Yet again, my brother, you make little sense to me."

"It can happen when times align," Jychanumun added. "If she can resist joining with the Old One in eternal slumbers, we may stand a chance."

"Could you not wake her from the Old One?"

"No. No one can. The Old One's dreams are too vast."

"What would that mean?"

"All would be lost."

"Oh," Mardoch frowned. His frown turned into an accepting smile. He shrugged. "Well, at least she is safe on Earth, now. I suppose all *we* can do is wait."

"Yes."

"And this," Mardoch looked around at the darkness and closed doors, "this really is it? Us three, here for millennia? Until the time is right, whenever that may be? Nowhere to go? Nothing we can do?"

"Yes," Jychanumun affirmed. "There are no exits until then. We either remain here in the paths, or return to the shadow. Those were always our only two options. Would you prefer us to return to the shadow?"

"No," Mardoch laughed. He was still recuperating and the laughter made him hurt, so he stopped. "I think we would not be welcome in the shadow realms. But another time perhaps, in the future, when we have had victory and peace prevails. I would like to see it."

"Remember it," Jychanumun corrected him. "It was our first home. We have just forgotten."

Jychanumun began moving his hands, signing the old kutu language that Mardoch had heard of, but never had the time or patience to study. As Jychanumun's hands deftly moved, black energy wove through his long fingers. Some residue of the black energy remained in the air, leaving faint shadows against the darkness, as if giving the darkness dimensional depth.

"There is much you will come to understand about these paths," Jychanumun spoke as he worked. "They are both nowhere and everywhere. We cannot interact, because we cannot make new doors, but I can still see."

He moved a hand before him, weaving energy once again, but this time the energy was pure white. The pure white became a fine sheet of light which lingered, unmoving in the space.

"I can always see through the darkness," Jychanumun continued. "So, I can view any place. For you, I can create a window."

Jychanumun indicated towards the sheet of white energy.

"Through this, my white energy, you can see into light and all that is now home for the Shaa-kutu. And this," he pointed towards the area of darkness that appeared darker than its surroundings, "is a window into the shadow. Here our fellow Nigh-kutu have returned. Arrunn will soon arrive. He will regroup his warriors. They will follow. But there are some, a few, whose choices will define them."

"And I can see too?" Mardoch asked, his interest piqued.

"Yes. Give me a point of origin, being, object, or energy."

Mardoch did not remember the original shadow realm to give a specific location. Object? None that were of significance. Being?

"Shemya," Mardoch decided. "Shemya of Arrunn-kin. He was one of my warrior-firsts. He had promise. You've mentioned that he was originally of the Gatherer clan. I remember that I liked the Gatherers. They had fortitude."

Jychanumun stood back, giving space for Mardoch to see through the shadow.

"Then observe. I show you Shemya, formerly of the Gatherer clan, and where he is now."

SEVENTEEN

The Shadow

Deep in the shadow realm, on the far side of infinity, where the dark was darkest and instincts limitless, Shemya, Nigh-kutu warrior, one of the first-caste warriors of Arrunn, stood poised, ready to defend. He had no weapons. His armour was gone. The clothing he had been wearing had vanished.

Shemya had stood unmoving, ready for attack, since he had found himself cast into this place of darkness. As yet, the attack had not come and the darkness had prevailed. He had no idea where he was.

All around was intense, black shadow: above, below and beyond. The shadow appeared never-ending, empty and soundless, without shape or horizon to give him any sense of perspective. He wondered if this was oblivion. This looked as he imagined oblivion would look. Perhaps it was. Perhaps this was his punishment. No, that would be too easy. Oblivion and punishment meant that he was paying atonement. He didn't want atonement.

Shemya knew that he had to remain cool-headed and assess his situation, but his anger conflicted with his need for calm evaluation. He was so angry that his instincts urged him to run, to fight, to strike out at anything that he might encounter with the brute, violent aggression that was surging through him. That human had done this to him. Those few words Tachra Iastha had uttered as she had died had changed him. Using her magic ways, she had whispered suggestions into his mind that had awoken forgotten nightmares. She had made him remember things about his past, things that contradicted everything he existed for. He now doubted himself. He doubted everything he had done. He mistrusted everything he believed in. Oblivion or not, he was surely cursed.

So he had once been a Gatherer. So what? That was long ago. That was a different life. He was no longer a Gatherer, hadn't been for a long time, and could never be again. Why should he be concerned about such a thing? Those memories were no longer relevant. But, they did have connotations. How could he remain a warrior for Arrunn now that he recalled the atrocities which had been forced upon him? He could not. He was Arrunn-kin no more. So, what was he now? Did it even matter? Now that he was in this place of eternal shadow, did anything matter? He didn't know that either. All he knew was that he was lost. Resentful. Condemned. Angry. Mistrusting. And lost. Lost in every sense.

Although he could see nothing within the darkness, Shemya knew he was not blind. He held up his hands in front of his face and they glowed with the familiar outline of his deep orange energy. He had not suffered deafness either. His ears heard nothing, yet when he concentrated, he perceived a drone that vibrated through him as well as around him. It was as if the darkness was an energy of its own. It was as if this never ending shadow was an energy so strong that it could conceal all else from sight or hearing.

Shemya's alertness grew. If this shadow could conceal, it might not be as empty as it appeared. It could be obscuring things, beings, enemies. He must create an advantage. To survive, *he* must be strongest.

With no tools to work with other than his own skills, Shemya began drawing in the shadow energy. It tasted of nothing and smelt of nothing, yet it was potent and invigorating. It was condensed, yet as weightless as bathing in the Dimaru currents. He let the energy saturate his essence, acknowledging its power, and the more energy that he drew in, the more his strength increased. His mind sharpened. His instincts honed.

Suddenly, Shemya halted. He sensed another. He was not alone.

Utilising his natural sensing skills and the stealth he had learnt from Arrunn-kin, he wove his energy outwards, sensing who or what was close by. There. He could definitely feel it now. There was another being within the shadow. Its energy was familiar. It was undoubtedly Nigh-kutu. This Nigh-kutu was alive, but not moving, emitting a strong emotional aura of tenseness and uncertainty.

Speculating that there might be more Nigh-kutu concealed within the shadow, Shemya let his senses ease further out. It wasn't long before he detected another Nigh-kutu, and then another. Beyond them, his awareness perceived at least twenty more. He didn't doubt that if he kept searching, he would locate multitudes of them. Perhaps even the entire army. They all emitted similar emotions of unease and defensiveness. Yet none seemed aware of the other, not yet. It seemed that whatever event had forced Shemya to this place must have happened to them all.

Shemya knew that with his skill at understanding energies, he could aid his fellow Nigh-kutu. He could. But he wasn't going to. As much as they might have been brother warriors once, that was then. Now, the situation had changed. He had changed. They couldn't be trusted. He felt no allegiance to them, or to Arrunn – not to anyone. He felt only loathing towards them all.

Mask my thinking, Shemya disciplined himself, knowing that such traitorous thoughts would be penalised if Arrunn or his kin heard them. *Conceal my intent. Create distance from all others. Be soundless. Be invisible. Others are too close. Move to an isolated place. Turn. Step away. Slowly.*

He turned and moved.

Be cautious. Another step.

Shemya cautiously eased away from all the other Nigh-kutu, keeping a steady pace, ensuring his actions were undetectable. Once manoeuvred into a position within the darkness that had no other Nigh-kutu close by, he felt able to focus.

First strategy, Shemya reminded himself, *is defence. If this shadow is energy, use it to conceal. Gather it unobtrusively, like any other energy. Let none feel the movement, because there are no ripples. Gather it and surround yourself with it. Become undetectable within the darkness.*

Shemya smiled wryly to himself. So he was once a Gatherer? No wonder he could do what he did so well and so veiled. It was a skill that had shrouded his free-thinking for millennia. It was a skill that had saved him in battle many times. Well, this now was also a battle. This time, Arrunn would not direct his fight. This time, his conflict was with everyone.

Having absorbed an abundance of shadow and used it to conceal his own energy, Shemya flexed his essence. He felt taller and stronger, basking in the power that surged through him. His senses were on high alert and his wings rippled behind him. He had gathered enough of the shadow to obscure his presence. He would be undetectable to any other kutu. The best defence, the first defence, was always invisibility.

Suddenly, a waft of hot air passed over the back of Shemya's head. It was so close that it made his hair move. Something was behind him. He froze.

The soft yet heavy pad of unfamiliar footsteps began sounding directly behind him. They were so close that the shadow energy rippled. It sent shivers down his back. How had something managed to get this close without him sensing its approach?

Whatever it was behind Shemya, it was not kutu. It sounded too large to be kutu. The heat he had felt on his head had been the warmth of breath, from something far taller than a kutu. Its breathing was extended and deep, able to draw in ten times the amount of a kutu, and hot. Its footsteps were quiet yet substantial, as if from something agile and heavy. Such a combination would be powerful, fast and strong. But the footsteps were not so much footsteps, as the softness and sharpness of pads and claws.

Shemya's instincts told him to turn around and face whatever paced behind him. But it sounded big. It sounded powerful. And, although such things did not daunt him, if he did not know what nature of creature this was, how could he choose his best line of attack? He had no weapons, only his bare hands. He was at a disadvantage. So, despite his instinct to turn and fight, he remained disciplined. This was not the time. That would come soon enough. Meanwhile, he was well hidden within the shadow. As long as he kept still, he was sure that the creature would not notice him and would eventually leave.

Keep still. Make no energy ripples. Stay invisible. Still your thoughts. Let the creature pass by, Shemya repeated to himself.

Yet, despite remaining concealed, whatever it was behind Shemya did not pass by. It lingered, shuffling around the spot directly behind him. Then, just when Shemya thought the creature would finally leave, its breathing altered. The long, relaxed, drawn out inhalations, changed to short directed sniffs. Its breath moved, progressing along the top of Shemya's head, down the back of his neck and across his shoulder. It was as if it was sensing its surroundings. Sensing him.

Suddenly, the creature let out a quiet, threatening growl. It *could* sense him.

Shemya's hands instinctively moved to his sides, where for so many millennia he had kept his throwing knives concealed within his armour. But his knives were not there. Neither were the discs in his breast plates, nor the long swords at his sides, nor the sonic reactors, nor the quakemakers. He wasn't wearing breastplates or armour. He was weaponless. But he was not powerless. He could still use his skills. Especially the skills of a Gatherer.

Draw off its energy, he told himself. *Absorbing its energy will weaken it. Weaken it, make it inactive, and then finish it.*

Shemya began slowly, deliberately, gathering energy. This time, he did not take energy from the shadow around him. This time, he directed his attention to the creature.

Bit by bit, Shemya unobtrusively siphoned the creature's energy. As he worked, the creature's movements slowed and its shuffling reduced. A bit more and its breathing grew heavier, and then more laboured. A bit more and it slumped down, too weak to stand.

Soon the creature would be immobilised.

But, as Shemya continued siphoning, getting ready to make his killing blow, instead of feeling stronger, he began to feel a strange, heady tiredness. The tiredness increased. He felt heavier, his thoughts less clear.

Shemya knew that only one thing could do this. His own energy was being drawn from him! Whatever this creature was, it was now mimicking his actions. It was now drawing energy from him.

Shemya fought against this draining, but to no avail. He was growing weaker. His energy barrier was the first thing to be affected. It thinned and fragmented, and then dissipated entirely. His wings became numb and could no longer taste the air. He began to feel heavy with the fatigue, as if he could sleep for millennia.

Shemya knew that he had little time left. If this continued, he would soon be emptied entirely. He had to make a decision before it was too late.

There was no other option. He was going to have to fight the beast with his bare hands.

He slowly turned, ready to confront his opponent.

Eskah's oblivion! It was a Nar beast!

A gargantuan beast loomed over him. Within the gloom, its potent power glowed around it, making it look immense. Its body was covered in rough, black scales. Its scales emitted a faint orange outline, showing its compact, rippling muscles. Its long neck was lowered, its face held at the same height as Shemya's, its large nostrils flaring, sensing and smelling him. The movement from its breath vibrated the darkness like a heat mirage. Its broad mouth was slightly open, revealing double rows of sharp, pointed teeth. And it could certainly see Shemya. Its long orange eyes were narrowed, watching him fixedly.

Shemya knew he could never win in combat against a Nar. No lone Nigh-kutu could expect such a victory, not even him. Nars were the most feared beast of Arrunn-kin. A Nar could turn its attacker's energy against them. And that was for the lucky victims, those who simply waned to nothingness. The unlucky ones would have a final memory of their own body being ripped apart. Thousands of warriors had died trying to conquer a mere handful of Nars. Yet these beasts were said to be extinct now, bar the pet Arrunn had kept locked in his vault. Was this that same beast? Either way, Shemya knew that this creature could cut him down in an instance.

Shemya did not attack, holding instead the stare of the Nar. Standing ground, without intent to attack, was his only chance of survival. Right now, his best hope was to adopt a passive pose.

"Leave," Shemya plainly stated.

The Nar's body shuddered with restrained energy, its scales flexing. It snorted a low, long breath, making its nostrils quiver. It was almost a growl. Slowly, its eyes never leaving Shemya, its muscles rippling, it crouched back on its haunches. It looked as if it was readying to attack.

"Leave." Shemya tried commanding the beast again. "I do not wish to fight you. Do not force me to defend or attack."

"You will not attack," a voice from the darkness suddenly spoke. "He will not harm you. He is showing himself to you. We will stop drawing your energy now. Please do not try to draw ours again."

From behind the Nar, emerging from the shadow, walked a Nigh-kutu.

Shemya knew all the warriors of Arrunn-kin, but he did not recognise this kutu. His look was distinctive. He was taller and leaner than most warriors. His huge wings spanned out behind him, moving like cloaks in a wind, their edges outlined in the same deep orange as Shemya's own energy. His hair was long, longer than a warrior's, tied into multiple plaits over the top of his head, creating a ragged mane down his back. His long eyes shone with the same orange as the Nar and his skin bore the healed marks of much violent warfare.

Between the strange kutu and the Nar was a line of orange energy which connected them. The kutu walked up to the beast, putting his hand on its neck and allowing his wings to drape over the creature's back. The Nar leaned into the kutu. Both were watching Shemya with the same orange eyes. Their deep orange energy rippled together so it was impossible to tell where one began and the other stopped.

"Take your beast elsewhere," Shemya stated boldly.

"My Nar," the kutu corrected. "But you know about Nars already, don't you?"

As he spoke, the kutu patted the Nar, his eyes never breaking Shemya's stare. "And yet you do not greet us fondly. Have you forgotten us so readily, Shemya?"

Shemya was taken aback that this strange kutu knew his name.

"Forgotten you? I do not know you."

"Then look closer."

Shemya shook his head, trying to contain his hostility towards this kutu who had invaded his space and knew his name.

"I do not need a closer look. I do not know you," Shemya repeated. "Has Arrunn sent you?"

"No," the kutu replied. "I state openly that I am no friend of Arrunn and stand against him. You and I. . . we are friends, though. We are both Gatherers. We have run, flown and gathered together, kutu and Nar. We are clan-brothers."

"I am no longer a Gatherer," Shemya retorted. "If once I was like you, now I am not. I have, and want, no clan."

"But you cannot change the essence of who you are," the kutu said. "Remember me. I am Herun, your friend and brother."

"I have no brothers. Nor do I want any. I stand alone."

This strange Nigh-kutu called Herun laughed, but then his laugh turned into a cough. The cough worsened until it was a guttural, hacking convulsion from deep within his chest. It clearly pained him, as he clutched onto his chest and his energy swirled chaotically around him.

Shemya took a step back. The racket this kutu was making was loud enough to raise Eskah. And if the noise wasn't bad enough, his obvious pain was vibrating the shadow energy. Any warrior would be able to detect such a commotion.

"Be quiet," Shemya growled. "Get away from me and take your beast before your noise attracts attention. You're creating enough commotion to raise all Arrunn-kin. Leave. Leave, or I will be forced to show you what I have learnt as a warrior-first."

Herun thumped his chest, trying to control the convulsions.

"And what is that?" he asked, managing to catch his breath. "What has Arrunn's army taught you that is so valuable?"

"How to destroy you," Shemya snarled. "How to send you to

oblivion. And then I'll turn my attention to your beast and destroy him too."

"Destroy us? One at a time?" Herun shook his head. "Then Arrunn has truly taught you the impossible. Or, more likely, you truly have forgotten. Watch, young Shemya," he nodded, "watch and remember."

The strange Nigh-kutu looked at the Nar. The connecting line of energy between them expanded, becoming so large that it encompassed them both. For a moment, it looked as if they were both standing amidst a dome of orange energy. The energy flashed, the brightness briefly concealing both kutu and beast. And then, as the energy flash subsided, the Nar had gone. It had only been an instant of blinding light. It had not been enough time for such a large beast to get away. Nevertheless, only the tall Nigh-kutu remained.

Herun of the Nigh-kutu Gathering clan walked forward, drawing in the remnants of his energy as he moved.

"You cannot destroy me, and then the Nar," he stated, "because we are one and the same." He held out his hands, palms up, the old kutu sign of open sincerity. "I am Nar."

"You mislead me with trickery," Shemya retaliated.

"No," Herun shook his head. "You too are Nar."

"Do I look like a Nar beast?"

"Do I?" Herun shrugged. "It is no trick. It is part of a Gatherer's skill. We gather and transform. We were a peaceful, reflective clan. With that, we must also embrace the opposite within ourselves. Mostly we are placid, gentle and introverted; we study and understand. Yet our potent skills must also have a release. For that, we transform to our Nar form to embrace and express that aggressive power."

Deep in Shemya's core something rang true. Images of horror filled his mind. The memory of the destruction of so many Nars as they defended their clan. Shemya remembered it now; standing with a Nar as the Nar defended him, taking blow after blow until it could defend no longer. Shemya thought that perhaps that was his Nar. Why did he think that? Why did it hurt his insides just to think about it? Was his defender not a beast, but a friend?

"We must stand together," the Nigh-kutu spoke. "I sense that Arrunn has arrived in this shadow land. Soon he will be at full strength. He will regroup his warriors. You must see that Arrunn's way will destroy all Nigh-kutu eventually. We Gatherers must stand together. It is time that you left Arrunn-kin and rejoined your true clan."

"No," Shemya was incensed. "I will not stand with you, or yours, ever again."

Herun was clearly shocked. He launched towards Shemya. He thrust his hands towards Shemya's torso, grasping his arm, and then his neck, looking for something.

"Where is that crystal embedded in you; the ones Arrunn uses to control?" Herun growled.

"Get away!" Shemya pushed Herun violently. "I have no crystal. I never have had."

Herun staggered backwards. "You mean that you will fight for Arrunn willingly? You choose to remain Arrunn-kin?"

"I am no longer Arrunn-kin," Shemya retaliated. "I will fight for no cause, ever again, except my own." He narrowed his eyes as long distant memories resurfaced. "Perhaps Arrunn-kin did cloud my mind. But the Gatherers were worse. I remember now, but I remember it all: you all forced me to surrender."

Oh, those memories were clear now. Shemya could feel his energy ripple with anger. His supposed brothers, his clan, the last of the Gatherers, had encouraged and pushed him to surrender to Arrunn-kin. How could such betrayal be his true clan? How dare this kutu come along after millennia and just expect allegiance?

"You all betrayed me."

"Betrayed?" Herun's energy flashed, rippling around him. "You fool. You were not betrayed. You were saved. You were the only one we could protect. You were the only one of us who could control their transforming well enough. It took the sacrifice of many to protect you so that your true nature was concealed. You forget how many gave their lives for you. You forget too much! We did not betray you. We saved you."

As Herun spoke, he grew visibly angry. His body started morphing, growing in size, his smooth skin gaining texture as if scales were forming, his eyes narrowing like the eyes of a Nar. He visibly took deep breaths, allowing some of the growing energy to dissipate into the darkness, trying to calm himself, containing the transformation.

"It is you who is now betraying what you truly are," Herun added. "You have concealed your inner soul, brother. Unchain it!"

"You should not have spared me," Shemya growled. "Your sparing me turned me into this: a killer for Arrunn. And when I did not kill, I did nothing while others did. My clan," he said the word derisively, "is to blame for making me what I never wanted to be. I do not need to be Nar to be a beast. I *am* a monster."

"You are no monster," Herun quickly rebalanced. "You had to survive. You do not know what a monster truly is. You think a bit of warring, a bit of conflict has made you a monster? You speak of terms that you truly do not know."

"I know better than you," Shemya seethed. "You did little more than conceal yourself in your Nar form, hiding like a spicket-doe in a shadow cave, letting Arrunn's guards carry you around in that crystal-safe. You are a coward."

As soon as the word was spoken, Shemya knew that he had made a mistake. To any Nigh-kutu the term coward was the greatest insult, no matter whether they were Arrunn-kin or any other clan.

For a moment, Herun's energy was so still that it was almost tangible. Shemya expected him to return to his Nar form and rip him limb from limb.

"If any other kutu had called me that, I would kill them," Herun shook his head. His tone was sad, not angered as Shemya had expected.

"But still," Herun continued, "I attempt to remove the blindness from your mind. Do you forget what your clan's kutu went through? We, your clan-brothers, were contained, held in stasis between kutu and Nar, and starved. We were fed nothing but hallucinogens, to make us angered. And then, in a frenzied state, somewhere between kutu and Nar, with our teeth and claws bared yet bound in the body of kutu, we were given our friends, one at a time. Our warped minds did not see friends, but food. We tore them apart and ate them alive. Their screams only propelled our deranged minds. Their pain fed us. And then, once satiated and fed, the hallucinogens were removed from our systems and we had clarity of the horror of what we had done. And then they did it again. And then again. We lived a repeated nightmare until we no longer knew reality. Forced by your Arrunn-kin, I have done terrible things. Who," he said, starting to cough again, "is the monster?"

Shemya did not reply. He just stood, agitated, as Herun thumped his chest to stop the coughing.

"Arrunn will soon start seeking," Herun continued. "I have no more time to convince you. I had hoped that you would join me. But, you have stated your wishes."

"Yes, and I stand by them."

"Then I was clearly wrong," Herun composed himself. "Shemya, once of the Gathering clan, once my brother, I am joyous that you live." He bowed a bow that Shemya had not seen for millennia. It was a bow of honour and respect. "Farewell," he concluded. "I will trouble you no more."

Herun turned and simply walked away.

Shemya watched as the Gatherer's distinct form grew smaller into the distance, merging within the darkness.

All was quiet once more.

Shemya should have felt relieved to be rid of the noisy, coughing kutu. He should have felt relieved that he had not had to combat a Nar. He had wanted to be isolated; now he was. This was what he had wanted, but so much bothered him. So much bothered him about what Herun had said, and even more about what he had not.

Herun had shown no hostility. In fact, he had spoken more truths in those few beats than Shemya had heard for millennia. Now here he was, having told himself that he was no longer of Arrunn-kin, but still acting like Arrunn-kin; with contempt for all others and little more than self-preservation in his heart.

Shemya felt an alien sensation. He felt ashamed.

Something inside him snapped.

He launched into the darkness and began flying. He had to find Herun. He should not have let him just walk away. This kutu was the one kutu who had shown honesty, and who knew of his past. This kutu even said they had been brothers. Brothers? Clans were real? They had really existed? If this Herun was his brother, he must not let him leave like this.

Shemya could not sense Herun's presence anywhere. The kutu was obviously concealing himself within the shadow. Nevertheless, Shemya wove the shadow energy around him and pushed forward, trusting that his instincts would locate him.

Despite leaving no trace, Shemya did not have to go far to find the Gatherer. He had chosen a path avoiding all other kutu, just as Shemya would have done. The Nigh-kutu was still masked by the shadow, but unmoving.

Shemya nimbly landed.

Herun was crumpled on the ground. It was clear that the kutu was in a bad state. His breaths were shallow and rasping, as if he could no longer draw energy into his essence. Shemya had not seen damage to a kutu like this before. In battle, injuries were visible, yet Herun gave no sign of outward damage; nothing that could be healed. His injuries seemed to be internal.

"What can I do?" Shemya asked.

Herun began to speak, but as soon as he tried talking, the coughing began again. He struggled to push himself to his knees and then feet, refusing to take Shemya's outstretched arm. As Herun stood, he pointed to his torso, and then grabbed Shemya's hand, placing it on his chest.

Immediately, with his hand on Herun's chest, Shemya felt energy rush through him. Herun's body stiffened, becoming rigid, his eyes wide and his mouth open. Shemya tried pulling his hand away, but the kutu's hold was firm.

Suddenly, Herun's body began shuddering into spasms. His head thrust forward as his body tensed and relaxed, partially morphing between kutu and Nar. As Herun's convulsing intensified, Shemya was sure that he could feel something in the kutu's chest, exactly where Herun kept his hand firmly pressed. Whatever it was within this kutu, it seemed to push at his energy, burning his palm, as if wanting to be removed. Herun began retching.

As Herun retched, streams of luminous orange energy spewed from his mouth, pooling onto the substanceless ground. More came, and then more, as if Herun's very essence was expelling itself. Just when Shemya thought the kutu could not possibly endure any more, the retching subsided. Herun sunk down, panting heavily.

There, amidst the pool of orange energy that had come from Herun's body, were life-crystals. Small, glowing life-crystals. Dozens of them.

Shemya drew a sharp breath. Life-crystals. These were dangerous things. A kutu could be killed for just setting his sight on them.

Herun should not have them. Owning such a thing was instant punishment.

Shemya went to pull away from Herun and his prohibited crystals, but then stopped. Why should he believe that all life-crystals were Arrunn's and Arrunn's alone?

Tentatively, Shemya moved in to take a closer look at the little gems. He had never seen life-crystals at such close quarters before.

None of the life-crystals had physical form any longer, but they still held their recognisable angled shape. Most were in varied tones of luminous orange, aglow like tiny beacons. A few had random colours dotted amongst the orange: one cyan, one blue and two pale yellows. But there were also four that were colourless; a matte, pale grey. Whereas the coloured life-crystals were glowing, swirling and oscillating like tiny electrical stars, the grey ones appeared dormant.

Herun, although clearly exhausted, leant over to the crystals. His face fell as he picked up the four grey gems.

"Be at peace," he whispered. "Join the great gathering in eternity."

Then he blew on the grey crystals, making shadow energy flow from his mouth. As the shadow energy touched the grey gems they disintegrated, turning into whispers of fine grey energy that simply absorbed into the shadow.

Shemya had so many questions that he barely knew where to start.

"Those four did not survive," Herun said. "Baraddan, Rylock, Gunn and Peeran. I will mourn them."

"Then have the others come to life?" Shemya asked.

"They were never dead," Herun replied. "I have carried them safely for millennia, but I could contain them no longer. They wanted to be released. They have chosen here and now. It seems that in this shadow realm, where our futures are unknown, here and now is the right place."

"The right place for what?"

"For them to come back."

Herun picked up one of the crystals, setting it into the centre of his palm. He then drew in shadow energy, pushing it into the little gem. In response, the entire crystal began spinning, its momentum increasing until it levitated, hovering above his hand.

Herun left the glowing gem suspended in nothingness and picked up another, following the same procedure. A few moments later, all the crystals hovered, spinning amidst dark nothingness, their luminosity growing. They were beautiful alight. Together they looked like a galaxy with many suns in perfect miniature.

"I have been waiting thousands of clicks for this," Herun said. "This is why I was picked to remain as a Nar. I have forsaken all else for this very moment."

Each of the gems now spun and swirled of their own accord, absorbing shadow energy from the atmosphere. And, as they absorbed more energy, they began growing. As they grew, they moved beyond the confined shapes, expanding upwards, elongating, still moving within their mass. Their size kept increasing. Shemya and Herun both stood. The energy from each crystal was now as tall as them.

Slowly, each mass of glowing energy began to take a form. The forms began to look like figures. Heads, arms, legs, became definable, and then wings.

"What's happening?" Shemya asked.

"You, my brother," Herun replied, "are about to re-greet Nigh-kutu that you thought long dead. Most are your clan brothers; a few are from allied clans. Re-meet your lost brothers and then choose. Choose if you still wish to walk away from the Gathering clan."

Shemya watched as the luminous forms became more distinct. Some had an energy that seemed familiar.

"I have made my choice," Shemya nodded. "If you agree to my terms."

Herun looked questioningly, waiting for Shemya to go on.

"If you teach me how to embrace the Gatherer within me," Shemya said, "then when I am both Gatherer and warrior, I will choose my clan. If that is acceptable to you, whatever that choice may be, I will swear never to turn my skills against you or any of your allies here."

Herun considered Shemya's proposal.

"It is a fair, well-measured choice," Herun decided. "So, yes." He nodded to himself, as if taking into account all the implications. "I will teach you. And Shemya," he added, "you will be formidable."

EIGHTEEN

The Light

Meanwhile, in the light...

On the opposite side of infinity, where the light was brightest and all light thoughts intertwined, Chia, Shaa-kutu, sensitive, trailblazer and chi master, stood watching, listening. He had no body suit to limit his sensing anymore. He had no eye-piece to restrain his inner sight. He felt everything. It felt as if he was drowning in luminosity.

Kraniel's plan had worked. Chia was in the light.

His vision had only just begun to clear. At first he hadn't been able to see anything except the brightest, most intensely luminous, colourless light that blinded all else from view. Its brilliance seemed to reach to infinity, overriding everything. This was more than the simple rays from a bright star or sun, or the illumination of some powerful device; this light also wanted to move through him. It wanted to soak through his very essence. This light had substance.

Yet everything here was energy. Nothing was physical. Matter did not, could not, exist here. Chia knew that; he had assumed this would be the case. He simply needed to learn, or remember, a different way of hearing, seeing and sensing.

Chia smiled to himself, remembering Tachra's tales of trying to learn how to use her inner sight. Sometimes, she had said, the simplest and most natural things were the most difficult to achieve. It was true. Instinctively, Chia had tried to repel the all-consuming light. It was not so easy to stop the habit of millennia.

I must stop fighting this, he firmly told himself. *This is my origin. I must trust that my energy will remember how to react.*

Feeling the dread of potential consequences, Chia took a slow, deep breath, absorbing the light deep into his inner core. At first he struggled against the strange sensation. Like an earth mammal drowning in water, his limbs stiffened, a sense of panic momentarily making him believe that he had made the wrong choice, or must be doing something wrong. Slowly, his panic calmed. He forced another deep breath. Nothing untoward happened. He felt no pain.

As Chia breathed, the light flowed through his entirety and, to his surprise, the sensation did not overwhelm him; neither did it affect his thinking. Instead, it felt clean, invigorating and whole. It even seemed to clear his thoughts. He was aware that he still held his form, but he was now part of the light. He felt the strength of the light, and that the light connected everything and everyone within it. And, although he could not yet see them, he sensed other Shaa-kutu: hundreds of them, thousands of them, all within the light too.

As he concentrated, Chia thought he saw indistinct shapes in the distance. At first, from the corner of his eye, he thought he saw what appeared to be the outline of a vast sphere. But when he looked directly, he saw nothing. Then again, almost immediately, he thought he saw the vague outline of a huge column. It was just the slightest change to the bright light, a brightness within a brightness, yet when he concentrated his vision, the light was continuous and never ending, with nothing inside it.

And somewhere close by, Chia could now hear humming.

Chia slowly turned, pushing out his senses to determine its source.

A short distance away, a vivid blur of luminous red was now unmistakeable. It could only be Orion. Chia focused his vision on it.

Orion was standing with his chin raised and his arms by his sides, motionless. He was humming as loudly as he could, as if the action calmed him.

"Orion," Chia called, his voice moving through the light in visible lines of violet. "I can hear you. I'm here; just in front of you."

"Chia?" Orion sounded relieved. "You're in front of me? You sound as if you are all around me."

Orion cautiously walked forward. "I am as blind as a dirk mole lost in the tunnels of Eden." He talked as he walked. "I had to trust someone would hear me. I was beginning to wonder if I alone had been thrust here."

Chia was already moving to meet Orion, touching his arm to reassure him of his presence as he reached him.

"Your vision and sensing will return," Chia told his friend. "Let the light move through you. Feel yourself as part of the light, not a singular being inside it. The way we translate information is different to what we have become accustomed. And this," he paused, "is very different."

"Can you see?" Orion asked.

"My vision is adjusting," Chia replied, looking around, "although I have no idea of our landscape yet. Plus, I am sensing things that I do not fully understand."

"I cannot help yet. I see nothing," Orion shook his head. His red hair tumbled around his form in strands of red pure light, as if they were sensing the new surroundings.

Chia caught Orion's arm and linked it through his. "Then hold onto me until your vision clears," he directed. "I am adjusting more quickly because I am accustomed to translating new energies."

"This place is as alien to me as a new world. I had expected I would remember, but I do not. And what concerns me is that I have very little sense of time. How long would you estimate you have been here for?" Orion asked.

"Not long. A few hundred beats."

"And I feel as if I have been here for a thousand times that amount." Orion seemed to be considering the implications. "I suspect time is less relevant here. Perhaps time has no relevance at all and is defined by nothing more than the perspective of the individual. Millennia could pass very quickly without physicality, matter, or energy restrictions to judge or guide by."

As Orion spoke, Chia glanced to one side, thinking once again that the shape of a vast sphere was inside the light. But again, there was nothing.

"The constant brightness of this light plays tricks with my vision," Chia voiced his concerns. "I keep thinking I see something."

"That, my friend," Orion replied warily, looking around, "I find alarming. This is still an unfamiliar place to us. We do not remember what it may hold. We must regroup everyone as soon as possible."

"I too feel urgency," Chia nodded. "I sense others. Thousands have survived and are here. But this place is vast and our fellows are scattered. Many feel fragmented, as if they had sustained injuries before arriving here. They need our help."

Orion rubbed his brow. "We have no tools at our disposal, so must find another way to regroup everyone. If I could connect with Una, the Supreme – if he has survived – then he has the ability to do it."

Orion fell silent. He was thinking so deeply and so quickly that his energy flickered around him. The sparks of crimson red energy seemed to ignite, falling around his feet in tiny shards that were absorbed into the light.

"I can do a mind probe. I have done one before," Orion suddenly decided. "If I can make a mind-connection to Una, if we can find him, then the three of us together should have enough connective ability to call all other Shaa-kutu to us."

Chia groaned. He disliked mind-probes at the best of times. He knew he would have to be the binding force if Orion performed one. The inevitable pain was not the issue. The issue was that, if done incorrectly or inaccurately, it could leave them both dislocated for a very long time. It could even leave them mindless for that time. And, if time here was inconsistent, then the potential disasters were incalculable. This place was an unknown commodity. Here, any aspect of a dangerous task could be greatly exaggerated. Nevertheless, they had to do something.

"It is dangerous, and I wish to argue, but I cannot," Chia decided. "If a mind-probe is our only option, so be it. I will be your binding force. I hope," he paused, "the Supreme is still alive. But be cautious. My senses are picking up things that I cannot explain."

"Then we act now," Orion decided.

Chia nodded.

Both Orion and Chia knew the procedure. Chia was already pushing out violet energy through his fingers. He clasped onto Orion's wrist, allowing his energy to twine around them both, tightly binding their arms together from wrist to elbow. Unsure as to how the technicalities of a binding worked in this place, he doubled the attachment, and then tripled it, until his right arm and Orion's left were fused together by energy.

Orion glanced at Chia, confirming he was ready, closed his eyes, and then bowed his head.

Orion's energy began shimmering – much faster than usual. The shimmering intensified, as if Orion was oscillating between existence and non-existence. Chia could sense Orion searching, pushing out his thoughts, trying to locate the Supreme.

Chia suddenly stiffened. There!

Orion's mind had located and connected to the Supreme. Una had survived! He was exhausted, but his bright, almost white energy was unmistakable.

Chia had to act fast. He was now responsible for Orion's essence. He was holding his mindless energy. Orion's bound essence was now as wispy as a dissipating cloud. Orion's mind was gone, far beyond them, to the place where Una had been located. Chia had to reunite Orion's energy with his mind before his friend lost himself entirely.

"I sense it," Chia confirmed, hoping some part of Orion could still hear him. "Hold the connection."

Chia was already running, running with his dispersing friend bound to him by energy, running in this place of light with no discernible floor or sky, running as fast as he could. As he ran, Chia let the light flow though him and around him, running faster than he ever could when partially physical. The two kutu, bound as one, launched into the light, soaring on Chia's energy wings.

"Hold on. Almost there," Chia calmly instructed his friend, quelling his own sense of urgency.

Chia flew fast. He couldn't tell if he was flying upwards or downwards. All he knew was that he was flying towards Orion's consciousness and that Orion was linked to Una. He flew and he flew, using the energy around them to act as a current to propel them. As he flew, his new vision scanned ahead for any sign that could be Una or Orion.

Finally, amidst the light, Chia was drawn to an area of crimson red next to a brightness that was surrounded by golden light. That was it.

Chia landed with nimble speed, his sole concentration now on reconnecting the fragmented Orion.

"Come back," Chia instructed. "Orion, come back. Now."

Orion's wispy energy, still bound to Chia, seemed to hesitate, and then flickered in response. It's vague glimmer of red grew in clarity.

Orion's form returned with a shudder.

"Are you fully together?" Chia asked hurriedly as he unbound their arms. He observed Orion's eyes, looking for any signs of recognition. "Speak to me. Orion, draw every last essence of your thoughts back."

"I am whole," Orion nodded. "Where is Una?"

In unison, Chia and Orion looked up. There, directly in front of them, were two Anumi warriors standing either side of the Supreme. Although both the Anumi were weaponless, they were crouched, ready to attack.

"Hold," Una stated to his Anumi guards. "This may be no illusion."

The two Anumi did not attack, but nor did they relax their guard, remaining crouched and ready to defend. One of the warriors was injured. What had been a flesh wound to his leg now appeared as vague tattered energy where his leg should be.

"Supreme," Orion bowed. "I rejoice that you live."

The Supreme looked at him cautiously. "Am I alive?" He did not return the bow.

"Yes, you are. There are many Shaa-kutu alive here," Orion replied.

"Forgive my wariness," the Supreme said, but showed no less caution, "but the last I remember, I was in refuge in the lower tunnels of Eden, knowing my time was limited before I was found by the Nigh-kutu. I trust nothing, or no one, except my own thoughts and these two Anumi who have never left my side."

"Kraniel found a way to draw all Shaa-kutu to the light," Orion explained. "It was the only way to bring us all back together, and the only way to escape defeat by the black-winged ones. This," Orion indicated around him, "is the light from whence we came."

The Supreme watched. His wary eyes observing Orion intensely.

"If you are Orion, forgive me, but I can no longer trust my sight," Una said guardedly. "Illusion is just one of the many tricks these Nigh-kutu have learnt in their warfare. I have even seen them wear the face of another."

Orion hung his head, appearing to collect himself, and then looked straight up at the Supreme.

"I understand," Orion said. "Then just see the truth of me. There are things that, unless you have broken your word, you, and only you, will know. A pretender would not be able to tell you these things. Only you know why I left the council. I nearly lost you as a good friend that day, but you trusted me enough to let me go. Eden3 was thought to be our greatest mission, but you trusted me enough to abandon the project. Only we know where sleeping beasts lay. . ."

"Enough," Una held up his hand.

Orion stopped talking as Una indicated to the two Anumi. "It is alright, my friends; stand down," he told them. "Orion and Chia are true."

The relief on the two Anumi's faces was clear. Although they visibly relaxed, glad to see two more fellow Shaa-kutu alive, it was apparent how truly exhausted they were.

"Orion, Chia," Una bowed. "Your presence is indeed a welcome relief. How are we here? What has occurred to bring this about? I have much to understand."

"There are many here who need that understanding," Orion spoke with urgency. "Most will not know where they are, or how they got here. And many," he indicated towards the Anumi guard's injured leg, "are wounded. We must call them all to one central place immediately. Then I can explain to all at once while we start to heal the injured."

The Supreme listened carefully. "Very well," he agreed, his

thoughts already moving to action. "To bring all Shaa-kutu together, I must create a calling circle. I will need you, Orion," he directed, "and you, Chia. Have you participated in a calling before?"

Chia shook his head.

"All will be well. You have natural skills. Just link into me and filter external energy into me. If this light. . ." he moved his hand through the nothingness as if the light were something tangible to him ". . .is as close to my own energy as I perceive it is, this should not be difficult. Both of you connect to the back of my neck, above my wing line." He indicated the point and then looked at the two Anumi. "Keep guard, my friends. I am afraid this is not quite the time to stand down yet. Break my connection to the calling if anything looks untoward."

The two Anumi took guard while Chia and Orion moved to stand behind the Supreme. Orion placed his hand first. Chia placed his hand above Orion's. Immediately, Chia felt as if he was being drawn inwards. Energy, pure energy, surged through him and into the Supreme.

Una began radiating light as fiercely luminous as anything Chia had experienced since first entering this place. The brightness shone from the Supreme's eyes, nose, and open mouth. The light from his mouth began resonating. It was as if Una were talking in light. Chia heard nothing with his ears, yet his mind heard the call as loud as his own thoughts. The call was vast, encompassing everything.

"It is almost palpable, is it not?" Orion whispered, still connected to the Supreme. "Una's call draws all together."

Una's calling continued. Chia could feel the presence of so many Shaa-kutu: their relief to hear the call of the Supreme. All had begun moving towards the source of the call.

Amongst the tumble of emotions and thoughts from the masses of his fellow Shaa-kutu as they drew closer, Chia could feel something else, something different. That something resonated with the same flavour he had sensed when he first found himself in this realm of light. It was unfamiliar to him. He did not know what it was.

"Orion," Chia whispered slowly and deliberately, "I sense the connection to fellow Shaa-kutu. I sense Una. I sense you. But it is not just these things I am sensing." He paused. "It is something else."

Chia's inner alarm heightened. Whatever this was, its presence was growing stronger. This unknown thing that he was sensing was powerful. And because of the Supreme's all-encompassing call, it knew exactly where they were and was drawing closer too.

Chia shot backwards, releasing his connection from the Supreme. He pulled Orion's hand away too.

"Cut your connection!" Chia instructed. "Una, stop the calling! We are not alone!"

Slowly, in front of them, the Supreme turned around. His eyes were still bright with the light; his light from within and the light around them were almost the same. He looked from Orion to Chia. "I also felt it. And I felt something else."

"What is it?" Chia's voice betrayed alarm.

"I do not know," the Supreme shook his head. "As I called, it was as if it called back."

"Eskah," Chia was horrified. "What have we done? Do we now also have to fight that which we do not know?"

Orion was already acting. "Supreme, I will guard your back," he directed. "Chia, you guard the Supreme's front. Warriors, flank the sides. Any suggestions?"

"We have nowhere to hide and no weapons," one of the Anumi flatly replied. "Whatever this might be, we must face it here, as we are."

"The Shaa-kutu come," the Supreme whispered, more to himself.

"Look, so many. It gladdens my heart. I had thought most of us lost."

In the distance, Shaa-kutu were already in sight and drawing closer: the golden rays of other Anumi; the familiar green of scientists; the blues of the trailblazers; all and every colour spectrum of light now filled the colourless brightness from all directions. The Shaa-kutu came at a pace, thousands of them, some shouldering others, their energies entwined like healing sheets. So many were injured.

The Supreme stepped out from his guarding friends, calling to the kutu to draw closer. Within the call he gave knowledge: knowledge that they lived, that this was a new place, but that they still must remain watchful.

The Shaa-kutu gathered. At first there were dozens of them, and then hundreds, growing to thousands. Expressions of exhaustion, pain, and confusion, all now laced with relief.

"You must explain," the Supreme indicated towards Orion. "Speak to them. We all need to know how and why we are here."

Orion began addressing the kutu as they arrived. Chia did not watch his friend as he spoke. Instead, he watched the horizon of never ending light for any sign that he did not recognise. As he watched, knowing that he sensed something, but not knowing what that something was, he listened.

Orion's tone was hurried, and Chia could feel the weight of urgency in his voice as he told of the last days on Earth after their home-world had fallen. He told of how the Nigh-kutu had been winning, of Kraniel's experiment, and how this experiment had brought them all here.

"Orion," Chia spoke under his breath. "Something else is listening. Hurry your words."

"The important thing is that we are here, together, alive," Orion concluded. "But this is an alien place and so we may not be alone."

The listening Shaa-kutu fell silent, their relief now replaced with a new trepidation. Orion began giving them reassuring words.

Chia was not reassured.

"It draws closer," he told Orion. "I feel intent."

Orion hesitated.

"Something has heard Una. It comes." Chia stepped closer to the Supreme in order to protect him. "It comes. It comes now."

"Draw in!" Orion shouted to the crowd. "Any Anumi warriors, guard the parameters. Draw in!"

The huge gathering of Shaa-kutu visibly drew in closer.

From within the masses of gathering kutu, the golden energy of the Anumi warriors amongst them moved outwards, taking positions of protection around the circumference. A small group of kutu seemed to break away, moving towards Chia, Orion, and the Supreme. Chia was relieved to see it was his companions, Kraniel and Stanze. With them was the Anumi leader, Peniva.

"Supreme, you should join the crowd," Peniva directed as he approached. "I will escort you. You will be better protected there."

Peniva tried to manoeuvre Una towards the huge gathering of fellow Shaa-kutu, but Una would not move. Instead, he gazed ahead in the same direction of Chia's sensing.

In the distance, the light on the horizon of light seemed to grow brighter still: brighter than a thousand flaring suns; brighter than the strongest burning star; even brighter than the heart of their home planet. The brightness continued to intensify, growing in strength, its unknown intention growing closer. Some of the kutu looked away, but Chia could not. For within the brightness was where he sensed the very thing that had struck his initial curiosity, the very thing he could sense.

From amidst the light, a form began to merge. It was big – easily larger than their largest warriors, and perhaps twice their height. It was walking just like a kutu. The form drew closer, close enough to be heard, yet its movements and footsteps remained silent. Its pace was constant, steady, and purposeful. And, although Chia was filled with trepidation, to perceive such power was compelling. He could not look away.

It was almost upon them.

Within the brightness, the form gained definition. Chia could almost see it now.

"Hold," Peniva spoke from behind them.

"Hold."

"Hold."

The unknown form stopped a short distance away. The light began peeling away from it, revealing an even greater brightness, but with the definition of lines. With each layer stripped away, the shape became more distinct. The last light peeled away like a finely obscuring sheath. It stood.

It looked just like. . .

How could this be?

It was a kutu.

It was a kutu, yes, but it looked like no other kutu Chia had seen before. Its naked skin glowed brightly, as if only made of light. It had not one set of wings, but two. Its long mane-like hair moved around its head and shoulders in gentle oscillating sways, framing its calm, expressionless face. Its eyes shone with a whiteness similar to the Supreme's.

In an instant, without any sign of movement, the strange kutu transposed itself from where it stood, a distance away, to directly in front of Chia. Chia instinctively put up his hands, ready to defend. He was the only thing standing between Una and this kutu-like creature made of light.

The creature stood in front of Chia, towering over him, poised, calm, considered. But its attention was not on Chia. It was looking at the Supreme. It appeared to be studying him.

Una remained behind Chia, holding the strange kutu's stare. Both Una and the kutu made of light were so close that Chia could have reached out and touched them both. How he wished that he had his vapour daggers.

"Una-sol-shirana," the huge kutu suddenly spoke without moving his mouth.

The Supreme walked from behind Chia.

"Supreme," Chia whispered through gritted teeth, "get back behind me."

But the Supreme did not retreat. Instead, he stood next to Chia, directly in front of the kutu made of light.

"Una-sol-shirana," the huge kutu said again to the Supreme.

Una didn't move, his own white eyes holding the gaze of the unknown kutu made of light.

"How do you know my true name?" the Supreme asked.

The kutu made of light tilted his head just a fraction. It was the smallest movement, but Chia noticed it nonetheless.

"We are harrtriel," the strange kutu replied, using a word that Chia did not recognise. The tone in the light kutu's words were strange, as if he was stating a fact that was obvious.

"Harrtriel," the Supreme muttered, shaking his head with doubt.

"Harrtriel," he repeated, as if questioning himself, as if the word was familiar, but only in the furthest reaches of his mind.

There was a moment of silence. A moment when Chia felt a connection.

"Harrtriel," the Supreme gasped, as if comprehension had struck his thoughts.

"Septa-sol-shirana. . ." the Supreme suddenly said aloud. "You are Septa-sol-shirana and I remember you."

The kutu made of light inclined his head. "We have been awaiting your return," he said. There was a sense of a shift in the energy, almost as if he was smiling.

Una's gaze moved from the kutu made of light towards Chia, and then Orion, and then out to the watching Shaa-kutu. His expression was one of realisation.

"I was meant to come back," Una whispered, although his words carried strong and true through the light. "I told them that I would come back. Millennia passed. I forgot," he paused. "I forgot about those who chose to stay."

The myriads of Shaa-kutu looked on in silence. Never had they seen something so familiar, so different, so beautifully pure, so alike yet unlike themselves. They understood now: this place, this light was their first home. Long ago, this one had chosen to stay.

While the masses watched in awe, there was one kutu who did not watch the light-dweller. After all, he was still just another light-dweller. All of them were going to die. He was going to die. None of them would be spared.

Shursa stood at the very back of the crowd, ensuring his face was not noticed. He too had felt Una's calling and had been compelled to come. But now he needed to get away. The other Shaa-kutu Arrunn had persuaded would soon realise that too. They would come to him for guidance. He would find somewhere out of sight for them.

So, as his fellow Shaa-kutu were enchanted by the strange, giant light-dweller, Shursa slipped away into the brightness of the light.

Nineteen

The New

Soul caught my hand, squeezing it consolingly.

"I'm sorry," she whispered.

With Soul and Iris beside me, I stared down at the small mound of flowers and bracken in silence. Pieces of dark brown bark reflected bright hues where the morning's first light touched them. Sprigs of blossom and leaves in every shade of green were woven amongst the deep brown like stars in the night. It looked sadly beautiful. It had taken the remainder of the night to cover my mother's ceased flesh.

After the shock of hearing of my mother's death, and after the awfulness of seeing her disfigured corpse, I had insisted I would bury her. I knew it was only her empty flesh. But still, I did not want my eyes to remember that as my last image of her. Neither did I want to leave her mutilated, ruined body on view for anyone else to see. So, using a broken piece of wood, I had covered her body in soil and added foliage, next to the remains of her old home.

Taking mother's spirit to Elysium and reuniting her with father had not negated the heavy heart of loss. The triumphant happiness of freeing Soul from Arrunn's grasp had faded. There was no lingering sense of glorious victory. There was only a deep, exhausted relief. I was beyond weariness. I didn't feel like talking. Nevertheless, as I dug, I spoke to Soul of the events that had led to this point. I wanted to give her any necessary knowledge before I left. I had made a decision as to where I would go. I intended on leaving soon.

Soul had recovered surprisingly quickly. Her remaining flesh wounds had mended readily with the use of our lone healing sheet, until the sheet was depleted. Now, having told Soul all I thought she might need to know, I had no more will to say more. Without the urgency of fight forcing me to act, think or feel, my mind had silenced.

It had only been half a day since I had taken my life at the bottom of the pit. I had planned to walk the death-path to Jychanumun, yet here I was. I should not be here. I should be with Jychanumun. Events had not occurred as I'd expected. So much had happened and in such a short space of time.

I heard myself sighing.

"Where shall we go now?" Soul quietly asked.

It took a moment for my mind to instruct my mouth to work. "Threetops is still a good village for you and Iris," I eventually replied.

"Perhaps," Soul contemplated, "but we'll go with you, wherever that may be."

I glanced at Soul, my friend, my beautiful, loyal friend, and then at Iris, the little one, whose will and compassion never failed to make me smile. They had such potential. They still had so much life yet to live.

"Iris," I spoke gently, "do you mind if I speak with your mamma? Perhaps you could find one last, extra pretty flower for the top? A blue one? It was my mother's favourite colour."

"Alright," Iris nodded, her little face looking grave. "But you won't move from here, will you?" she asked.

"We won't move at all," I promised.

Iris walked towards the trees where the season's last blooms of wild flowers still grew in abundance. She moved with a new wary caution, her eyes casting glances into every shadow. Events had taken their toll on her, but her spirit was not weakened. On the contrary, I sensed a new, unwavering strength in her; a determination beyond her years. It was a noble and beautiful thing to behold, yet I wished it had not been forced upon one so young. Iris deserved the chance to live the life of a child. A life just to play and laugh and not to worry. Here, in Threetops, she could still have that life, now that the kutu were gone.

I turned to Soul, once Iris was beyond earshot. "It's best that you do not come with me. You'll be well cared for here, in Threetops. You'll have everything you need," I said. "The villagers will build you a new hut in no time."

"I don't care for things like huts anymore," Soul frowned. "You are the closest thing that Iris and I have to family. That's what matters. We go with you."

"All my family loves you. Any of my siblings would be happy to have you," I urged. "My sister, Dih, her daughter, Hiela – both love you. Dih has mostly boys. She'd welcome more female company gratefully. You would. . ."

"Tachra," Soul interrupted. She put her hand gently on my arm to stop me talking. Through her touch, I felt her deep sense of dread. "You do not know?"

Whatever Soul was about to say, I knew that I would not like it.

"Hiela is no longer here, nor her boys, nor Dih." Soul spoke apprehensively. "Five nights ago, one of Arrunn's guards came. He collected your family. None of them have been seen since. I thought you knew. But of course," she shook her head, "how could you?"

Arrunn had collected my family? Why would he do that? My stomach churned at the thought. "Who did he take?" I asked.

Soul closed her eyes and bit her lip, as if not wanting to speak.

"All of them," she replied. "Your brothers and sisters, their children, even the babies. . ." her words trailed away. "He took them all, except your mother."

"All?"

"Yes."

I could say nothing. It was too much. Just too much.

"We never found their bodies," Soul added. "Your mother and I searched and searched, but found no trace except the strange grey dust."

Soul looked to me, a knowing glance. We both understood what that dust meant. That dust meant they were ceased. That dust would be all that was left of them.

I stood numbly. Images of my siblings and their smiling faces flashed through my mind and then stopped. Blank. All of them. Dust.

"You still have us," Soul said softly. "We will come with you."

"You shouldn't," I looked to the ground. "Not because I do not want it, but because my time here is limited. You and Iris need a permanent home. Where I am going, you'll not have that. My flesh will not sustain me for much longer. I'll walk away and do what I can until this body can do no more."

"You can heal yourself!" Soul replied crossly. "If you can revive me from death, surely you can heal some damaged limbs."

I wished Soul's words were possible. Mardoch had done what he could to mend me. I was grateful for the reduced pain, for the blood in my veins, and for the tongue that allowed me to speak again, no matter how odd it felt in my mouth. The healing sheet had mended what was broken: bones, skin, ligaments, muscle. But much of the damage to my body had left it not broken, but decrepit. The kutu had designed human bodies to deteriorate as they absorbed toxins. Once a human's flesh had deteriorated past a certain point, it returned to the earth; it died. I knew not what the Nigh-kutu had done to me while unconscious in the pit, but I did know that I had sustained too much toxin damage to heal from. I could feel it. Nothing could mend that. Even if it could, my place was with Jychanumun. I had to find a link to him again. My place was by his side in the death-paths.

"I cannot," was all I could reply to Soul.

"Then get the Old One to mend you. He can do anything."

I shook my head. "It is not that simple. A body, this body, means nothing to the Old One."

Soul went to object. I knew she could not understand. "Don't fret," I intercepted her. "It's alright. And," I paused, "you and Iris can still build a new life; a long, happy, healthy life."

"Do you really think a long, happy, healthy life is likely for me?" Soul replied vehemently. "My mind was overrun by Arrunn with his rotten heart. I have barely any memories left. My hands have done terrible things. I have loved two beings; one a man who is no longer a man, and now made of fire, the other a kutu I will never see again. And Iris has seen things that no child should see. Don't think you can go bringing me back from death only to go away and leave us! We have nobody else! No one else would understand." She sounded desperate. She stood, trembling with tension, her hands clenching and unclenching at her sides.

Soul was probably right. As much as I wished a normal, happy life for her, she would never live a normal human life, not any more. Nor would Iris. Too much had happened. With time, much would heal, but they could never go back to how they were.

I picked up Soul's hand, placing it between both of mine.

"My dear friend," I spoke from my heart, "we are both changed. But, in many things, we are not changed at all. Soon you will go to the ravine, as Jychanumun requested. That journey we will do together. Take that time to think and decide. Once at the ravine, you can choose. Either return to Threetops, or continue journeying with me, which I urge you not to do." I smiled at her, trying to be consoling. "Know that my time here is limited and my path ahead will be arduous. I'm going to walk to the place where the Nigh-kutu warriors camped. There are no villages there. And it will be a difficult journey, especially for one so small as Iris."

"And where is this camp?" Soul asked.

"Near the Temple," I replied. "If I can get to the Temple, I'll know my way."

"But that walk will take many moons. It is too far!" Soul exclaimed. "You will cease!"

"Probably," I shrugged.

"I don't understand," Soul shook her head. "If the Nigh-kutu are gone, what's so important about that place, so important that you'd walk to and face certain ceasing?"

"They took human prisoners," I replied. As I spoke, the terrible images of the slave camp flashed through my mind. "I could not save them and they would not have survived. So, I will bury their flesh and guide their souls to Elysium. I could not help them in life, but I will help them in death."

"Oh," Soul sighed.

"I did not expect to be here," I explained. "But now I am. I'll use this time. I will do what I can, while I have this body to move and act."

Soul contemplated this for a moment. "Do you have a plan?" she asked.

I shook my head. "No," I admitted. "Just get there."

"It's a start," Soul accepted with a shrug. "Then I'll agree to your suggestion. I'll make my decision at the ravine. And we should go soon. I promised Jychanumun that I'd go at first light."

Iris rejoined us, clasping a large, pale-blue flower. She placed the bloom atop mother's grave and then turned, telling us that, even though she was tired, it was time to leave, because she wasn't too tired to walk. I think she had heard every word that Soul and I had said.

It was a good time to walk. The new day was starting to lighten the land, although the sun had not yet passed the horizon. It was going to be warm. From the scents in the air, I guessed it was early autumn. That was good. That meant that the worst of the summer heat had passed. Walking the flatlands to the Temple would be through autumn and winter.

With no possessions, except one spent healing sheet, I knew I must retrieve what I could from the burnt remains of the hut. It was going to be a long journey. We would need supplies, especially containers for carrying water. I remembered too well how thirst had been the greatest challenge when travelling before. Then, I had started the journey strong and healthy, but still the thirst and hunger had almost killed me. Now, I had two companions and the disadvantage of a frail body. Anything I could salvage could make the difference.

The remains of my old home was now a ruin. The blazing fire had gone, leaving little more than smouldering cinders. Black smoke wafted into the clearing sky. Glowing embers crackled as they gnawed away at the once heavy beams of wood. Little else was recognisable, just a blackened mess. It was still hot underfoot as I began picking through the debris. I held scant hope for finding anything of use. Nevertheless, inside a burned pot I found twine that was still flexible. The pot too was whole. It was a start.

Without asking, Iris collected her dropped berries, repacking them into her little berry-bag. Soul talked to herself as she scoured through the hut's wreckage, scolding bits of wood as they burnt her fingers. As she talked to herself, another noise in the background made my ears adjust away from her voice.

I quickly shook Soul's shoulder, putting my finger to my lips to indicate quiet. She immediately fell silent. Through the dominant sound of crackling wood, I could make out a series of blips.

"It's your communication port," I exclaimed, heading in the direction of the sound. It was emitting from within the burnt debris.

I used my senses to detect the energy of anything kutu. My eyes could not see it, but my senses told me that a communication port was there. It was buried deep under the blackened ruins and emitting the same kutu energy of all their machinery.

After moving several pieces of incinerated wood, which had once been the roof, I finally uncovered the port. I rubbed the soot covered screen, not making it any cleaner, and moved my fingers over the embedded crystals. My mind raced; what if the Shaa-kutu had managed to send the black-winged ones home, but had found a way to remain themselves? The thought of seeing those friends again made my heart leap.

I knew, by memory, most of the connecting codes for my old friends. One by one, I inputted those codes, hoping to find someone on the receiving end. Chia. Orion. Stanze. Kraniel. Una. Nirrious. Peniva. I tried them all. But nobody picked up my communication. I had one last hope. I inputted a code that Una had given for use in a time of crisis. If any Shaa-kutu, any at all, were in the realms of the physical, then they would respond to that calling.

I waited tentatively.

No response came.

In truth, I didn't expect a reply from the Shaa-kutu. Nevertheless, a part of me dared to hope. The other part simply felt compelled to try.

Although there was no response from any kutu, the port did indicate that there was a postponed message stored within it. The message was for Soul. I handed her the device. Immediately, Stanze's deep, choral voice began speaking a fragmented version of our human language.

"Heart Soul," Stanze's message began. "By arrival of new day this message plays and I will be gone. It grieves that we will not converse again." I heard him laugh a small, thoughtful laugh. "My human speak requires much improve and only you have patience to teach this kutu. But," he paused, "our leaving is necessity. It creates new chance for us all. I wanted to say goodbye." Stanze then spoke a Shaa-kutu word that meant that he hoped he would see her again, although futures were unknown. "I will miss your face. Be joyful. Be strong." He concluded. "Live life."

The message finished.

Soul held onto the port. She said nothing of her message from Stanze. It was not a thing that needed to be discussed. I could see it in her face. Some things were just too deeply felt.

In those moments of thinking about the Shaa-kutu, I realised then what had been different this last night in Threetops – the blue kutu lights had not appeared. Their absence was indicative of so much more. The harvesting ships that made those blue lights would never appear over any village ever again. There were no Shaa-kutu to guide them from their home-world. The Shaa-kutu home-world was empty. The kutu were gone from their world and from ours. All kutu were gone. Foe and friend. For better or worse, we humans were alone now. It felt strange. Yesterday they were here. Now they were not.

In silence, I collected up the few items I had salvaged from the hut: just two blackened pots and a piece of twine. I used the piece of twine to secure the spent healing sheet around me, and tucked the pots into the folds. I would collect food as I travelled, I decided. And, if my old knives were still at my place at the ravine, I could always carve out more pots.

I paused, glancing around. I was ready to leave.

Soul, Iris, and I crossed the village unnoticed and headed towards the ravine. We moved through the tall berry bushes and into the fields where the flower covered trees crowded above our heads. Very little had changed here and the sweet smell of early autumn fruits filled the air, just as I remembered. It was still a beautiful, bountiful place. I breathed in the scent and committed the scene to memory. I knew that I would never see this place again.

Beyond the cultivated area, the long, untamed grasses were waist-high. Young trees and fruit bushes poked their leaves above the green, vying to take hold. We passed through the long grasses and over the small mounds that acted like a natural wall to the village. There, in the untamed land, something caught my attention.

Just beyond the mounds, standing amidst a randomly scattered collection of deep green pine, gera, and belee trees, was a tree so luminous and white that it looked unnaturally bright against the morning sky.

Our footfall naturally took us past the strange, white tree. I stopped at the foot of its trunk, observing its position. Yes, this was the tree I had expected.

I remembered this tree, but it was indeed much changed. The last time I had seen it, it had stood green and healthy except for the half-burnt branches. The burned half had been my fault, a result of my untamed use of the Voice. It had been the first time I had used the Voice of the Old One. It had poured forth from my mouth with such wild power that it had burned half the closest tree. That tree still stood. This tree. Its shape had regrown like any normal tree, but now all its leaves were pure white and its bark a pale silver that shimmered with many colours.

"The people of Threetops call it the moonlight tree." Soul stroked the tree's bark. "It reminds me of the fabric the kutu made your dresses from."

I reached up, touching a small branch. It seemed to bend into my hand, severing from the trunk, as if my thought to remove it had made it happen. I ran my fingers over the bark, watching the energy move in response. The branch was still a branch, a branch from a tree. Yet its energy was now saturated with an energy not unlike my own.

I knew instantly that my connection to the Old One had done this. The Old One's energy, through me, had touched the tree and changed its constitution, similar to what had happened to Wirrel. Just as touching Wirrel with the energy of the Old One at the point he was dying had changed him forever, this tree was also forever changed. This consequence of my actions I had not foreseen. The tree was beautiful, yes, but the thought that my actions could have such unforeseen effects was unsettling.

We left the white tree and continued in silence towards the ravine, but I did keep that slender branch, as it would make a perfect walking stick, and the tree did stay in my thoughts.

By the time we reached the ravine, the sun was peeking over the horizon. Our long, stark shadows cast behind us like the memories we were walking away from. We paused at the top, looking down at the dense foliage. Soul told me that she had never made the walk to the bottom. She said that she only knew of my old hideaway because Stanze had taken her there. She didn't think any human legs could descend such a steep, deep gorge.

It had been several turns of the seasons since I had last visited this place. The area at the top of the ravine now looked very different from my memory of it. New undergrowth and small new trees now covered the path once worn by the familiarity of my footsteps. I observed with broader sight, remembering the pattern of the huge old trees. They had not changed. The patterns they created still framed the route we should take.

We began the careful, winding descent, with me leading the way. Almost immediately, the familiar sweet yet earthy scent of the ravine filled my nostrils. I felt the energy of the trees, strong and gentle, connecting to the air, the soil, and each other. To my

time: the immortal divide

senses, it sounded like they were singing in low, flowing tones. From habit, I touched their trunks as I passed, greeting them like old acquaintances.

Our surroundings grew darker as the denseness of the trees blocked out the sunlight. The long tufts of grass gave way to cool, soft moss underfoot. There must have been rains in the preceding days, as the moss was damp and slippery, often forcing us to crawl the steeper sections. Our knees complained at being skinned so often, but we continued down and as we descended, I could sense the river below.

It took longer to descend the ravine with the three of us, but eventually, after navigating the steepest section, we reached the bottom. Here, the scene had changed very little. In the tiny clearing that overlooked the river, the trees still spanned their branches low over the rushing water and the rocks still protruded from the centre. There were still remnants of my previous life, just a few, in the places where I had left them. I collected two blunt, but usable, flint knives, from a hollow in the roots of an aged tree. A particularly beautiful broken branch that I had collected when I was a girl still stood propped against the tree. The wood had greyed with the seasons, making the knots and natural turns even more defined. I had intended on carving the entire branch. I had intended many things back then.

"This is the place," I told Soul and Iris. "If Jychanumun told you to come to my favourite place at the ravine, this is it. That's the shilimar tree with the sitting area."

Soul glanced around, a frown creasing her brow.

"He said I would know what to do," she shrugged. "But I don't."

"What did he say?" I asked. "What were his exact words?"

Soul rolled her eyes, thinking.

"He said, 'At the morrow's first light you will be at Tachra's favourite place, at the ravine,'" she recited. "Then he said, 'It will be clear what to do. The ravine. Do you understand?' And I just said, 'I understand.' That's all."

To me, Jychanumun's words did not sound like an instruction. Knowing how he spoke, it sounded more like he was informing her.

I observed our surroundings. Admittedly, I couldn't see anything different from the usual scenery. But when I looked with my true vision, I could feel the presence of something. I opened my senses wider. What I sensed, to my surprise, was instantly recognisable. It was a kutu ship.

Almost immediately upon having the thought, the smooth curve of a matte-grey kutu pod started to rise above the line of the river. As it arose, small rocks and silt tumbled off its curves and back into the water. It hovered, and then moved towards us, coming to a halt over the small clearing.

I took a step towards the pod. As I moved, the side and top folded away, opening expectantly. There was no kutu pilot inside. The pod was empty. Nevertheless, it was waiting for us to enter.

Although I felt nervous at boarding a pod that would fly without kutu to guide it, I had no hesitancy in climbing aboard. As soon as I entered, I noticed something. There, by the streamlined controls, were Jychanumun's two black inscribed armlets. I would know those armlets anywhere. They were the only items Jychanumun had retained from his home-world. He had carved them himself. He never took them off. Not even when he slept.

I picked up the armlets. Wrapped around them, holding them together, was my old necklet; a piece of fine earth-twine with my pendant on it. The pendant had been a gift from Una. It was an ornately carved symbol that, in kutu, was my given title, Iastha. I had given that pendant to Jychanumun for safe keeping when I had left to infiltrate the Nigh-kutu camp. He had said he would give it back when I returned.

Only I knew the meaning of the pendant.

Only I would know the significance of the armlets.

Only Jychanumun could have put them here in the pod.

Somehow, I realised, Jychanumun knew that I might end up here.

My mind spun with the concept. Jychanumun knew my being here was a possibility. He once said that he could see some of the potential outcomes of my choices. He must have seen this as one of them. But he would never tell me, lest it affect my choices. I raced over possibilities and questions. It made my mind spin.

"What is it?" Soul asked, looking into the pod.

I held up the armlets, showing her.

"Jychanumun knew I would be here. The message that he gave to you, he knew that you would tell me."

Soul shook her head, as if the idea did not want to stay inside her mind.

"Where will the pod go?" she asked.

I tucked Jychanumun's armlets into the folds of my makeshift garment and tied the pendant around my neck.

"I do not know for sure," I replied. "But if Jychanumun arranged this, then I expect it will go exactly where I am trying to get to. This, my friend, is where you make your choice."

Without a word, Soul picked up Iris, placing her in the craft, and then climbed aboard herself.

I guessed that was my answer.

With Soul and Iris next to me on the bench, the pod automatically sealed and began rising. I could hear the brush of branches as it pushed through the dense foliage of the ravine. And then, causing a bracing jolt in my stomach, it raced forwards and up at an incredible speed.

As we travelled, I could not watch our direction; neither could I recall how to change the settings of the pod to make the panels viewable. Nevertheless, wherever we were heading, the little craft had a specific destination. It flew gracefully and with speed, and in no time I sensed it descend.

The pod landed so gently that I could barely tell we were no longer moving.

The sides silently unfolded.

I didn't need the familiar scent of grasses, punni berry, or pure water to tell me where we were. It smelt like home. Nor did I need my ears to hear the call of forest birds and the breeze through the tall trees to inform me. It sounded like home. My eyes saw it. My heart felt it. My valley.

But of course! I only knew my way to and from the Nigh-kutu camp via this place. Of course Jychanumun would arrange for the pod to come here. He would know that from here, the walk to the warriors' camp was but half a day's journey. He would know I would need provisions. I could collect provisions from the Temple. I could stay in the Temple and travel back and forth to the Nigh-kutu camp until my tasks were done.

This was heart-hope incarnate. A journey that would have taken a full turn of the seasons to walk, and would probably have seen the death of me, was now accomplished in mere moments. It was all thanks to Jychanumun that I could do this last task. If he were here, I would have kissed him.

"Wait here," I told Soul and Iris. "The Nigh-kutu should be gone, but I'll use my senses to search the Temple, just to be sure."

Neither Soul nor Iris objected.

Soul nodded, passing me the branch from the moonlight tree. The gesture made me smile. She wasn't giving me the stick to aid my walking, but because it was the only thing available that looked remotely like a weapon. What did she think I would do with it? Pop a Nigh-kutu over the head? Nevertheless, a stick was better than nothing. So, I clasped it tightly like a cudgel, climbed down to the grass, and cautiously headed towards the Temple.

On one side, the scene and smells of my valley – the trees, lake and sloping banks that were covered in punni berry bushes – were mostly unchanged. But on the other, where the Temple stood amidst a backdrop of trees, much had altered. The Temple looked ravaged.

As I walked, using my true vision and Earth sense to detect anything untoward, I picked up essence of kutu everywhere. Their resonant energy lingered upon the ground and in the air. Discarded items that had once been theirs still felt like them. Equipment and armour infused with their energy littered the grass. My senses were assailed by it.

There was so much kutu essence. But so far, no kutu.

The once beautiful Temple of Learning was indeed ravaged. The smooth golden walls now had great gouges out of them, as if a giant beast had taken bites. Jagged fragments of the beautiful golden stone now lay all around. Some were partially buried in the ground, as if trampled by a creature taller than the skies, and others were piled on top of each other. The colossal statues that framed the doorway were in pieces. Huge sections of stone that had once been part of a face, or arm, or body, now lay in oversized, fragmented chunks on the ground. A particularly large piece, which had once been the head of one of the statues, was now broken off and embedded in the soil. It looked as if the earth itself had a face, staring up to the sky, snarling.

I noticed a golden Anumi helmet laying discarded. I picked it up, quickly putting it down having noticed the stain of Shaa-kutu blood inside it. I knew Jychanumun and the Shaa-kutu had attempted several attacks here. From the scene around me, I could see that the battles had been ferocious.

I picked my way through the ruins and headed up the once smooth steps, now an uneven mess of rubble, and towards the Temple's entrance.

The huge doors were ajar. I entered with caution, clasping the branch, ready to strike.

Once inside the Temple, I paused. Even though Arrunn had inhabited this place, it still felt like a good building. I was glad of that. The main hallway looked much the same. There was no sign of kutu.

I cautiously progressed, passing the entrance to the central chamber, pausing at its opening. There, just inside the doorway, were the discarded weapons and armour of two Nigh-kutu warriors. The armour was positioned on the floor as if the bodies had simply been removed.

Close by was yet another array of Nigh-kutu attire. The leg armour and coverings were perfectly poised in a kneeling position. It looked strangely unsettling.

The central chamber itself was a ruin. The glistening domed roof that had once let in spectrums of light was now darkened, making it difficult to distinguish anything inside with precision. Nevertheless, it was easy to notice that most of the huge columns had collapsed. The stone and uana that had once formed the vast pillars were now broken boulders, heaped to one side like discarded rubbish.

In the gloom at the far end of the central chamber, behind the broken columns, I sensed the presence of a strong Nigh-kutu device. Whatever it was, it reeked of Arrunn. I considered investigating the source, but then spotted the well. That well. That stinking prison. I would not venture inside.

I moved quickly through the remainder of the Temple's lower floor. There was no sign of any kutu, and thankfully, the rest of the building appeared intact. The inner walls were still sound and the beautiful carvings and pieces of human and kutu art still adorned them. In fact, other than the central chamber, little had changed. Most rooms still had the exact same layout. Weaponry was gone, but other Shaa-kutu equipment was still there. Kutu recliners were still positioned, their sumptuous hangings in the same place. It felt like a strange juxtaposition of desolation and beauty. It made me realise that Arrunn really had no interest in belongings. These kutu objects of grandeur meant nothing to him.

I went to the room that had once been mine, lingering in the doorway for a moment. Every storage space had been emptied and my old belongings had been rifled through; many of them were now in pieces on the floor. It didn't matter. What mattered was that the space, my old room, still felt strong with my energy and the energy of Meah, the valley and the forest. Here, I could work with precision.

I stood motionless, threading out my senses beyond the physical confines of the room: up the walls, along the floors and beyond, through the rest of the Temple. I felt the energy of the floor above and the cellars below. I sensed no life other than the insects and small creatures that had crept in and made this place their home. There were no humans here. More importantly, there were no kutu.

Assured that the Temple was safe, I made my way back to the pod, knowing Soul and Iris would be anxious until my return.

"The Temple is in better condition than it looks," I told Soul. "I shall remain here. I'll gather provisions and leave for the warriors' camp later this morn. It's not far. Are you sure you do not wish to return to Threetops?"

Soul tutted, climbing out of the pod, and then lifted Iris down to join her. "Kutu or not," she decided, "Iris and I have always loved the Temple."

Iris announced that she was both hungry and thirsty, so the three of us headed directly to the old kitchens in the great cellars.

In the kitchens in the Temple, the kutu food had gone, every morsel of it, but I was grateful to find the food vaults for humans undisturbed. It seemed that human food was of no interest to

Arrunn or his warriors. There was an abundance of supplies, enough to feed Soul and Iris for many turns of the seasons. With this, and the natural fruits and vegetation of the valley, as well as the fresh water of the lake, they could stay here as long as they wished and never have to worry about hunger or thirst. Even once I was gone, they could easily reside here.

Having gathered a selection of food, I led the way to my old room, ignoring the broken remnants of my possessions and placing our supplies on the floor. There we just sat for a while, too tired to talk. I sipped slowly at cool, refreshing water. Soul picked at some sweet-meats. Iris ate heartily from a plate of berries and cake, and then climbed onto the recliner, insisting she wasn't tired, but falling asleep virtually the moment her head touched the pillows.

While Soul searched for a change of clothing and re-familiarised herself with the room, I gathered some left-over sweat-meats, opened the double doors and headed outside.

My old room in the Temple had been designed with a set of personal doors that led directly outside, to the cusp of the forest. As soon as I stepped inside the boundary of the trees, the world changed to one that felt most like home. Here was the place where I would always be most at peace. Here, even when the Old One was sleeping, I could feel his presence. This place was filled with only good memories; memories that had helped to shape Elysium. Even Meah's essence would be forever ingrained here.

Meah, I called softly with my mind, reaching out to her essence.

I instantly felt her presence. The connection between us would always be strong, through life and death and all realms. Meah moved from the world of Elysium to be back by my side. Her spirit brushed against me, welcoming me in her familiar way, and then trotted ahead, her pale fur appearing luminous in the gloom of the forest. She looked around as she moved, glancing at me with her amber eyes, egging me on to increase my step, leading me to where I needed to go.

I entered one of the many small clearings to see Valiant, Meah's cub, clambering playfully over the spirit of Meah. It lifted my heart to see such a thing, both flesh and spirit. To Valiant, Meah was as real as when she was alive, and I realised then that animals could see each other's energy just as acutely as they could feel skin and bones.

I quietly placed the sweet-meats on the ground and stepped back. The cub went to the treats, sniffed them, pulled his head back as if they were not edible, and then continued brushing up against Meah. I had expected he would be hungry.

Meah stood, and then moved deeper into the forest, leaving Valiant sitting, watching. Valiant waited expectantly, looking in the direction of Meah's exit. My ears were listening to the movement of the forest. My true vision was watching Meah's trail of golden energy as it dispersed into the thickness of the trees.

From the trees, Meah re-emerged. Behind her was another female wildcat, one in the flesh. This one had her own cub. I knew instantly that the second adult cat was Mah, Meah's twin sister. It was the first time I had seen her since the kutu had come to the valley. It was wonderful to behold the two wildcats together again.

Mah also treated Meah as if she were there in the flesh. She pushed her head against her, and then moved towards Valiant, sniffing the air around him, pushing her nose into his fur. Valiant sat obligingly, taking the nuzzling inspection until the smaller cub bounded towards him, distracting him, encouraging him to play. Mah nuzzled them both. She was accepting Valiant, accepting him as her own.

In that moment, that one precious moment, I remembered joy. I had not expected this, and it was beautiful.

I let the moment of unexpected happiness fill me with hope.

I was in my valley with Meah.

I had not thought my flesh would see this place again.

This last day has felt like ten thousand turns of the seasons, I thought. *And it is not finished yet. I still have one last thing that I need to do.*

I left the wildcats, spirit and flesh, in the forest, and returned to my old room. I would gather supplies, take a short sleep, and then leave for the old Nigh-kutu camp. My last task.

I knew my direction. My path would be over the rock-land, away from the valley and in the opposite direction from the tall mountains and the long-away village of Hollow. Reaching the Nigh-kutu camp should take half a day.

I only hoped that all the Nigh-kutu had gone. The Temple was clear, but most of the Nigh-kutu warriors had been based at their camp. There, there had been many. I hoped by the skies that Kraniel's device had been effective on them all. And then, if the skies continued to be good to me, my gruesome final task of burying the ceased bodies would go swiftly.

TWENTY

The Army

Jin and Jan, the two brothers from the town called Hollow, were deep in discussion. Both were tense, knowing that the task ahead would likely see the end of them. Both wanted the other to go home and be safe. Each wanted to raise their voices and insist, but they could not speak any louder than a whisper. They were too close to the Temple. They did not want to alert any black-winged ones.

Jan stood just inside the tent's entrance with his arms crossed. "Do not be so stubborn," he insisted.

Jin didn't reply. He merely paused the sharpening of his spear and raised his eyebrows.

"Can I do nothing to convince you to go home?" Jan asked.

"No."

"But you realise that this will probably leave Hollow without a chief."

"Yes."

"I can lead the army for the attack. I'll not fail you."

"I know," Jin said. "But I'm not returning to Hollow until I've freed Tachra, or died trying. You return. You are just as much Hollow's leader as I."

Jan conceded with a grunt, with clearly no intention of returning to their home village. "I owe Tachra my life," he shrugged, picking up his head protector and checking its tightly woven wicker for the umpteenth time. He turned, glancing yet again out of the tent's entrance.

"Have you noticed how quiet the skies have been tonight?"

"Too quiet," Jin agreed. "We're close to the Temple. I would have expected Nigh-kutu above our heads regularly, yet we have seen none this last night. Not one."

"Perhaps their attentions are elsewhere. It could be to our advantage," Jan considered. "We should make our move against them soon."

"How many men have now arrived?"

"Four hundred." Jan moved to get a better view of the map etched into the sand. "Another one hundred have reached here," he pointed to an area beyond their current encampment. "They'll join us around dawn tomorrow."

"Not sooner? Then it will be another day lost."

"We must calculate the best odds," Jan said. "Which is to our best advantage: one hundred more men, or one day sooner? Either way, we must attack when we are strongest. We will only get one chance."

"I know," Jin nodded. "It concerns me to have so many men in one place, especially if we wait another day. Travelling in groups of fifteen made us insignificant to the black-winged ones. But now we come together, our numbers are conspicuous."

The brothers' conversation was interrupted by the noise of sudden shouting.

Jin and Jan were both immediately up, grabbing their spears, and sprinting out of the makeshift concealment. All the men had been instructed to strict silence. Concealed whispering only. No one should be talking, yet alone shouting. Something was amiss.

Jin and Jan both expected to be thrown into a turmoil of

attacking Nigh-kutu, but there were no black-winged ones in sight. Instead, a group of their men appeared to be tussling.

"Silence!" Jin projected between gritted teeth, running towards the commotion.

A dozen of Jin and Jan's men pulled back, standing in a circle, surrounding the source of the disturbance.

Amidst their circle, several more men now held onto a small group of unknown humans.

There were six unknown people. All looked as if they had been running. None appeared injured, although all were filthy. Each one was now held firm by a soldier, with the soldier's hand clamped tightly over their mouths.

"You must be quiet," Jin whispered, walking towards the unknown people. "We are within the roaming plains of the Nigh-kutu. Do you want to call their attention and see the death of us all?"

The people shook their heads, clearly fearful. Slowly, under careful instruction not to start shouting again, they were released.

"Who are you?" Jin asked the closest person; a middling woman of fair skin and hair. "And what brings you to this remote place?"

"I am Seeta from Himsfields," the woman nervously whispered. "But I come from the Temple. I was taken to the Temple by black-winged ones. But then something happened and they were distracted. The people in front of me just died. . . poof. . . gone." She gestured with her hands. "I ran while I could. The black-winged ones did not come after me. Others ran too. Some people headed over the rock-land. We," she indicated to the others, "were heading towards the mountains."

Jin was suspicious.

"No one can survive climbing the mountains unaided," he said.

"Better to cease on the mountains than at the hands of the black-winged beasts," the woman vehemently replied. "I tell you truths." She repeated her words. "The people in front of me. . . poof. . . gone. We ran while we could."

Jin studied the woman's face, watching for signs of untruths, just as he had been shown how to do.

"And tell," he asked, "what distracted the black-winged ones to enable such an easy escape?"

The woman shook her head.

"Kutu magic," she looked to the others, unsure. "Bad kutu magic. Or Iastha Tachra magic."

"Explain," Jin prompted.

The woman moved her fingers through the air, watching them as if entranced. "They filled the air. Without wings, they flew up."

It didn't make any sense, but, as much as Jin questioned the woman, her answers, and the answers of her companions, all, though strange at best, told a similar story.

Jin beckoned to his brother and walked beyond earshot of the group, also calling one of the men, Trell, to join them. Trell was a strong, quiet landsman, who now bore the task of overseeing the wellbeing of all the men. Trell was good at reading the truth of people's words.

"I agree, it makes little sense, but I too saw the certainty of her words," Trell confirmed. "I do not think they are infiltrators."

"Then this could be fair news," Jin whispered. "If the Nigh-kutu have been distracted, it could be our best time to strike."

"It is still a risk," Jan said. "Whatever the distraction to the black-winged ones, it may be over. Plus, we do not know what this new magic is."

"In your opinion, is it a risk worth taking?" Jin asked. His brother was more cautious than he was. He already knew that for him, it was.

Jan considered for a moment, his eyes narrowing as they always did when he thought deeply and with calculation.

"Yes," he nodded.

Jin did not need to ask twice.

"Trell," he immediately began instructing him, "assign one man, whoever is least adept at fighting, to escort these people to Hollow. Send with him a message: when he passes the one hundred men en route they are join us in battle at the first opportunity. Once you have done that, gather all the men. We still have some ground to cover if we want to strike during bright sun."

Trell gave a curt nod and left.

In silence, Jin and Jan returned to their makeshift concealment and donned their armour. The hushed activity outside told them that their men were gathering into formation. They too covered their boots in cloth to silence their footsteps. And then, leaving the concealed tent to act as the last in-betweener hut, they stepped out.

This was the last stage of their three-moon journey, and the most dangerous. Four-hundred men must remain undetected until they had attacked the Temple and liberated Tachra.

TWENTY-ONE

The Temple

I returned to my old room in the Temple. I didn't want to rest. I wanted to leave for the Nigh-kutu camp as soon as possible. But for the tasks ahead I knew I needed sleep or I would get no further than the valley's edge. So, I found a compromise. I made my way to one of the store rooms and found a sleep-sheet that the kutu had designed for me.

I had never liked sleep-sheets. In the past, I'd found them disorientating. They were designed by Kraniel to speed up my sleep and its effects. With a sleep-sheet, I could attain a full quota of sleep in a quarter of the night. The kutu had thought they were a more efficient use of my time. I had thought they tasted strange. I had refused to use them, much to Kraniel's dismay. Now, for once, I was glad to see the small supply that had languished in the store.

Back in my room, Soul and Iris were both curled up on the recliner, already asleep. The kutu sized recliner was plenty big enough for us all, so I climbed up, wrapping the sleep-sheet around me. I took Jychanumun's armlets from the folds in my wrap, my fingers tracing the inscriptions etched into them. I searched my mind for any trace of my connection to him. Nothing. I felt no sense of him. Our link was truly broken. Nevertheless, just holding his armlets was comforting, as if a part of him was still close. I would find a way to join him in the paths again; soon this flesh would cease.

Convinced that I would not slumber, once I relaxed my head into the cushions, it felt as if I could sleep forever.

My sleep soon fell into dreaming. Gone were the nightmares of the Temple filled with painful screams or of the never-ending corridors. Instead, my dreams were filled with images of horrors that I could not stop from my position at the bottom of the well.

I awoke with a jolt, the tumbling of my thoughts tormenting me that I must not sleep, that I had to stay awake, that there were important reasons why I should not sleep. For a moment, in my half-dream state, I did not know where I was. I thought I was back in the pit. I was relieved to see my old room.

The room was dark, except for the gentle glow of the memorite statue. I knew that outside would be the bright, early morning light, but the window coverings had been activated, making it feel like it was night. To my side, Iris slumbered deeply. Soul, however, was neither sleeping nor resting. I could hear her hushed activity at the far end of the room.

I quietly slipped from the recliner.

"You look terrible," Soul said when I reached her.

She moved a chair, indicating that I should sit, and proceeded to wrap a healing sheet around my shoulders. It was a crisp, unused sheet, and I immediately felt the nanos relieve my aching flesh like a drink of the freshest water when thirsty. But then my thoughts turned: with the kutu gone, there would be no new supplies of such valuable items. I should not waste any. My body would suffice as it was. I only needed it to get to and from the Nigh-kutu camp once or twice.

I pulled the healing sheet from my shoulders, folding it and placing it on the table.

"You need that," Soul stated.

"My flesh is well enough for what it has to do. Save them for someone else."

"You're not 'well enough' if you don't heal!" Soul retorted. "What about after you have been to the black-winged ones' camp? What about all the tomorrows? Anyway," she indicated towards a pile of healing sheets and strips on the table, "I found a good supply; we have plenty."

Soul pushed a bowl of watery looking substance under my nose.

"Eat this," she nodded. "It's plain, but looking at you, it's all your stomach will accept. And put this on." She handed me a piece of red kutu fabric. "I adjusted one of Orion's gowns to fit you and stitched pieces of healing sheet into it. And these," she handed me two odd-looking bags, "are made these from pieces of healing sheet too." She raised her brows at me, as if expecting an objection. "And I have already cut the healing sheet, so there's no point telling me to save it for someone else."

I held up the misshapen bags. "What are they for?" I asked.

"Slippers," Soul replied, a little indignantly. "For your feet."

I pulled on Orion's adjusted gown, placing Jychanumun's armlets in the deep pockets. The slippers were different sizes and oddly shaped, making my feet look like they belonged to different people. But, knowing the consideration that had gone into making them, they were the best I had ever seen. At least, I told Soul as much.

Soul leaned forward and pulled the hood of Orion's old gown up so that it covered my head, tucking my hair in.

"The more of you we can cover with healing fabric the better," she said. "And, if I remember rightly, these kutu clothes clean themselves and clean the wearer." She chuckled quietly. "Which you need greatly. Almost as much as you need food."

"You've done all this while I slept?" It was more a statement than a question. "You should be resting too."

"I will," Soul said. "I have to make sure you are well first. After that, it will just take a little time to relearn how to rest. It will come."

As Soul continued sewing, the plate of watery broth was nudged towards me again. I had no appetite, but had a spoonful anyway. The broth tasted surprisingly sweet. Or rather, I realised, my mouth tasted surprisingly sour. Soul was right. I was filthy. For now, Orion's nano-embedded gown would suffice to cleanse me, but I made the decision that I would bathe in the lake upon my return from the warriors' camp. One last swim in my beautiful lake. Relishing the thought, I finished a good amount of the broth. It felt as if I had eaten a feast.

"Promise one thing," Soul suddenly spoke, pausing in her task.

"I'll do my best," I responded.

"Find a way to heal yourself."

I sat in silence for a moment. Soul didn't say any more. She just picked up the needle and began sewing again. She purposely didn't look at me and purposely kept quiet.

Could I heal myself? I wondered. More importantly, did I want to? I was weary of the fights of the flesh. I yearned for a path where I could rejoin Jychanumun, or sleep with the Old One and dream his endless dreams of everything.

What if I at least tried to heal my flesh? I thought. The notion did not fill me with joy. I had to *want* to try.

I stood up. "I'll be back shortly," I stated.

Soul nodded, saying nothing, watching me as I walked from the room.

Wearing my new slippers, and an adjusted crimson kutu gown that had once belonged to Orion and was still far too big for me, I walked through the Temple. On each side of the corridor, the golden-clad walls gave off a pale light. The art and sculptures that still adorned them emitted colours and shapes that told stories of adventures, and spoke of meaning and intent. It was a visual feast and I had sight that had hungered for beauty. I let the harmonic essences calm my apprehension as I headed to the place I wanted to go least: the central chamber.

It took little time to reach the central chamber. I stood in the main doorway, looking in with trepidation. It sickened me to see the old water well, my old prison. It brought to the forefront of my mind all the atrocities Arrunn had done, and all the grief, anger and hatred that I had felt. I *still* felt.

I didn't want to feel them. I didn't want to have to think about my time in the well, let alone face it. I just couldn't.

Perhaps, I considered, I was forever changed, and never would be able to accept that part of my past. Perhaps I did not need to tackle such things anyway. Once I had discovered a way back to Jychanumun and his death-paths, things like this would mean nothing.

I didn't have to think about it, if I didn't want to.

I didn't even have to look at it.

I could close this place from my sight.

I could seal the doors to this room and would never have to look at that well ever again. That, I decided, was something that I could do. It might not be the absolute resolution, but it would make me feel better.

There were many doors into the chamber from different hallways. All of them were constructed from an unusual composite kutu material that was both energy and matter. They were huge and heavy, very heavy, especially the main doors that led from the long hall. I started the task by pushing aside the discarded Nigh-kutu armour and weapons that now littered the floor, blocking them.

Most of the entrances into the central chamber were single doors, yet still colossal, with their handles placed at a height suitable for kutu, well above my head. I struggled with these, using all my weight, pushing with both feet against the wall and coaxing their energy until they finally closed. With those closed and sealed, I moved to the main doors. These were the difficult ones. These double doors were so large that even a kutu would strain to close them. At a point high above me, each was secured with a fine energy tether. I could not reach. I needed something to stand on.

I crossed the hallway and into a room that had once been used for teaching. The room was mostly intact and there were plenty of seats, both kutu and human. A kutu seat with a human one on top of it should be high enough.

I picked one of the tallest seats, dragging it noisily across the hall, positioning it in front of one of the chamber's open doors. I then placed a human-sized chair on top of it. Having climbed up, I released the energy tether and pulled. The door budged a fraction, and then, with the weight of its own movement propelling it, it swung shut with a gentle thump.

I climbed down, moved the chairs, and then set about untethering the final door.

The final door was more fixed than the first. From its unwillingness to dislodge, I guessed it had never been closed.

As I pulled, suddenly, the door jolted. I stumbled. The hood of the gown fell over my face. The door swung shut with a thud. My hood trapped itself in the door, almost strangling me. I tried to pull my head back, but the hood didn't release. I tugged and tugged at the closed door, but it was now firmly shut, with the fabric of my gown acting as a securing wedge. I tried wiggling out of the gown, but the trapped hood had tightened the neckline and I could not get my head through. I tried to rip the neckline, but the fine kutu fabric was stronger than it appeared.

TWENTY-TWO

The Rescue

Jin pointed to his eyes, and then pointed to a direction in the open land to one side of the Temple.

Jan strained to see. The sun was bright, bouncing light off the golden stone and the luminous pieces of armour littering the ground, making precise vision difficult. The sun's reflection on the rippling water cast movement where there was none, and the shadows within the trees made his heightened senses think there were a thousand Nigh-kutu waiting. But there, just where Jin had pointed, once his eyes had adjusted, Jan could see the matte-grey hub of a small kutu ship concealed behind a fallen rock.

"It looks empty," Jin whispered, "but avoid getting close. Those things have perimeter sensors. Are the men in position?"

Jan nodded. And with that he silently stepped back, taking position with the army.

There were no goodbyes between the two brothers, and no speeches about if they didn't make it. Neither did they say how much they trusted and loved one another. It wasn't necessary. And, even though neither of them thought they would survive this, both wanted the other to believe that they would.

Jin nestled further down into the cover of the bushes.

Silence requires stealth, and stealth does not rush, he told himself.
He was ready.
He held up his hand.
Now!

TWENTY-THREE

The Friends

I had been so intent on releasing my gown from its trappings in the door that I had not initially heard anything. Now, what sounded like hundreds of running footsteps, like kutu charging into battle, were coming this way.

My instinct was to run and hide. I tugged frantically at the trapped gown, desperate to be released. The footsteps grew louder. They had entered the Temple and were racing rapidly nearer.

Suddenly I heard a faint whistling sound.

I sensed a weapon aimed my way.

I ducked down, suspended by the trapped fabric. A spear hit above my head, missing me by less than an arm's length, embedding itself deep into the door. And then, bellowing out, the deep roar of approaching warriors thundered closer.

I covered my head with my arms, pushing flat against the door, and pulled the earth energy to me.

Please make this fast and painless, I thought.

The running footsteps came to an abrupt halt.

"Kutu," a deep voice shouted. "Step down slowly and turn around!"

Kutu? They thought I was kutu. It must be the gown.

"I'm not kutu," I called out. "I'm human."

"Where are your black-winged masters?"

"They're gone," I replied. "All the kutu are gone. And I can't get down; my hood is stuck."

I heard movement, and then someone's spear slicing at the fabric above my head, releasing my hood. I let what remained of the hood hide my face, unsure as to whether these were friend or foe, and slowly turned around. I held out my hands to show that I carried no weapon.

There, filling the entire width of the corridor, were men; battle ready, armour clad men. They were human, not kutu. All of them clasped weapons: swords, daggers, spears; some even carried axes and giant hammers. The closest men had swords and spears pointing towards me. I couldn't see any of their faces, as they were covered in full masks. I'd never seen armour like it. It was fashioned similarly to Anumi armour, yet made of tightly woven wicker. They were all covered in dust and baked-on mud.

"Move," one of the wicker-masked men directed towards me. "You cannot protect your master."

Something in the voice was familiar. I was sure that I recognised it. That, and the beautifully woven wicker that the men wore as armour. A long time ago, I had seen a man weave intricate shapes with wicker just like that. His skill had fascinated me.

"Jan?" I stated. "Jan of the in-betweener huts?"

I pulled the hood from my head, showing my face.

"Tachra?"

Simultaneously, the two closest men lifted their wicker masks.

I recognised those faces. They were Jin and Jan, the two beautiful brothers.

Jin stepped forward, helping me down. He had an expression of bewilderment.

"We came to rescue you," he simply said.

TWENTY-FOUR

The Camp

The men who had travelled with Jin and Jan were too charged for battle to rest. So, having surprised Soul as I led them into the vast kitchens, I showed them the well-stocked supply stores. They heartily helped themselves. They were not tired, but they were hungry.

I stood with Jin and Jan amidst the noisy bustle in the kutu kitchens, but it was as if a part of me was beyond my body, detached, just watching. Neither Jin nor Jan wanted to eat. Although happy, they seemed disjointed. I wasn't surprised. They said that they had not expected to survive this day. I knew that feeling well.

Jin and Jan spoke of how all the men had volunteered, despite their negligible chance of victory. It transpired that even more were on their way. They would wait here, Jin told me, until the last of their men joined them. Then, he decided, we would all return to Hollow. I did not reply to that.

In turn, Jin and Jan had many questions. I gave them the briefest of summaries. I told them how the kutu had been drawn away. I told them how I had come to be here.

Although Jin and Jan wanted to know more, I did not discuss my future plans. I did not have the time. The men who had travelled with them wanted to greet me, or ask how I was, or where the kutu were, or how had I escaped. It was a wonderful thing, but with so much talk I was soon exhausted. So, knowing that the men would be here for a day or two, I excused myself. I left Soul preparing yet more food, and Iris, who had joined us, enjoying the attention of so many.

I returned to my room, glad of heart to have seen Jin and Jan, glad that Soul and Iris were safe, and glad of the peace. I opened the windows to let in and relish the day's scent. The morning air smelt of long grass and punni berries. It was the perfect time to start walking again.

If I left for the Nigh-kutu camp now, I considered, I could be back within a day. I could be back before Jin, Jan and the soldiers had left. And I would need very little for the journey. Just some water, my knife, and a tool.

I selected a tool that the kutu had designed for planting young trees. Having found some kutu twine to make a strap, I fastened the tool across my back and tied several water flasks around my waist, along with a knife. And then, just in case, I put some healing sheets into a bundle.

I slung the bundle over my shoulder, smiling at the familiarity of the action. I had not thought I would be doing that again. Well, one last time.

Deciding to quietly slip out via the Temple's main entrance and follow the route exactly as I remembered, I stepped from my room and closed the door.

Jin, Jan and Soul were waiting in the corridor.

"I had intended on a quiet departure," I admitted sheepishly.

"Soul told us where you are going and why," Jin said. "A group of us will go instead."

"Thank you, but this is something I must do," I replied. "It is not just about burying ceased bodies."

"Then we will accompany you," Jin answered firmly. "Would we be a hindrance?"

I shook my head, indicating not.

"A group of us will escort you and assist," he decided. "And if you insist that we do not, we will merely follow two strides behind."

I could not help but laugh.

"Very well," I bowed. "I accept with gratitude."

In truth, I did appreciate the offer of an escort. As much as I had the desire to walk alone, I knew the upcoming task would be difficult. There could be up to eight-dozen people's bodies. Once I had shown their souls the way to Elysium, those bodies should be buried. It would be an arduous and horrible undertaking. Also, somehow, I had to free a Nar beast. That would be no small task either. I was thankful for the physical support from such strong, able-bodied men, and the mental support from friends.

At the Temple's main entrance, ten more men, still clad in their beautiful wicker armour, stood ready, holding their headwear. I recognised some of them from their attending studies at the Temple over the years: Tan, Jandan, Trell and Trell's son, Shaul, plus others whose names I did not yet know. They had all made good use of the short time they'd had in the store rooms, and now carried a supply of food and water. Several also carried digging tools. These ten men, Jin and Jan informed me, would also be part of my escort.

With no reason to delay, I bade farewell to Soul, and we headed out into the mid-day air – twelve wicker-clad men, and me wearing Orion's crimson gown that cast a red glow on the ground as I moved.

I wanted to walk fast, and my anxiousness to get to the Nigh-kutu camp made my gait seem far too slow. The men did not find fault, patiently allowing me to set the pace and direction. Jin walked by my side. He seemed to sense my reduced strength, lending me his arm over the more demanding terrain; terrain that previously

I would have found easy. The men around us walked deceptively casually, yet were vigilantly alert, constantly observing the skies and the horizon for any sign of kutu.

The walk seemed to take far longer than the movement of the sun indicated. We passed mainly through barren land, where the only vegetation was the tiny yellow flowers sprouting scraggily from rocks amidst flat, hard sands. The afternoon moved on and we stopped twice, briefly, allowing me to rest when my determination could no longer sustain my footsteps.

We eventually entered a small area of greener land, where resilient trees and bushes were randomly scattered amidst hardy grass. It was landscape scarred by the kutu war. Land where once had grown rangy grasses and wild flowers was now disfigured. Areas of sandy soil were churned up, some now forever changed by huge craters. The greenery around the craters was blackened by burning, now hardened, dry rocks. Some of the craters were several men deep; others joined together to make crevices running through the land. It was unusually quiet. No birds were singing here. Only the buzz of flying insects indicated any sign of life.

In the distance, I saw a small hill and a dense patch of trees. The hill was a mess of thrown up dirt, and most of the trees had been felled. I recognised that area. Battles had been fought there.

I spotted a discarded kutu weapon. A Nigh-kutu weapon.

"We're almost there," I told Jin. "Beyond that hill is where the Nigh-kutu camped."

Jin scoured the immediate surroundings and then caught my arm, changing direction towards one of the craters. He indicated towards Jan, and then the hills.

In silence, Jan led all ten of the wicker-clad men in a soundless jog towards the battle-scarred area.

"For safety," Jin said, as we climbed down inside a crater. "Just in case not all the black-winged ones have gone. We don't want to walk into their midst. As much as the men have trained, I think the chance of success would be against us."

"I sense so much kutu essence that I cannot tell if it's live kutu or just their resonant energy," I said.

"They'll go with stealth," Jin assured me.

And indeed they did. Although my senses felt their movement, my ears heard nothing. These men were able-bodied and well prepared, even after such a long journey from Hollow.

"I didn't tell you how we managed the near-impossible journey from Hollow to the Temple and keep in good health, did I?" Jin asked. I could tell he was trying to alleviate my anxiousness.

"You didn't," I replied, although my senses were beyond me, searching for signs of trouble.

"We used the principle of the in-betweener huts," Jin continued. "Make-shift huts, well concealed, every two days' walk. Each hut is manned by two or more people. They hold some supplies for the army for when they pass through, and move the rest of the supplies along to the next hut."

"That's well planned," I nodded, genuinely impressed.

"You have no idea," Jin smiled.

It was good to see Jin smile. It lifted the concerned crease on his brow and made his eyes shine. He was very handsome.

The sound of someone running towards us made us both freeze until Trell's face appeared over the side of the crater.

"All is well," Trell announced. "Not a black-winged beast in sight."

He held down his hand, helping me up to level ground.

"It is a sight my eyes can barely believe," Trell continued, as he helped Jin up to ground level too. "Never, under all the skies, could I have imagined such a thing."

"People?" I asked. "Bodies?"

"No," Trell replied. "Nothing at all. No human or kutu, living or ceased. Just armour and weapons everywhere. Most of it is laid out as if the wearer just disappeared from it. It is the strangest sight to behold."

"Tell the men to keep vigilant," Jin instructed. "Do not let your eyes convince you of anything."

Trell nodded and then, as he sped ahead, we followed him towards the hill.

I was not sure what to think as we climbed the hill. But as usual, when it came to the Nigh-kutu, my mind jumped to the worst conclusions. I was not surprised at the description of the armour laid out, as if the kutu inside it had simply disappeared. I had seen similar at the Temple. But no human bodies? I knew that the humans could not have survived the ordeals that the Nigh-kutu had put them through. There should be bodies. Surely the Nigh-kutu would not have eaten them. Would they eat humans? It was a terrible thought, and I did not want to think such a thing, yet alone voice it aloud.

Despite Trell's report, and despite having seen the empty kutu armour at the Temple, I was still shocked at the view from the top of the hill.

The Nigh-kutu warriors' camp appeared larger from the raised viewpoint. In the vast expanse, from one end to the other, were what looked like kutu bodies. But there were no bodies. It was just clothing and armour and weapons, laid out on the rectangular sleeping mats in the shape of kutu bodies. At their centre was the huge, black octagonal structure that housed the Nar. To one side were penned areas, which had once contained some of the humans and now were empty. At the far end were the food preparation tables that I had once worked at. Several tables still had trays of half-prepared food on them. Except for the abundance of fat, buzzing flies, there was no sound. Nothing moved. It was an eerie sight.

I hurried down the hill, moving past the threshold of the

wooded area, my eyes scanning for any sign of corpses, also pulled towards the octagonal containment that I knew housed the almost starved Nar beast. I couldn't detect anything within the octagonal container. Not dead or alive. The Nar was gone. Such a powerful beast, yet I could sense no trace of it anywhere. That puzzled me. And humans? Even at closer inspection, there were no ceased bodies. Not one set of remains, or even partial remains. Trell was right. This place was empty.

I stopped in my tracks, annoyed at myself for acting so human and relying on the vision of my eyes.

Look, I thought. *Not with your eyes, with your true vision.*

As the twelve men walked on, I opened my true vision to the land. Immediately, my senses were bombarded with the residue of the past horrors that had occurred here. There had been so much fear. The residue of fear from the humans was still so potent that it overpowered the remnants of the aggression from the Nigh-kutu. It saturated the ground and lingered in the air like stagnant, murky clouds. The clouds of fear were drenched with images and actions of past terrors. It was like souls without thought or consciousness, only dim, directionless dread. It was terrible. Even the purity of the land did not rebalance it. Such a potent, negative energy would take many turns of the season to disperse.

I braced myself, pushing past the clouds of terror, widening my true vision to search for any indication of life.

The response was instant. Although there was no trace of the Nar beast, far or wide, I sensed humans. There were some close. Very close. Not from a village, as no village existed for many moons' walk, nor the Temple, as that was much further than what I was sensing. Neither was it Jin and Jan's men, as they were all directly ahead of me. What I was sensing was coming from behind me. This had to mean. . .

By the skies! There were survivors!

Survivors! I wanted to rejoice, I wanted to run to help them, yet I maintained prudence. Survivors from this terrible place, full of fear, would be in an appalling state. Perhaps they would be suffering madness from their traumas. They could attack any who came close. And, if humans could remain concealed, there was still a chance of Nigh-kutu among them too.

I scanned the presence of the survivors with more precise control. There seemed to be over a dozen living people in close vicinity to each other, somewhere in the broken remnants of the wooded land. I felt that some of the people were seriously injured. All of them were hurt. Most of the energy felt feminine. Within that, I detected something else. Some had a very strange energy. It was almost Nigh-kutu. But it was not the usual Nigh-kutu energy. It was diluted, changed.

Looking deeper at those survivors, yes, something did indeed sense of Nigh-kutu. But it was faint, almost hidden.

Perhaps, I considered, *some of the people have been possessed by Nigh-kutu, just as Arrunn possessed Soul.* The thought was not a pleasant one.

I concentrated on the small pocket of life, searching for more than just existence to sense the one thing that told me everything about a life: intent. A being's intent could never be masked or falsified. If these people had been possessed, I would feel the intent of the possessor.

I searched with the deepest part of my true vision within that group of survivors, but I could not sense any bad or malicious intent. The main thing I sensed was despair.

I pulled back, returning my consciousness to my body.

Jin had stopped walking and was standing ahead of me, watching me attentively.

"You sense something?" he asked as he approached.

I indicated towards the woodland.

"Yes," I replied. "Humans."

"Any black-winged ones?"

"No, but something is not right. There is Nigh-kutu energy. But no Nigh-kutu that I can detect. Perhaps it is just residue on the humans."

Jin turned, about to indicate to Jan to join us. I caught his hand, stopping him.

"We go in alone, to ascertain the situation first," I said. "I can mask myself within the energy of the forest. I can make myself undetectable. I can conceal you too, but twelve men would be difficult."

Jin nodded.

"You must walk like a cat," I instructed. "Do not speak, and follow my lead exactly."

And with that I walked, knowing that Jin would follow.

I entered into the woodland, pulling in the energy of the trees to conceal us, ensuring both mine and Jin's energies were masked by the land. I kept my senses high, my eyes alert, my ears sensitive to any change of sound, my footsteps light, and my true vision expanded far beyond us. The energy here was not the usual strong peacefulness of a forest, but chaotic and unsettled from the battles that had assailed it. It unnerved me, heightening my uneasiness.

The woodland had sustained grave damage. Most of the tall, old trees were shattered or broken, some at the roots, some midway up their thick trunks, their bark burnt and black. Huge, dislocated branches hung down like giant shards. One area of trees now leaned tentatively against one another, as if pushed over by a giant hand. Their colossal, gnarled roots were now exposed, ripped from their hold in the soil, like fingers from the earth clawing towards the skies for hope. I picked my way tentatively, knowing that some areas were so finely balanced that a mere stumble could bring them crashing down.

My true vision led Jin and me into the thick of the broken forest. I held up my hand, indicating to stop.

We were almost there.

I could feel them clearly now: thirteen humans grouped in one place. Thirteen living people. Eleven women and two men. All were hurt. Some were near starved. Most were injured and broken, like the forest around them.

I still detected Nigh-kutu energy. But were there black-winged ones present? No. This place was devoid of those shadowy beasts. Nevertheless, I did not relax. I could not, because there was indeed something. I could taste it like rust on metal. The dark shadow energy was coming from within the humans themselves. Five of the women had it coursing through them. Now that they were close, they reeked of Nigh-kutu.

My hand subconsciously touched the hilt of my knife, my other remained raised to tell Jin to keep still.

Not moving, maintaining silence, I concentrated on the energies of those five tainted women. Within their energy, I saw what they had endured. They had been used for pleasure by the Nigh-kutu warriors. They had been taken for lust, and taken repeatedly, saturated with the energy of those who had forced themselves upon them. Those five women had endured terrible ordeals every day, for days, moons.

I pulled my senses away from the group of survivors, trying to shake the revulsion from my mind. No wonder those women reeked of dark energy. They were not possessed. They reeked of Nigh-kutu because they had been used for lust. Their minds and energies were troubled beyond hurt. They desperately needed help.

"There are survivors," I whispered to Jin. "Thirteen of them. They are hurt." I put down my hand. "No kutu. No dangers that I can detect."

Jin nodded, indicating that he understood.

"Hello," I called into the forest. "We have come to help."

The forest seemed to silence. They had heard. I could feel their tentative hesitancy.

"We have supplies and healers," I called in their direction.

After a pause, I detected the cautious, slow movement of someone coming towards us. They stopped, concealed. They were watching us.

"The Nigh-kutu have gone," Jin spoke clearly into the trees. "I am Jin from Hollow. I have people here to help escort you home."

More hesitancy.

"Are they really gone?" A woman's voice finally spoke from behind a fallen tree.

"Yes," I replied. "All of them. They will not be back." *Not for a long time,* I thought.

A weather-beaten, dirty face, which I did not recognise, slowly showed itself. A woman cautiously emerged, her gaunt expression and tattered tunic only hinting at the horrors she must have endured. She was thin, painfully so, and only her voice indicated that she was female.

"There are more of us," the woman said. "I am Doe. My third brother, Doro, he is near ceased."

I hurried my step towards her, untying a flask of water from my waist. I held out the flask, handing it to her as soon as I reached her, and she drank with urgent thirst. Still drinking with haste, she led us towards an area of thick bushes and into a small, gloomy den.

The small, makeshift den had been fully covered with brush, concealing it within the broken forest. Inside, it smelt of bad flesh and desperation.

As my eyes adjusted to the dimness and took in the compact surroundings, my fingers could barely move fast enough to undo the bundle of healing sheets. Most of the women sat huddled to one side. Two other women and the two men were laid out on the ground, too wounded to sit. They were almost ceased. The men's wounds were the worst. Their faces were barely recognisable as men, their emaciated bodies a mass of sores, cuts, stabs, burns and bruises. It was a wonder that they still breathed. It was a wonder that any man who had been used for sparring practice by the Nigh-kutu had survived.

I tore the water flasks hastily from around my waist to give what I had. Jin emptied his supply pouch, and the food was readily grabbed and devoured. Having given out all the food and water, I covered the two wounded men with healing sheets, and then the two laid out women, handing out the rest to the others.

"Let the healing sheets do their work. Do not move," I told one of the men as he tried to open his congealed eyes. "You are safe now."

The man tried to nod and closed his eyes again.

"Her? Do not let her near me," someone spoke with surprising vehemence.

I turned. The words had come from a large woman who was laid out at the end of the line. She was badly injured and covered in sores amidst sunburn and dark, mottled bruising. I could feel that something was broken in her back. Despite the woman's dirtied, bloated face, I now recognised her. It was Mags. Mags from Meadsins. Her open, swollen eyes were looking at me with abhorrence.

"Mags," I went to her side, ignoring her attempted struggles of protest. "It's alright. You'll be alright now."

Jin heard the fuss and came over. "You're Mags? Mags from Meadsins? Ren's mother?" he asked.

"You know my Ren?" Mags stopped struggling, her tone softening. "My little Ren is alive?"

"Alive and well," Jin confirmed. He crouched down to her, brushing the hair from her face with a damp cloth. "And Dinah and the babies are well too. They will be overjoyed to know you live. Please," he spoke cajolingly, "let the healing sheets do their work. Ren would not forgive me if I did not bring you home to him."

As Mags relaxed acceptingly, I turned to a woman who seemed surprisingly uninjured of flesh, yet her mind felt forever scarred. "Are there any others alive?" I asked.

The woman shook her head, indicating not.

"Yester-eve the black-winged ones turned into mist," she waved her hand through the air, "and disappeared. We escaped and hid here. This morn they hadn't returned, so we dragged the ceased into the trees." She indicated in one direction. "My mate, Yew, had already been ceased for eight days. They cut his throat and let his blood flow because he was too hurt to fight back. I watched his flesh rot and could do nothing. When I dragged his corpse into the trees this morn, his arms just separated from his body. They just pulled off." She stopped, unable to continue. Images flooded my mind, making me witness the dreadfulness she had seen.

"What is your name?" I asked her.

"Ada," the woman replied. She closed her eyes and hung her head. "I was taken on my choosing night. I'd only just chosen Yew as my mate. He was a good man."

Ada looked up at me, tilting her head to one side, her eyes registering recognition.

"Don't I know you?" she asked. "Yes, I remember. You were here too, serving food. You tried to get away. I thought they killed you."

"They almost did," I replied. "Ada, you are safe now. No one will hurt you again."

I leaned forward, touching the side of Ada's face, sending her soothing thoughts. As I touched her skin, I felt a surge of Nigh-kutu energy from within her.

Jin touched my arm, breaking the connection with Ada.

"I'll inform Jan and get more food and water," he said.

It was a timely idea. Jin's food had already been devoured. The water was down to the last flask. We desperately needed more.

Having assured me that he could retrace his steps back here without difficulty, Jin left, and I returned my attention to the survivors.

There seemed so much to do, yet so little that I could do for these poor, wretched people. The healing sheets were already doing their work on their bodies. Only time would heal their minds. So, I tucked the healing sheets underneath those who were laid-out, knowing it would speed their repair, and found a piece of discarded cloth and dampened it, wiping their faces, cupping water into my hand, dripping it into the mouths of those who could not tend to themselves. They truly were in a terrible state.

Jin returned in no time, quietly entering the cramped den with Trell and Jan, and more food and water.

"They others await just outside," Jin told me, handing out the new supplies. "We are lacking space here."

"They could start by carefully removing the bush and bracken from around us," I suggested. "The stench in here is foul. These people need clean air."

Before Jin could pass on the request, one of the women started shaking. Her shaking grew more fierce, as if a fit had overtaken her. She collapsed sideways from her sitting position, convulsing, the healing sheet falling behind her. Jin automatically twisted around, quickly getting behind the woman, wrapping his arms around her to prevent her juddering spasms from damaging her any more than she already was. Her convulsing seemed to quickly calm. Jin pulled the healing sheet back around her. As soon as the healing sheet touched her, her convulsing accelerated again. She shuddered violently, her arms twitching, as if trying to flail. Her eyes bulged wide and foam began frothing from her mouth.

Reacting only with what my senses perceived and ignoring my

logic, I pulled the healing sheet off the woman. Immediately, her convulsing stopped.

I stood, healing sheet in hand, observing the person who now lay limp and exhausted in Jin's arms. She was a fair haired young woman with large, round eyes and pale eyebrows. I recognised her as one of the women who had been used for lust. She still reeked of Nigh-kutu. The healing light of the sheets should have cancelled out the shadow energy that coursed through her. But it hadn't. Somehow, the shadow energy within her had been repelled by the healing sheet. This woman had not appeared to be badly hurt in body before the healing sheet was put around her. Now, she had suffered a bad reaction to it. That should not be.

I glanced around. Five women seemed in relatively good physical health compared to the others. The one in Jin's arms was one. She had been fine until the healing sheet had touched her. Doe, who had come to us, was another. And three others. Five in total. None of them chose to use the healing sheets given to them. Although these five women had minds that were forever scarred, they did not appear to be outwardly injured, as I would have expected. Those five women were the same ones that reeked of Nigh-kutu. Somehow, the shadow energy within them had accelerated their healing and kept them in strong physical health. All of them were the five surviving women who had been used for lust. It could not be a coincidence.

I turned to the woman whose energy was most saturated by Nigh-kutu. She sat silently clasping her knees, her grimy, haunted face gazing into nothingness. She told me her name was Pallyn, and that she was from Meadsins too. Her body looked surprisingly undamaged, albeit emaciated. She too had discarded the healing sheet given to her.

"Do you not want the healing sheet?" I asked Pallyn.

She shook her head.

"No, it made me feel worse," she said.

I nodded, saying nothing, and then picked up her unused healing sheet, placing it over one of the men whose own had almost depleted.

I did not want to alarm Pallyn by staring at her, so, while my body and eyes moved in one direction, my true vision looked closer at her. Her belly was the source of the shadow energy around her. Her belly. And she had been used for lust by the black-winged ones.

It looked like... surely it could not be possible.

But it was. I could see it clearly now that I knew where to look. Pallyn was with child.

In Pallyn's belly, where the shadow energy was strongest, was another life – a new life – a child. But this was no normal human baby. Its energy was not just the energy of a human. This was part Nigh-kutu too. This was where the shadow energy I was sensing stemmed from: an unborn child.

I observed the bellies of all the surviving women. All five of those who had survived being used for lust were with child. All their unborn ones were not just human. They were half Nigh-kutu.

It felt as if the air was being sucked from my lungs.

I stood, holding onto the side of the den to steady my legs.

"Can you manage a moment?" I asked Jin.

Jin nodded, observing my expression with a concern of his own.

I excused myself, moving out of the woodland to stand in the sunlight. I closed my eyes, my hands deep in the pockets of my gown, clasping Jychanumun's armlets. How I wished I could converse with Jychanumun. But I could not. And, even if I could, in this instance, I think even he would not know what to do. And me... I did not think such a thing possible. Kutu did not have the same biology as humans. Nevertheless, my true vision had seen the impossible and I did not know what to do either.

"What is it?" Jin's voice came from behind. He came to stand beside me. "As pale as you are, I noticed the colour drain from you. Something is amiss."

"I am shaken by something I do not understand. I do not know what to do," I replied.

"Is it potentially dangerous?" Jin asked, matter-of-factly.

"I do not know."

"Then do not hold your tongue," Jin urged, a frown spreading across his brow.

"What do you call those huge brown birds that fly highest and hunt and feed on other birds and small animals? The kutu called them rapereals. I've seen them in the desert, near Hollow," I asked.

"In Hollow, we call them the giant hunt-wings."

"And you know the small animals, like rabbits, hares, or woodnoses, which they prey upon?" I continued.

"Of course."

"Do you think that a rabbit and a giant hunt-wing could mate and produce offspring?"

Jin laughed, as if I was jesting, and then stopped when he saw that I was not.

"No, of course they couldn't," he said. "What are you trying to tell me, Tachra?"

"The survivors in there. Some of the women were used for lust by the Nigh-kutu," I paused. "Those women are now with child – with child from a Nigh-kutu. Part human. Part kutu."

Jin stood for a moment, his gaze fixed ahead. He did not seem as taken aback as I was.

"Is that the Nigh-kutu energy you were sensing?" he asked.

"Yes."

"How many of them?"

"Five. The five women who appear least hurt in body."

Jin remained silent for a moment, considering the information.

"Do they know?" he asked.

"No, I don't think so."

"Then they will need to be told."

Before I could reply, the sudden sound of bracken snapping made me turn around.

One of the surviving women, one of the ones who was with child, Ada, was several strides behind us. She had stumbled over a broken branch and was struggling to regain her footing. From the look of sheer revulsion and horror on her face, I guessed that she had heard what Jin and I had said.

Ada stumbled sideways a few steps, and then launched forward. She was running away from the woodland and into the Nigh-kutu camp with agile speed.

"Ada!" I called, following her.

Ada was fast. She ran, stopping at one of the closest Nigh-kutu sleeping mats that still had the armour laid out upon it. She glanced down.

"Ada, don't!" I shouted, trying to reach her.

I could see in her expression that she was going to do something terrible. I could feel it.

Jin realised something more was amiss and began sprinting to catch up with us both.

Ada fell to her knees. She picked up a knife, a long Nigh-kutu knife. And then she looked at me, put the knife to her throat, tilted her head to the sky and drew her hand across her throat in one swift move.

The kutu knife sliced deep into her flesh.

Blood spurted from the cut, gushing down Ada's front. Her eyes rolled up. She slumped forward.

By the skies! No!

I reached Ada's body at the same time as Jin. I flipped her over, immediately clamping both my hands over the long, gaping wound across her neck in order to seal it. There was so much blood already; more blood than I thought any one body could hold. Jin was acting fast, ripping a piece of his tunic.

"Get me a healing sheet!" I shouted to anyone. The blood was beginning to slow its gushing from the gaping wound.

Jin held out the piece of cloth to hold against the long cut. He paused, checking Ada's wrist for a pulse, feeling her mouth for breath.

"Tachra," Jin spoke, "she has ceased."

"No," I protested. "The blood is slowing."

"She cannot heal from that. She has lost most of her blood. She has ceased, which is why it slows."

I knew Jin was right. I saw Ada's energy disperse into the ground around her and the shadow that coursed through her wane to nothing. She was dead. Her child was dead.

Jin leaned forward, closing Ada's staring eyes.

I sat next to Ada's ceased flesh, knowing she was gone, with my head in my blood-covered hands, wishing I had the tools and skills of the Shaa-kutu, angry and frustrated with myself.

"She heard me," I was fraught. "She heard what I said about being with child. She was with child. She could not bear the thought of it. This is my fault."

"It is not your fault," Jin assured me. "The Nigh-kutu did that to her. Not you. You cannot take responsibility for what damage the Nigh-kutu have done."

"But she endured moons of torture, she survived, to come to this." It was heartbreaking. "Poor Ada. Poor, poor Ada." I looked up at Jin. "What do I tell the other survivors? What do I do?"

Jin picked me up, making me stand.

"We," he said calmly, "will clean you up. Then we will return to the other survivors. Once there, you will give them some of that soothing Earth energy you have given so many lectures about. Once done, and they have ears that are ready to hear with reason, we will tell them the facts and the truth. With the truth, subsequent actions become their choice: their consequence, not yours. We will simply try to guide them to good choices until they are strong enough to make their own."

"And when did you become so wise?" I asked, feeling wretched.

"Tachra," he looked at me, with conviction, "those were your words once, not mine."

Jin stayed while I washed the blood from my hands and face. Then, once I was cleansed enough, and while the soldiers began the arduous task of locating and burying the bodies of those who had not survived the Nigh-kutu, including Ada, we returned to the survivors in the woodland. I had to brace myself for the task. It took all the courage I could gather from the chaotic, war-assailed land, to speak to them.

I told the remaining survivors that they were safe now. I told them that the Nigh-kutu were gone, that their flesh was healing, and that with time, their minds would heal too. I reminded them that they still had families – parents, siblings, offspring – who loved them, and whom they would see again. I told them that they needed to stay strong. And then, while sending them soothing energy, I told them about Ada. After that, I had to tell them why. All were justifiably distressed and it took a great deal of Earth energy to calm the with-child women enough not to follow Ada's path.

The ray of hope for the women who carried a Nigh-kutu child came from Jin. As I sent calming energy to them, he told them that in Hollow was a man who knew herbs. He told them that if their choice was to be rid of their unborn child, herbs could be mixed to make it happen. He spoke with reassurance and confidence, and I could see that his words were both authoritative and comforting. He had an air about him. Nothing seemed to daunt him. The four afflicted women sat listening with grave apprehension, rather than having life-threatening, panicked reactions.

"We will all return to the Temple, where you can rebalance and decide," Jin concluded. "Then, if and when you are ready, if you wish, you can be escorted home. So now we will make litters for those too injured or exhausted to walk, and we will all leave this forsaken place."

With no more that could be said, I guided those who could walk out of their make-shift den, out of the broken forest, and into the early evening.

It was still gloriously bright, and I hoped that the gentle warmth of the sun's last rays would lift everyone's thoughts. They didn't talk very much, choosing to stay huddled together, as if comforted by each other's presence. Pallyn was the only one to speak, telling them that they had all fought to stay alive, and that she didn't expect them to have any different thoughts now. The rest of them listened to her. While they listened, they watched with blank eyes as several of the wicker-clad men gathered wood and fastened litters.

Before we were ready to leave, I walked the length and breadth of the Nigh-kutu camp. I thought that perhaps I should collect anything that could be of use. The abandoned weapons could be stored for the needs of future generations. The armour was made of the toughest yet flexible substance, unlike anything I knew of on this planet. Surely people could benefit from such things. It was tempting. But, everything I considered taking felt too contaminated, and I realised that nothing here should be taken away, no matter how useful it may appear. It should all be left exactly as it was. Left for nature and time to cover.

As I walked through the camp, Trell and Shaul saw to the difficult task of burying the ceased bodies. The survivors had said that they had dragged several into the forest. There had been twenty-six ceased bodies in the forest in total. It was far fewer than I had expected.

Despite searching with my true vision, I could not find any souls to take to Elysium. I scoured the land, but not one ceased spirit lingered. That saddened me. None of the dead had retained any essence. The Nigh-kutu had broken their bodies, their hope, and then their will. Twenty-six deaths and none had retained a soul.

I saw Jan and Trell deep in close discussion. They both looked solemn. They indicated that I should join them.

"What is amiss?" I asked as I approached.

"We have discovered something," Jan informed me. "We were debating whether you should be shown, or just told."

"Both," I replied.

Jan directed me towards an area of natural dips and small hillocks where fat flies gathered in abundance

"We have found more bodies," Jan said. "Human bodies. It is unpleasant," he warned me.

But Jan's words did not prepare me for what I saw.

Between the small hillocks was a large pit, concealed by the natural lay of the land. Inside the pit were strange, grey shapes. When I looked closer, I could see that the pit was full of ceased humans. Limbs and torsos wound around each other in odd poses, making it impossible to tell where one human stopped and another began. The dead had been covered in a fine layer of grey powder. It almost did not look like people. It looked more like one huge, grey, multi-limbed, sleeping creature.

"We estimate around three hundred," Jan told me.

"I was going to remove the bodies to start burying them," Trell added. "But as soon as I touched one," he looked at his hand, "this."

Trell showed me his hand. It had a piece of healing sheet around it. I carefully unwrapped the healing fabric. Underneath, his palm and wrist had developed large, odd-looking, blackened blisters where once there had been skin. I carefully re-bound it.

"They are healing," Jan indicated to Trell's blisters. "When

Trell first showed me a few moments ago, I thought he might lose his hand."

I had to make a decision.

"Then the bodies must remain where they are," I decided.

"We can put earth over the top," Jan suggested.

"No," I shook my head. "The risk to the living is too great. If the powder is disturbed, whatever caused that," I indicated towards Trell's hand, "could become airborne. We leave this as it is." I looked down into the pit. "Once we leave this place, I will ensure that no man will ever tread here again. I will mask this land from all eyes. It is wounded. Only time will heal it. We can do no more here. We must leave. Soon."

Both Jan and Trell agreed. They would clearly be glad to leave too. And, having seen the strained brows and grim expressions on the rest of the men's faces, it was clear everyone would be keen to depart this wretched place.

As one of the soldiers was sent ahead to the Temple to give instruction to prepare a healing room, I returned to the survivors. The four who could not walk were now carefully laid out on the roughly constructed litters. Healing sheets were wrapped tightly around them. Those who had been so badly hurt that they were barely conscious were now awake.

I tended to the man who had sustained the worst damage. His cuts had healed well, but the deepest wounds were still fragile. Next to him, Mags was alert, but could not sit. Her spine had knitted, and thankfully the nerves were mending. I told her that in no time she would be chasing her grandchildren. She didn't reply. She still seemed to dislike me.

As the sun was about to leave the sky, twelve survivors, eleven healthy men, and myself, began our return to the Temple. I was relieved to leave. Everyone was. We did not even care that a wind was starting to blow, whipping up the leaves and grit, threatening a sand storm. We got to the top of the hill that looked down upon the Nigh-kutu camp. There, while the others walked on, I paused for a moment, turning to face the wounded land.

From the hilltop, I sent my energy through the deepest part of the earth and towards the wounded land. I imagined a barrier around the warriors' camp, making it invisible to any creature's eyes.

No one would come here again. Not for hundreds of generations. Not until time had allowed nature to bury the past forever.

TWENTY-FIVE

The Book

The walk from the Nigh-kutu camp was slow but steady, and the soldiers took it in turns to drag the litters. The unaccustomedly unkind winds blew against us, making every step an effort. Twice I had to remind the brothers that I could do nothing to ease the winds. Still they asked.

By the time the night was at its prime, and we had just stopped for the third time, all the survivors were on the litters. Four were still laid out, with the rest now perched on the sides, too exhausted to continue. It put more strain on the soldiers, and everyone was exhausted, but no one wanted to stop for the night. We had no wind protectors, no blankets, and the water supplies had been consumed. So we pushed on. Jin, Jan and the men dragged the litters, and the gritty wind prevailed. My legs grew numb with exertion, my face grew numb from the grit that assailed it, but I pulled my hood down and walked on, determined not to be the one to delay us.

I was relieved when the luminosity of the Temple was eventually in sight.

I was even more relieved when we entered the peace of the Shaa-kutu building.

And I was even more relieved again to see Soul and a group of well-rested men waiting to escort the survivors to a healing room.

"No, we can manage," Soul insisted as I went to go with them. "You go and rest. Eat. Sleep. Truly, Tachra, we can manage without you."

I stopped arguing. I clearly was not needed.

As Soul and the group of freshly allocated men escorted the survivors into a nearby room, Jin and Jan ushered their exhausted men into another for debriefing. I stood in the corridor alone.

I wasn't sure what to do.

I had done what I needed to do. Soul and Iris were in a safe place. I had been to the Nigh-kutu camp.

There was nowhere else that I needed to be.

My work here was finished.

My directionless feet took me back through the Temple's entrance and into the quiet of the night outside. There was no one else around, and I found myself staring blankly at the lake.

My feet carried me forward, past the ruins, across the patchy, war-torn grass, and down the slope that led to the water. One last bathe.

I carefully removed Jychanumun's armlets from my robe, put them to my lips, and placed them on the bank. I then waded into the lake. As soon as the water was deep enough, I submerged, wiggled out of Orion's gown, and threw it onto the grass.

I gently paddled in the water, staying afloat. As I swam, I looked around the dark valley. The beautifully crafted Temple was now so damaged. It would never be the same.

Nor would I.

I could just stop paddling, I thought. I could just stop and sink into the water.

I pondered on that for a moment. If I just let my body go and left this mortal life, what would I do? What if Jychanumun could no longer open a death-path for me? If I cannot speak with him anymore, how will he know to open a path for me? I could not go to the Old One. Not until this war with the kutu was over, and that would not happen for thousands of years. What was left for me? This mortal life? Could I ever feel the joy of mortal life after all I had seen? What was my joy of life anyway? No longer guided by others' needs, did I know? I had done everything that I had to do. Perhaps, without having to help others, I was lost.

I think I was lost.

I had not been lost before now.

I tried to imagine what it would be like just to give up this mortal life. I let the thought dwell for a moment, deciding how I felt about it.

I realised that I didn't like it.

I didn't like it at all.

But here, in the flesh, I had nothing left that I needed to do.

I thought about the fact that my decisions and actions had for so long been directed by others' requests or needs. Orion had often spoken about that, referring to himself. He said that was why he turned down being the Supreme, because he was the type of kutu who would lose himself in the needs of others. Orion had often said that life was a delicate balance between striving for ascendancy and the simple joy of living. Sometimes, he would say, just to live for the joy of living can get forgotten when striving for greater things. I hadn't understood those words. Now, I think I did.

Life was not just about being needed, or doing what you had to do. Life was also about the simple happiness of existence. Perhaps I had forgotten this. I think I had.

Surely I could still experience the beauty of life. I didn't need war, conflict or disaster to direct my purpose. I could simply live.

And the people here now. Jin and Jan and several hundred men had been prepared to sacrifice their lives fighting the Nigh-kutu.

Now they looked forward to going home, to live the lives they had chosen. And Soul and Iris, they were determined to embrace a full life. They were prepared to walk into the unknown for the potential of their tomorrows. And those survivors from the Nigh-kutu camp, they had given their strength to one another when it appeared that there was no hope. They knew there was always hope to find joy in life again.

I looked at the valley once more. It didn't matter that much of the lush grass had been burnt by the attacks that had occurred here. The grass would regrow. And it didn't matter that the broken rocks from the Temple littered the ground. In time, those rocks would become part of the landscape, covered in moss, giving home to small creatures. It was part of the changes in everything, the changes that passing time brings. Just as my valley would heal, but would never be the same, so too the twelve survivors would heal. No one could say who they would become. Only time and their choices would reveal such things. The same for me. I didn't know what time would bring for me. But for the first time in a long time, my choices felt like they were truly my own.

I could do anything, I thought. Tomorrows are full of potential. Beautiful, unknown, untouched potential.

The thought was exhilarating.

I stepped from the lake, re-dressed in Orion's old gown, and headed back towards the Temple. My feet walked with purpose this time; a newfound, determined, animated purpose.

Inside the Temple, I almost bumped into Soul. She was hurrying from one of the rooms with her arms full of bright kutu fabric.

I think I was smiling as I hugged her.

"I want to live," I laughed.

Her frown turned into a smile. "Of course you do. I knew that," she said as she rolled her eyes. "You just needed to stop moping about yesterdays and realise it for yourself."

"Can I do anything to help?" I asked.

"Don't be silly," Soul chortled. "I have half an army asking the same thing. I have far more help than I know what to do with. You do," she shrugged, "whatever you want to."

I smiled at my friend and watched her walk away. She turned before she reached the end of the corridor.

"Jin was looking for you," she said, raising her eyebrows.

"I'll find him shortly," I replied. "There is something I want to do first."

Soul laughed to herself. It was wonderful to see my friend laugh again.

I knew exactly what I wanted to do. There was something I could now face.

I made my way to one of the side entrances to the central chamber. No one else was in sight. I released the energy seal from the door, and then slipped into the gloomy, damaged room.

I walked towards the old well and stood for a moment, holding onto the wall that encircled it. Then, I looked down.

Far below me, too far for my eyes to perceive anything other than darkness, was the place that had been my prison. I loathed it. It had almost made me doubt everything. It had almost made me give up.

I made myself stare into that pit. I visualised myself down there, naked, starving, maimed, near mad. I made myself relive the fears that had tormented my mind. I forced those thoughts through my head again and again, like a never-ending loop. I did this until my mind stopped fighting it and my heart accepted it. In response, my heartbeat slowed. As my heartbeat slowed, time slowed.

Slower. Slower. Stop.

It felt as if time stood still. And then, in that moment devoid of time, knowing that I had completely accepted the memory, I embraced it.

I was down there but a day and a half ago. A time so close I can almost touch it, I thought. *But yesterdays are past. I made it through my yesterdays. It is today that matters.*

As I embraced every aspect of that past, instead of feeling weak, I felt empowered. It was like rocks being lifted from my shoulders. It was like a constant dull ache that had suddenly gone. My energy seemed to react, moving more freely again. I felt like I was sunbeams on water. I remembered feeling like this when I was a girl, and it was wonderful.

I stood awhile, motionless, allowing the moment to matter.

This place was no longer one to be feared.

It was just a well. An unused, empty, water well. Nothing more. I turned to leave.

As I walked away, my attention was drawn towards a source of energy coming from the back of the chamber. It was the same energy, from a kutu device, that I had felt when first entering the Temple. It was just as powerful now as when I had first felt it. It still reeked of Arrunn.

This time, my curiosity led me to locate the source.

I found the source of the kutu energy almost immediately. It wasn't hidden, merely concealed by the natural shadows of the darkened chamber. The energy was coming from a small yet strong force-field barrier. It was a dark, Nigh-kutu barrier, nothing like the bright repelling energy that the Shaa-kutu used. This was what tasted of Arrunn. But although the barrier was strong, it was what was inside that caught my interest.

Inside the barrier was what looked like a large, black cube. It was quite beautiful and elaborately decorated. The cube was the span of four of my hands and covering every side were complex layers of engravings and embossing. Some of the carvings looked like old Nigh-kutu script; most I did not recognise. Through the shadow of the barrier around it, I could see that the cube's dense, dark substance wasn't pure black. Within the black it appeared to have tiny specks of white.

As I moved in closer for a better view, the white specks within the cube changed. With each new perspective they changed again, creating different shapes and patterns. The patterns seemed to constantly move.

I walked around the cube, considering it. I'd never seen anything like it.

The ornate black cube was certainly Nigh-kutu in origin. That much I could tell. But I had no idea *what* it was. It could be a weapon, or used for storage; it could be a regenerator, a duplicator, a communicator, a portal, or even simply a piece of art. It was kutu, therefore it could be many things, significant or insignificant. But, I reflected, it was positioned exactly where Arrunn used to stand. The energy barrier around it was just like Arrunn's energy. This had clearly belonged to him.

Not only had this object clearly belonged to Arrunn, he had used his valuable resources to bring it with him, into the light and here to Earth. If he was prepared to use his valuable resources, then this interesting black cube had to be important to him.

If this object was important to Arrunn, I determined, I wanted to know what it was.

I decided to remove the cube from its energy barrier for better inspection. I lightly touched the force-field around it. It made my skin tingle. The tingle rapidly progressed to a cold burning. I quickly pulled my hands away. My fingers were bleeding. The healing sheet Soul had sewn into my gown quickly soothed the pain and mended the skin.

I considered again. If I was quick, the healing sheet would do its work and no lasting damage would be done to my hands. It was only pain. It would be worth the pain to know what this object was.

I rolled up my sleeves, and then, opening my true vision, threw caution to the skies. I thrust both my hands straight into the shadowy force-field.

Immediately, the pain from the energy barrier was excruciating. I worked fast, trying to push the heavy cube out from its retaining hold. The cube moved, but the barrier moved with it. My hands manoeuvred within the force-field, feeling with my fingers through the crawling pain, trying to locate where the energy felt strongest, most condensed. There. The force-field was emitting from this place. It was flowing from one specific area like water from the mouth of a waterfall.

The force-field around the black cube was controlled by a small black disc that was attached to it. The disc had been cleverly constructed to look like part of the cube's design. I hit the disc.

The disc dislocated from the cube and rolled along the floor. The force-field moved with it. It hit the wall and deactivated.

I didn't want to look at my hands. I wrapped them in the hem of my gown and sat cross-legged, rocking, as the sticky, sickening agony slowly subsided.

It took a while for my hands to be soothed enough to function again. While they healed, I sat observing the ornate cube.

Without the shadowy force-field around it, I could see the black object much clearer. Its engravings were more intricate and the moving flecks of white were more defined. They looked like morphing, unknown scripts, moving in all directions across and around every surface. I still did not know what the object was. But, whatever it was, it was far greater than it appeared. I felt compelled to examine it.

With my hands almost healed, I gently touched the cube, running my fingers over one of the many embossed sections. The white flecks moved under my fingertips in response, reshaping to create what looked like different words. As the words formed, my mind became filled with the image of a beautiful pale-yellow planet. I touched another section, my mind picturing a moving constellation, sped up in its transition, as if propelled by time. I drew my hand away and sat, considering.

I must have sat studying the black kutu cube for some time. I was pulled from my deep contemplation by the sound of Soul calling my name. I returned her call, pushed one of the heavy doors ajar just enough for her to get through, and then returned to the intriguing black object.

Soul did not seem surprised to find me in the central chamber.

"The twelve are finally sleeping, even Pallyn," she said, as she squeezed through the door, carrying a large pile of healing sheets. "And look," she held up the healing sheets, "I found another unused supply."

She stopped walking. Her words paused. She glanced around, taking in the severity of the damage to the once magnificent room.

"You should not be here," Soul decided, looking at the ruins. "It doesn't look safe."

Soul then noticed the object of my consideration. She moved in closer for a better view.

"What is it?" she asked.

"That is what I'm going to find out," I replied. "It was in a force field, but I've managed to disable it. It was Arrunn's."

Soul immediately pulled back.

"Tsst," she hissed. "Then we should put it as far away as possible. You find an item of Arrunn's and remove it from its containment? Tachra, what were you thinking? Have you lost your senses?"

"I did act hastily," I admitted, "but not entirely foolishly."

I brushed my fingers over the surface of the cube. Soul saw how the flecks of white moved in response to my touch, creating new patterns.

"This was Arrunn's," I explained. "As yet, I have found no weakness in him. He has consistently dominated and conquered all other kutu and humans. If this object was important to him, it might give information to help me understand him."

"But you beat him," Soul protested. "You sent him away."

"Not really," I replied, wishing Soul's words were true. "His options were limited, but he still chose to leave. At some time, in long away futures, he will be able to return. If someone does not find a way to conquer him, he will see the end of us all."

Soul sighed. "I know," she seemed to slump, "these are important matters. You speak like a kutu so often now, but the kutu are gone. I just thought perhaps you could have a life free of kutu troubles. A normal life."

"All *is* well," I tried to reassure her. "Perhaps I just have to find my new normal. Or perhaps," I indicated towards the cube, "this is my normal. Either way, I admit, my friend, that it fascinates me."

As I spoke, I leaned forward, moving the cube to view it from different angles. This time, I did not watch the moving shapes, I looked at the engravings.

I noticed that one well-defined area had embossing that encircled a large, deeply carved ring. Inside the ring were engravings. On the opposite side of the cube, I had noticed a similar pattern, almost identical, except the engravings inside the ring differed.

I looked closer at the engravings. I was sure that I had seen those symbols before.

Jychanumun's armlets!

Suddenly, everything added up.

"By the skies," I gasped, suddenly standing, taking a step back.

"What is it?" Soul asked, taking several steps backwards too.

"No, it's not dangerous," I reassured, realising I had caused alarm. "I think it's a book."

I stepped in to look at the cube again. "Kutu don't do things like us. Everything is multi-dimensional. This cube – I am sure it's a Nigh-kutu book."

I pulled Jychanumun's armlets from the pockets in my gown. "And, if I am right," I added. "Jychanumun's armlets are part of it. And if it is, it may be the answers I seek."

I studied one of the deep circular engravings on the cube, selecting the armlet with the matching symbols.

I held up Jychanumun's armlet to the cube. The engravings were an exact match. And the deeply engraved ring at the centre was of an identical size. I aligned the two, carefully slotting Jychanumun's armlet into position. It fitted perfectly.

I took the second armlet, turning the cube around, aligning the armlet to match the opposite deeply engraved ring. With ease, I slotted that armlet into position too.

On placing the second armlet into position, the patterns on cube seemed to go wild, changing and morphing at a pace so fast my eyes could not keep up.

"What. . . ?" Soul began to ask, crouching down beside me.

"This is it," I whispered. I could barely believe what I was seeing. "This is the Book of Fate."

I had heard much about the Book of Fate from Jychanumun. Never did I think I would see it. Now it was here, in front of me.

I explained that Jychanumun had written this book from his predictive visions, long before he had chosen to join the Walker clan. He had only ever written one book. This book. The Book of Fate was multidimensional, constantly changing, its changes affected by fate. From that one book, copies were made for the great Nigh-kutu libraries. But those copies were flat, unchangeable, just linear details of specific predictions. Over time, Arrunn had destroyed all copies. All that remained was the original, and Arrunn had appropriated that for himself.

"This book is sacred to the Nigh-kutu," I said. "Even to Arrunn. It's what Arrunn has used to know what fates were to come. No wonder he wanted to capture Jychanumun so badly. It wasn't just the death-paths, it was this. This book. He needed Jychanumun, or his armlets, to see the complete works. Now here it is. We have the complete book."

"Can you read it?" Soul asked.

The question quickly quelled my enthusiasm.

"Not yet," I replied. "I barely know any Nigh-kutu spoken words, yet alone their ancient languages. But I can study it. Just think, Soul: the Book of Fate. The book of tomorrows."

Soul stood, clearly not as impressed as me.

"Then if it needs to be studied, it is something that can wait until your tomorrows. There's an army out there, waiting for direction from Jin and Jan. Jin and Jan are waiting for direction from you. You must leave this for now."

Soul had clearly taken an instant dislike to the Book of Fate. No matter if it was written by Jychanumun, she said, it had been in Arrunn's possession, and she wanted nothing of Arrunn's anywhere near her, or her daughter, ever again. She did not want to keep it in the Temple. And she absolutely did not want it anywhere that she or Iris might wander.

Eventually, we compromised, agreeing that the Book of Fate could remain in the central chamber on the condition that the chamber would stay sealed. Once we had agreed to this, Soul told me that she was going to change the survivors' healing sheets, and then I was to meet her in the kitchens. Meanwhile, she decided, I was to reseal this place straight away.

Soul left me in the central chamber. I wanted to start studying the book right away. I was keenly anxious to discover how it worked and what it said. But I knew such a task could be a long one. Learning how to read the words could take seasons – longer, perhaps – and that was only if it was possible at all. Nigh-kutu was such a complex language, and most of the script was nothing like any kutu language I had ever seen before. Discovering the secrets in this book would take time. Right now, Soul was right. I had more imminent matters to attend to.

I carefully removed Jychanumun's armlets from the cube. In response, the volatile writing calmed, resuming its gentle morphing.

I got up, tucked the armlets back into my pockets, left via the door through which I had entered, secured the room, and made my way to the kitchens.

TWENTY-SIX

The Survivors

The twelve survivors from the Nigh-kutu camp were all sleeping, having been well fed and cleansed and their wounds tended to. Jin and Jan's army had grown by another one hundred men while we were away, taking their total to over five hundred. They had all been allocated comfortable accommodation, and the bulk of them were resting, having finally stopped after a long journey. It was bright morning and, for such a full Temple, it was surprisingly quiet.

Soul, Jin, Jan, Trell and myself had been deep in discussion in the kutu kitchens for some time. We were trying to work out the best way to attend to all the differing requests of the twelve survivors, plus the army of men.

All the army were Hollow men, keen to return to their mates, parents, or offspring, and the lives they had left behind.

Of the twelve survivors, all bar one originated from Meadsins. It appeared that Meadsins had been singled out by the Nigh-kutu and many of its occupants taken. Despite being ravaged, all the survivors wanted to return home to rebuild their lives. Thankfully, Meadsins was close enough to Hollow to make this possible.

Four of the survivors were healed enough to travel and wanted to return home as soon as they could. They were fit to do the journey, although it would be slow, and they would need at least ten able-bodied men to escort them.

The four survivors who had been too injured to walk still required a great deal of recuperation. They were equally anxious to return to their village, but none had the adequate strength yet to travel. It would be too dangerous to carry them on litters over the mountain. Therefore, they would have to stay in the Temple for a while longer, until they were strong enough for the journey.

Of the final four – the four women who were each carrying a half-Nigh-kutu child – three were from Meadsins and one, Doe, was from a nearby small off-shoot of Meadsins. All four women wanted to take the herbs to destroy their unborn half-breeds. None wanted to return to their homes until this was done. All wanted to stay here, at the Temple, until they could return to their villages. But there was a problem. Here in the valley we had neither the herbs nor anyone who knew how to mix them.

The man in Hollow who knew how to mix herbs was old. He would only be able to travel at a slow pace. Soul pointed out that if he was brought to the Temple, he would arrive too late to do what he needed to do. For a moment, the five of us had fallen silent, deliberating how to overcome this dilemma.

"Who is your fastest runner?" I asked.

Jin and Jan looked at Trell.

"My son, Shaul," Trell replied. "And there are several others who can almost match him."

"We could put a team together of those fastest to get to Hollow," I suggested. "Would the herbs or potion keep fresh enough, if made at Hollow, for the return journey?"

Everyone thought that this was possible. In fact, they thought that it was the only solution that had a chance of working.

So it was decided. Jin and Jan would send a group of their fastest runners back to Hollow: six men. Six, they explained, would ensure safety and success. The runners would fetch the required potions, and then return. If they were fortunate with the weather, the conditions, and no injuries, the journey there and back would take them less than three moons. There and then, Trell selected the men. The men were summoned, given instruction, and told to ready themselves. They would leave tomorrow at first light. Shaul would oversee the group. Shaul was a good choice. Trell had trained his son well.

It was also decided that Jan would return to Hollow with the majority of the soldiers. They would leave tomorrow at high sun, allowing the runners to get ahead, informing the in-betweener huts that the entire army would soon be passing through, and to have provisions ready. Within the army, a group would be selected to oversee the wellbeing of the four survivors who would be leaving with them.

Jin would remain here at the Temple with twenty men. Those twenty would be selected from volunteers. Trell insisted he would be one of them. He argued that all his eight sons were grown men now, and his mate had ceased before he had come to Hollow, so he had no commitments there. And, he pointed out, of everyone present he had the most experience in helping with childbirth. He was quite matter-of-fact about it, telling us that if the herbs did not work for any of the women, as their effectiveness was not always certain, then he would oversee any babes being born. It was this talk that made me realise we could well have half Nigh-kutu, half human beings brought into the world. I was not sure how I felt about that.

Of the remaining eight survivors that would stay here at the Temple, when they were healed enough to travel, Jin and his men would escort them home. We did not decide a time-span for this. It could only be determined once the four with-child women were ready, or once the most injured were healed enough. If necessary,

Jin's men would divide into two smaller groups for separate leaving dates.

When the men spoke, they assumed that Soul, Iris and I would return to Hollow with the final escort. Soul had glanced nervously at me when this was mentioned. She did not have good memories of Hollow. Neither did I. So, I simply said that it was something Soul and I would discuss. It was not something either of us had contemplated.

With arrangements in place and all of us seemingly satisfied that the right solutions had been found, the discussion ended.

The rest of that day I was busy. I had needed sleep. I had needed a proper bathe. I kept going back to the gloom of the central chamber, attempting, without success, to read the Book of Fate. And I kept visiting the twelve survivors. They slept deeply all day, so my visits were more to ensure they were healing well. Before the night fully drew in, I paid them another visit.

As I approached the healing room, instead of the usual hush, I could hear talking. I even heard someone laughing.

I entered the healing room to find Trell, Soul, several soldiers and the twelve survivors all awake and chatting. Four were still on recliners with healing sheets over them. They were sitting now, even Mags, eating from an array of healing foods. The rest were up and walking about. They had been bathed, and each now wore a short tunic made from bright kutu fabric. They were all still painfully thin, but they appeared much refreshed already. And, now that I looked, I could see the indicative curve of the bellies of those who were with kutu child.

As I entered, one of the women turned and came to greet me, throwing her arms around me.

"Thank you," she said.

At first I hadn't recognised her face, but I recognised her voice. It was Doe. The very first survivor we had met. She looked unrecognisable from the person who had cautiously come to us in the broken forest. She was still far too thin, and the outline of her shoulder bones poked at her tunic leading to scrawny arms, but she looked so much recovered already. Her mouth smiled, her large hazel eyes sparkled, and her wild hair was now a glossy taupe brown that fell around her face in large curls.

"You saved my brother," Doe hugged me again. "You saved us all. Soul has told us how you insisted on returning to the camp. If it was not for you, we would have ceased."

It was wonderful to see the change in Doe. All of the survivors now seemed in better spirits, even Mags, although she still would not talk directly to me. I stayed with them, listening to their chatter about returning home and their plans now that this world was rid of the Nigh-kutu. Doe mimicked spitting every time that the word Nigh-kutu was mentioned. Although I understood her abhorrence, it made me feel a sad for my Nigh-kutu friends; Jychanumun, Mardoch and Dragun. They were wonderful beings. It was true what Chia had once said: "The balance of greatness can be tipped either way." I hoped that one day, everyone would understand that.

I stayed in the healing room until the night was in its prime, eventually retiring from the merriment and returning to my room. Soul had pulled in additional recliners for her and Iris, and all were now lined up against the same wall, with Iris already sleeping deeply. My recliner was at the far end, by the external doors. The doors were ajar, letting in the autumn air. I welcomed the comfort of the soft cushions and drifted into sleep while listening to the subtle sounds of the forest outside.

I slept well that night; better than I had for many moons. For the first time in a long time, I had no nightmares. Just a deep, restful slumber.

I awoke much later than I expected. Soul was shaking my shoulder.

I didn't want to rouse. I wanted to stay in the comfort of the pillows and enjoy the pleasant sensation of rested sleepiness.

"I'll just doze a little bit longer." I turned over, closing my eyes again.

Soul laughed, shaking my shoulder again.

"Come on," she said. "I've been trying to wake you since sunrise. Have you forgotten that the army will be leaving soon? And the runners should have left already."

Oh, yes. I sat up.

"Or are you just going to let them leave without a word, after they thought they were going to die trying to save you?" Soul was smiling. I could see that she was teasing me.

Soul thrust a piece of iridescent white fabric in my direction and told me to hurry and dress. I was very happy to see that the piece of fabric was actually a gown of my own.

"Where did you find this?" I asked, amazed to see it. I didn't think any of my own clothes still existed.

"It had been slashed, but I mended it. I can't get used to that red gown. You make everything glow red around you. You illuminate everything with a crimson incandescence. It's disconcerting."

I laughed. It was true. I did.

"Crimson incandescence?" I said teasingly. "Who's talking like a kutu now?"

Soul conceded with a grump, happily so, telling me that if she talked like a kutu then it was clearly my fault anyway.

We were in good spirits as we went to see the bulk of the army from the Temple. I would be sad to see Jan leave, and all the others who I had come to call friends in this short space of time. But, I was happy for them to be in good health and going home to the things that were important to them.

Outside, Shaul and the group of runners were already waiting in their faction of six, talking amongst themselves. They no longer wore their wicker armour, opting instead for plain, loose clothing and hardy boots. They carried little more than a day's supply of food and water each, draped across their bodies in flat satchels. They would eat at the make-shift huts, they told me.

The runners were enthusiastically anxious to get going, so we bade them well on their journey. They left the valley in a steady trot and in good spirits.

Jan and the main bulk of the army were convening outside too. As the men gathered, they checked they had everything they needed. The four surviving women who were also leaving on this day were noticeable amongst the men. Their tunics were made from bright kutu fabrics that glowed under the morning sun, contrasting with the deep sandy brown and beige that the army wore. I said my goodbyes to them. One woman, Jenev, did not stop crying. They were tears of relief and happiness, not tears of sorrow.

Once those who were leaving were ready and waiting outside, I returned to the Temple's entrance, standing at the top of the steps. Jan gave me a long hug. He whispered how glad he was to have seen me, how he knew that the healing on his legs had been my doing and that he would be forever thankful. He then walked down the Temple steps, standing at the bottom, pausing.

Several hundred men stood in formation in front of him. They silenced.

Jan held up his spear.

"Everlong Iastha Tachra," he called, to my surprise.

"Everlong," the men shouted back, lifting their spears too.

Jan walked forward, past the formation, and spoke a word that I could not hear. The furthermost line of soldiers turned and, in single file, began walking up the valley's edge. It all happened in perfect synchronicity, and in silence bar their footsteps.

Very soon, the army was walking away, with Jan standing at the top of the valley as they filed past. Up the valley's slope and over the edge they marched. As the last man moved from view, about to pass the cusp of the valley, Jan turned before he joined them, saluting his brother. Jin returned the gesture.

All the army was now out of vision. I stood for a moment, listening to their fading footsteps. I had always felt an odd sense of emptiness with goodbyes. It was happy and sad at the same time. Jin was standing by my side, holding his wicker head protection, staring at it. Everyone else had gone back into the Temple.

"I have no use for this now," Jin spoke.

"I am glad of that," I replied. "I've seen enough war-wear to last a hundred life times. I am relieved you had no need to use it."

Jin contemplated this in silence. He had a thoughtful, poignant air about him. I guessed he was both happy and sad too.

"Would you like to pick punni berries with me?" I asked. "I want to replenish the store room while the bushes have so much fruit."

Jin nodded and we wandered across the valley.

On the far slopes, the punni bushes that had caught the most sun had a full quota of fat berries on them. Jin decided that it would be a good use of his wicker head protector, so we picked berries together, filling the new head-shaped basket.

"I wished to speak with you," Jin suddenly spoke, "to ask if you were intending on returning to Hollow with us."

"I had not planned to go to Hollow," I replied.

"Hollow has changed much since you last saw it," he explained. "We have irrigation to the fields and orchards, which are expanding. We have created a list called the Rules of Fairness, which apply to all townsfolk. No one is forced to take a mate. We select chores that suit the person, and certainly no burnings or exiling of those who are infirm. And we have built our own place of learning. Not a magnificent building like this, of course, but our own version. We have two teachers. People come from many villages to attend."

He stopped, waiting for my response.

"It does sound as if Hollow has changed a great deal," I said. "I'd happily visit to see the wonderful changes, but this valley is good for me." I paused picking berries and looked around. "It's my home," I simply added.

"I understand," Jin replied. "But would you just consider it? Perhaps to return to Hollow and see how you feel about it? If you didn't like it, I'd escort you back here whenever you wanted."

"Thank you. I'll give it consideration."

Jin fell silent once again.

"Once, I let you walk away," he spoke after a while. "You probably do not remember it; it was when we first met. I do not think I could let you walk away so easily this time."

"I'm not going anywhere," I said.

"Tachra," Jin tutted, "You know exactly what I mean."

"Yes," I said, feeling self-conscious. "I do."

I knew then that this was the reason I felt so. . . so something, around Jin. He had always made my heart flurry. But how could I ever consider pairing with any man? Surely that would be dishonourable both to him and to Jychanumun.

Jin sensed my hesitancy.

"Just give my words deliberation," he said. "There is no hurry. I'll be here for a while. Anyway," he changed the subject, "what say we take some of these berries to the remaining survivors? Punni berries are always best when freshly picked and warm from the sun."

I gladly agreed, and together we headed to the healing room, where it transpired that several soldiers and Soul were already gathered. All those freshly picked berries got eaten that day, and none ever saw the store room.

The rest of the day passed swiftly. As did the proceeding days. And, as the days passed, a new routine developed.

To start each day, I slept late, past sun-break. The spirit of Meah was usually curled up on my recliner when I awoke. She would venture into the forest, and I would take my morning bathe in the lake. I found it was the best way for me to wake up.

Once dressed, I would visit the remaining survivors. I would stay with them until high-sun, talking about anything and everything. Jin would usually join us, and he came to be the centre of attention with his stories. The survivors were healing well. Only Mags was still confined to her bed, but she too was mending. Because the four with-child women, Pallyn, Doe, Gale and Coran, could not use healing sheets, and my Earth energy gave them nausea, I would spend time teaching them how to focus their thoughts to heal their minds. It helped them greatly.

After attending to the survivors, I would visit the wildcats in the forest. Sometimes I forgot that Meah was spirit only. We would run together, chasing leaves, and time would pass like a breath. Sometimes I would take Iris into the forest with me to teach her how to read the signs of nature. She learnt very fast.

From mid-afternoon, I spent time alone in the central chamber. I would sit staring at the Book of Fate, trying to force my mind to understand the strange language it was written in. The understanding did not come, but still I tried. And even though I could not read the words, I never tired from looking at that beautifully ornate cube.

The kutu kitchens had become the new gathering place, with everyone convening at sundown for nourishment. Even Mags was wheeled in, on a makeshift arrangement of kutu chair and manoeuvrable wheels. That time was always relaxed and enjoyable.

My last task of each day was a private one. I would return to the central chamber, where I had collected a selection of items to remind me of the kutu: a corvidae feather for Jychanumun. A piece of brown clay for Dragun. Green jade for Mardoch. One of Chia's gloves. Red kutu fabric for Orion. Kraniel's retuning disc. A golden arrow for Stanze. The discarded Anumi helmet for all the Anumi and, at the end of the line, I placed the communication port. Each night I would try contacting the kutu via that port. When none responded, I would whisper to the Old One to keep my friends safe. It was a sentimental gesture, and I knew that. Nevertheless, it made me feel better.

Finally, at the end of each day, I would return to my room and fall asleep holding Jychanumun's armlets. I would sleep deeply, closing my mind to nightmares, letting my slumbers heal my body instead.

The days rolled by with this new routine.

The weather stayed fair.

The survivors healed.

I grew stronger.

On the thirty-seventh day, after the bulk of the army had left, the eight survivors were offered their own rooms. All bar Mags were now healthy enough not to need monitoring in the healing room. Most happily accepted their own space. The four with-child women chose to take a room together.

On the thirty-ninth day, the resident men began clearing up the valley. The discarded kutu weaponry and armour was carried over the lip of the valley and into a pit in the rock-land. I also sent the little kutu pod home that day. When I had touched the pod, stroking its side as I would a horse, I had sensed its pining. So, assured it that it could find its way back to the kutu home-world, I bade it goodbye and watched it disappear into the afternoon sky.

On the forty-third day, I made my first breakthrough with the Book of Fate. I had been day-dreaming while staring at the black cube when I glanced a moving word that I recognised: Iastha. I only recognised that word because Jychanumun had once shown me how to write my name in many ancient languages. He had called this one the Language of Intent. At first, recognising a word had excited me. But then I quickly realised that the Language of

Intent was like none other. I only understood intent via emotion and sub-conscious thought from living things. A book had none of those. A book could not have intent. It was my first breakthrough. I hoped it was not the last.

On day forty-four, three of the survivors left the Temple to go home. The two men, Doro and Erek, and one of the women, Linsi. All three had been near dead when we found them. Jin allocated ten of his twenty men to escort them and they left the valley, happy to be returning to Meadsins to help rebuild their town.

On day forty-eight, Mags took her first unaided steps. She was so intent on being well enough to go home that she stubbornly made herself walk around the entire valley's edge. It took her all day. That evening we celebrated. I arranged for everyone to have food outside and we lit lanterns and found some honey mead. It was an evening filled with tales and laughter. Even I told stories, recounting the day when I had first met the kutu. When Soul joined in, playing the part of the humans they had taken to examine, I laughed so much that it made my stomach hurt.

On day fifty, we made a discovery. Of the four women who carried a kutu child, one of them was carrying twins: Pallyn. She was shocked. I was not so surprised, as the shadow energy in her was strongest. The three other with-child women consoled her. The bond between them had grown strong.

On day fifty-five, I heard shouting coming from the front of the Temple. It was shouts of excitement. I slipped from the central chamber and ran down the corridor to see what the commotion was about.

Standing in the Temple entrance were Jin and several soldiers with two sandy-clad men. One of the men was bent over, panting heavily. The other was laying on his back on the floor, gesturing frantically while Jin poured water over his face, telling Jin to "keep it coming." I saw it was two of the six runners, Shaul and Brennal.

Shaul pulled a sack from his back and put it down. He was handed water and paused his gasping to take long, welcoming swigs.

"Herbs," Shaul panted, indicating towards the sack. "One portion per pouch inside. To be eaten. Not to be taken until nightfall and sleep."

Soul hurried to join us, carrying more water. I looked out of the door, expecting to see the remaining runners heading up the Temple's steps. No more were in sight.

"The others?" I asked, concerned.

"Returning to Hollow," Jin informed me, "there was a rock-slide. Two were injured and returned to the closest in-betweener hut."

"They'll be fine," Shaul added. "A broken ankle and a head cut. I left Sachan and his brother with them; they know healing."

Shaul moved to sit with his back against the wall, still drinking deeply and with relish. Brennal picked himself up and joined him. Other than their immediate breathlessness, they were in good form; thin, but strong, with lean muscles like a sprint-beast.

"Well done," I said. "You've made short work of a long, difficult journey."

"Easy," Shaul shrugged confidently. "Although we lost two days with the rock slide. How many days have we been gone?"

"Fifty-five," I replied. "Trell will beam with pride."

"To the skies with pride," Shaul grinned. "Where is he? He bet that I could not do it in less than two moons. I made him bet his best spear." He laughed. "I'm going to plant that spear outside my hut and hang a shirt on it when I get home."

Trell had been at the back at the Temple with his maps. He ran up the corridor, slowing to a casual yet proud walk when he saw his son. He was indeed beaming. He greeted Shaul with an uncharacteristic hug.

Seeing that they were well and being tended to, Soul picked up the sack, inspecting its contents, and then tucked it under her arm.

Together, we left the men to their merriment and headed deeper into the Temple. Although it had been fifty-five days since the runners had left, we had not discussed how we would proceed if and when they returned.

"This," Soul indicated to the sack of herbs, "I do not feel easy about. I've heard of these herbs. I've heard they're not pleasant. They will make pain."

"Do the women know this?" I asked.

"Yes. The herbs originate from Meadsins. Before Hollow was a good town, some women chose not to have so many children rather than send some to Hollow. They know."

"I do not," I confessed. "On this, you'll need to direct me."

"I'll do my best," Soul nodded. She paused. "There is something that concerns me. I have only seen the herbs used on women whose bellies barely show. Our four are larger. The herbs may not work. Either way, taking them will be especially painful."

"I wish they could use healing sheets; they'd help," I considered. "Or my Earth energy, but they say it makes them feel sick. We'll just have to inform them so they're aware. They must all be sure of their choices. And if they go ahead," I added, "we must all be prepared for a long and difficult night."

Together, we walked in grim silence to the four women's quarters.

The four with-child women had picked a bright, quiet room on the ground floor. It was the same room that Chia had used for meditation. He used to say that it had peaceful chi. That was good. I got the feeling we would need all the peaceful chi we could get.

The door to their room was closed. I knocked.

After the four women had shouted 'hello' in unison, Soul and I entered.

Pallyn, Doe, Gale and Coran were sitting together, sewing. When Soul and I walked in holding a dusty sack, they knew that the runners had returned.

"These are to be taken at nightfall, just before sleep," Soul explained as the four women opened the herb sack, inspecting the contents.

There were four portions of herbs, each in separate bags. I too opened one, inspecting its contents. The herbs smelt very bitter. They didn't smell like something that would be good for any flesh.

"Please," I requested, looking to the four women, "do all be sure of your choices in taking these."

"And do know that there's a chance they might not work," Soul added.

"I took them once," Doe admitted. "They worked for me."

"I've heard they cause great pains," Gale considered.

"Oh yes," Doe's eyes went wide as she nodded.

Doe began telling the others in grisly detail how agonising it had been and how long the pain had gone on for. I left them to their talk, deciding to look for anything in the Temple that might help ease their impending distress.

As I turned the corridor away from the women's room, I heard someone calling my name. I turned to see Pallyn, holding her overly large belly, trying to catch up with me.

"May we talk?" Pallyn asked as she approached. She glanced up and down the corridor, looking anxiously. "Somewhere private?"

"Of course," I replied, taking her arm. We turned and headed back the way we came. I explained that if she didn't mind the gloom, we would never be disturbed in the central chamber.

Once in the central chamber, Pallyn began pacing. Even if I could not see the turmoil of her energy, she was obviously fretful about something.

"I've lost my mate. He died in the Nigh-kutu camp," Pallyn suddenly spurted out.

"I know. I'm sorry," I replied.

"We had lost six babies before they were born. Each one I could sense I was going to lose. They felt weak and sickly, and my body has never been a strong one. But these twins," she touched her stomach, "I feel their strength. They do not want to die."

I took a deep breath, considering.

"You have my support for whatever you choose," I said, "but I cannot tell you what to do. You must decide."

"I know," Pallyn sighed. She then paused, looking around the chamber. "I came to the Temple once," she continued, "Although you were away visiting family. I remember the first time I met a kutu. His name was Orion, and it was like looking at sunset and sunrise at the same time. And I met a Nigh-kutu too. His eyes sparkled like laughter. He was beautiful too, yet he was Nigh-kutu. You yourself have said that the Nigh-kutu are capable of as much beauty as the Shaa-kutu." Pallyn paused, putting her arms over her belly protectively. "What is to say that my twins would be terrible beings? These children may be beings of beauty."

I did not say anything. I knew that right there and then, anything I said could sway Pallyn's decision.

"Can you tell?" Pallyn asked, looking at me beseechingly. "Can you tell if my babies are bad beings?"

I calmly cupped Pallyn's face in my hands and spoke gently, looking into her eyes so she would truly hear.

"My heart wants to soothe you and tell you words of comfort," I said, "but no one should tell you words just because you want, or don't want, to hear them. No one can say what any child will become. Every child is unique. Yours especially. This is a first: babies that are both kutu and human. These are your children. This is your decision."

Pallyn seemed to slump.

"I don't want to kill them," she said miserably. "These are *my* babies. I've felt this way since Soul told me it was twins. But I couldn't say anything. What would the others think?"

"I believe," I replied, "that they would understand your choice. They have grown to love you."

"I want them," she stated.

"Then you have made your choice," I replied.

"Yes, I have," Pallyn sighed, closing her eyes, as if just saying the words was a relief. "I'll tell the others. After that," she smiled nervously, "how they treat me is their choice."

At Pallyn's request, I accompanied her back to her room. Her energy was in turmoil. She could barely walk for her wobbly legs. She was nervous and anxious and excited and relieved, amongst many other things. Even the shadow within her seemed to react, as if sensing her decision.

When we arrived back at the women's room, Pallyn immediately told the others her decision. She blurted it out before her lips could silence her. On hearing the news, Doe instantly declared that Pallyn was being stupid. Gale was very sympathetic, rubbing her friend's shoulder and telling her it would be alright. Coran became very quiet, listening to everyone else talk.

"I'm not going to take the herbs either," Coran suddenly voiced.

"What?" Doe seemed even more outraged. "You want to have a Nigh-kutu monster?"

"It won't be a monster," Coran replied nervously.

"Has Pallyn's choice swayed you?"

"No."

Doe looked confused, shaking her head to herself as if trying to loosen her thoughts. "Then you're the fool," she frowned.

I glanced at Coran, seeing now her quiet resolve.

"Are you good?" I asked.

"Yes," Coran nodded.

"All of you?" I looked to all four women. "Have you all made your decisions?"

All four women nodded. They had independently made their

choices. Pallyn and Coran did not wish to take the herbs. Doe and Gale did. I felt the resolution from each of them.

There was little more that could be done until nightfall, so Soul and I left the four women and headed back to my room. Ahead of us was a long, arduous night. We decided to rest while we could.

But back in my room, while Soul lightly slumbered, I found it impossible to relax. Instead, I spent my time picking and poking at various things with restless interest. I was too concerned about many things to concentrate on any one thing. I was concerned that there would be much pain for the women who took the herbs. I was concerned that for those who chose to keep their child, giving birth to a very large half-kutu could be dangerous. I was concerned that no one could say what type of creature a half-breed would be, or become. That was if it lived at all: once the child was born and no longer protected by its mother's energy, its shadow energy could just dissipate, just like a kutu's. Whatever the outcome of this situation, it would bring difficulties.

Eventually, I climbed onto my recliner and I too drifted into restless sleep. I did not dream. Nevertheless, something in my slumbers felt wrong. The sense of wrongness churned through me until it urged my mind, forcing me to wake. It felt like the world was screaming.

I came to with a start. It was early dusk outside. I quickly shook Soul from her slumber, telling her that I felt something was amiss. Together, we hurried from the room.

I sent my senses through the Temple, searching for the source of the disturbance. There was a chaotic energy everywhere, as if the Temple was arguing with itself. Through the discord, one energy shouted louder than all else. Its shout was not aggressive, more pleading, as if beaten into desperate submission. From its colours, I knew it was Gale.

It did not take long to locate Gale's distinct mix of shadow-kutu and human energy. She was somewhere near the kutu kitchens, in the great cellars, and in pain.

As soon as we were at the top of the deep stone steps that led down to the cellars, I could hear Gale groaning. The noises from her energy and mind were far greater than the muted whimpers that spilled from her lips.

I ran down to Gale's side. She was positioned halfway down the steps, on one of the wide turning squares, curled up, holding her stomach. A plate of flat breads was strewn across the floor.

"It hurts," Gale gasped. "Hurts too much to scream."

"It must be the herbs," Soul said to me.

"No," Gale interjected, wincing. "I've not taken the herbs yet. None of us have."

As Gale and Soul spoke, I looked into Gale's belly. The child within her was very active. It appeared to be kicking, as if trying to fight its way out. It was as if the unborn child was fighting against Gale.

I knelt by her side, touching her face so that she looked at me.

"Are you injured elsewhere?" I asked.

"I don't know," Gale gasped. She was clearly in a great deal of pain. "I slipped."

"I am just going to check you for wounds," I told her.

With the lightest touch, using my hands and eyes more than my Earth sense, I examined Gale's limbs, torso and head, checking for breakages or damage that would prevent her from being moved. She had scrapes down one leg, with dust and grit embedded into the cuts from slipping on the steps. She had a few bruises that were yet to colour. And she had three broken fingers on one hand where she had tried to soften her fall. There were no other injuries from the fall. But when I lifted her tunic, her belly was moving. And where her belly was moving, it was already showing signs of bruising.

I put the smallest, gentlest healing energy into Gale's torso, avoiding the unborn child. Immediately the movement of her belly increased. She let out a scream of pain. I quickly pulled the energy back.

I looked at Soul. "She has broken fingers on that hand," I indicated. "The child inside her fights. It fights against her."

"We need to get her somewhere more comfortable," Soul directed.

"Don't move me!" Gale exclaimed.

"You are in birth time," Soul said calmly. "It has just started. Your child wants to come this night. We must get you to a recliner."

But Gale would not move, fighting off the attempts to lift her.

Soul changed position, sitting and placing Gale's head on her lap.

"I'll stay here. You rally the men experienced with birthing," she told me. "And bring cushions. This child comes tonight, no matter what anyone else wants."

I quickly headed back up the stone steps, away from the great cellars and towards Jin's room. Before I got to his location, two soldiers ran around the corner.

"You were not in your room," one soldier said. "The three women, Coran, Doe and Pallyn, have all started signs of birthing."

"All of them?" I asked, taken aback.

"Yes, all."

"So has Gale; she is half way down the cellar steps," I hurriedly informed them. "She is in pain. Get one of the litters and move her into the room with the other three. Be gentle with her," I added. "She is hurt and something is amiss."

The soldiers nodded and immediately headed towards the storage rooms to collect a litter.

I returned to Gale to oversee her being delicately transported back to her room. There, along with Doe, Coran and Pallyn, the soldiers who knew birthing were now in attendance. The room was a bustle of activity and they were all already busy. There were six soldiers, plus Mags, who said she'd delivered all her children's children. Trell took charge. He had previously talked to me about the fact he had delivered many of the babes of Hollow. I was glad to see he already had a plan of action if events came to this.

Soul and I were ushered from the room, being told that it was already too cramped and that they knew what they were doing. We left, deciding some cool evening air would do our nerves good.

At the Temple entrance, Jin was sitting alone on the top step, just overlooking the dusk-lit valley.

"You've been told to become scarce too," he said when Soul and I joined him.

"Yes. Although in this, I think I am glad to be considered useless," I replied.

Jin's expression was grave. "What are their chances of survival?"

I considered the odds. "We can't use healing sheets. I can't use Earth energy. I have hope, but only time will tell. I feel useless."

Jin nodded, so did Soul. None of us were accustomed to feeling this way.

"It's coincidence that all are in labour at the same time," Jin remarked. "Did the women take the herbs and bring this on?"

"No," I replied, "they did not."

I decided to voice all my concerns. "Nor is it coincidence," I added. "I think those unborn children sensed that some of their lives could be at risk. I think they knew. The energy feels as if they fight for life. Somehow, they are aware of each other, and already those unborn babies are working as a unit."

"That does not bring me comfort," Jin said.

I did not reply. All of us were aware that these children had the potential to be powerfully destructive beings. Already they felt like warriors.

We sat atop the Temple steps, the three of us, and time gradually moved on. Dusk gave way to night. The stars glowed. The stars gave way to the first signs of dawn.

None of us wanted to sleep. None of us could sleep even if we wanted to. All we could do was wait for news. Even Iris came to join us in her nightwear, sitting patiently until the wait grew too long for her and she fell asleep sitting up. As the night surrendered entirely, the first rays of sunlight cast shadows into the awakening valley.

From my position sitting atop the Temple steps, I could turn to see into the Temple, down the long corridor and to the door that led to the four women's room. I regularly glanced back, checking for any sign of change. All had been quiet for some time. The door had remained shut since Soul and I had left. Finally, I heard it open.

I turned to see Trell emerge. He had blood on his tunic. He looked exhausted. He acknowledged me with a smile-less nod. Instead of joining us, he held the door open.

From the open door, one of the soldiers emerged, his face grave. He was carrying a litter. On the litter was a cloth-covered, adult-sized body, with another of the soldiers carrying the other end. Sombrely, as Trell closed the door, they headed towards us.

I moved, allowing the men carrying the litter to pass.

No one spoke. The men looked grim as they headed down the Temple steps. Trell came to sit with us.

"Pallyn, Doe and Coran are doing well," Trell said. "Exhausted, but well. Their bodies are now accepting healing sheets, so are mending. But," he shook his head, "Gale did not survive. Nor her child. I tried everything. Everything."

We all fell silent for a moment, letting the news sink in.

Trell rubbed his forehead. He was very perplexed. I put my hand on his shoulder.

"When I last saw Gale, it was as if mother and child were locked in conflict," I said. "Neither wanted to submit."

Trell nodded. "Her body could not cope. The child suffocated within her."

"The other children?" I barely dare to ask.

"All healthy boys."

I glanced; an apprehensive look.

"They all look like normal children," Trell responded. "So far, they sound and function like normal children too. But," he added, "they are larger than any I have delivered before. And a strange thing was," he paused, "all were birthed, and let out their first cry, at the exact same time. Gale's child would have been a boy too."

We fell silent again as the men carried the litter holding Gale's body across the valley. They gently placed it on the grass.

"I have said to bury mother and child just beyond the valley's edge," Trell sighed. "Is it appropriate they be buried together?"

"Yes," I nodded. "It is only empty flesh."

And I knew that it was. As I had sat watching the litter carrying Gale's body being transported across the valley, my true vision had noticed something else: Gale's essence. Gale had retained a soul.

The soul that was Gale now stood in the valley next to her empty flesh. She was looking directly at me. She looked confused.

I excused myself from the others, walked down the Temple steps, and stood next to Gale's essence.

It's alright, I silently told her.

Is it? she asked. She could hear me. *The others couldn't see me. I kept trying to tell them I was here. But,* Gale looked down at the cloth covered corpse, *I know that is my body, so I'm not quite sure where 'here' is.*

For some people, ceasing is not the end, I explained. *It is just becoming something different. There is a place where you can go. It is a place of beauty, called Elysium. It is where souls can go to be happy, reunited.*

Gale looked unsure.

You can leave whenever you wish, I assured her. *If you wish to go there, I can call someone to guide you.*

Yet I did not need to call my father. From the edge of the valley I noticed him, the spirit of my father: strong, handsome, marching his long, purposeful strides, walking towards me as if he had merely been toiling the land for the day. Next to my father walked the soul of another, a young man with sandy hair who I did not recognise. As father stopped, his serene gaze held upon me, the unknown man continued forward.

The unknown man walked up to Gale and held out his hand. Gale took it. She was smiling. He was smiling. These two clearly knew and loved one another, their energies winding around each other as if in a gentle caress. Together they walked away, joining my father, and then all three walked up the valley, their energies fading from view. They didn't look back. They didn't need to. Nothing in Elysium needed to look back.

I paused for a moment. Even though I knew that Gale would be happy, that my father and even my mother were happy, I wanted to mourn. I was happy with my beautiful Elysium, yet grieved for another physical loss. Life here was so fragile. Time was so short.

I looked over at Iris and Soul, sitting atop the steps. They were watching me, but they had not seen what I had seen. Iris was under Soul's arm, like a small bird under a wing. They were luminescent to my true vision in blues and pale gold. Their souls were already strong and defined. Jin too was luminous, in vivid shades of teal and silver that wove around him, curling outwards like the flames of a sun. From his colours, I could see that he was honourable, passionate and strong. Trell too shone in many shades of deep green. Peaceful. Earthy. Giving. I could already see their souls. All of them. Together, they looked like beautiful, glowing butterflies, poised and ready for flight.

I realised then that we humans were not born with souls. Something in us, some strength, bond, or good intent, created one. But not everyone had the feelings or intentions strong enough to create a soul. We, as humans, became the sum of our choices. All humans, any human, had the potential to be more than the mere harvesting bios that the kutu had designed them to be.

Surely, I considered, this was something that Arrunn had not foreseen. He had not equated the strength of Iris' will, Wirrel's passion, Soul's love, Jin's intent, Trell's altruism. These strengths, just like Gale's and my father's, meant that some humans had developed to have undying souls.

A wave of realisation washed through me there and then: it was humans, not kutu, who had the capacity to tip the balance in the future war. The warring between the shadow dwelling Nigh-kutu and the light dwelling Shaa-kutu could remain equally balanced. It was nothing to do with numbers, but intention. Yet the beings that could make or break that balance were here, my fellow humans. Every single human had the potential to be more than they were made to be – to create a soul, to become immortal. Every single human had choice.

And here was I; even I had not seen that before this point. I saw it now, like a perfectly balanced equation with an element that could make the difference: the unknown. In this instance, in the war between shadow and light that was still to come, the unknown was humans.

I must have stood staring up at the Temple's entrance for some time, deep in my contemplations. Soul came to join me, asking if I was well. I had watched her walk down the steps, her luminous energy glowing around her like a gold and blue moon. As she approached, her energy tentatively moved ahead of her, brushing against mine.

"I am very well," I assured my friend. "I have realised something I had not realised before. This," I waved my hand around the valley, "this world is special, unique. And everyone, every single human being, has the ability to be great. Perhaps even greater than a kutu. I see now that it is humans and their choices that will tip the balance in any future war."

Soul took my arm. "But that's good, isn't it?" she asked.

"I believe so," I said. "Our choices could make the difference. But humans are such a young race. Young with the potential of greatness. And the balance of any greatness can be tipped either way."

"I think I understand," Soul contemplated. "But what about these new babes? There is now something new in this world. Half kutu, half human. Where do they fit in?"

"I do not yet know," I replied. "But I shall know when I see."

TWENTY-SEVEN

The Murderesses

I quietly opened the door to the room where Pallyn, Doe and Coran were with their newborns, conscious of not wanting to wake the exhausted new mothers. To my surprise, all the mothers were awake, wrapped in healing sheets, with a generous array of food and drink by their recliners. All appeared well.

I remained quiet and observed.

Pallyn sat dozing in the nearest recliner, two bundles in a make-shift crib by her side. Next to her was Coran, sitting up, engrossed by the swaddled babe in her arms. At the far end, Doe was half sitting, half lying, her back turned to the crib by her side.

I unobtrusively sent my energy outwards, looking at the energy of the newborns. They felt like human and kutu. But, whereas humans had energies that were based on light, like the Shaa-kutu, these four babies had a shadow-based energy. They were far more aware of their surroundings than any normal human baby would be. It was as if they already had souls. Yes, I was sure this was true.

I opened my true vision further, tentatively feeling for the potential of what these four new souls could become. Suddenly, an image came into my mind so strong that I could barely tell whether I was still in the room or part of the vision. My inner sight saw the babies as four young men. They stood, shoulder to shoulder; tall, noble and rippling with energy that was both powerful and peaceful. They were wonderful beings: beings of beauty and ascendancy, beings that embraced the best of both Nigh-kutu and human. In that vision, I loved and trusted them, and the love was so pure that I felt it even now.

I pulled away from the vision. Pallyn had looked up and was smiling.

"Would you prefer that I come back later?" I asked, suddenly conscious of the vacant expression I probably wore.

"Oh no, come look," Pallyn serenely replied. She leant over, pulling the cloth from the faces of the two swaddled babies in the crib, indicating to me. "They are both beautiful," she smiled.

And indeed the two twin boys were beautiful. Trell was right. They did look like normal human babies, although they did not look like newborns. Both Pallyn's two sons were awake. Their eyes were open. They had the same eyes of darkest brown, and the same black, wavy hair. The only apparent thing that differed in them was that one had a nose covered in freckles. They laid next to each other in their crib, looking at their surrounds and then each other. I was sure they were smiling. When I looked with my true vision, those two boys had a very unusual energy: shadowy yes, but within the shadow it morphed between silver and grey. It looked like their energy was breathing.

I see you, I spoke to the newborns with my mind. "Have you decided what will you call them?" I asked Pallyn aloud.

Pallyn stroked her babies' hair away from their faces. "Yes. Although I always imagined that I would call my first son after my mate, these sons are mine alone. I've named them Pall and Lyn."

"I like that," I said.

"Pall is the one with the stars painted on his nose," Pallyn added.

I liked that too. Now I would know how to tell them apart.

"And what about you, Coran?" I moved to Coran's side. "Have you decided a name?"

Coran's son was contented in her arms. His large green eyes were already open too, watching her. He had a thick mop of curly golden hair. His physical appearance was like a baby version of Coran. He, too, looked just like a normal human baby, but his energy was already strong. I could see vivid swirls of green and gold within his shadow. And, while I was observing him, he looked at me. He knew I was watching him and in return, he was watching me.

"I want to give my son a name to be remembered, because he will do great things that people will remember." Coran announced. "Tachra," she asked, "is there a kutu word for memory?"

"There is," I considered. "The Nigh and Shaa words for memory are quite similar. In Nigh it is 'ach-viir-an' and in Shaa it is 'viir-iel'. They both have 'viir' as the directed intent of the words."

Coran laughed. "I have no idea what you've just said," she shrugged, still laughing. "But I like the sound of the word 'viir'. And he," she looked at her son's expression, "seems to like it too. That's what I shall call my son. Viir."

Having stayed a moment more with Coran, I moved on to see Doe. Doe had been very quiet, lying on her side, facing away from her child. Her energy was a turmoil of negativity. Without realising it, she had put up an energy barrier between her and her son. She clearly was not happy that she had given birth to this child.

I sat by Doe's side, talking quietly so that no one else could hear. I told her to give herself time and that she would heal. I told her that no one was going to force her to look after her son, if she did not wish it. I also told her that he, along with the other newborns, was a beautiful being who would grow to be a beautiful man. But, I also said, if she chose not to look after him, we would find someone else who would. Doe listened, but she did not give an opinion.

"Can I do anything to help?" I asked her.

Doe did not reply.

I placed another healing sheet across her, hoping its effects would soothe her mind as well as her body.

Iris had happily entered the room, cooing over the newborns. She came over to see Doe's baby. He was another beautiful child, with thick mid-brown hair and wide blue eyes, just like Doe. His energy felt gentle, almost earthy, in tones of sandy brown.

"What is this one going to be called?" Iris asked. She began playing with the child, making him curl his hands around her fingers.

"I'm not calling it anything," Doe tersely replied without turning around.

"Oh you must give him a name," Coran brightly chirped. "Everyone has to have a name."

"*It,*" Doe emphasised the word, "Is not an everyone. I'm not naming it."

"He has lovely brown hair, just like yours. You could call him Brune," Coran encouraged.

Doe did not reply.

I sensed the tension in the room tighten.

"Then how about we call him Brune; just for now," I cajoled, trying to placate. "You are right, Coran. Everyone should have a name. With the sound of a name, all molecules move when that sound is made. To each of us, our name is the word we can hear through space and time. A name, our name, is the sound that stirs us."

As if sensing the tension, Brune started crying.

Doe did not turn around.

"He wants to be held," Coran suggested to Doe.

Doe ignored both Brune's cries and Coran's suggestion.

"I'll hold him awhile." Coran indicated for me to pass the babe to her.

I picked up Brune and passed him to Coran, so she sat with a swaddled babe in each arm. Brune silenced immediately.

"You'll feel better soon," I whispered to Doe. "If I can do anything to help, just ask. Meanwhile, would you like to be moved to a room on your own?"

"Just leave me alone," Doe managed to say, and then she would say no more.

Sensing that Doe was not going to accept her child any time soon, if at all, I moved the crib from her side and towards Coran. Coran nodded acceptingly, giving me a look that said a great deal more. She would look after Brune too.

"I can see the truth of these four babes," I spoke to all the women. "And be assured, all of you, that these four boys will all grow to be beings of beauty in energy, spirit, mind and flesh."

"I know," Coran smiled, and I could tell from her eyes that yes, she did indeed know.

"Can we get you, any of you, anything?" I asked, sensing it was time to go.

"Just sleep," Pallyn replied. "I am so tired."

Coran nodded in agreement.

I sent them all soothing, peaceful energy, noting that the Earth energy no longer had an adverse reaction on either child or mother. And then, having calmed them so that they could sleep if they wished, I left.

As the sun rose to its highest point, the men dug a grave to bury Gale and her child. I collected flowers and leaves for the burial place. Jin taught me how to weave, and we crafted leaf stems into garlands wound with wild flowers. It was a bright, cool day and I told Jin and Soul what I had seen of Gale's soul and about Elysium. It was the first time I had spoken about Elysium in any detail. Jin and Soul listened with fascination.

"Will I go to Elysium when I cease?" Soul asked.

"My friend, I have no doubt that you will. How could souls go to Elysium if Soul, the namesake, is not there?"

"But what if you cease first?" Soul asked worriedly. "Who will guide me there?"

"All souls can guide," I replied. I laughed. "Although my father seems to have taken the task upon himself. But if I cease first, I will come and find you; if not, you can always find me."

Soul made me promise on that. I didn't doubt that with the connection between us, I would feel her in both life and death.

Having buried Gale and her son, I chose some solace in the forest. I came across a fledgling with an injured wing and healed it, although birds were never easy to work with. I did not usually interfere with the balance of nature, but I could not turn my back on it either. So, I asked the wildcats to give me distance, much to their disapproval, and by the time the evening beckoned, the fledgling flew to join its parents. And then, watching the wildcats roll with undignified fervour in the leaves that the bird had hopped in brought a welcome smile to my lips.

That evening, the mothers took supper in their room with their children rather than joining us in the kitchens. They were still very tired. I paid them a visit to say goodnight before retiring.

Doe's attitude continued to trouble me. I had sent her a great deal of soothing energy throughout the day, yet her tension and anger had not abated. It was as if she found strength and power in her self-pity. It was as if she enjoyed her resentment. She took her tension out on the other women, snapping at them with snide remarks at every opportunity. Pallyn and Coran were very tolerant, but I knew it still affected them. Although Doe said that she did not want to move to a room on her own, I could see that we might have to move her anyway, if her foul mood did not calm. I had faith that her mind would heal. I just hoped that she wanted it to heal.

Mags especially fussed over Doe and every time I visited, the two were in hushed conversation. Mags seemed to be the only person Doe wanted to talk to and would be affable with, so I appreciated Mags tending to her, but was wary of Mags' continued pessimism. I hoped that the two women would help to heal each other. Doe had not bonded with her child and did not want to. She wouldn't even look at him. Her resentment towards him was almost palpable, making snide remarks when the babe cried or needed something. Mags seemed to encourage Doe's bitterness. So, Coran oversaw to Brune's needs as well as the needs of her own son, Viir.

Something else, something more than Doe's attitude, was troubling me before I retired for the night. I had spent much of the evening with an anxiety that I could not work out. I had learnt enough about myself not to ignore such a feeling, but no matter how much I tried to look at it to decipher it, I still couldn't uncover what it was.

I still had not fallen into slumber when Soul turned in for the night. It was very late – nearer dawn than dusk. Soul crept into the room, sliding quietly onto her recliner.

"Is all well?" I asked, turning around.

"Did I wake you? Sorry."

"No. I can't sleep."

"All is better than well," Soul said. "Doe has finally eaten. I was starting to think she would starve herself. And even better, when I just checked on them, she had Brune sleeping next to her."

"I think that is good," I replied. My head told me that I should feel relieved, but for some reason, I was not.

"Sleep well," Soul bade me.

"Goodnight."

Within moments, Soul's long, deep breaths told me that she slept. I closed my eyes, determined that I too would have some rest.

I did eventually sleep, but it was not a sleep for my mind so much as a rest for my flesh while my mind roamed. I dreamt that I wandered the Temple. I knew that it was a dream. I knew that the dream was real. Sometimes when I dreamt, it was not a dream but my energy moving from my flesh, roaming, restless or curious. In this dream, my energy and awareness were roaming the Temple.

In my dream, I heard whispering. I was drawn to the source. The source of the whispering was Mags and Doe. I stood invisibly, listening, watching.

Mags and Doe were standing at the Temple entrance in their nightwear, in the dark. They stood close, leaning into each other. They were talking in hushed tones.

"What about the lake?" Doe suggested. "I can just say I tripped."

"Yes," Mags replied. "You were taking him for a walk and stumbled. We could even do the others tonight too."

"Ach," Doe rolled her eyes. "I tried to move Coran's hand from hers, but she stirred. And Pallyn's cry whenever I go near them. I'll be heard if I get them."

"There'll be time enough," Mags said. "A chance will present itself. I'll see to it. They'll just look like accidents."

I knew that they were taking about the newborns. I became aware that Doe was holding Brune in her arms. Even in the dream, I knew those words were real. I knew this was happening now, as I slept.

Doe and Mags were planning something terrible for Doe's son and for all the newborns. I think they were going to kill Brune. No, they *were* going to kill him.

I had to wake up.

Wake up, I told myself.

Now. Wake up!

I struggled to rouse my flesh, pulling my energy and thoughts back into my body, forcing it to react.

I got up, my heart racing with an anger of injustice. I did not have time to find footwear, to wake Soul, to find help anywhere. I had to act now.

I slipped out of the external doors and into the edge of the woodland, running as fast as my sleepy legs would carry me. I raced along the edge of the Temple, ignoring the brambles trying to catch my feet. By the skies, why did this building have to be so large!

I got to the front of the Temple, just in time to see Mags and Doe carrying a bundle – I guessed Brune – across the valley and towards the lake.

"Stop!" I shouted, running towards them.

I could feel the protective anger welling within me. "Mags, Doe, stop! I can see you. Stop now!"

Mags and Doe stopped in their tracks, turning to face me. Their expressions were filled with guilt and resentment.

I raced towards them, snatching Brune from Doe's arms.

"We were just going for a walk round the lake," Mags lied. "We couldn't sleep. The child needs fresh air."

"You," I seethed, "you horrible, conspiring, lying being. You would kill such an innocent!" I backed away with Brune. "You were given the choice of rooms on your own and never to have to care for this babe, yet you choose to murder him! And Coran and Pallyn's babes too? This day," I growled, "you both leave this place. I do not care if you are not fit enough for the journey. This is my home and you are no longer welcome."

Mags tried to protest.

"Not another word," I scowled. "Lest my anger makes me do something I would regret."

And with that I walked away. I had to walk away lest I harm the two women. The feeling of fury welled in my belly and the energy oscillated wildly around me. I could have woken the Old One. I could have called Wirrel to claim vengeance. I was incensed. Kill an innocent? Kill this babe whom I could see would become a being of beauty? Kill the others too? Mags and Doe had been cared for and only kindness shown to them – how dare they.

My legs were shaking with adrenaline as I walked through the Temple. I entered Jin's room, holding Brune, and stood.

"Jin!" I called out from the open doorway.

Jin came to with a start, sitting up quickly.

"What is it?" he asked.

"I almost lost my temper."

Jin quickly got up. He pulled on a gown, walking towards me.

"Mags and Doe were going to drown Brune," I continued, still shaking with anger. "They were even planning to murder the other babes. Such destructiveness cannot remain here. They must leave."

Jin didn't question me. He didn't argue. He just caught my arm and said, "I will sort this."

We headed back towards the women's room, knocking on the doors of several soldiers as we passed. We waited a few moments for the soldiers to get ready.

"Find Doe and Mags," Jin ordered all the men bar Trell. "They were last seen in the valley. Bring them to room three. Do not let them out of your sight."

The men nodded and immediately left.

Jin escorted Brune and me to the women's room.

"Guard this room," Jin told Trell, who nodded sombrely.

In the room, Pallyn, Coran and their babies slept soundly. Jin nudged Coran gently awake.

"Coran," he called softly.

Coran came to.

"Will you look after Brune for a while?" he asked.

Coran nodded sleepily and shifted in her recliner, creating a space between her and Viir, patting the bed next to her. I placed Brune between him and his mother.

Jin and I headed towards room three.

Back in room three, the soldiers had found Mags and Doe. They sat next to each other. They didn't look remorseful. Their energy still felt defiant, not repentant. Thankfully, I had calmed. Jin's authoritative, composed manner had helped that.

Jin showed his fairness and experience. He asked Mags and Doe what had occurred that evening. Mags and Doe both gave the same account. Surprisingly, this time, they did not lie. It was as I had seen; they were going to drown Brune.

"That beast shouldn't be alive," Mags scowled. "None of them should. I was doing us all a favour."

"Such decisions are not yours to make," Jin frowned. "And Doe, I understand you were offered the chance to relinquish your child."

Neither Doe nor Mags replied.

"You will both leave this place tonight," Jin told Mags and Doe. "You will be escorted from this room to gather your belongings, and then you will be led away and to your homes. I will send half a dozen men with you for your journey. But know this, I do not send a guard for your benefit. I do it to ensure you do not return."

"But my legs are still weak," Mags protested.

"You were not too weak to murder," Jin stated matter-of-factly.

"It's her fault," Mags sneered at me. "If she'd been drowned as a babe, none of this would have happened."

Mags' vehemence towards me, once again, surprised me. "Mags," I intervened, drawing a deep breath. "I have tried to help you and yours. I have saved your life. I have healed you. Yet you consistently turn my goodwill against me. Legs or not, you are no longer welcome in my home. But," I paused, "your son, Ren is my friend. I will give you supplies and a healing sheet, because despite your attitude, I still wish you well."

I turned to Doe, shaking my head.

"Doe, I feel sorry for you, because I know you have been through terrible times. I know your mind is hurt and I wanted to spend time with you to help heal you. But," I frowned, "you have become destructive. I can only hope that returning home to those you love will heal you."

I looked at both the women. My heart felt calm.

"May the Old One protect you both, and may the energy of the Earth heal you enough to help you to see the error of your ways," I said.

I took a step back. I had no more to say to them. I had no more that I wanted to say, lest the anger within me rose again.

"And," Jin added, once I had finished speaking, "if you attempt to harm the men who escort you, I give them advance permission to abandon you." He paused. "Do you understand?"

"Fools," Mags uttered under her breath, and then resentfully affirmed that she understood. She muttered to Doe that they would both be better off far away from such evil creatures anyway.

"These two men," Jin curtly continued, ignoring Mags' remarks and indicating to two burly soldiers, "will escort you to gather your clothing. Do not speak to the other women. Do not wander. Do not delay, or you will be leaving here with nothing."

While the two women were chaperoned away, Jin instructed another soldier who was going to oversee the group of six. The soldier, a tall, quiet man, listened, nodding dourly.

Thankfully, the ordeal seemed to go without further incident. Both Doe and Mags were sensible enough not to do anything else foolish that might harm themselves. With a bag each of supplies, in the prime of night, they were escorted from the Temple and from the valley by six soldiers.

Jin and I stood at the Temple entrance once again, watching the group leave. A part of me felt pity for Mags and Doe. But, for the safety of all others, they could not remain. They would be escorted home. In this difficult situation, I could not think of a better solution.

"Do you think that some people are born to cause trouble?" I thought aloud.

"Yes," Jin considered. "I do. But, there is a big difference between trouble and slaughter. I have no tolerance for murder. None at all."

Coran had walked up to us so quietly that it took me by surprise when she tapped me on the shoulder. I spun around. When I saw her without her babe, my mind immediately thought there was problems.

"Viir and Brune sleep," Coran quickly assured me. "Have Mags and Doe really gone?"

I told her that yes, they had left to go home.

"What about Brune? Who'll look after him?"

"He'll be looked after here."

"I already love Brune," Coran blurted. "Viir already seems to love him too. I really don't want to separate them. I could take him as my own. Can I, could I, be his mother?"

Oh relief.

I gave Coran the biggest hug.

"You give me hope," I said gratefully. "Just when my heart feels cold and sore, you have warmed it. Yes, of course you can."

"Oh, that's good," Coran beamed. "Well, I'd best get back to them." She fidgeted on the spot. "My boys know when I am not close. They don't like it."

Jin and I watched Coran walk away.

"My boys," Jin sighed. "Did you notice that Coran already referred to them as 'her boys'? This is good."

"Yes. And once again, I must thank you for your help."

"Let us hope the remainder of our time here is smooth," Jin said. "I am reduced to four men plus the two runners."

"There won't be any more trouble," I replied. "The anxious twisting in my belly has gone."

"Good," Jin nodded. "Still, I'll arrange a rota so there is always someone on patrol through the Temple. I'll walk you to your room and take the first watch."

I didn't argue. After this night, the thought of always having someone maintaining safety in the Temple was deeply reassuring.

Over the next few days, there was no further trouble. On the contrary, although everyone was shocked to hear about Doe and Mags, the atmosphere and energy lifted significantly. There were now sixteen of us residing in the Temple. There was much interaction between everyone, so it felt like a great deal more.

Jin now had six men, seven including himself. Trell was the natural nurturer, and everyone treated him like a father figure. He and Jin had taken over room three, at the front of the Temple, and spent time creating plans for the next developments in Hollow. Jin had even created a miniature three-dimensional version of Hollow on one of the tables.

Soul and Iris flourished. Soul spent most of her time keeping everyone else organised, either alongside Trell or with Coran and Pallyn. We shared a great deal of laughter together. I even started teaching her more complex reading and writing.

Iris spent most of her time with the newborns. She would tell them stories, play with them and talk to them, trying to teach them things she thought they should know. She loved them. She told them every day how much she loved them. She treated them like her little brothers.

Coran, Pallyn and their four baby boys were all healthy and active. The two women began to pick up weight at last, and stopped looking like walking skeletons wrapped in skin. They seemed content. They were good friends to each other. They loved their sons.

The four boys grew at an alarmingly fast rate; much faster than a standard human babe. Every day I saw the change in them. And goodness, they loved their food. They were sitting before they were a week old, and then crawling by two weeks. As soon as they could move about, their growth accelerated even more. It was as if they were determined to explore the world. They were curious about everything and everyone. The boys were so active with their crawling, often all four going in differing directions at once, as if making a break for freedom, that everyone took turns in helping tend to them.

By the time the boys were a turn of the moon old, they had started to walk.

By the time the boys were two moons old, they had started to talk.

At three moons old, the boys looked much more like children of three or four years of age. They grew taller on an almost daily basis. It wasn't just physically that the four boys were developing fast, it was mentally and psychologically too. They were clever, asked constant questions, and were able to hold conversations using thought and reasoning. They were all charming, good natured, loving, kind, funny, cheeky boys, and they loved their mothers vehemently. I saw in them the basis of the beautiful beings from my vision.

It was when the boys were four moons old, spring was starting to blossom, and the Temple had been peaceful throughout winter, that the changes really began.

TWENTY-EIGHT

The Teachings

"Are you sure?" I asked.

Coran and Pallyn nodded.

Jin and Soul had sat silently as the discussion had taken place.

"Yes, we're sure," Pallyn spoke. "The boys need the company of more humans and more children. No matter how much we teach them, they believe all the world is like it is here in the Temple. They are surrounded by too much that is kutu. They need to experience how real human villages work. They need to learn how to interact, plant crops – everything a normal boy would do."

"When were you thinking of leaving?" I asked.

"Soon," Pallyn replied. "Before the hot summer months are upon us."

That was not far away.

"And," Coran added, "we have to think ahead. At the rate they are growing, they will be young men by next spring. Then they'll start thinking about mates and children of their own." She laughed, relishing the notion. "They all love Iris, but at the rate the boys are growing, Iris will still only be seven once they are young men. Even if they all wait for her, she may want none of them. Even if she does choose one, what would the other three do?"

It made sense. Still, I did not like it. Here, the boys were happy. They could learn about kutu as well as human. Here, they were safe.

"Will they be safe in Hollow?" I asked Jin.

"Yes, I believe so," Jin replied. "Hollow is a good town now. It is a fair, open-minded town. It embraces kutu history. The boys should thrive there."

Jin pulled out a piece of parchment from his tunic, unfolding it to show me a complex line drawing with notes.

"Viir drew this," Jin indicated to the paper. "He had been listening to Trell and I discuss how we could improve Hollow's irrigation. It is a water pump. He designed it. He drew it. He even calculated how much water it could pump over a given time. He told me that when he goes to Hollow he wants to help make it more like the Temple."

I sat looking at the line drawing. It was a complex yet simple device, unlike anything any town or village had. The skill of the design reminded me of a kutu's, yet this took into account only earth substances. It was quite brilliant.

I examined my own attitudes. Pallyn and Coran were right: the boys did need to be integrated into a normal human life in order to have the chance to flourish. I didn't want Pallyn and Coran to be right. I wanted to find a good argument why they should not leave. The truth was simple: I would miss them. I loved the people here. They had become my family. And I loved the four boys. Not only were they like family, they represented everything I loved about all people and kutu.

I nodded, feeling a little sad.

"They are only four moons old," I thought aloud, "but no longer babes. They are children. They love to play make-believe and draw and learn. But you are right: these children do not age as we do. Soon they will be young men. Decisions must be made now for their best futures."

I looked to Soul. "What are your thoughts?" I asked. She knew exactly what I meant.

Soul contemplated my words. "Iris has been around many children, but she has loved none like the four boys. To her, they are her brothers. But," she took a deep breath, "she loves you even more. I will have to give it some thought."

"Of course," I nodded.

I turned back to Coran and Pallyn. "Then I suppose we start making arrangements for your departure," I shrugged acceptingly. "How long exactly do we have?"

"Shall we say the day before the full moon?" Pallyn suggested.

The full moon? That was so soon. It was only six days away.

"Six days?" I confirmed.

"Yes," Pallyn agreed. "It will give us time to gather provisions."

The impromptu meeting suddenly halted as the four boys and Iris, with Trell in tow, ran into the room in a skirmish of noise and laughter.

Trell was trying his best to gather the children into some sort of order. But the children were having none of it. The more Trell tried to gather them together, the more the children laughed and ran.

"We can draw outside," Trell said, exasperated yet smiling. "Let's leave the grown-ups to their talking."

The children ignored Trell and raced ahead, pleased with themselves, putting their books and papers on one of the tables next to us, climbing up onto the kutu seats. Trell followed, giving us a good-humoured shrug.

The interruption to our meeting was good timing anyway. For the moment, all that was needed to be said had been said.

Coran and Pallyn naturally migrated to their children's sides, asking them what lessons they had learnt so far that day. Trell, laughing to himself and shaking his head, helped himself to sweet-meats, and stood back, talking to Jin, allowing the children to take a break from their teachings. It was a beautiful afternoon and the sun was streaming through the windows. The energy around us was vibrant and positive, filled with talk and laughter. I felt happy and at ease with all the people here. My heart hurt to think I would only have six more days of moments like these.

I looked around, my thoughts so deep that they could be considered empty. Soul caught my eye. She was watching me. She had her knowing look on her face.

"Brune!" Viir suddenly exclaimed, making the energy of the room flicker.

I looked over. Viir was tutting, nudging Brune in a playfully indignant manner.

"I can't draw there now," Viir told his brother. "It's not smooth anymore."

Viir moved his parchment and leaned to one side, continuing his sketching. Next to him, Brune was sitting with his arms spread wide and his palms flat on the table. He was looking at his hands, concentrating deeply.

Suddenly, I saw a flash of shadow energy. It was fast – so fast that I would have missed it if I had blinked. It was like a sun-berry popping. Brune then lifted up his hands, smiling delightedly to himself.

There, where Brune's hands had been pressed against the granite table, were now two indented hand prints.

I swivelled around to better observe.

Coran and Pallyn moved to see what was catching the boys' attention. They saw the hand-shaped indents in the stone table and Brune looking at them, seemingly pleased with himself.

Coran glanced at me questioningly. I nodded to her. We had discussed what we would do if anything like this ever happened.

"Show me that again," I said, ensuring my manner was nonchalant.

Brune put his hands flat against a different place on the table. He concentrated again. Again I saw his energy flash. He lifted his hands. Again he had indented the stone.

Brune, it appeared, had the beginnings of a skill like a Nigh-kutu Weaver.

The other children had stopped what they were doing to watch Brune's act. They then also put their hands on the table, pressing down as hard as they could. All were indignant when they couldn't make the same indents.

I moved to join their table, taking a seat among the children.

"All of you are special. You may find that you have special skills," I told the four boys. "Everyone's will be different."

"Ours are the same," Pall suddenly announced.

Lyn nudged him, telling him to 'shh'.

"It's Tachra," Pall told his brother, shrugging. "She'll notice anyway."

I moved around to kneel on the floor, between Pall and Lyn.

"Come on then," I encouraged. "If you tell me about your skills, I can help you to refine them. And I will tell you about some of mine."

Pall and Lyn looked at each other. As they did, I opened my true vision. They were talking to each other with their minds!

"You talk with your minds, not words?" I asked the twins.

Pall and Lyn shot me a look, surprised that I knew such a thing.

"Yes," Pall said sheepishly, "but that wasn't what we were going to show you."

I remained quiet as the boys stared at each other. I glanced from Pall to Lyn, and then Lyn to Pall. For a moment I could not see that anything had changed. Then, I realised, Pall's freckles had suddenly disappeared. Or was it Lyn who had suddenly gained freckles? Or had they invisibly swapped places? I had to use my true vision to tell which boy was which. They were still the same boys, but now Lyn had freckles and Pall did not.

"How clever: you have lost your freckles, and you have gained them," I laughed.

"No," Pall corrected me indignantly. "I took his face."

Lyn shook his brother's arm. "You look too much like me," he frowned. "Let's do someone else."

I heard the boys say my name with their minds. Both started giggling. Pall thought this was a brilliant, hilarious idea. Both boys turned around, staring at me with intense concentration.

Suddenly, I saw the boys' faces change. Their skin paled to near ivory. Their dark, curly hair lengthened and straightened. Their faces became more angular, their eyebrows arched, their brown eyes turning to green. They even had the familiar silver scar on their foreheads.

They looked like me!

This shocked me even more than Brune having some, or all, of a Weaver's skills. I could make my face look as if I was someone else, but I had never personally known any kutu who could do such a thing. Jychanumun had told me stories, but I had thought it was a rare talent, and that any Nigh-kutu that had such ability had been stamped out by Arrunn.

"We're getting better at it," Pall said, letting his face return to his own. "At first, I couldn't make my eyes change colour. Now I can."

"That," I told the boys, "is remarkable."

"Now tell us one of yours," Pall said.

"Well," I considered, "I can become invisible by pulling energy around me from my surroundings. I'm not really invisible when I do it, but no one can see me. They just look past me."

"That's a good one," Lyn said approvingly. "Will you show us one day?"

I told the boys that yes, one day I would.

"I can't do anything special," Viir announced as he nonchalantly carried on his drawing.

"Sometimes," I said, "The most special skills are the most hidden ones. You'll have them. They will come when the time is right."

"You can already do things," Brune said encouragingly. "You can draw anything. You can read and speak anything. The way you think is special."

Viir accepted this with a shrug. I looked at his energy, concerned that he may be aggrieved that he couldn't change faces or shape stone. But he genuinely didn't mind.

I stood up.

"As from today, I too will be teaching you all," I told the children. "I will teach you a little more each day, to help you understand your special skills. And remember, you can always ask me anything."

"Yes, Tachra," the boys replied in synchronicity.

This, I knew, was the day the boys' instruction would really need to begin.

I glanced at Coran and Pallyn. They both looked a little wide-eyed and startled. Up until now, they had just had accelerated growth to contend with. Now they had the emergence of kutu-like skills too. I did not worry. The mothers loved their children more than life itself. The boys loved their mothers. With this, everything else would be conquerable. I told them this much.

Iris moved to stand beside me as I spoke to Coran and Pallyn. She took my hand, standing silently. I felt her energy. She was more than a little dejected. I asked her if she wanted to have a break from her lessons, and for me to show her how to make punni jam. She didn't reply, but bit her lip, just like Soul bit hers, and nodded. I made my excuses to the others and guided Iris towards the kitchens, squeezing her hand as we walked away to let her know that I understood.

I didn't press Iris, although I knew exactly what was wrong. I waited until she wanted to talk to me. It took until we had almost finished making the jam. She stood on top of a stool, stirring the hot substance in a simmering pan. We both tasted a little, and I told Iris it was the tastiest jam ever. It was true. The berries had been in storage over winter, making them particularly strong and sweet, and we had added more honey than usual. The jam was exceptionally good.

"When I grow up, am I only going to be good at making jam?" Iris asked.

At last, I thought, she was ready to talk about what was bothering her.

"Of course not," I replied. "Not only are you good at many things, you are also unique."

Iris kept quiet, waiting for me to go on.

"Do you know," I considered, "that you are the only person, other than Jychanumun, who can just talk to me in my mind, whenever you want to?"

"No," Iris shook her head, but it didn't make her feel any better.

"Did you know," I tried again, "that you are the first ever child born from love?"

She shook her head to that too, still not feeling better.

"That is a very unique thing," I said. "All tomorrows and yesterdays, there will never ever be another like you. You should really be impressed with yourself at that one."

Iris sighed.

"Or that you have the ability to call fire to you at any time." I gave her another.

"But I don't know how to do that. And anyway, that's not mine; that's from my papa."

"Of course it is yours," I said. "Just like my Earth energy skills are mine. I have them because of the Old One, but they are still mine."

I could have given Iris many additional things about her that made her unique, but I saw it was more a case of her feeling sorry for herself. I could have told her that she could swallow the Earth and she still would not be impressed.

"Do you want to be the best? At everything? In the whole world and all worlds and all yesterdays and tomorrows? The biggest and the smallest and the fattest and thinnest?" I asked her.

Iris started giggling. Her giggling turned into belly laughter.

"I think I must do." she said. "I want to fly like a kutu, heal like Chia, fight like Stanze, paint like Orion, use Earth energy like you do, and cook like my mamma. I want to do them all."

"Then you will," I told her, helping her from the stool. "If anyone can, I do believe it's you."

Iris looked up at me, studying my face with her questioning dark eyes. "You really mean that, don't you?" she said.

"Yes," I replied. "Because another unique and very special skill that you have is that whatever you want to do, you can. But," I said, "there are still only twenty-eight days for each moon. So you will have to choose what to learn and how to spend your time."

"But everything takes too long to learn," Iris protested. "I'm impatient."

Her blunt honesty made me laugh.

"It's not just about having a skill," I told her, "it's the understanding of its application as you learn it; it's that which makes all the difference."

"Are you going to tell me it's about choice too?" she asked.

"Yes," I nodded. "As you grow up, you will learn that once someone is aware of choice, they become responsible for the consequences of their actions."

Iris frowned, giving that consideration. I knew I was talking deeper than her young understanding. For now, it did not matter. What mattered was that she was happy, and understood that she too was unique.

The jam was made. Iris no longer felt left out. She gladly left the kitchens to rejoin the boys for better fun than cooking. I went with her to the classroom where their studies took place. Each day, Iris and the boys had been in a routine of being taught. Everyone took turns teaching them. As from today, so would I.

The boys were back in the classroom with Trell, having regrouped from their disorderly mischief. Iris returned to her seat, picked up her drawing pens and returned to the day's lesson. Seeing Iris and me enter, the boys were momentarily distracted, suddenly wanting to talk about everything and anything. Once their exuberance had calmed, they resumed their studies, and I sat at the back of the room. As Trell taught them, I observed the children's interaction with each other and their tutor. I opened my true vision to feel their energy. I needed to see who they truly were, and had the potential to be, if I was to help guide them.

Trell's discussion was on the process of designing and building huts. The boys listened respectfully. While the boys' attention was on Trell, I opened my true vision further. I could hear Pall and Lyn's innocent chatter with their minds as they talked silently to each other, and listened with amusement into the thoughts of the others. I could feel Brune's intense desire to learn every word as accurately as he could. Viir's mind was very different: simply open, absorbing.

As my true vision felt the movement of energy within the room, my eyes were drawn to watch Viir sketch. His sketches were of dwellings, but no dwellings like any I had seen. As Trell discussed wooden huts, Viir drew magnificent, multi-levelled buildings with art and statues, and courtyards filled with hanging gardens.

Jin entered the room, standing at the back beside me. After Trell, Jin was readying to spend some time with the children, to teach them something else.

"One at a time?" Jin quietly asked.

"Yes."

"Any specific order?"

I shook my head, indicating not.

When Jin took over from Trell, he told the children that they would each be spending time with me this day. He asked them who wanted to go first. All of them did, except Viir. I had no preference, so Jin played the fair-game. Brune won.

While Jin started his lesson with the others, I took Brune's hand and led him into the room next door. I had no plans as to what I would teach. Not for any of them. I had just decided I would know at the time.

Brune, Coran's adopted son, reminded me of Dragun in many ways. It wasn't just that he clearly had Weaving skills; he too was quiet, the tallest, and very empathic. As a babe, he had seemed the most human by his nature, and at first I had thought that he did not have many kutu abilities. But now, not only could I see his skills starting to emerge, I could see his depths. He had passion and intensity, and felt things acutely. His empathic nature meant that he sensed the feelings of seemingly inanimate objects, as well as other living beings.

"You feel more than you can express," I told Brune. "Today, I will start teaching you how to speak how you feel without using words."

We sat at one of the stone tables. It was a table made of rough grey earth stone, not a kutu substance. It would be the best place to start. I told him that many kutu were great artists, and that art was a way to express feelings without words. I pointed to the table, running my fingers along it.

"Do you feel what this is made of?" I asked.

"Stone," Brune replied.

"And how does that stone feel?"

Brune put his hands on the table and thought about it for a moment. "It's kind and gentle," he told me. He then considered further. "And young for stone. And a little bit sleepy too. As if it's not properly awake."

"Yes," I agreed. "Keep your hands on the table. Feel how it feels. Unite that with how you feel."

Brune nodded, moving his hands over the rough stone surface.

"Now, use your fingers and hands to reshape the stone so that it feels that it is in the right shape, as if you are the one who can help it show how it really feels."

I pushed energy out to Brune to guide him. But he didn't need any guidance. He began digging his fingers into the stone, sweeping his hands in wide arcs, leaving deep swirls in the table's surface. I just sat and watched as the table was gradually reshaped.

"I want it to stay as a table," Brune told me as he worked. "It is content being a table. But I want it to show its true nature."

Brune gathered momentum, fully immersed in what he was doing. I observed his energy as he worked. The way he pushed his energy out, connecting to the material, understanding it, was wonderful to watch.

I did not expect Brune to be able to work so fast on his first lesson. I expected this first project might take several lessons. But once he had started, Brune didn't want to stop. In no time, the table was a gloriously carved tribute to earth stone. At its centre, he had shaped a statue that looked like a waterfall. He had even smoothed the stone in places so that it glistened like water.

Brune stood back from his work, satisfied with the result.

"You can practice that," I said. "Tomorrow we'll see how you feel about metals."

"Can we do that now?"

"We could," I replied. "But perhaps a little bit at a time. And I do have to see the others today too."

"Oh yes," Brune accepted. "It wouldn't be fair otherwise."

I opened one of the concealed panels within the wall of the

room, showing Brune some of the kutu items stored there. Most of the items were dismantled bits from Kraniel's research. I picked out two small pieces of metal and showed them to Brune.

"Do you want to take one of these so you can practice feeling what it is made of?" I asked.

Brune's face lit up, his eyes fixed on the items in my hand. Neither of the pieces of metal were anything special to anyone else's eyes, but Brune saw their potential. He picked the piece of matte-grey metal, a surprising choice as the alternative was speckled with golden uana, and tucked it into his tunic.

"Shall I get Iris now?" Brune asked with satisfaction. "She was next."

I said yes, and as Brune returned to the teaching room, I waited in the corridor for Iris. For Iris, I had just decided, her first lesson would be best held outside.

Iris and I ventured out of the Temple into the cool spring sunlight. I guided us to sit by the lake. It was a purposeful decision, just in case we had need of water. And there wasn't much of a breeze, which was good.

"Is this extra special teaching?" Iris asked.

"Today it is," I replied. "Because you and I learn things together every day. But there is one thing I have promised someone that I would show you."

Iris sat straighter, expectantly.

"Can you speak to your papa? With your mind?" I asked.

She shook her head, indicating not. "He came to me before, but I don't know how to go to him."

I sat on my knees, one hand out in front of me, palm up. I concentrated on Wirrel. I found him. I told him what I was about to do, and that he was to be moderate.

"Ohh, look," Iris suddenly gasped.

There, in the middle of my palm, a tiny flame now flickered.

"Your papa exists within fire," I told Iris. "You can call him to you at any time. His flame will never burn you. But it is still a flame. It can burn all else."

I picked a long piece of dry grass, holding it over the flame. Iris saw how the piece of grass immediately curled and incinerated.

"Your mamma, you, your bloodline to come. . ." I paused. "Do you understand what I mean by your bloodline to come?"

Iris nodded.

"Only those will be able to see Wirrel, your papa. But for you, the connection will always be unique. You are his daughter. Yours is a voice he will hear. That means that you will be able to talk to him. . ." I paused again, "and call him to you."

"Is that my papa?" Iris asked, referring to the flame in my palm.

"Not entirely," I replied. "Any flame is a connection to your papa. Through a flame, you can call him. Through a flame, he will come. But," I warned her, "your papa is very, very strong. His flame is very powerful. You must only call him when you understand how powerful he is."

I let the flame extinguish in my hand.

Iris looked disappointed. I made her repeat what I had told her, to ensure that she had listened, and then asked her why she should not always call her father.

"I saw what he did to our old hut," Iris replied gravely. "He's so powerful that sometimes other things, like the hut, get hurt."

"Clever girl," I smiled. "Exactly right. Now that you understand that, you are going to do a palm flame, just like I did."

Iris held out her hand, closing her eyes and holding her breath. No flame came. She shrugged when she opened her eyes and saw that a flame did not spring from her palm. I told her to remember her lessons on seeing energy and pulling it towards her. I told her to pull a small, gentle flame into her hand.

As Iris sat with her eyes tightly closed, concentrating, I could see that she was doing it right this time. Small specks of energy drew in towards her, settling in her hand.

"Keep going," I encouraged as I shuffled my position, ready to spring up. It was just in case I needed to throw her, or us both, into the lake.

"Gently," I told her, observing the energy was moving a little too fast. "Remember, gently, like breathing."

A tiny flame rose up in the centre of her palm.

"You can open your eyes now," I said, and Iris looked at her palm with pride. "Now make the flame go away."

Iris made the flame disperse immediately.

"Now call it to you again, but this time with your eyes open."

"That's too difficult," Iris protested.

"Then practice," I said firmly.

It took several attempts before Iris could call a flame to her palm with her eyes open. We went through this process over a dozen times until she was comfortable calling a flame and extinguishing it. When she could do the task with her eyes open, and with nothing more than a thought to make it happen, she was ready.

I sat cross-legged and made Iris sit directly in front of me with her back to me, almost on my lap. I put my arms around her. It was a safety measure: Iris in my arms and water close by.

At my instruction, Iris called another flame to her palm.

"Look at the centre of the flame. Think of your papa."

Iris nodded.

"Can you speak to him?"

"I just did."

That was faster than I'd expected.

"Now, gently and peacefully, call him to you," I said calmly.

There was nothing gentle about it. Almost instantly, Iris and I sat amidst a blazing inferno. Neither of us were touched by the flames.

Within the fire, Wirrel stood in his flame-form. I was not

shocked. I knew what Wirrel now looked like. Iris was not fazed in the least. She just sat looking up at her father with love and acceptance.

Wirrel smiled at his daughter. "Now you can call me to you when there is need of justice," he told her.

"Yes, papa," Iris replied.

And just as fast as it had come, Wirrel and the inferno sunk back into the earth.

Having explained to Iris that Wirrel was now a being that existed for justice and vengeance, Iris was content, understanding why the visit from her papa had been so short. She extinguished the flame in her hand, and then we cleared up the burnt grasses from around us, ensuring that no tinder remained that could catch light anywhere. Iris' lesson for the day had finished.

I had spent more time with Iris than I realised, but I determined that I would spend time with each and every one of the children that day. So I sent Iris to get herself some food, and asked her to send the next child to me.

I had expected only one child to come for the next teaching. Instead, two walked down the Temple steps together. To my eyes, they looked like Iris and Viir, with all the right physical attributes and even the right clothes. But I was also watching with my true vision. It was really Pall and Lyn.

The twins were an active bundle of mischievous brilliance. Being twins seemed to give them both more courage for acts of daring and simple naughtiness. They were a handful, but never bad, and I loved their mischievousness, just like I loved the mischievousness of the wildcat cubs. The twins already had potent skills. They could clearly mind read. They also had another remarkable skill: they could control their energy. They could control it to such a degree that they could make themselves look like someone else. But so far, they had not understood the potency of what they could do.

As the two boys, still trying to look like Iris and Viir, walked towards me, they were too engrossed in their own chat and giggles to notice me. I moved quietly to sit by one of the punni berry bushes, calmed my energy, threaded my essence through the soil and up the roots of the punni bush, feeling the essence of the lush green growth, and sat still. To all eyes, I would simply now look like part of a punni berry bush.

A few moments later, the two boys reached the area where I had been sitting and stopped talking, looking around.

Where did she go? Pall asked Lyn with his mind.

I don't know, Lyn replied, looking around again, turning a full circle.

"Tachra," they called aloud in unison. "Tachra!"

I let the boys search for me for a few moments.

"Tachra, we're here!"

"And so am I," I eventually said aloud, without revealing myself. It made the boys jump.

I released the energy of the punni bush, allowing the boys to see me.

"That was brilliant!" they exclaimed. "Do it again."

I sighed and laughed at the same time.

"Come here you two," I said. "Pall and Lyn. And yes, I know it's you."

Pall and Lyn looked disappointed that they hadn't fooled me. They dropped their false appearances and came and sat on the grass, handing me a flask of water, telling me that they thought I might be thirsty and asking me if I wanted any of the snacks they had brought with them. I thanked them for the water and sat while they heartily ate their food.

I had moved from beside the lake to one side of the valley where the punni bushes were thick and already full of early blossom. The late afternoon sun was making their scent fill the air. It was a beautiful spring evening and all the plants in the valley were budding with life.

"Being twins makes you special," I told the boys. "You two will always share a unique connection. Today, I will teach you together. But, from the morrow, I would like to teach you separately."

The boys groaned at this. They clearly didn't like the thought of doing anything separately.

"When you grow up," I added, "you will sometimes want to do different things. You may even disagree with each other. You both have to learn that this is normal, and not a reason for ill thoughts. On the contrary, the differences in you will be the very things you love most about each other. But that is not for today's lesson," I realised the subject was too deep for this moment. "Today we will talk about energy."

"Why can't every one see it?" the boys suddenly asked.

"Because everyone is different."

"Everything must look really flat and empty and uninteresting to them," Lyn considered. "Or they are just stupid."

"Well," I considered, "there are things that *you* do not see. Does the world look flat, empty and uninteresting to you? Are you stupid?"

That caught their attention. I realised that I was going to have to be sharp with these two. And fast. Their minds whizzed through information so quickly that they were like light moving through air.

"You two," I told them, "are two of the cleverest boys that have or will ever exist. You both have many skills and you know that you do." I looked at them, putting on my best serious face. "But, because you know you have skills, you don't think you need to perfect any of them. Do you want to be so good at what you do that you are the best at it?"

The boys nodded fervently.

I started with an easy one, picking a piece of blossom, putting it in my hand. I pushed my own energy through to my hand, saturating the blossom with my energy. To all eyes, the blossom seemed to disappear.

"Look at the energy," I said. "What do you see?"

"Just your hand," Pall replied, not bothering to push his senses out. "You made the blossom disappear."

"I didn't. The blossom is still there." I held my hand further out to them, indicating that they should take the blossom from my palm.

"There's nothing there," Pall shrugged again. But then he put his hand out, touching my palm, gasping when he felt the shape of the blossom. He picked the flower off my palm. As soon as he moved it from my hand, releasing my energy from it, he could see it was a flower. We could all see it.

"Energy is not just about looking like something. It's about feeling like it too," I told the boys. "This is what I am going to teach you, to begin with."

"Yes, but how do *you* see things?" Pall asked. "If you don't see things the same as us, what's the point of you teaching us?"

Lyn nodded, agreeing with his brother. It was a pertinent question, especially from one so young, and not something I had ever had to vocalise to another. This was not something I could pass off to these two. They were too astute, too curious, and could see the truth of my energy, even if they did not yet understand it. I could also see that they needed to respect their teacher or they would have no desire to listen.

"I am me, in this flesh body, with eyes that see, ears that hear and a heart that feels, just like any other human," I replied. "Yet I also have true vision. My true vision is similar to yours, but more encompassing." I pointed to my own shadow, stretching out beside me. "My true vision is like my shadow. It walks everywhere with me, yet unless I look, I am not aware of it. If I look, I can become it. My shadow sees and hears much more than the flesh. It sees energy, thought, intent; past, present and future; and many other things. It is the greater part of me, capable of great thoughts. If I were to become simply my shadow, I would forget about matters of the flesh. That is similar to the Old One, but he is superior to all beings. He is the shadow and the light everywhere, and all things in-between."

The twins nodded solemnly, their small, beautiful faces looking at me with acceptance and respect. Now, I knew, their teaching could really begin.

I made a bit of a game of the day's lesson for the twins, picking out items such as leaves, stones, sticks or water, teaching them how to look at the energy of each thing and understand it. Some aspects they were quick at learning. They could push out their energy and saturate an item quickly, but in reverse, drawing in the energy of something to become it, did not come so easily to them. They loved the lesson, and loved the opportunity to learn something that they found difficult. It made me realise that the boys could easily become bored if they did not have something to learn, or follow some creative pursuit.

Before the lesson was over for the day, there was one last thing that I wanted to try. I was not sure if it was within their skill set or, more importantly for these two, something that would interest them enough to try. The two boys were busily occupied trying to meld with the same punni bush that I had melded with. They were not looking. Good.

"Ouch," I suddenly said loudly, tucking my knife back into my pocket.

I had made a deep nick on my thumb. It wasn't really a bad cut, but in exactly the right place to make blood drip quickly. The blood made it look worse than it was.

The two boys came running over.

"Oh Tachra," the boys fretted, when they saw my bleeding thumb. "That's bad. It's bleeding. We'll go and get mamma."

"It's alright," I said. "It's a good opportunity to try out another skill with energy."

The boys were anxiously standing over me. They wanted to go fetch their mamma to help mend the cut. They were worried that I was hurt. They were worried that not getting their mamma was the wrong thing to do.

"Truly," I patted the grass with the hand that wasn't bleeding, "sit. It's alright."

The boys tentatively sat down.

"I want you to try, one at a time, to use your energy to heal it."

The boys nodded, anxious to help.

Pall went first. He desperately pushed his energy out to my bleeding thumb. I could feel that he was trying to wrap his energy around the cut, like a bandage. But the cut was flesh and matter, and an energy bandage wasn't going to seal that. I then felt him make his energy into a small clamp shape, attempting to close the cut. It made a quick pinching pain that transferred to my energy and came as a surprise. A squeak escaped my lips.

"You're hurting her," Lyn said, fretting. "I'll do it."

Lyn took my thumb, holding it close to his face, inspecting it. He sat there for several moments, not talking, just looking. Then I felt something. I opened my true vision. Lyn was using his energy in the layers of the skin on my thumb, making the binding cells in my blood push forward. The bleeding on my thumb stopped, but Lyn continued, still holding my thumb close to his face. He was making my skin knit over! It was crude, yes, but he was doing it exactly the way I would have done; exactly the way I had watched Chia work. Lyn was a natural healer.

"It's not quite as good as new," Lyn said, letting me have my hand back.

"It's perfect, thank you," I said. "And I didn't feel any pain."

"I didn't want it to hurt," Lyn frowned. "I wanted to take the hurt away."

Pall held out his hand.

"A present," he declared proudly.

His palm was empty to my eyes.

I played along with the game and put my hand in his empty palm, feeling something. I lifted off the concealed item to reveal some tiny daisies that had been twined into a head circlet. I put the circlet around the top of my head.

Pall and Lyn both sat looking at me, their eyes wide with earnest integrity. It was the first time I had seen this side of the boys. It was beautiful.

"You wonderful boys," I said. "How much does Tachra love you?"

"Loads," the boys broke into a smile.

"How do you feel about lessons separately from tomorrow? Or shall we keep them together for now?"

The boys glanced at each other.

"Separately," they replied in unison.

I nodded, telling them that I would see them tomorrow. I told them that if they were good, I would introduce them to Meah, who was energy only. They sat eagerly when I mentioned her.

The twins' lesson was complete for today. I asked them, if they didn't mind, to ask Viir to meet me in the kutu kitchens when the moving sun shaded tree four. The boys knew what I meant. Here at the Temple we had grown accustomed to coordinating meeting times by the movement of the sun on specific trees.

The boys confirmed, and then ran back into the Temple.

I washed my face in the lake, approvingly inspecting my mended thumb once again, and then made my way to the forest. I had a short while until tree four was shaded and I wanted to do nothing more than empty my mind. Teaching was harder work than I had expected. It wasn't that it was difficult, but it took a great deal of concentration and energy, especially with such bright students.

I made my way into my favourite clearing in the forest, laying in the dry leaves that were almost disintegrated. Meah joined me, tired from the antics of her own cubs, and we both lay awhile, not doing anything, barely moving. I was so relaxed that I almost fell asleep. I eventually got up, knowing I had stayed as long as time would allow. Meah was too lazy to move, so I pushed some leaves up against her like cushions. She liked that. I decided that I was hungry. I had forgotten to eat all day, so I was glad that I had said to meet Viir in the kitchens.

I was early enough into the kitchens to find nourishment. I had just finished clearing away when Viir entered. He had been the only child, when asked, who hadn't wanted to go first with his teachings. It wasn't that he was shy. Nor was it because he wasn't eager to discover new things. It was because he was not competitive. And, from observing his energy, he wanted to learn as much as he could in order to make the world a better place for everyone else.

Viir, Coran's son, reminded me more of a Shaa-kutu in his looks and nature. Of the four, he was the sharpest, most imaginative thinker, as well as considerate, kind and astute. He was the one who could already surpass the adults in conversation. Already he had asked many questions about the Old One, about the kutu, and about humanity too. He would listen and, as he listened, in his mind he would paint pictures. I had regularly found him in one of the kutu teaching rooms, reading books. He had already grasped the basics of the Shaa-kutu language.

"Good evening, young Viir, son of Coran," I said as Viir entered.

Viir stopped in his tracks. I had welcomed him in the formal Shaa-kutu manner, speaking the Shaa-kutu language.

"Good evening, my friend and teacher, Tachra," Viir replied, also speaking in Shaa-kutu, although a fragmented version.

Viir did a small bow of honour. The bow was one that had been described in the Shaa-kutu books. It was beautifully endearing. I had to try hard not to smile – it was not the done thing in Shaa-kutu culture to smile at such a gesture. Instead, I bowed in return.

"And good evening again," I spoke, this time in Nigh-kutu.

Viir looked at me quizzically, not understanding.

"That was Nigh-kutu," I informed Viir. "The Shaa and Nigh languages are very different. Shaa has one language, which has not changed much. Nigh has many dialects which have moved from their original meaning."

Viir hurriedly sat by my side, already keenly interested.

"I've read lots of Shaa-kutu," he said. "But this is the first time someone else has spoken it. Can we keep talking in Shaa-kutu?"

I agreed that we could, and we had a general conversation about the Temple and his return to Hollow, all spoken in Shaa-kutu. Viir would keep asking if he was pronouncing the words correctly. Mostly he was. Occasionally I would correct him where he had the sound of a word wrong, or the rhythm incorrectly placed in a sentence, and he grasped each new thing immediately.

"Did you know that there are fewer than sixty words written by the people here at the Temple? Other than by you, that is," Viir sagely informed me.

"Perhaps, when you are older, you could design a written language that is suitable for people," I suggested.

Viir thought this was an exceptional idea, and far more beneficial than water pumps or buildings. He said that a good language could unite people in every town and village everywhere. I listened to him as he spoke with such passion. He had such grand ideas for the world.

"When you have learnt more Shaa-kutu, I will teach you what I know of the modern Nigh language," I said. "Once you understand all the aspects of Shaa, Nigh will be easier to pick up."

Naturally, Viir wanted to know why. I explained that the Shaa language was based around truth and the shared perception of a fact or of intent, and of past, present and future, whereas Nigh had corrupted many of its words so they no longer related to how they sounded or felt – rather like human dialect. Viir thought that must be very confusing as a language. I had to agree.

"If I had books, I could learn," Viir frowned. "But I can't find any written in Nigh-kutu."

For a moment, I considered telling Viir about the Book of Fate. It was the only book that I knew of that was written in any Nigh-kutu language. But Viir was young and innocent, and I still had no idea what this potentially powerful book might say. I decided against it.

"Once, the Nigh-kutu had many books," I eventually replied. "In great libraries. Some books were just words. Some were magnificent sculptures that reflected parts of stories according to the energy of the reader. Even the buildings themselves were stories. Their stories covered everything: facts, fiction, ideas, thought, visions. They were places of great beauty."

"Were?" Viir asked.

"Yes. They were destroyed. But," I paused, "that will be a lesson for a very different day. We have not yet finished with language. I want to teach you how to push your energy out with a word so that your intent is felt. Although most people will not be able to reciprocate, or see what you are doing, their sub-conscious will feel the intent. It will help them to understand what you are trying to explain."

I looked at Viir and said 'understand' with both my mouth and my mind while pushing out my intent.

"I felt that!" Viir exclaimed. "I felt you sending understanding."

Viir was the fastest learner. And he had an amazing skill where he could still his mind enough to concentrate on one thing at a time, while retaining a million thoughts in a separate part of his head. I enjoyed spending time with Viir, and speaking kutu once again. It was a language that flowed easily from my lips and had little leeway for misunderstandings. Sometimes, when explaining a new word, I forgot I was talking to one so young, such was the level of his communication.

Viir did not want the lesson to end. But, when the sun began leaving long shadows through the window, I told him the day's lesson was finished.

Viir stood and gave me a perfect kutu bow. I returned the bow. He then smiled the biggest smile, hugged me, and thanked me for such a wonderful tutorial.

The day's instructions were complete. It had been both tiring and rewarding. The four boys and Iris were only going to be here at the Temple for another six days, and all of them still had much to learn. For now, I decided, I'd make the most of it. If I had only six days, I'd teach them as much as I could and would enjoy all the precious time they were here.

The next day went far too swiftly. I barely slept, waking with those first up. I swam in the lake with Coran, Pallyn and Soul, and Pallyn showed me how to braid my hair. I kept my daily lessons with the five children, and all developed their skills, not wanting their lessons to end. We all had our evening nourishment outside, together, enjoying the spring air and happy talk.

The following day, I arose first again, enjoying the pre-dawn outside with Meah. I helped with making new attire for the fast-growing boys. Shaul and Brennal cooked their first ever meal, which tasted delicious, but looked like mud. I taught the children through the evening, choosing dusk to show them differing movements of the land's energy. Pall was very distracted, and kept asking if I wanted to take a pause. The first time he asked, I just thanked him for the consideration and told him that I didn't need a break. By the third time he asked, I started to wonder if my teaching was not stretching his mind enough.

My final student of the day was Pall's brother, Lyn. While teaching, he too asked the exact same question: "Would you like to pause?" Unlike Pall, Lyn could not stop his cheeky grin from spreading across his face. When I asked what he was really referring to, he sincerely told me that he wasn't being naughty, but just wanted me to say the words. And, when I did say the words, he had a fit of giggles. I knew that he and his brother were up to some sort of mischief.

Later that night, while everyone else slept, I decided to see what the twins were up to. I knew they didn't sleep much. They didn't need as much rest as the others, although I had noticed they had been uncharacteristically tired that previous day. Usually they played in their room together. This night, I could sense they were not in their room.

The Temple was dark, with only the faint moonlight glow through windows illuminating my way. I kept quiet as I walked, ensuring my bare feet made no sound and my energy remained concealed. My legs guided me to where I sensed Pall and Lyn. They were at the front of the Temple, in one of the disused teaching rooms.

The old teaching room was dark and the door was firmly closed. I slowly opened the door and slipped in unnoticed.

Pall and Lyn were sat on the floor, with a shared blanket around them. In front of them was a speaking three-dimensional image of myself. They were playing one of the kutu recorded lessons. This particular recording was about understanding the energy of plants. They were both engrossed.

I let my energy show gently, so as not to startle them, and then bid the boys hello.

Pall shot up, putting his hand against the three-dimensional image of myself. As he did this, the image said, "Would you like to pause?"

Now I remembered where I had heard that phrase from.

"We weren't being naughty," Lyn explained. "We just wanted to learn more. If you're not coming with us to Hollow, we have to learn while we can."

I sat down next to them. "I could come and visit."

"It's not the same," Pall frowned. "Like this," he pointed to the three-dimensional image of me, "isn't the same. But it's better than nothing."

"Shall we watch this together?" I asked them. "Unless of course, you would like to take a pause?"

Once the boys had managed to stop giggling, having spent several moments making the image say, "would you like to pause?" and making me say it too, the three of us sat, the blanket shared between us, watching me speak until the sun began to rise. I then made them return to their room and to bed. They were to sleep, I told them, even if just for a short while, and lessons would only resume once they were rested.

I was particularly tired the following day, although everyone else was busy and buoyant. There were only four days left until my friends left the Temple. I started dozing when teaching outside in the afternoon, so took my classes into the Temple and found some of the kutu coffee. I decided I could grow quite fond of the unusual bitter taste.

That day, when Brune arrived for his lesson, he presented me with a gift. It was a fine sheet of circular stone and metal. In the centre was a raised angular shape. All around the edges were tiny, intricately shaped, raised trees. He had made it himself. It was a beautiful work of art.

"It's functional too," Brune explained. "The way we count the moments here is by the sun touching or leaving the trees. When we want to know what moment it is, we have to go outside and all the way to the lake to look. Here," he moved to the side of the room that had the sunlight streaming in, placing the gift on a table, "you don't need to go so far. I've numbered the trees. And this," he pointed to the raised angular shape in the centre, "will tell you what tree the sun is closest to."

I looked at Brune's gift in the sunlight. There, a shadow from the central point was casting across the smooth metal, almost touching the tiny sculpture of tree five.

"It's a time counter," Brune proudly announced. "But it has to stay in the sunlight. It's for the front of the Temple."

It was a beautiful gift, expertly designed and crafted, and made with love.

I thanked Brune, and together we made our way to the front of the Temple. We chose a spot at the bottom of the steps, so the counter could be viewed from the Temple entrance. As Brune positioned it, he signed his name in the stone. It read, *from Brune, to Tachra*.

"I don't want you to forget us," he said.

I told Brune that never could I forget him, or any of them. I told him that once I loved someone, that love lasted beyond eternity and never declined or altered, and that I loved them all. Brune was content with that.

Three days before my friends were due to leave the Temple, it was early morning. I had just had sun-break feast with everyone and I was on my way to another sitting in the central chamber with the Book of Fate. As I approached the chamber, two children, looking like Brune and Viir, came running up to me, skidding to a halt.

I stopped, folded my arms, and put my head to one side.

"I know it's you two. Young Pall and Lyn."

Pall and Lyn dropped their disguise.

"Will you teach us intent again?" Pall asked. "The classroom is empty. Or we could go outside."

"You already know how to use intent, both of you. You mastered that yesterday." I looked at them, reading their energy. They were desperately trying to cover something up.

"What are you up to?" I asked. "I sense even more mischief than usual."

The boys both looked guilty. Their energy reeked of conspiracy. Neither of them could hide their thoughts from me. I picked up that they had released the energy seal from one of the doors into the central chamber for Viir. Viir was now in there. They were acting as lookouts.

"You know that room is out of bounds," I told the boys. I was genuinely dismayed. "It's dangerous in there."

"We didn't go in," they defended themselves. "Viir wanted to go in."

"With your help," I said sternly, letting the boys sense my firmness. "That room is damaged. I can go in there because I can see the danger areas. Viir cannot. He could get injured or hurt. You should not have opened the door for him."

The twins looked suitably remorseful, declaring to me that they didn't realise it could be dangerous. They were both suddenly anxious that Viir should come out.

"I'll go fetch him," I told the twins. I also told them that they were to go and help their mother prepare supper. Pallyn knew that if the boys were naughty they were given kitchen chores.

As Pall and Lyn ran towards the kutu kitchens, I entered the central chamber.

Sitting in the gloom, Viir was so engrossed in staring at the Book of Fate that he did not hear me enter.

"You know why this room is closed off, don't you?" I asked Viir as I approached. "Because the damage makes areas unstable. And,"

I added, "because of this," I gestured towards the black cube. "It's called the Book of Fate."

Viir went to get up. I indicated to stay sitting and sat down beside him.

"This is a very old Nigh-kutu book," I said. "Written in one of their ancient languages. Jychanumun calls it the Language of Intent."

"I can see that it's written on two levels," Viir considered. "One is the surface engravings, which I can read, but that's just an introduction and doesn't say much. The other is the changeable script, but I cannot read that. What does it say?"

"I don't know yet," I replied. "I have been trying to study it. Without success."

Viir looked at me. His expression was one of confusion and surprise.

"Of course you can read it," he said. "According to the engravings, you are one of the keys."

That took me by surprise.

I ran my fingers over the cube's surface, making the morphing script move around at my touch.

"See," Viir said. "You are a key. Any of the three keys can read the book, or parts of it. One key is the person the book was written for. I cannot see his name. And the two other keys are the people who wrote the book. You," Viir said matter-of-factly, "are one of them."

That took me by surprise even more.

I thought about this. Viir had to be wrong. This book was written millennia before I existed, and written in a language I did not understand. There was no way I could have had any inclusion in its writing. What Viir must be sensing was my energy around the item. Most likely, I had sat here so often and for so long, my energy was now saturated into the cube too.

"Come, Viir," I told him, "you are not to be in here alone. But if you wish, you can join me here the morrow to study this further."

"Can I not stay a while longer?" Viir asked. "I like it here. It's peaceful."

Viir did not want to leave the chamber, but I insisted. It really was too dangerous. With the columns destroyed, the domed roof could collapse if a storm blew or rains came down hard. Only one who could sense movement, such as myself, would have time to leave and secure the chamber in safety.

I escorted Viir from the chamber and resealed the door, ensuring it was a much stronger seal this time, and with an energy that would make a resonance to alert me if tampered with. My thoughts were preoccupied. It bothered me what Viir had said about me being a key to the Book of Fate. He was an intelligent boy, and I had never known him to be wrong. But, knowing that the Book of Fate was written before I existed, Viir could not be right. The conflicting facts were unsettling.

With two full days before my friends were to leave the Temple, I was up first again, well before sunrise. I wandered through the Temple, as I often did when all else was quiet.

I passed the disused lecture room where Pall and Lyn now often came to listen to pre-recorded talks. Usually it was quiet inside. This time, I could hear banging and scraping.

Inside the lecture room, I found Pall and Lyn with digging tools, trying to pry one of the kutu panels from the wall. They had made a lot of dents and scratches, but the panel was still firmly in place.

"We're trying to get it out," Pall and Lyn explained, although it wasn't much of an explanation. They then pointed to two well-constructed back-bags.

"Mamma made these bags for us. She said we could only take what we could fit in."

One of the boy's bags was already filled to the brim with kutu data crystals. I recognised those crystals. They were recordings of the lectures by me and the kutu.

"We need the device that will make them speak," Lyn added. "It's in there," he pointed to the panel in the wall.

He was right; it was in there.

"It would be very heavy to carry," I mentioned.

"We'll manage."

"And I don't think it'll fit in your bag," I added.

"We'll manage."

Pall picked up the digging tool again, trying once more to wedge it into the panel of the wall.

"If you are not coming with us," he said as he worked, "then if we have these, you can still teach us things."

"True. But it's very late. You should really be asleep," I said.

"We are nearly finished," Lyn replied. "We'll be in bed before mamma awakes."

"Promise?"

"Promise."

The twins weren't doing anything that could harm themselves, and I had no heart to tell them to stop. So, I left them to their efforts and headed out into the warm night and into the forest.

I had already bathed and played catch-in-the-dark with Meah before the others awoke. I think I must have fallen asleep. I came to. I heard someone call my name. It sounded like Jin. It was now bright morning.

"I'm here," I shouted, quickly making my way back to my room.

Jin was entering my room from one door as I entered from the external doors. He had a worried look on his face.

"I couldn't find you, and you weren't in the lake. I scoured the Temple looking for you," he said. "I was concerned you were trapped in the central chamber and I could not gain access."

"Apologies, I fell asleep in the forest," I explained. "I arose early, too early it seems, as I didn't want to miss a moment of seeing everyone before you left."

"I do not think Soul and Iris will be returning to Hollow," he announced.

"No?" This was not as I expected. "But Iris and the boys are such friends. I assumed they'd travel together."

"As did I," Jin replied. "But you are their friend too. Soul and Iris would worry about you if you were left here alone. They've said they will stay here with you."

I wasn't quite sure what to say. I let the information sink in.

"It would trouble me also," Jin added. "What if you were taken by illness? Or did not have enough food over winter? Or if something happened to you? Or to both you and Soul, leaving Iris alone? I think I should return here after escorting the others to Hollow."

"But you belong in Hollow," I replied. "You've such plans for expanding the town. You've spent much time developing those plans. It's your aspiration."

"It is," Jin agreed. "But I can help elsewhere too. I could rebuild this Temple to be the place of learning it was designed to be. I could ensure the huts between Hollow and the Temple operated well. I could ensure you remained well."

"Jin. . ." I interrupted.

Jin stopped talking. He was so sincere and such a good man.

"You would truly give up your plans and ambitions, just to ensure I was well?" I asked.

"Easily," Jin replied.

I looked up at him, stood on tip-toes, and then kissed him on the cheek.

"Please do not," I said. "I have heard you. I have heard Soul and Iris' needs. I have heard the boys' needs. I think it is I who must make changes, not you."

Jin looked at me, waiting for me to go on.

"I must confirm my thoughts first and speak with Soul," I said. "We will talk again after that."

Jin nodded, and as he returned to his tasks, I went looking for Soul.

I assumed that Soul would be in the children's classroom, as it was her turn to teach this morning, but she wasn't there, nor was she in any of her usual places. The Temple was a huge building, and I grew fed up of searching with my legs, so I sent out my senses to locate her. I sensed her outside, by Gale's grave.

Outside, Soul was sitting quietly on her own, weaving a fresh garland for the grave.

"People forget too easily," Soul said as I reached her. "I don't want to forget."

"I don't forget."

"That is one of the many reasons why I love you," she said.

"Soul, you know that you are my friend, always, no matter where you choose to live. . ." I paused.

There it was – Soul bit her lip.

I knew that the best way to tackle anything with Soul was directly.

"Do you want to return to Hollow?" I asked bluntly.

"Wherever you go, Iris and I go too," Soul replied.

I sat down, picking up some of the loose vines, starting to weave another garland.

"My friend, you didn't answer the question," I said.

Soul placed her finished garland atop Gale's grave.

"If you want to stay here at the Temple, then that is where Iris and I will stay," she determined. "But, I do have a question."

"Speak, my friend," I told her, "and please don't look so worried. Nothing you say could be bad."

"Would you mind if Trell stayed too?"

"Of course I wouldn't. Does he want to stay?"

"He wants to be where I am." Soul rolled her eyes and smiled coyly.

"Trell? You and Trell?"

It made me laugh with joy. Soul and Trell. I knew they got along and had spent a great deal of time together, but I hadn't realised it had grown into this. But now, seeing my friend's content yet coy expression, it was so clear. I was pleased. Pleased for them both.

I hugged Soul.

"My friend, that is wonderful news. Trell is a fine man."

"He is," Soul agreed. "And handsome too." She laughed to herself when she said that, as if it was the first time she had said it aloud. "He lost his mate with the birth of his last child. He says he has never looked at another until me. And he loves Iris. He would make a good mate, and a good father. You know," she considered, "I may even like a brother or sister for Iris. Seeing her with the four boys has made me realise it would be good for her. Trell would be a good father to more children."

"Are his first children all grown?" I asked.

"Yes, Shaul is the youngest at fifteen and still to find a mate. He has said that he wants me to help him find one."

"In Hollow," I added.

Soul nodded.

I thought about this, and I knew my heart confirmed it: Trell would benefit from being around Soul and all his family, in Hollow. Trell would be wherever Soul was. Soul would be wherever I was. Iris would miss the four boys, because they were in Hollow. The boys really needed my guidance with developing their new skills, but they would be in Hollow. Jin would now be where I was too, but his future was based around Hollow. And I would miss the four boys, and Coran and Pallyn, and all the people here whom I had come to consider as family. They would be in Hollow. It seemed that in this matter, it was where I wanted to live that was causing the problems. I loved the Temple and the valley. But my choice to stay here would not be so good for those that I loved.

I considered the prospect of living in Hollow too. It made sense. Had I not realised that it was humans who were the key, the future, of all things? Surely my future must be to embrace humanity and embrace my own human aspects. If I shut myself away here in my valley, isolated and alone, wouldn't that be like turning my back on my human side?

I had a choice, yes. But really it was no choice at all.

"What if," I thought aloud, "we all travelled to Hollow together?"

"You would consider it?" Soul asked. I saw her eyes sparkle. I saw it was what she truly wanted.

"Yes," I replied. "Temporary at first, and I would have to see how I felt about it. But I could ensure that you and Trell were settled. I could also ensure that the boys were taught."

"Oh, they will need to be taught." Soul sounded excited. "I know Pallyn and Coran want them to learn agriculture, but I even caught Viir reading a kutu book on universes. Only you can teach them understanding of the kutu, of everything. It would be perfect. You could live with me, Iris and Trell. Or, if you didn't want that, Jin said you could live at Hollow's temple if you wanted. Or you could live with Jin. Whatever, we would all be together. It would be perfect."

Soul's energy was bubbling like the kutu drink kiyala. It was the happiest I had seen her in a long time.

I placed my garland atop Gale's grave, alongside Soul's.

"Come on," Soul stood, taking my arm. "Let's go tell Iris and the others. They'll be so pleased."

And everyone was genuinely pleased. They all wanted to tell me how happy they were about it, and how we as a group had all come to love and rely upon each other, and that their world would not be the same if we split up. It was wonderful to hear, and it filled me with joy. I smiled and laughed when they told me how glad they were. But along with my own gladness, another part of me already pined for my valley. I reminded myself that I would not be saying goodbye to my home. I reminded myself that I could return whenever I wished, and that it was good for me to embrace my human side. In Hollow, I knew that could do that.

There was only two days until we all departed for Hollow.

Those last two days in the valley passed quickly.

Far too quickly.

Today, we were leaving.

I had my bundle packed. I had everything ready. I had been up since dawn.

I now lay in the leaves, revelling in the warming forest air. Meah was by my side, having been running with her sister and the cubs for most of the night. She was sleepy. I was wide awake.

I didn't need to worry whether Meah would be travelling with me or not. Over the months, we had developed our way together. With just a thought, she would be by my side. With just a nuance, my energy would be by hers. Where my physical body existed was no longer important to either of us. She would come to me whenever she wished. I would never again have any reason to miss her as our bond was eternally aligned.

I stood up, stretching. Meah lifted her head lazily, watching me with her sleepy amber eyes. I smiled at her, telling her that I would see her soon. As I walked away, she casually relaxed, back to her dozing.

I could already hear the shouts of the four boys at the front of the Temple. They had packed their bags the day before, excited for their new adventure. Thankfully, I had persuaded Pall and Lyn not to take an entire kutu three-dimensional teaching system. Instead, they had packed several changes of clothes. Not so much for cleanliness, but because they were growing so fast. It would not be long before all the boys were taller than Iris.

Once back in my room, I picked up my bundle. It was fortunate that we did not need to take many provisions. The in-betweener huts would give us what we needed, and after the mountain, the make-shift huts were every two days' walk apart. Never before had I journeyed anywhere in a way that was so well prepared. Still, along with a few items that I felt were too precious to leave behind, including the Book of Fate, I had packed knives, twine, water and food. Cautionary habits would not fade so easily for me.

My bundle was heavy. Very heavy. But, as Pall and Lyn would say, I would manage.

I made my way to the front of the Temple. I met Trell, Soul and Iris en route, talking together. It seemed that everyone was excited for what their tomorrows might hold.

"Look," Iris ran up to me, amused with herself that she was wearing trousers. "I like them now."

Iris did a twirl before running off to join the boys. It was good to see her so excited. At first she had refused to wear what she considered to be boys' clothes, and had spent much of the previous evening sullen when seeing her travelling attire. But, having watched me refashion my white robe into trousers and a tunic, she had decided that she would be an explorer too.

At the Temple's entrance, Soul looked up at the colossal main doors.

"Do we close these?" she asked.

"They've never been closed," I considered. "Not while the Shaa-kutu lived here, nor Arrunn, nor us. Let's leave them open, just as they've been designed to be."

Soul nodded her agreement. In truth, even if we could budge such huge doors, closing them simply felt too final. It would feel like I was saying goodbye, as if I was never coming home again.

We started the walk. Sixteen of us. Soul and Iris. Coran, Pallyn and the four boys. Seven Hollow soldiers. And me. The sun was rising. It was a bright, cool spring morning, and the ideal season to travel. Now, to get to Hollow, all we had to do to was put one foot in front of another.

I had travelled the route between Hollow and the valley once before, in reverse, but I remembered little of the specifics – more the sensation of starvation and thirst. Nevertheless, I could not forget that crossing the mountain was an almost impossible task. Neither could I forget that the dry flatlands were gruelling and hot, and appeared never ending. Even in spring, this would not be an easy journey.

Six years ago, when I had travelled away from Hollow, I had done so to walk away from my fellow humans. This time I walked back, not just to be among other people, but to embrace my own humanity.

TWENTY-NINE

The Journey

On the first day of our journey to Hollow we found our pace, which was guided by the children's capabilities. We passed through the trees beyond the valley and into the land where the only thing ahead of us was rocky terrain and the looming mountain. Everyone was buoyant, talking and laughing.

That first night we slept out under the sky. The soldiers carried fabric for make-shift tents, but they were not needed, and we chose instead to make the fabric into sleeping cocoons. Jin ran through the outline of our journey while the children gathered dry sticks. Iris showed off her skill of making a fire with no more than a thought and we consumed some of the food rations, toasting root vegetables and breads in the flames. Everyone seemed in good spirits; tired, but satisfied.

Our second day of walking was simple again. The weather was fair. The windy air smelt of potential rain. Other than a few new blisters on our feet, everyone remained in high spirits. There was still a great deal of talk and laughter.

By the third day, the reality of travelling hit hard with a sudden downpour of rain. We didn't stop when the rains came down harder, as there was nowhere to shelter and the tents would have gotten soaked through. Our legs complained at the rocky terrain. Where the rocks were not freshly slippery from the soaking, the ground turned to gritty mud. The mud worked through our foot coverings. Any talk was saved for the short moments when we paused so the slowest could take breath.

The rains didn't stop through the night, so we found a place where the muddy puddles were better than the little torrents of draining water and set up camp. Not wanting to drench all the tent fabric, the men erected a single large canopy and we all huddled underneath in wet clothes. It was too sodden for even Iris to make a fire, so we ate cold, damp breads and raw roots. No one slept well.

As the days continued, the land grew sparser and rockier and the incline increased. The rain, so welcome in the valley, continued. I tried comforting my friends, telling them that as downpours were so seldom, at least we would be getting them through the early part of our journey. Better to have them now than on the mountain, I said. It didn't make them feel much better.

As our supplies of food dwindled, the mountain loomed ahead. But I no longer thought of the difficult climb with trepidation. Instead, the knowledge of soon coming across the first in-betweener hut, with hot food and fresh supplies, spurred us all on.

Eventually, the rain clouds passed to welcome a bright afternoon. And there, brightening our spirits even more, ahead of us, at the base of the mountain, was our first in-betweener hut.

The first in-betweener hut had, it seemed, been much changed over the months it had been inhabited. From Jin's discussions, I had expected a tent. Now, what had originally been just fabric was entirely made of wood. If it wasn't for its sparse surrounds, I could have imagined it was one of the temporary huts in Threetops. There were small look-out windows with thick canvas coverings, and a doorway opening in the middle, again covered by thick fabric. The land around the hut had been partially cleared, except for an array of rounded boulders. A small canopy to one side covered a mottled selection of dried sticks that had been collected. Smoke wafted from an opening in the roof, bringing smells of cooking vegetables to my nostrils. It was a welcome scent, and my stomach started rumbling in anticipation. We trudged on through the fast-drying mud towards it. We were all hungry, damp, weary and quiet.

As we approached the hut, we were greeted by a middle-aged couple with pleasant round faces, raven hair, and athletic bodies. Their attributes were so similar that I presumed them to be brother and sister. It transpired that these two were mates, their children fully grown, and volunteers to live in this remote place. They, Ben and the beautifully named Runs-with-sun, greeted us with such genuine smiles that it lifted all our moods. They had seen us approaching and were well prepared for our arrival.

We were sat down on rounded boulders, given rough but welcome dry blankets and hot food. Propped on a boulder in the warm evening sun, pleasantly full with fresh broth, I could barely keep my eyes open.

That evening, we sat outside wrapped in blankets while our clothes dried on the rocks. I helped to tend to everyone's feet, binding fresh blisters and preparing for the climb ahead. The rains stayed away, so we camped outside in our small tents. I pulled my dried clothes into a pillow and slept so deeply that I didn't even notice the hardness of the ground.

I awoke to a bowl of steaming tea. My limbs were stiff and I longed for a soft kutu recliner to fall upon, or my refreshing lake to bathe in. But, having dressed and forced my sleepy body to consume a hearty sun-break feast, I was ready for the day ahead.

Beyond our tents, Jin and Ben were deep in discussion. When they noticed that I was awake, they called me over.

We moved to a position where we could better view the incline of the mountain. Ben then pointed out a deep russet-red spot in clear view, a short way up the slope. The rich colour stood out against the pale natural rock.

"Painted stones." Ben pointed to several other red dots on the lower sections of the mountain. "They are markers. It's taken months to discover the best route up and down. The red stones show the safest and quickest path."

I looked further up. There, all up the mountain, to a point beyond where my eyes could see, were more painted red dots.

"They go all the way up?" I asked, impressed.

"Yes," Ben replied. "And the other side. You'll also come across red crosses painted on ledges," he added. "These are the safest places to sleep for the night. The first day on the mountain, you must push on to reach the first sleep area or you'll be stuck on small ledges in darkness. After that, each day is still difficult, but more attainable."

"How long do you think it will take us?" I asked.

"If you reach the sleep zones, it's possible to get to the other side in three days."

Three days! This was so much less than I had anticipated. But I then compared Ben and his strong physique to my friends. Coran and Pallyn were still very thin, with little muscle. And the five children were so small. What took one such as Ben three days could take us ten times more.

"Even with young ones," Ben indicated to the five children, noticing my concerns. "Just follow the markers. Walk softly. Three days is still possible."

I noticed the relief on Jin's face. It was just the way he nodded and closed his eyes for the briefest moment that made me realise the acute sense of responsibility that he too felt.

"This is welcome news indeed," I said gratefully. "You have indicated a safe route. Ben, thank you. From all of us, thank you."

"It is still dangerous," Ben's tone became grave, speaking quietly.

"Do ensure that you follow the markers and do not let the little ones stray. I've seen more than one stone slide up there."

"Then I will lead the way," I decided. "With your markers and my true vision, I can hopefully guide us safely."

"Runs-with-sun has told me about your true vision," Ben said. "She too feels the movement of the land. Not like you, of course, but she has saved my life more than once."

I looked over to Runs-with-sun, who was sitting with the children. They were grouped around her, crossed legged, immersed in something she was showing them. I opened my true vision, observing her energy. Her gently luminous multi-colours were balanced, curving around her and encompassing those close by. It was like seeing a softly fused rainbow.

Runs-with-sun looked up to me. She had felt that I was observing her.

"Will you both be returning to Hollow?" I asked.

Ben shook his head, indicating not. "We are happy here. We will see our days out here."

"I understand," I felt a little sad. I would have liked the opportunity to get to know these two people better. "I hope to see you both again."

"You will," Ben nodded. "There are no goodbyes."

"True." I glanced at Ben. I sensed that his words were loaded with deeper consideration. His inner strength and love of the land reminded me of my father. His energy, like Runs-with-sun's, was a beautiful fusion of many colours.

Yes, I thought. *I see your essence, your souls, already. Even if I do not see you in flesh again, I will see you both in Elysium.*

Jin asked Ben further details about our mountain route. I left the two men to their discussions and returned to the others, swiftly repacking my sleep items. We distributed the children's bundles between us adults, ensuring no-one had more to carry than they could manage. And once our bundles were on our backs, Shaul moved through us, checking that each bundle was secured and balanced. I noticed he spent more time with Coran than the others. I noticed too the shy smile between them. It was like seeing a sheath of green, only to find it was really a flower in bud.

Runs-with-sun had given each of the children a gift: a piece of fossilised bark whittled into beautiful abstract shapes. She came over to me, kissing me on each cheek before handing me something too. It was a perfectly smoothed, tiny circular stone with a natural hole through the middle. Inside the hole were flecks of crystal.

"For you, a piece of the mountain," Runs-with-sun said.

She helped me to untie my pendant, threading the stone alongside the ornate symbol from Una the Shaa-kutu. Once around my neck, I looked down at them. The two items were so opposite in many ways, but perfect in every way: kutu and human, new and eon-aged.

"Because you carry the land in your heart," Runs-with-sun told me. "And this is from the heart of the land."

"It's perfect, thank you," I replied. "But I have nothing to give you." I wished that I had. "Can I do anything for you instead?"

Runs-with-sun's eyes glazed as she thought.

"You can," she replied. "When the world is full, my children's children will hopefully be many. If they ask for your guidance, please hear them."

And as she spoke, my mind was filled with the image of many faces.

"I will," I simply replied. And I knew that I would not forget those faces. Neither would I forget her request.

I was sad to leave these two extraordinary people after knowing them so briefly. But our objective was to get to Hollow and we had barely begun the journey. We were given a good supply of food and water, and then said our goodbyes.

We began our ascent up the mountain in single file formation, with the strongest placed between the weakest climbers and me leading the way. The climb was difficult, although not as difficult as my memory told me, mainly due to Ben's markers. Although I used my true vision to see the stability of the land, each marker was on solid ground and then followed a straight line from one to the other. Climbing at an angle proved true. Those little red painted stones mapped our way like stars through the cosmos.

As the evening wore on, we all climbed beyond exhaustion. My legs changed from pain to numbness, and I had to be extra vigilant. I could not relinquish my heightened awareness, as we were all growing clumsy and the night was drawing in. I made us press on, remembering Ben's instructions. By the time we reached the marker indicating a good sleep area, where a gently sloping ridge overlooked a steep drop, it was almost dark and my legs felt like hot water. I dropped my bundle, helped those behind me to climb the last section, and then slumped down to sleep.

On the second day, we reached the mountain's summit. There we stood for a short while, taking in the panoramic vista. This was a view that I remembered. Behind us, my fruitful valley was now concealed. Only a distant patch of green indicated the trees behind which it lay. Ahead of us, the pale, sparse land had a dark line of green weaving through it. This was the wiry growth either side of the narrow stream. I knew the stream would widen to the river. The river would lead us through the flatland and on to Hollow.

When I had last stood here upon this mountain summit, thinking death was upon me, it was also the first time Jychanumun had spoken to me. He had told me to live. I missed him. It felt like grief and loss and yearning all rolled together. But I had lived. And, looking around at my friends, a mismatch of people thrown together by circumstance and events, I felt lucky. These were people I had come to love. I was lucky to have their company. The skies had blessed me.

Embracing that positive feeling, I stepped down from the summit and led the way for our long descent.

Descending the mountain was far worse than the ascent. I realised that I did not like these types of heights. Soul thought that was funny, coming from someone who had regularly flown with the kutu. I told her that I trusted a kutu's arms much more than the unstable rocks beneath our feet.

Jin did not want me to take the lead with our descent. He thought it too perilous, and wanted to take my place. But I knew I was the best person to keep our path safe. So he put the strongest man, Trell, directly behind me, and kept reminding him to watch my every step.

Very little of our downward path was sloping; it was more a mixture of staggered drops of craggy, layered stone with loose stone and shingle in between. Low mists and rain had made areas of the rocks damp. The spring heat had not yet burnt away the fine layer of moss-like growth that thrived in the shadowed areas. These were now dangerously slippery. If it was not the slippery moss on the sloping, craggy ledges, it was the loose stones that could tumble. Every place to put my feet had risk. As I found our path, I kept reminding people to stay vigilant. We stuck close together, aiding each other.

Once we had passed the craggy upper ledges, our way grew more unstable still. With my true vision I could see where the land could move under the pressure of a footstep. We remained in single file formation and I used my Earth sense to find the best path from marker to marker. It was not an easy task – sometimes I had to take a long route just to descent a small amount – but we kept safe.

That night, when darkness was almost upon us, we discovered that our sleep marker was no longer in place. Instead, the wide section of stone had tumbled far down the mountain, taking rocks and shingle with it.

I had to make a difficult call, selecting three small ledges that I hoped were sturdy enough to sleep on. I shared with Coran, Viir, Brune, Jin and Brennal. There was barely room enough for us to lay down. Below us was a steep drop. So, for safety, we fastened twine around our wrists and secured lengths to one another to prevent anyone from rolling off the ledge.

The following day, we all had to be extra vigilant. We had slept badly. Our minds and bodies were near spent. Whether clumsy, argumentative or sullen, tiredness had its differing effects. Most of my companions were quiet but for Trell; the more exhausted he became, the more he tried lifting everyone's morale. Eventually he began singing at the top of his voice, making up rhythms and words about our adventures. He added little repetitive sections and made the others join in.

I had been navigating a particularly difficult section of loose stone when I stopped. Nowhere in clear view was any other of Ben's markers.

The others stopped behind me, waiting.

From our position, I guessed that the rock slide above had taken out a section of markers that we were now wanting to cross.

"There," Shaul pointed to a marker far below us.

Between us and that marker were only small rocks and stone. To my eyes, it looked traversable enough. But it was loose, and freshly fallen from the rains. If that way had once been safe, it was no more.

"No," I shook my head, "it will slide."

I looked to both sides and below. Nowhere looked safe to my true vision. I attempted another tactic, threading my energy out at different angles, trying to foresee a point that we could reach.

No route ahead was safe. Not even for one as light as Iris.

I turned to face the others, feeling unhappy at being the bearer of bad news.

"We have to go back up, to a point that will offer another route," I said.

I felt their hearts sink, and saw the looks of dismay on their exhausted faces. But no one argued. No one complained. They simply nodded and, one by one, turned around.

As lightly and nimbly as possible, I began moving out to pass our formation in order to take the lead once again.

As I moved out to pass Trell, my peripheral vision caught sight of moving shingle. It was only a small slide, ten strides directly above.

"Budge along, three strides," I spoke loudly and calmly, knowing this was the only small area of safety we currently had.

Everyone moved across in turn. It was too late for me. The shingle was already passing over my feet.

I felt one foot give way and I could do nothing to stop it.

The moment seemed to go in slow motion. I knew I was about to slide with the stones. I did not allow my instinct to get the better of me. I did not put my hands out to those nearest for them to catch me; that would simply take them with me too. Instead, I closed my eyes, accepting what was about to happen. One foot slid down. The other followed. Trell reached out to grab me, but I shrugged off his grasp like a reed bending with the wind.

I felt myself fall.

For that moment my mind was blank. I just felt acceptance.

Suddenly, my descent stopped.

It felt as if I had hit a solid ledge. I fell hard on my side. I expected the stones and shingle to keep coming, but they too stopped.

I looked up. There, directly above me, Brune was crouched, his hands flat against the ground. His face was tight with concentration. His energy spanned out before him, coming from his hands like rays of shadow light, binding all that it touched. He was fusing the falling stones! He had halted the slide.

I could see the effort Brune was making was great, and that he could not hold what he was doing for long. I quickly clambered up the fusing shingle. As soon as I passed the area of danger and onto safer ground, I told Brune to let go. Brune sank down, the sweat and energy trickling down his face with exertion. But we could not stop for him to rest, as the land above us was still perilously fragile; even more so now movement had shifted the balance. I asked Trell to aid him, and deftly wove past the formation line to take the lead once again. Without a pause, I then led us away from the unstable area at the fastest possible pace.

It was not long before Jin, now directly behind me, pointed out that my leg was bleeding. I knew that it was. I could feel the pain of something sticking into my calf and the wetness of blood oozing into my foot covering, but I did not stop. I had to find a safe area.

I walked with my energy threaded out in all directions, feeling for an alternative route. I was exhausted, but I could not drop my guard, for every footstep had to be checked before taking it; not just for myself, but for the moments that would pass as the others walked there too. Bar the soldiers, the others were far more fatigued than I. So, as I sent out my energy in one direction, trying to keep us safe, I gave whatever energy I could spare to them, ensuring their legs and minds remained focused.

Darkness was almost upon us. I headed across the slope, having spotted a craggy ledge that was stable enough for us all to sleep upon. I was so tired that I could no longer speak. A fever had started to cross my brow as a result of my draining reserves. Eventually, exhausted, once my feet touched that solid sleeping ledge and all the others had joined me, I dropped to the ground. I was too tired to do anything else. Soul kindly tended to my leg, but was quickly taken over by Lyn. The healing nanos of my kutu fabric had tried to mend the wound, but had partially knitting the stone into my flesh. Lyn painlessly removed the sharp object and healed the wound with ease.

That night, overlooking the sheer drop to the lands below, and with a clear, star-filled sky above us, we ate the last meagre portions of our food. We should have been at the next in-betweener hut by now, enjoying a hot meal and flatter land. I didn't doubt that the hut was somewhere below us – frustratingly close. Nevertheless, I thanked the skies that we were safe. As the others drifted into deep sleeps, I lay down, using my hands as a pillow, glad to be on solid rock. I breathed in the air and let the energy of the land restore my ravaged own. The world fell into silence, bar the deep breaths of my fellow travellers and the gentle breeze brushing past the stone.

"This place is dangerous," I heard Pall whisper to his twin, not realising I too could hear. "I saw how draining it was for Tachra."

Lyn moved in closer to his brother, taking hold of his hand for comfort. "Tachra will keep us safe," he replied. "Don't worry."

"But who keeps her safe?"

"We do, of course." Lyn yawned.

And then even the twins fell into a deep, worn-out sleep.

Knowing how all my friends relied upon me, I did not sleep. Instead, I sent my energy into the rock below until I had found a path that would take us safely down.

The following morning, despite my body's fatigue, I knew the course we needed to take. Just like Ben's red painted markers had mapped out the way physically, my mind held tight to the route I had found during the night. As we sun-break feasted on the last of our water, I outlined our path. If we were careful, it was not too far, I told them. If we regulated our strength and remained alert, we should reach the bottom of the mountain before nightfall.

I walked silently, bar the occasional description of how everyone needed to tread, or how wide or safe our route was when it grew narrow or fragile. Finally, the steep descent began to level. The land, at last, was stable. And there, nestled into the slope, was our next in-betweener hut.

It was a happy relief to see that little make-shift building. The mix of fabric and wood had been bleached pale by the sun. Newer canopies each side offered additional sheltered space. There was smoke coming from a cooking fire. We were greeted by another strong-looking woman with an equally strong-looking mate. The woman, Dana, emerged with breads in a basket in one arm and a newborn babe in the other.

Dana and her mate, Yemmal, looked after us that evening. They nurtured us like plants thirsting for water, although I did notice they were wary around the four boys. We slept under their canopies, with extra blankets and pillows made of grasses. It felt so good to close my eyes and not have to concentrate on anything.

After staying at that second in-betweener hut, we reached the start of the stream that in my previous travels had led me to the valley. Other than the stream itself, and the small amount of growth immediately around it, the landscape was flat and dry, with little of note on any horizon other than rocks and stones of differing shapes.

As my legs grew stronger, the days rolled together.

There was little variation to each day, other than the people we met at the in-betweener huts. They were a varied assortment. I particularly took to the couple, Rill and Mena, and also Judia, with his mate Little-smile. Little-smile was Ben and Runs-with-sun's youngest daughter, which I should have guessed by the beautiful name and rainbow-coloured energy. Judia could mimic the different sounds of the insects, teaching us the sounds of the flatland. Further along, Urtia and Yem, with their nine children, treated us with wary caution, especially the four boys. While their children wanted to spend time with Iris and the four boys, the parents ushered them away from any interaction. There were many people of different types looking after the in-betweener huts. It was fascinating to meet them all. Nevertheless, I could not help but notice the guardedness in some of them, especially when dealing with the boys.

Despite still only being spring, the flatlands were hot. I could not get accustomed to the blazing sun, choosing to move my headwear through the day to best cover my skin. For Soul, the heat and brightness made her thrive. She would tie up her hair and roll up her trousers, often walking barefoot on the hot ground, her olive skin turning to a deep golden brown.

The journey was a good opportunity to continue the children's lessons. Sometimes I would use the land around us to teach them, sometimes the movement of the stars, sometimes more specific subjects; or I would just talk about the kutu or the Old One. When I talked, especially of the things closest to my heart, all my companions would listen. They were most enamoured with my stories of the Old One's dreaming. I would close my eyes and imagine I was dreaming with him, speaking of what it felt like, forgetting all about the passing of time and the monotony of our footsteps.

All five of the children were learning fast. The boys were growing fast too. By the time we had been travelling a full turn of the moon, Brune was a full hand taller than Iris and the rest of the boys' height now matched hers. Iris thrived with the boys, and with Trell. Soul and Trell had become very much the couple. They shared the same stubborn humour and strong heart, and now the same sleeping tent too.

Our landscape changed little: sparse on all horizons bar the stream that we walked alongside. And, just like the repetitive, sparse landscape, our pattern for each day was much the same. We would wake with the sun, eat a hearty sun-break feast, pack our items, walk until sunset, eat supper, and then sleep.

Wake with the sun. Eat. Pack. Walk more. Eat. Sleep again.

Wake. Eat. Pack. Walk. Eat. Sleep.

Wake. Walk. Sleep.

By the time two full moons had passed, the stream had widened to a river. The land was mainly sand with large protruding rocks and occasional tufts of long wiry grasses.

Just before we had been walking three moons, one little in-betweener hut looked different to the others. As with many of the huts on this river route, this hut had also been placed alongside the supply of fresh water. Yet this little abode appeared to have a section that was built into the river too.

As we approached the hut, a very wrinkled older woman with wild, curly grey hair and a huge wide smile came to greet us, introducing herself as Mane.

Mane announced that our timing was perfect, but wouldn't say why. Instead, she sat us under the canopies by the river, on land that had been cultivated with wild-flowers, and gave us all sweetened apple water.

"Are you here alone?" I asked Mane, wondering how one of such mature years could cope on her own.

"Oh no, my young Tachra," she replied. "Mane is never alone." She laughed to herself, as I came to discover she did often.

The woman, Mane, wouldn't stop grinning at me. I made small talk with her. Still, she kept grinning her big grin. It was quite disquieting. She reminded me of a woman called Tooth whom I had met once before. Although still old, she looked similar enough to be her younger sister.

Then, during our small talk, I noticed something. On the wooden table was a beautiful little array of dried flowers. Tooth had loved her dried flowers too.

"Do you know a woman called Tooth?" I asked, wondering if they could be related.

Mane suddenly jumped up and did a little dance, seemingly very pleased with herself.

"Ha! Dint recognise me, did you girl! Thought I's someone else!"
"Tooth?"

It was! Oh, by the skies! Eccentric, wonderful old Tooth. I got up and hugged her. Tooth, or rather Mane, kept doing her little dance, so she jogged about in my arms. She looked up at me, grinning, and squished the sides of my face with her fingers. My friends looked on, bemused.

"I's not Tooth anymore, girl," Mane told me. She did another big grin.

Now, when I truly looked, I could see that her large, perfect teeth were made of something else: bone, or wood perhaps. She was wearing false teeth! And, now that I'd noticed, this was even more disquieting, in a comical yet odd way, than the gappy, gummy smile she had worn the first time I had met her over six full summers ago.

Tooth, or rather Mane, noticed that I was looking at her mouth.

"Looks," she grinned. She turned her head away from me, did something that I could not see, and then turned back, holding up a perfectly carved set of teeth.

Mane grinned, showing me her gummy smile. She no longer even had one tooth left.

"That's brilliant!" I couldn't help laughing. "So now you are called Mane. Is that," I pointed to her hair, "not real either?"

Mane pulled hard at her hair.

"That's all mine girl," she said proudly. "Ain't no one with a mane like Mane!"

I started trying to relay the story of how I had met Mane to the others. Suddenly she sprung forward, towards the riverbank, and started doing her little hopping dance again.

"Oo, here he is," Mane was so excited. "My handsome mate. Handsomist in all the flatlands my mate is. Here he comes."

I couldn't see anything or anyone approaching as Mane continued her dancing jig, looking excitedly down the river.

I turned to Jin. "I thought her mate had ceased," I whispered.

"He had," Jin replied under his breath. "This is her new mate, Sail. They met during the kutu war. Sail arrived in Hollow, demanding that he be allowed to fight too. Tougher than old runi bark. When those two met they were like a couple of young fire-hearted lovers. Couldn't keep them away from each other."

The thought made me start laughing with unexpected delight. Mane had stopped dancing. I looked down the river to where her gaze now watched with bated breath.

Coming into view around the curve of the river was the corner of something made of wood. Or, rather, many branches, bound together in layers. On top of the floating bits of wood, a wiry yet muscular old man with a bushy white beard came into view. He had a long, sturdy stick and was slowly drifting along the water, his focus on us.

"Guests, eh?" The old man called as he approached. "Welcome, welcome."

As the old man on his flat boat drew parallel to us, he threw a piece of woven twine towards Mane. Mane caught the twine, pulled it, and then knotted it around a tree stump. When the twine grew taut, the wooden barge came to a halt.

The old man climbed off the raft, gave Mane a big kiss, and did a sweeping bow before us.

"I see my beautiful mate has made you welcome already," Sail announced. "And I have got fresh supplies from the next hut down. We'll feast well this night."

And feast well we did.

We set up a small fire, away from the wooden dwelling, and ate bitter-sweet fruits and sweetened cake. Sail had a wonderful way with the five children, treating the boys like normal children, yet also as if they were special. He and Mane sat with us, telling long, winding stories that both fascinated me and made me want to sleep.

Sail had a low, gruff voice that was so soothing that sometimes I forgot to listen to the words and just drifted with the sound.

I awoke at dawn, realising that I had fallen asleep without setting up my camp properly. Someone had tucked a blanket around me and put another under my head. To one side was a wooden screen, stopping the direction of the breeze.

"Morning, sleepy girl."

Mane had heard me stir. She was walking around her hut, vigorously brushing the outside of the wooden walls with a long-handled bristle broom.

I got up, wrapping the blanket around me.

"Bugs, bugs, bugs," Mane muttered. "All this land and they want to come in my house."

She glanced to me. "Made you something," she said, looking pleased with herself.

Before I could say anything, Mane had thrown down her broom and darted around the corner, out of view. She soon returned with her hands hidden behind her back and her wide grin showing off her big white teeth.

Mane held out a small, intricately twined array of dried flowers and leaves.

"For you," she said, handing me the posy.

"For me? Thank you."

I looked closer at the arrangement. All around the edges of the dried purple blooms were distinctive yellow-green leaves in a triple, pointed spray. I would recognise those leaves anywhere. They were from a tachra tree. I didn't think any tachra trees could grow in a land as dry and hot as this.

"It's beautiful," I said. "And these," I pointed to the leaves, "are a wonderful co-incidence. They're from a tachra tree."

"I know that, girl," Mane tutted. "Co-incidence," she tutted again. "Tachra tree for Tachra girl, of course."

Mane picked up her broom and paused, giving me a sideways glance. "Tachra girl remembered Tooth," Mane nodded to herself. "Tachra girl helped Tooth. Made her happy. Mane remembers."

Now, looking at Mane, I realised that there was nothing mad about her at all. When I had first met her, as Tooth, I thought she had partially lost her mind. But now I realised that she was just eccentric. In the same way that Orion always wore long red gowns, or Chia insisted on sleeping in his bio-suit, Mane had her ways, and simply didn't care what anyone else thought was normal. Mane was as sound of mind as me.

"I'm glad you are happy," I said. I felt a lightness of heart. Seeing her again, seeing her content, was not something I had expected.

"Got me the handsomest mate in all the flatlands," Mane grinned. "Oh," she jolted, "he's got fair news for you!"

Mane disappeared off into her hut. I waited, expecting her to return, but then heard her busy with chores around the other side of the hut. Laughing to myself yet again, I returned to the remainder of my friends, who were all now waking up.

"I think I slept deeply," Soul yawned. "How are you?" she asked.

"In good spirits," I replied. And I was.

Once we had eaten sun-break feast, packed our camp, and gathered enough supplies to last until the next hut, Mane announced again that Sail had fair news. He stood in front of us, as if about to tell another story, cleared his throat and indicated to his flat-wood boat.

"This sturdy float, made by my own hands, can carry more than one person," he announced. "Sail can take some of you fine folk to the next hut by water, if you would like." He glanced around at our eager faces. "So," he clapped his hands together, "who would like to travel with Sail on the water?"

All the children's hands shot into the air and I could tell that everyone liked the idea, allowing the children priority.

"I can take up to six," Sail told us. "More, if it's you skinny ones. Sail can get you to the next hut in a good timely manner. Takes 'bout the same time as walking. But," he grinned, "much, much nicer."

"We men will walk," Jin decided.

"Then all you little uns," Sail looked to the children, "and skinny uns," he looked to us women, "will travel with Sail. Come along," he indicated to the raft, "the day's already started; on you get."

That decided that.

Once I had said my farewell to Mane, and as Jin and the men began walking along the route of the river, the rest of us climbed onto the floating wood. Sail told us to just sit and enjoy.

I unravelled my feet coverings and sat on one edge of the raft, dangling my feet in the water. It was a hot morning, but I didn't care. I wrapped extra fabric around my head and neck to block the flying, biting insects and enjoyed the wonderful sensations as the world passed by.

At dusk, Sail moored his floating wood and we rejoined the men on dry land. We made a small fire and Sail told us more stories of the village where he had started his life. I learnt that as a young man he had chosen to travel the waters, exploring the new lands that he could access from the rivers. He wove fantastic tales into his recounting, using his imagination to make mountains into sleeping monsters and clouds into flying spirits. It was enthralling to listen to. Then, once we were all pleasantly sleepy, we made up our camp; and Sail insisted he would sleep on his barge.

The following day I was up early, greatly looking forward to another day of travelling by barge.

Travelling by water and seeing the world from the river looked different to when walking on dry land. I found the gentle tilt and sway of the barge was relaxing for both body and mind. As a result, my thoughts wandered into half-awake half-asleep imaginings. I understood how such a mode of travel was a stimulant for waking dreams.

I was most heartened to hear that Sail was making wooden boats for the next huts along too. I had decided that this was a wonderful way to travel. I took the opportunity to ask Sail questions about his life. I discovered that he was from a village far north of Threetops. It sounded like that village was one of the original human encampments, and that the land was as green and fertile as my own old home. I asked him why he had chosen to leave and travel.

Sail had just shrugged. "The world is far too big for me to sit in one place," he had replied.

I was quite disappointed when Sail dropped us off at the next in-betweener hut, bid us farewell, and I had to rebind my feet and walk on sandy ground again.

Our next stop was tended by a young couple who welcomed us eagerly into their chaotic home. Their hut was a random mix of everything they found interesting, from pieces of strangely shaped wood to segments of unusual coloured fabrics. All they had collected were placed around the walls and in every available space. Where there was not an item of interest, their six energetic children had painted images. It felt like walking into a human version of a kutu art gallery, yet without order or arrangement. I found the couple difficult, yet not unkind; just strange. They constantly watched us like vultures, as if expecting marvels or mayhem to drip from our fingers. And once the couple realised the four boys were the half-kutu children they had heard about, they wanted them to add their own pictures to the walls, insisting on it even though the boys were not keen. The following morning, I was quite relieved to leave.

Having spent two days travelling by water, our routine re-established itself once again. Wake with the sun, eat a hearty sun-break feast, pack our items, walk until sunset, eat supper, and then sleep.

The days passed. I kept count by numbers and the position of the moon. We had been walking for three full moons. During that time, I would often forget that we were travelling to Hollow. When I forgot, a sense of unknown adventure filled me. Now, Hollow was close, along with a realism that I could not forget. We would arrive there soon.

I could sense Hollow. I could smell that town in the air. We had almost reached the last in-betweener hut.

The last hut before Hollow was placed next to the river, with a surrounding area that had been cultivated into lusciously thick gardens and foods. The garden was beautifully tended with blooms of every colour in staggered heights. Around the flowers, the area of produce was thick with root and vine vegetation, and leafy shrubs with fat berries in them, all sheltered by canopies. Outside was a glossy horse, with a wooden trough of water to one side and hay on the other.

A little girl of about two summers old came running out of the hut, shouting for her 'dada' when she saw us. Her thick mop of brown curly hair bounced around her face as she jumped up and down, waving excitedly.

Out of the hut door stepped a man. My heart stopped.

Huru.

Huru, the man who had murdered Wirrel. The man who had raped Soul. The man I had tried to kill.

I glanced back at Soul. Soul had seen him too. I slowed my walk, waiting for her to catch up.

"Is that definitely Huru?" I asked Soul.

"Yes," Soul frowned. "I would never forget his face."

We paused our walk.

"Is everything alright?" Jin asked us.

"I don't know," I replied. I discreetly nodded towards Huru. "Is he alright?"

"Oh yes," Jin said. "A good man; helps with crop design and field management, and oversees the building of huts."

"You know he killed Soul's love and Iris' father, Wirrel?"

"No." Jin faltered. "Oh."

Soul looked at me, clearly anxious, clearly hesitant. "We both know that Huru is a changed man. You saw to that," she told me. "I can do this. Can you?"

I nodded. Yes, I believed I could. It was more my friend I was concerned for.

Soul took my hand. "Do not fret for me. Perhaps the skies are blessing me with an opportunity to forgive him."

What courage and open heartedness my friend had. I looped my arm through hers, sent her energy for a calm head, and we continued towards Huru's hut.

By his mannerisms, I would never have recognised Huru. He warmly greeted us alongside his mate, Rian, and their three children; all pretty, curly-haired girls. Both Huru and Rian recognised Soul, welcoming her, telling her how well she looked and how beautiful Iris was. Huru clearly adored both his mate and his daughters. I watched his energy constantly move out to them, ensuring they were well. I watched vigilantly for any sign of incongruities from him, or discomfort from Soul. Soul concealed her angst well. Huru and Rian seemed nervous yet genuine.

Huru and Rian had prepared a mini banquet and had harvested their best fruits and vegetables. As we enjoyed our feast, Huru spoke of how he wanted to help Jin expand Hollow's place of learning so that more people could attend. At one point, he lowered his eyes, and said:

"If one such as myself can learn to be a better person, anyone can. I would like the opportunity to help make that possible."

He appeared genuine. His energy appeared genuine. Huru was indeed much changed.

Even so, as much as Huru was a changed man and his family a loving family, I was glad there was not enough room in their hut for everyone to sleep. So, Coran, Pallyn and the four boys were to stay in the hut while the rest of us slept outside.

Outside, I found Soul. She was sitting alone, beyond the grounds of the hut, contemplating the stars. I quietly joined her, sitting silently.

"I don't hate Huru anymore," Soul said. "I just hate what happened."

"Although people can change, the past cannot," I replied.

Soul thought about that for a moment. "I always wondered what I would do if I saw Huru again. Now, I am surprised that I feel only calmness," she said. "It's the same feeling that I get when looking at the stars."

"That's your inner peace," I said. "With inner peace we are strong, yet we do not need to prove that strength. Inner peace is a calm strength."

Soul rolled her eyes good-humouredly. "Do you know everything?"

I laughed at the thought. "I know that with each thing I learn, I discover ten more things that I need to learn," I shrugged.

"How frustrating," Soul looked at me, her eyes sparkling with mischief. "Then best not teach me anything. Least that way, I can have a nice, simple life."

Trell came to join us, asking what this talk of a simple life was all about. Soul teased him, telling him that now they were paired, she was doomed to live a simple life and would probably be a farmer's mate planting corn and baking bread. Trell put his arm around her, tenderly kissed her, and then told her that if she wanted to bake bread then, as long as it was with him, he would be a happy man. It was good to see that my friend had found what her heart needed.

I slept that night under a warm sky, with the biting flies enjoying me for food far more than was comfortable. Having been awakened to the smell of fruit tea and hot breads, and given an ample supply of water for the last segment of our journey, we left Huru's abode. His was the last in-betweener hut. From this point we were leaving the trail of the river.

We threw our bundles over our shoulders and walked away from the water. Now we were crossing the dry sands towards Hollow.

I was not sure what to expect of Hollow. One part of me expected a town of greatness, with people of learning and broad thinking, having heard the plans and stories from Jin. The other part of me expected the same dry, foul smelling, ugly assortment of people and dwellings that I had visited before.

The reality was somewhere between the two.

THIRTY

The Hollow

From a distance, Hollow looked like a haze of brown shadows on a colourless, flat landscape, exactly as it had the first time I had seen it.

As we neared the town, I noticed subtle changes. The farmlands encircling it had expanded, and were now twice the width.

Closer still, directly ahead of us, the same dusty path ran straight through the sprouting pale crops and towards the huts.

We reached the crops, where several young men noticed our approach. They stopped their work and joined our walk. They didn't talk, choosing instead to follow a few strides behind. It felt rather like we were being chaperoned towards something unpleasant.

Past the crops, where the dusty path ran between closely built wooden huts, and more people joined us, leaving their homes or the tasks they were doing. Our small group of travellers was clearly expected here in Hollow. It was as if people had been waiting. As we walked, there was a hush around us bar concealed whispers. It felt surreal.

I was relieved when someone with a friendly voice called Jin's name, and a man whom I recognised as one of the soldiers came to greet us. From there on, we felt a little less apprehensive, with talk around us and several people handing out flasks of fresh water. I was glad to see the attire of the townsfolk had changed. Gone were the long red gowns I had seen on my previous visit. Now, there was no uniform. Most wore shades of pale, loose, sandy-coloured clothing with head wrappings to shade from the sun.

As we passed through Hollow's outskirts, the dusty path that kicked up fine sand with our footfalls changed to smooth, cobbled stones. The huts nearer the centre looked more tended, with small fruit trees in raised urns around the outside, and canopies placed over doorways for shade. Bunches of dried lavender hung from windows, repelling the flies and lacing the smell of dried faeces with deep floral notes. Hollow still smelt of waste. Still, it was not as bad as I remembered.

Our small group was now surrounded by hundreds of Hollow's inhabitants. There was pushing and bustling amongst them. I could pick out words from their hushed talk; whispers of kutu and black-winged ones. Their faces strained to better glimpse us. Their eyes scanning past us adults, lingering on the children, as if looking for something. I didn't like it. Many were looking for signs of the half-kutu babies. They did not realise those babes were the four boys.

At the centre of the town, the huts stopped, opening up to a large circular space paved with cobbled stones. This was where I had previously witnessed Wirrel's burning. Now, in the midst of that space, was a single wooden building. It was too large to simply be a dwelling, built on two levels, with multiple small windows and several doorways. There, standing in one of the doorways was Jan. He was watching our approach, smiling.

Jan came forward to greet us, directing us towards the central building. As we got to the doorway, the crowd that had joined us came to a halt, and Jan turned around to face them.

"Hollow welcomes all," Jan declared loudly. "Some come home, while others are new, welcome faces."

There was a ragged cheer from the crowd.

"To celebrate," Jan continued, "we all feast together tonight. Bring your suppers to the town circle and we dine as one. We'll have singing and dancing and wine; a proper Hollow celebration."

There came another, more enthusiastic cheer.

I felt more than a little uncomfortable with so many faces staring at us. I had hoped that we could make a modest entry into Hollow. I had hoped that we could just quietly join the townsfolk and settle in, unnoticed. It seemed that Hollow had its own ideas.

The crowd didn't disperse. I forced a smile, hoping my uncertainty wasn't creating a grimace instead. Thankfully, Jan ushered us into the wooden dwelling, and the crowd did not follow.

Inside the wooden dwelling, there was one large open area with doors to smaller rooms at either end. In the central space, there were two people teaching. Around each of them, sitting on the floor, was an assortment of people of all ages, listening. It was a good, airy space, with a calm atmosphere, and tiny candles flickering in the gloomier corners. This, I realised, was Hollow's own version of the Temple of Learning. Jin had spoken about this place.

Jan directed us towards one end of the building. I thought I recognised one of the teachers: I was sure his name was Findal, a kindly, tall, elderly man who had regularly visited the Temple of Learning. He was sitting on a short wooden stool, engrossed in his talk. He glanced up when we walked past.

It was definitely Findal. He recognised me too. His intense concentration broke into a genuine smile. It was good to see him. He was a good man, and I was relieved to see another face that I knew. Findal nodded, and then as we passed he resumed his talk. I heard him say the words 'bios' and 'harvesting' and guessed he was teaching human origin. A part of me wanted to stop and listen.

We entered an off-shoot room where cushions had been laid out for sitting; blankets were heaped in one corner, and nourishment was laid out on a central table. I also noted four empty cribs.

"Brother," Jan welcomed Jin first, and then turned to us all. "To those new here, welcome to Hollow. To others, welcome home. Please, you've had a long journey, make yourself comfortable. If you will be happy to stay here for a short while, once I am told your requirements, I will arrange more permanent living space. So eat. Sleep. Or have a look around the town. We've brought in changes of clothing if you want them. And there's cribs for the babes. . ."

Jan paused, glancing between us. I could see he was noticing that there were no infants present. News would have travelled with the earlier soldiers about the four baby boys. Jan would be looking for four babies of around seven moons old.

"Jan," I intercepted, before he could ask.

"Tachra, my friend," he bowed.

It was a little disconcerting to see my friend being so formal. I smiled, giving him a hug, and then looped my arm through his, standing next to him.

"Jan, may I introduce you to the four babes," I said.

I beckoned to the boys, indicating to them to walk forward.

"Pall, Lyn, Brune, Viir," I introduced the boys in order, "this is Jan, Jin's brother. Jan," I nodded, "these are the babes. But they are not so little anymore."

The four boys, all now taller than Iris, performed perfect bows, greeting Jan and thanking him for his kind hospitality. Jan's mouth fell ajar, but he quickly gathered himself, bowing in return.

Once all the newcomers had been introduced, several of the soldiers who had accompanied us left to return to their families. The four boys wasted no time finding the largest plates so that they could stack them with food. Coran and Pallyn nestled into a corner, watching their boys. Iris went to find the cleansing area, insisting that she did not need an escort, so Soul and Trell cuddled up on some of the cushions for a doze. The cushions did look alluring: extra-large, very plump, and soft too. They were the first proper cushions I had seen since leaving the Temple, and even their rough hessian covers looked good enough to fall upon.

Before I could nestle down, Jin lightly touched my arm, indicating for me to follow.

Jin and I joined Jan in a small, quiet room at the very back of the temple.

"I know what you are going to ask," Jin spoke to his brother as soon as the door was closed. "And yes, those four boys truly are the half-kutu babes. They are good boys. They are keen to help, and keen to be part of a good community. When you get to know them, you will come to love them too."

Jan nodded, assimilating the information, and then looked at me.

"I see their energy. They are good beings," I affirmed. "Just children really, with heightened skills."

"That's welcome news." Jan's concerned expression lifted a little. "Gossip here has been rife."

"Is there anything I should be made aware of?" Jin asked.

Jan paused, considering. "When news came that you would be arriving soon, some townsfolk did have a problem with the new additions of half Nigh-kutu beings. I told them that if they were no longer content to live in Hollow then they should leave."

"And did they?"

"Yes. Around a dozen. Mainly from the Udan family."

Jin shook his head.

"What better choice did I have?" Jan responded. He then looked at me apologetically. "It is sometimes difficult guiding people, especially where fear is concerned."

"A thing I know well," I sympathised. I paused, thinking. "Jan, do *you* think we have done the right thing in bringing the boys here? Will they be safe? Will the people be open enough to see them for who they truly are?"

Jan did not answer at first, giving my question consideration.

"If they are good beings, which you assure me that they are," Jan replied, "given time they will be accepted."

"What can I do?" I asked.

"If you can aid in integrating them."

"Of course," I said. "And you know these townsfolk, so any guidance will be gladly heard."

"Hollow is more open minded than most towns. And," Jan added, "although some have left, we have new arrivals daily now that news spreads that we have built a place of learning."

"That is fair news," I replied, glad to hear that even since the kutu war, so many still wanted to learn.

"Yes and no," Jan replied. "Hollow expands beyond its capabilities. We cannot produce enough crops, no matter how fast we try planting them."

I could see the potential problem. In this dry, arid area, increasing crop yield would be difficult at best.

We continued our discussion, outlining suggestions such as Viir's water pump, and how establishing some of his inventions would be good for the town and the boys. There seemed to be many things that could be done to integrate the boys while showing their true natures. Jin and Jan naturally fell into deep discussion about Hollow's growth. I was tired and hungry and overcome by so many new people that my mind wandered. I apologised when Jin and Jan paused their talk, looking at me expectantly. They had just asked me a question and I'd not heard a word of it.

"Please, it's me who should apologise," Jan said. "You've just completed a three-moon journey. You need rest."

"Thank you," I bowed, appreciative that he'd not been offended at my inattentiveness.

I left Jin and Jan, passing back through the main open space in the centre of the building. I noticed Pall and Lyn sitting among the group of students, listening avidly to Findal. I was relieved to see that neither Findal, nor their fellow students, treated Pall and Lyn any differently to the others. I hoped that it stayed that way once they all realised who and what the four boys were.

I went to stand outside to observe the movement of the town and take in some quiet air. The cobbled centre was a bustle of activity. Some people were swapping items; others were making things such as buckets, baskets or cloth. I had never seen a town operate like this. In Threetops, each household grew everything it needed, wove its own cloth, and made its own utensils. Whatever we had extra, we gave away to those with young ones. Here, people appeared to do just one thing, and lots of it, in order to swap their extras. Although it appeared to function, I imagined that making the same item day-in day-out could become very tedious. Not only that, but meant each individual and each family lost the ability to be independent if they wished. Their existence here in Hollow now relied upon having others of different skill sets around them.

As I stood, simply absorbing my surrounds, someone suddenly grabbed me from behind.

I felt someone's arms firm around my waist, lifting me from my feet.

Before I could protest, that someone was swinging me in a circle.

I was put down, my hand grabbed, and then spun around to face my assailant.

"Ren!"

"Hello Tachra green-eyes."

"You got tall!"

"Perhaps you got small," Ren ruffled my hair. "I cannot tell you how happy I am to see you! Dinah will be delighted too. When we got news that you lived, we thanked the skies a thousand times."

Ren caught my arm, threading it through his as we walked across the busy cobbled marketplace. I noticed quite a few eyes glance at me, unsure. I now felt very conspicuous in my travelling clothes. The luminous kutu fabric made me look as out of place as I felt. Such obviously kutu attire would not help me, or any of my friends, to settle into this rough desert town.

"I hope to see lots of you," Ren told me. "I am a man of Hollow now, so no avoiding me."

"I heard you were injured," I looked at his hand. It still had splints on it and up his lower arm, as if trying to straighten it. Around the splints were thick fabric bandages.

"Yes," Ren held up his bandaged hand. "A point to remember: a hand cannot stop a kutu laser. My own fault. Wasn't thinking. Happened in one of the last assaults of the kutu. Stanze got me out. I owe him my life."

"You know that I can mend your hand," I said. "A few days. A bit each day. I can make it as good as new. But," I teased, "I can't do anything about that new silver streak in your lovely sandy hair."

"That," Ren shrugged good-humouredly, "was not the kutu war. That was when Dinah told me another baby was on the way. Happened there and then."

Ren's joy and humour were infectious. He had me laughing at him and myself, being cheeky and feeling totally at ease. I almost forgot about the cautious stares and hushed talk that seemed to follow us.

Ren stopped walking, indicating to one of the narrow huts that overlooked the central area.

"This is where I now live," he announced. "So, now that you know, you will come to supper tonight after the feasting, which for you won't be so much of a feasting. For you it will be more a case of everyone wanting to talk to you. Or," he nudged, "just stare at you. It seems that all eyes are upon the guest on my arm even now."

Ren performed a bow, and then another, turning in a full circle as if bowing to all those who were staring. Although I felt a little embarrassed, I was grateful that he was being so bold about the guarded glances from so many.

"You are so badly behaved," I tutted under my breath.

"So Dinah keeps telling me," Ren cheekily winked. "She'll be back with the babies before supper. She's gone to the weavers for new tunics, to look especially nice for you when you come to supper tonight. When she sees you, she'll tell you that you look far too thin and what you need is some of her hot-pot."

I went to request if such a wonderful meal could be on a later night. The morrow perhaps, once I was rested. But Ren would not take no for an answer.

"Dinah will make my life a misery if she finds out I saw you and did not invite you. And," he added cheekily, "if you don't come, she will tell me that I must have said something wrong. So, I cannot win unless you join us."

I agreed that supper would be lovely.

"How is your mother?" I tactfully asked. What I really wanted to know was whether Mags, Ren's mother, was now living with Ren or not. I knew Jin had banished her back to Meadsins. Nevertheless, Mags had a way of not doing what was best for her, or anyone else. I really did not want to have to face her.

Ren became very solemn. He assured me that Mags did not live with him. He said that the entire town had been publicly notified about what had happened. Apparently, Mags had not wanted to return to Meadsins. But return to Meadsins she had, although forced, and despite her aggressive protests.

"I love her," Ren shrugged, "but I am ashamed."

"Do not take it upon your own shoulders," I said. "Hopefully, with time, she will see the error of her ways."

"I do not hold my breath for it."

I squeezed his arm, giving him reassurance.

I could see that Ren was hurting. To my true vision, hurt of the heart looked similar to hurt of the flesh. I pushed some healing energy into that cut heart, making a note that I would do that each day too.

Before we could talk any more, a short, placid-faced, stocky man came up to Ren, slapped him on the back and told him he was needed to resolve a fruit-swap dispute. Ren rolled his eyes, saying that he bet it was old woman Lever again and that she was never content. I waved Ren away and headed back to the wooden temple.

Before I could get back into the wooden temple, I bumped into Trell, hurrying across the town centre. He made a beeline for me when he saw me and asked if I could spare a moment. Although I was desperate to change my conspicuous attire and bathe, none of those were as important as Trell's anxious expression.

Trell guided us past the wooden temple and into another area of huts. These huts were small, but placed a little further apart. I guessed they were some of the older abodes, being less angularly placed, and their wood had paled to a silver beige with age.

"Jin and I marked up a plan of Hollow," Trell spoke as we walked. "I will build a new hut for Soul and Iris. But for now," he pointed at one of the very last little huts, "do you think they would like this?"

The little hut Trell pointed to was clearly in need of fixing. But, despite its tatty appearance, I knew Soul would like it. It was at the end of the higgledy row, looking out onto the newly planted orchards. There were long-beans dangling from the stems of climbing vegetables to one side, and a stone rockery with the remnants of its planting on the other.

"Of course I shall fix it straight away," Trell fretted. "But do you think Soul would be disappointed? It's not grand like the Temple of Learning."

I saw Trell bite his lip, and it made me smile that Soul's habits were already being picked up by him. His usually confident, calm expression looked so concerned at the idea that he might disappoint her.

"I think Soul will love any place that you choose so considerately for her and Iris," I said. "And," I added, "I think that nothing I say will take away that anxious face you're wearing. So, I think you should bring Soul and Iris here straight away and show it to them. I am sure you'll make them both happy."

Trell agreed, albeit reluctantly. I knew that Soul would see Trell's thoughtfulness and that would make her love him even more. I knew that my friend would be happy in a tiny cave up a desolate mountain if her heart was fulfilled.

I was thankful to return to the quieter anonymity of the wooden temple. Before I could be called elsewhere, I found the cleansing room and a change of clothing, and thoroughly refreshed myself. It felt odd to stand in the wooden square and pour jugs of cold water over myself once again. I had not done this for a long time. I had become happily accustomed to both the vast expanse of my lake and the wonderful kutu hot cleansing stands. I realised I had a great deal of adjusting to do. I had not lived like a normal human for a long time, if I ever had at all.

Having washed a great deal of sand out of my hair and off my skin, despite the rough drying clothes and soggy pre-used soap leaves, I felt much better. The dress I chose was the plainest one I could find. Here, in this town, until I knew the ebb and flow of its people better, I wanted to be as invisible as I could. I was sure I would adjust, but it would take time.

When I returned to the welcome room, I realised that I was not the only person who needed to adjust to this new town. Both Coran and Pallyn looked wide-eyed, like unsure animals. They had neither changed or moved from their corner on the cushions.

"There are rooms here, on the upper floor," Coran told me when I sat with them. "We will stay here while. . ." she paused, searching for the right words.

"While you get accustomed?" I suggested.

"Yes," she nodded. "Pallyn and I were wondering if you would stay here too? Just until we are settled into our new homes? I know it is a big task that we ask of ask you. You have already done so much for us."

Poor Coran. She was so anxious. She was so nervous.

"It is no burden," I assured her. "Of course I'll stay here too. I'll stay until you are settled in. And even once you've settled in, I will make sure you remain well."

"Oh, thank you," Coran sighed with relief. "This is so different from Meadsins. It's so busy. And so noisy. I feel like it's swallowing me up."

"Do you remember how to contain your energy?" I asked.

Coran nodded.

"Then practice that. It will help a little. And you know," I tilted my head, considering, "if you do not settle in, you do not have to stay here. There are other towns and places of all types to live."

"I know," Coran looked reassured. "Although the boys already appear content. Despite the strangeness of some people here, they've had three plates of food each and have already made themselves at home."

I had noticed that too. All four boys were now sitting listening to Findal speak. I glanced through the open doorway, observing them. They were engrossed. To my true vision, their shadow-light energy glowed around them, spanning far beyond their flesh, touching the energy of their teacher with integrity. Those four were already at ease, blending with their new surroundings. I just hoped that their new surroundings would be equally as open in adjusting to them.

The rest of that day moved so fast that I could barely think. Jin showed Coran, Pallyn, the four boys and myself to the rooms on the upper floor. I chose the smallest room, as my needs demanded nothing more. Before I had even put my bag down, Jan called us all outside where tables were being arranged for a welcome feast.

At the feast, all, if not most, of the town came bearing foods. A young girl and boy took it in turns to sing some enchanting melodies. Jin encouraged Brune to show off his skill for shaping stone, creating a magnificently bold statue of the sun for outside the Temple. Jin talked to the crowd about Viir's plans for installing water pumps. The crowd was in high spirits, laughing, jesting, shouting to one another. I felt uncomfortable to be around so many people, but I concealed it well, smiling and saying hello to so many people that I lost count.

The crowd clapped eagerly as three men finished playing a strange melody on some reeds with holes cut into them, an instrument rather like a kutu fluchean. They were still clapping when Pall and Lyn walked forward to address them. I had been midway through thanking a young woman for her welcome when I glanced up. Pall and Lyn had changed their faces. They stood there, in front of the masses, and made themselves morph to look like mini versions of Jin and Jan while everyone watched.

It was too late for me to stop them. The twins were so caught up in the moment, the applause, and the general good spirits, that they wanted to show what they could do too. They did it with such innocent intention. They did it with no badness in their hearts, just wanting to join in to show their skills too. But the moment they walked forward wearing the faces of Jin and Jan, I felt the uncertainty of the crowd and a sudden hush.

I nudged Jin hard in the ribs. Jin moved forward, clapping enthusiastically, as did I. After an awkward moment, some of the people cautiously clapped too.

"Pall and Lyn," Jin announced, "have a unique understanding of energy. The skies bless us because Lyn is a healer. And Pall has said he will aid locating underground water sources for our water pumps."

The crowd clapped again. A few more this time.

I suddenly felt sorry for the boys. All of them. It was as if they were having to prove themselves to be worthy of acceptance into this dusty little town. No one should need to prove themselves to another. The boys seemed oblivious. Of course they would be, as their childish innocence still accepted everything as good. And I understood why Jin was doing what he was. This was his way of helping them become accepted as quickly and openly as possible. Jin knew these Hollow people better than me. I would stand by his decisions. Still, it would not stop me seeing with my own eyes. If I had to make a stand to protect them from becoming spectacles, I would.

As the evening wore on, most of the people retired to their huts for the night and there were no further incidents. About thirty villagers remained behind with my group of friends, continuing the merriment, encouraged by honey mead. Iris and the four boys had gone to bed while Trell sung some of his songs, making Soul join in, and everyone appeared to be enjoying themselves. I was ready for sleep, but Ren came to greet me, escorting me across the cobbles where Dinah and the twins waited in new dresses.

It was refreshing to see the genuine affection and movement of energy between Dinah and Ren. The two twin girls, with their sandy red hair and freckles, reminded me of a young Ren. Neither wanted to go to bed while I was there. Their resolute difference of opinion concluded with Ren chasing them around the table with a blanket over his head. Although I was weary in mind and body, it ended up being a charming supper with the buoyant company of two old friends.

I eventually left Ren and Dinah, crossing over the cobbles to return to the wooden temple. Hollow was quiet now, bar the muffled talk from inside some of the huts, and it appeared that all the townsfolk had retired.

"Take the nigh-kutu half-breeds back whence they came!"

The abrupt shout had come from nowhere.

I immediately stopped walking, sensing my surrounds like a cat wary of potential threats, and tentatively glanced around.

My eyes could not see anyone within the gloom and shadows, but my true vision could see the energy of two teenage boys lurking to one side of a hut. I could see the similar colours of their energy. I guessed they were brothers. I did not sense evil maliciousness, more ignorance. Even so, such ignorance could escalate. I turned to their position.

"You two brothers," I said calmly. "Come to the temple tomorrow and I will introduce you to the boys properly, after we have had a polite discussion on understanding. Meanwhile, I guess your parents do not know that you have snuck out of your beds. Shall I rouse them and let them know?"

There was a short pause, and then I heard the boys run off, believing that I knew who they were.

I waited a moment, sensing for any other people lurking in the shadows. All seemed quiet.

I quickly entered the wooden temple without further ado, realising that I would need to keep my senses and true vision alert. The night was in its prime, and those in the temple were asleep. I quietly tip-toed over squeaking wooden floors and up to the small space that would be my room for a while. I closed the door. At last, for the first time in three moons, I had a moment alone.

I carefully untied my bundle, removed the layers of protective fabric, and took out my precious cargo. The Book of Fate had been heavy to carry for so long.

I placed the Book of Fate in the corner of the room, ran my hands over the surface, and then covered it with a blanket to conceal it from prying eyes. The small mementos of my kutu friends were arranged on the floor, next to my mattress. I performed my evening ritual, first trying to contact any kutu on the communication port, then touching each of the keepsakes. And then I covered those too. Finally, exhausted with the long journey, tense surroundings, too much conversation, adjustments to change, and a multitude of other tiring endeavours, I fell into a deep sleep.

The following day was busy again. There was so much occurring and so much to absorb while keeping my senses alert, that my mind spun. Jan asked me if I would consider teaching the townsfolk occasionally. Of course I said yes, although I suddenly wished that we had taken along the kutu's three-dimensional teaching system. I watched the four boys vigilantly and watched the differing attitudes of people around them. Trell showed Soul and Iris their potential new home and the three of them began immediately repairing and cleaning. I helped them for a while, being pulled away by Shaul, who was looking for me on behalf of Jin.

Jin's hut was a small, modest home behind the wooden temple. The door was fully open. Inside, Jin was standing over a table, dressed in a long sarong skirt, in a single room with a curtained area for bathing. In one corner, his wicker armour stood like an empty guardsman, with his spears and a sword propped against it. He bade me enter when I knocked on the already open door.

"You never need to request entry to my home," Jin looked up, beckoning me over.

As I approached, I could see that Jin was looking at a large piece of parchment, which I saw was a map. The map was human drawn, not kutu. It was the first time I had seen one drawn by a fellow human.

"Did you do this?" I asked.

"Yes, with help from others," Jin replied. He looked at me and smiled. His dark, curly hair had grown long with our travels, and it fell over his face. He pulled it back, tying it into a tail like the kutu would often do. He held my stare for a bit too long. I looked down to the map to stop myself from blushing.

"It's a good map," I said. "I guess this is Hollow," I pointed, "here."

"Yes," Jin replied, turning back to the parchment. "And this is the river. You know maps, and have travelled; does this look accurate to you?"

I looked closer. The land drawings around Hollow were accurate. And the area west of Hollow, towards the valley, was accurate too, although not to scale. But there was much missed out to the East and North. Some of the areas I had traversed. Some I had seen from the skies, when Jychanumun had taken me flying.

I pulled up a stool and sat down.

"Here," I pointed, "the river is wider and it forks north here. And here," I pointed again, "is a small area of sparse land nestled in overlapping hills."

Jin marked on the map as I spoke, asking questions about verdant areas, lakes, hill heights and scale. Before long, he too had pulled up a stool and was making notes over the parchment.

"New people arrive in Hollow regularly," Jin talked as he worked. "The town's population grows rapidly and does not look like slowing down. Although," he shook his head, "another seven townsfolk left this morning."

"Because of the boys?" I asked.

"Yes. They said the face-changing unnerved them. It's a shame. But I think all is settled now."

I nodded, finding the news disquieting. Jin however, seemed confident that the matter was finished.

The afternoon went swiftly while working with Jin. It transpired that his plans were to be fast-tracked. If they wanted to ensure enough food for all, they needed to farm more fertile land.

"Growing produce closer to the river has not been as successful as hoped," Jin informed me. "The soil here is unforgiving."

He then confided that with current crop yields, there would not be enough food by the time the seasons had fully turned. I could now see this was an urgent dilemma.

I rubbed my brow, trying to think of a solution.

"Where I was born, crops would grow even where we didn't plant them. But Threetops is much too far."

I paused, remembering something that Sail had said. It might work: it was a distance away, but surely was close enough.

"Here," I pointed to the map. "East of Hollow, this fork in the river. Take the other fork, heading north, and it is all fertile land. Sail told me about it. He said there wasn't a town or village for several moons, yet the land was green as far as the eye could see. And I've seen it from the skies, when flying with the kutu. It is luscious and fertile. One area here is packed with nut trees. And here," I pointed again, "I'm sure this land is full of wild junir."

Jin made me mark on the map where these areas of land were. I circled two large areas that both went off the parchment and were criss-crossed by the river. Most of the untouched, fertile land was far too far from Hollow, but some would be accessible.

"It would be a difficult journey for carrying food and grain," Jin considered. "Too far to walk."

"It would be," I admitted. "To carry grain such a distance would be near impossible. But," I raised my eyebrows, "if you were Sail and had a raft, it would not."

"By the skies!" Jin thumped his fist on the table. "Of course! We build rafts and traverse the river. Tachra," he beamed, "you beautiful, remarkable woman; here is something that may save Hollow's folk from starving."

Jin felt that there was no time to waste. He rolled up the parchment, gathered the writing tools, and we hurriedly left his hut in search of his brother, Jan.

Jin wanted me to join him in the meeting with Jan. We passed a young man en route to the town circle, and Jin asked him to fetch Trell, Shaul, and several others whose names I did not yet know. In no time we were all grouped in the small, now cramped, room at the back of the wooden temple.

During that meeting, I listened more than I talked. The door was open, as the room was so hot, and young Viir came and sat with us, listening while sketching on one of the rolls of papyrus that he carried everywhere. I glanced at Jin when Viir entered. This boy had a brain that when it came to designing the rafts would know instinctively what would and wouldn't work.

By the time dusk was dimming our surroundings and Findal came to light the lamps, my friends had the first stage of their plan. Originally, I had thought they would simply travel to the green lands, collect any available edible vegetation that grew naturally, and bring it to Hollow. It transpired that their objective was even grander. They had decided to develop a whole other town in the green lands. They said that it was the only way to ensure a constant supply of food for the people.

"We have families here that are good lands-men," Trell explained, "yet the land here is not good. Those families don't want to leave Hollow entirely; they want their children and their children's children to spend time learning at our little temple. So, we will set up one small town, the new town, for growing crops. And this place, Hollow, will be where people come together to study, find mates, and learn."

"Those who wish to farm will set up this new farmland. We'll bring their children back here to learn over winter," Jin added. "At the same time we can transport grain and produce."

"Yes. . . one town, split in two locations," Trell agreed. "Hollow and New Hollow."

It sounded like a good idea. I understood why they couldn't just move everyone to greener land. Hollow was part of a larger network of villages with expanded families settled across those villages. And even if it hadn't been, this was where they called home. Most would not want to leave.

The group of men were enthusiastic. Everyone had different points to make. No one could find any insurmountable problems with the idea. My mind whizzed as I listened to their discussion, often trying to listen to several people talking at once.

"There's not enough trees to make the rafts," Viir suddenly spoke.

That silenced everyone.

"One of the consequences of desert land is lack of trees," Viir shrugged. "Most of the few that did grow here have already been cut down to make the huts."

It was true. The landscape here was sparse.

"Any thoughts?" I asked.

"Well, if it were me, I would not have cut down so many trees without ensuring I was cultivating new ones first," Viir replied.

The simplicity of Viir's words made me laugh. I nodded, agreeing with him. "Thoughts on going forward?" I asked.

"Well, if rafts are now more important than huts, we'll have to use the wood from some of the huts," Viir replied. "And while we're doing that, start planting trees for future needs."

Jin said that he would organise a group to oversee a planting regime for more trees. But, even if he started now, those little seedlings would not be mature for many turns of the seasons.

Jan had been quiet for some time, just listening to the plans as they developed.

"I know that there are those who would share living space, for a while," Jan said. "If many of our families will be moving to the new farmland, it would only be temporary. I can make at least twenty huts available for their wood fairly quickly. Maybe more."

"Twenty huts will make you five to eleven sturdy rafts," Viir replied, "depending on the size of the hut and the cut of the wood."

Viir carefully tore off the end of the roll of his papyrus, placing the small piece of paper on the table. On it he had sketched a design for a wooden raft. The drawings showed the raft from different angles, with measurements and descriptions.

Jan studied the plans, taking in the designs and absorbing the realisation that Viir, although young, truly was a forward thinker.

"Perfect," Jan affirmed. "Viir, would you help ensuring they're made correctly?"

"Yes, with Brune," Viir agreed. "Brune knows how to shape wood. And Pall and Lyn can see the energy of everything; they can help."

It was ideal; all the boys working together with the leaders of Hollow for the greater good of all. I could not have arranged such a good result if I had tried.

The meeting could have continued, there was so much to discuss. But Coran came looking for Viir, telling us that it was well past his sleeping time. It was dark and quiet outside, and it seemed the entire rest of the town was already asleep. None of us had realised how late it had grown. We all dispersed, agreeing that this room would now become the central place for organising this grand new venture. Here, this group of us would hold council once a day.

I returned to my little room on the upper floor. I was exhausted, but content. It was not just the fact that the boys had a positive project to work on together. Nor was it because the leaders of Hollow had found a way to protect their townsfolk from going hungry. It was because I felt hope: real, tangible hope. Here, in this seemingly dismal, dusty, dry town, despite the difficulties and adjusting, were some people who strove to do good things, with good hearts, and good intentions. And this was just the beginning of humans living without the kutu in their lives. With time they could flourish to be so much more. Arrunn had to be wrong. People would not turn on each other. They would follow the Shaa-kutu's existence and work together in harmony.

That night, I think I slept with a smile on my face.

The following day did not get any less hectic than the previous one. There always seemed to be someone wanting me to attend a meeting, or someone asking me to teach a subject to some students. Brune and I inspected and selected empty huts that had the most suitable timber to make rafts. I helped to set up a space where Lyn could work his healing energy. I had stomach-ache from having eaten mainly sour apples. I had never liked sour apples. The tension in the town towards the boys had softened a little. It was still there, along with the hushed whispers and occasional pointing, but I had hope that given time there would be acceptance.

The next few days passed quickly, blurring together in a mass of activity and people. During this time, no matter how busy I was, I made sure I kept my lessons with the four boys and Iris. The boys had started to ask pertinent questions: about their futures, their fathers and their origins. I spoke to their mothers, and it was decided that they needed to know the truth. So, Coran, Pallyn and myself gathered the four boys together in a room that was private and we told them how they had come to be.

With the news, at first, the boys fell quiet. Then Pall confessed that Viir had already told them as much, having calculated that this was the most likely explanation for their origins. Apparently, Pall had refused to believe it at that time. Now he, particularly, did not take the confirmation well.

"I hate them," Pall declared. "All the Nigh-kutu do is hurt people. And in the future they intend on coming back to hurt people again. That's not right."

The other boys agreed.

"When I am older," Pall said with vehemence, "I am going to travel to the shadow and kill them all."

I felt the determination behind Pall's words. I saw his energy gathering around him like dark storm clouds. Coran and Pallyn looked to me for help.

"You would do more good here," I said, "where you are loved and cherished."

"No, I wouldn't," Pall disagreed, not accepting my reasoning. "If the Nigh-kutu are going to return, I'll do better if I can kill them first."

"Those Nigh-kutu are trained warriors," I tried explaining further. "They have trained for thousands of years in the art of war."

Pall looked at me adamantly. His expression changed and a frown creased his brow.

"That is not what you are thinking," Pall said slowly.

The look that Pall had on his face when he said that was heartbreaking. As if I was one of the few people he expected plain truth from; as if he trusted me to give him the truth and I was breaking that trust. I should have been blocking my thoughts. I had grown lax.

"You're thinking that I would never get to the shadow because I'm only half Nigh-kutu. You're thinking that even if I could, I would be recognised as different and killed straight away. You're thinking I wouldn't be strong enough." Pall shook his head.

"That is true," I sighed. "I was trying to be gentle and kind."

Viir halted his sketching and glanced up. "We've just been told we were made from pain and suffering. I do not think this is the time to coddle us with words just to be gentle."

"Fair point," I acquiesced. "Apologies."

Whether I liked it or not, and no matter how much I wanted to protect these boys, I knew my best route was plain speaking.

"Firstly," I told Pall, "you would need to learn how to fight the Nigh-kutu way. You would need to be so good at it that you could win against many warriors at once. Secondly, you would need to be able to disguise all that is human in you so that to them you looked like them and could get into an advantageous position. But," I shook my head, "thirdly, that's if you could even get to the shadow. Your humanity binds you; that is how you came to be at all."

"The second and third points I will be able to do," Pall determined. "Not yet, but with practice I will. The first point," he looked to me, "tell me who can teach me. I want to learn how to fight."

For a moment, I cloaked my thoughts and let them race. If the townsfolk saw Pall learning to fight, would it increase their wariness of him? No. That could be overcome, as Jin and Jan taught fighting to many of the boys and young men – Pall would be no different. But could his learning to fight awaken dormant warrior traits that could corrupt him? No. Not Pall. Not any of them. I alone could see the full truth of who they were.

After a moment of consideration, I saw no reason why Pall should not learn the art of fighting. I asked his mother if she too would find it acceptable.

Pallyn agreed. I was glad that she did. Even if the training came to nothing, the physical and mental requirements would be good for one as active as Pall. And anyway, I saw his determination. If he was told he could not learn to fight, he intended on doing it anyway.

"Well," I decided, "I know that Jin and Jan teach combat to several of the boys here. It would not be out of place in Hollow for another to join that learning."

"Do they teach the kutu way?" Pall asked.

I considered this. Jin and Jan were not hugely familiar with the kutu methods of fighting. Of course, if I could choose anyone to train Pall, it would be Jychanumun. But that was wishful thinking.

"There is one man here who has been directly trained in fighting techniques by the kutu: he was shown the Shaa way, via Stanze, and Nigh, via Jychanumun," I thought aloud. "That one is Ren. He was among the first humans to help in the kutu war, so has considerable first-hand experience. Perhaps he could train you to some extent."

"When?" Pall asked.

"Shall we ask him directly after this?"

Pall nodded.

"Although do remember that, even if he does agree, he is no kutu. He will not be able to show you everything."

"I can work out the rest by myself," Pall determined.

I could see from his energy and resolve that yes, indeed, he would.

"Would you mind if I joined you, Pall?" Viir enquired.

"Of course not," Pall replied. "Once I get good, I'll need someone else strong to practice with."

Viir's request surprised me. He noticed my surprise.

"How can I be all that I could be if I do not embrace my shadow too?" Viir shrugged. "We four are all part warriors, no matter what other skills prevail."

"Do you all wish to learn?" I asked.

All the boys said yes, they did.

I told them that it was good that they would learn together.

"I don't see why we have to stay in these bodies anyway," Pall shrugged. "Our energies are stronger than our bodies. These bodies just hold us back. I'd learn to fight much better if I learnt more about fighting with energy."

The other boys readily agreed.

That gave me food for thought.

"Then there is one vital lesson you must learn now," I considered, looking at the four. "To energy, time goes much faster than to physical matter. That which is physical matter only is timeless, because the movement of time has no relevance to it. But energy, however, is dynamic, and for that, time moves fast. We," I indicated to all in the room, "are all a blend of both matter and energy. If you can learn and train while you have these physical bodies, you will have more time than if you were energy only."

"So we could train more, longer?" Pall asked, piecing together these new facts.

"Yes."

Pall looked at the others, nodding.

We all sat in silence for a while, and it felt as if the talk had naturally concluded. Just as I was about to suggest refreshments, Brune asked if he could ask a question. Of course, I said yes.

"Will we four die soon?" Brune bluntly asked.

"Of course not," I exclaimed.

"What Brune means," Viir intercepted, "is, will we continue aging quickly? Will we be old men and then be dead before our mammas are old?"

The other boys nodded vigorously. This was clearly something that had perplexed them.

"I do not believe so," I told them. "I think you'll live longer than most. Your energies are forcing you to reach adulthood quickly in order to protect you. But once your body is in an optimum state, you'll age slowly because you have unique self-repair systems."

"Are you sure?" Viir asked.

"As sure as I can be," I replied.

"Good," Viir said matter-of-factly. "I don't want to die soon. I have too much to do."

The rest of the boys agreed. They all seemed relieved.

The meaningful questions continued until the boys could think of nothing else to ask. I waited for a while, ensuring no deeply felt insecurities were being masked, and our talk naturally concluded. It had been a long discussion, although one that I knew would eventually come. I was glad that it had not been as difficult as I had expected.

Pall and I left in search of Ren. We found him fixing the worn floorboards in his hut, and he readily agreed to teach all four of the boys any fighting techniques he had learnt. He told Pall that it would be a good excuse for him to get out of a house full of girls. Pall found that funny, and the two instantly made a good connection. I could see that they would get along together perfectly.

The day had passed swiftly. It was already early evening. Soul and I had arranged to meet. Soul was expecting we would do chores together. I had other ideas.

Soul arrived after supper. She always looked at ease now, but this evening she looked particularly content.

"Guess what?" Soul asked as she sat herself down on the lone stool in my tiny room.

"You are with child?"

Soul threw her hands up in the air, pretending to be exasperated. "Can I not surprise you with anything?" she exclaimed.

"But my friend, delight is so much better than surprise. And I am delighted," I laughed. "Truly, this is the best news."

"It's another girl," Soul touched her belly.

"I guess Trell is overjoyed."

"More than I can cope with," Soul laughed. "I told him at first light. Now he won't let me do anything. I had to sit doing nothing all day while he looked after me. Please, my friend," she shook her head, "please give me some chores!"

"No," I replied. "The evening is too fine and your news too delightful to spoil with chores."

Before Soul could question me, I picked up a blanket, the small bundle I already had prepared, and guided her outside.

Soul and I wandered through the huts, ending up in the small orchard amidst the young sour fruit trees. It was almost full moon and the evening was particularly light and cool. When I showed Soul the small but appetizing picnic I had made for us both, it was her turn to be delighted. There were no sour apples in sight, although I had made sweetened apple water, and I had found some scented spices to make cakes. I had known that Soul was with child since we had arrived in Hollow. I'd readied the picnic earlier that day, knowing she would announce it soon.

We relaxed back on the blanket eating spiced cakes and talking about everything and anything. Her risqué humour made me laugh. My observational humour made her laugh. We made up stories about our surrounds, told our dreams for our tomorrows, and simply found joy in the moment.

"This," I lifted my mug of apple water, "is the joy of living. I am lucky to have a friend such as you."

"And I you. . ." Soul nodded. "To friends."

"Friends," I toasted. "And their growing families."

Soul's expression quivered a fraction.

"What is it?" I asked.

Soul looked to me, tilting her head. "Are you not lonely?" she asked.

"By the skies, no," I laughed. "I've never been lonely."

"I know there are many who love you," she said. "But you have never given your heart to a man. It is in our makeup to have a mate, yet you are alone. It makes me sad."

"Do not be sad, my friend. I am joyous that you've found love. But for me, it's not that simple."

"Yes, it is," Soul shrugged. "Is there no one who has caught your eye?"

"Once there was," I said. "But, as you said, it is in our natures to be attracted to others."

"Tachra," Soul exclaimed, "why are you not with him? Did he die? Did he already have a mate?"

"No," I shrugged.

Soul seemed momentarily speechless. Then her mouth fell open and she sat up straight. "Please do tell me that it is the most desirable, brilliant man in Hollow, bar my Trell of course. Please say that it's the beautiful Jin."

"Yes," I smiled. "But I'm not like others. My mind is connected to Jychanumun. He is like my twin. And my soul belongs to the Old One. And my heart is with Meah, my wildcat. . ."

"Stop talking," Soul interjected, waving her hand dismissively. "You've chosen bonds with beings that are alone by nature. The Old One, Jychanumun; even Meah is a type of wildcat and not a pack animal. But we humans were made to work together. You deny what could be the greatest part of you. You once told me that the kutu had a word for the type of passion between humans."

"Ros," I stated.

"Ros," Soul paused. "You have never felt ros. How can you embrace your human side if you don't allow yourself to feel human things?"

Soul had a point, I knew that. But I also knew that I too was a singular being. I couldn't help it. All the things that I was created their own conflicts. Did I like Jin? Yes, of course I did. And yes, I loved him too. But did I want to be with him?

"Now you're thinking about it too much," Soul tutted. "Sometimes you have to stop thinking and just feel. You do not give Jin a chance."

It was true. I didn't. Why didn't I? And then I knew.

"I love Jychanumun," I simply said.

It felt strange to say the words aloud.

"With all of me, through all times, and all existences, I love him completely," I said. "He is my fate and my choice. His is the face I see, no matter how beautiful a man may be, or how much that man desires me."

Soul nodded acceptingly.

"You must miss him," she contemplated.

"Yes, but it's not a sad thing," I replied. "It is a thing of beauty. And this," I held up my mug, "is not a night of sadness, but one of joy and laughter."

I was glad that Soul left the subject of mates, that our talk moved onto more general things, and we quickly resumed our laughter and banter. Eventually, having eaten all the spiced cakes and drunk all the apple water, the night was in its prime. The town had silenced and we were both sleepy.

Soul and I had both fallen asleep when we heard Trell's call. He had come looking for his mate, worried that she would not have enough rest.

I sleepily gathered my items, bid Soul and Trell goodnight, and then made my way back to my little room in the wooden temple.

It took me only moments to fall back asleep that night, with my blanket pulled around me on the grass mattress in my tiny room. I assumed I would sleep deeply, but my dreams returned and I tossed restlessly. Sometimes in my dreams I was running across sands, trying to catch something that I could not reach. Sometimes I was trying to say something but no sound would leave my lips. Sometimes someone was calling me and I could not wake. They kept calling and calling.

Tachra.

Tachra.

Tachra!

By the skies! This was no dream! This call was real.

I shot from my bed, disorientated, bumping into the wall before realising I was not in my big room at the Temple of Learning.

Iris? I searched with my mind.

I felt around in the dark for the door, pushing the door open and running towards the stairs.

Where are you? I called. "Iris!" I called aloud.

I did not get an immediate response, so I followed where my instincts were leading me. I ran down the rickety stairwell in the temple and across the dark, empty floor. It was pitch black everywhere. The moon's glow barely lit the inside of the building. I headed to where my memory told me the exit door was placed, feeling for a handle or something to get out. I could hear noise outside in the far distance; strange, muffled noises and movement. I heard someone cry out. The cry sounded like one of pain.

I ran to the source of the disturbance, calling loudly to any friends that might hear as I ran.

"Jin, Jan, Trell, Ren. HELP!" I shouted as my legs moved as fast as I could make them.

I could hear doors of huts being opened.

I ran through a section of huts towards the area where my ears were telling me the sound was coming from.

"I'm coming, Iris!" I shouted with both my mind and mouth.

I could now see torchlight.

There was a group of people just beyond the huts and a small person running towards them. A child. Iris.

The group of people looked as if they were throwing stones.

I could barely think.

I could only act.

My legs moved faster than I thought possible. I reached Iris just as she reached the crowd of people. The group of people were angry. I heard Mags' voice among them.

In front of the mob were Pall and Lyn. Lyn was on his knees, holding his shoulder. Pall was standing in front of him protectively.

"Get away!" I shouted to the people, going to stand in front of Pall and Lyn.

Iris ran to join me. "Get Jin," I instructed Iris through gritted teeth. "Now!"

I shoved Iris away as one of the rabble threw a stone, narrowly missing her. Iris began running back to the huts, shouting frantically for help.

"Stop this. Now," I instructed the crowd.

"See," someone – it sounded like Mags – said. "Even now she protects the black-winged beasts' spawn. Those two beasts can wear the face of another. They can take over your mind. It was them who made me sick. They'll get inside your mind and take you over 'till you're dead. That's if they don't eat you first. They are monsters who wear the face of men and eat people. And she, Tachra, is as bad as them."

It was definitely Mags. I'd know that voice and energy anywhere.

"That's not true. None of it." I replied, raising my voice.

The crowd began shouting different words, and I could make out none of them. I felt their fear. Over their fear, I felt their ignorant anger.

"Get away. Go home. This is. . ." I began to speak. But then a stone launched, hitting my knee and stopping my words.

I knew then that these people would not have ears to hear reason. Another stone narrowly missed me as I stood in front of Pall and Lyn.

"Move," I told Pall and Lyn. "I'll protect you, but move."

I leant over the boys as they hunched down, moving as fast as they could toward the closest hut. It was chaos. The people were shouting even louder. More stones were coming our way: some fast and small, others larger rocks.

From between the huts, I noticed Jin and several others emerge. They sprung forward to contain the crowd, but they were outnumbered. A scuffle started.

I could hear shouts and cries and protests and the sound of physical contact. The shouts and chants were layered into confusion. Another stone launched towards us, narrowly missing us. And then another. This one hit my hip, sending a thumping pain through my body.

I pushed the boys hard into the shadow of the closest hut.

Another stone hit the side of my head. A sharp pain shot through me. The strength went out of my body. I slumped to my knees. My legs wouldn't respond. Then, mustering every morsel of my strength, I forced myself up from my knees, stumbling forward, throwing myself over Pall and Lyn to protect them, imagining my energy was as strong as a kutu force-field barrier.

I could make out that more people were arriving. It was more of Jin's soldiers. The boys were concealed behind the hut, partly protected by the hut walls, wholly protected by me. I was furious, but I would not move; not until I knew that Pall and Lyn were safe.

The rabble had hushed. Jin, Jan, Ren and the soldiers had quickly contained over a dozen people, including Mags. Ren had her secured on one side and Jan on the other. Ren was shouting at Mags, telling her how stupid she had been. I was sure he was going to punch her, but he did not. I had never seen Ren angry like that before. His brow was furrowed over his narrowed eyes, his energy flickered angrily around him as he berated his mother. Jin and Jan ran over to where some of the soldiers were in a small group, hunched over something.

No one was coming to see if Pall and Lyn were alright. All eyes were looking to one side, where Jin and Jan now stood.

"Are you alright?" I whispered to Pall and Lyn, slowly getting up, checking them for cuts.

Pall and Lyn stood up. I could see that Lyn had a nasty cut that was already blackening into a bruise on his shoulder. His energy was pushing into the cut, trying to heal it. Other than that, both the boys were intact.

Seeing that they were well enough, my attention turned to Mags. I was furious.

"You stupid, ignorant, atrocious *achstahnnson* of a *larieliun*," I walked towards Mags, shouting in a mix of kutu and human. "I could wring your neck with my bare hands."

Mags didn't respond. She didn't even look at me. She looked beyond me. Everyone standing with her looked beyond me. It was as if I wasn't even there.

Lyn suddenly shot past me in the direction of Jin and Jan, who were still hunched over something with several men.

"Let me!" Lyn insisted, pushing through the others.

"Jin!" I called.

Jin did not respond. He was too engrossed in whatever he was hunched over, now letting Lyn squeeze past him and in front of him.

I guessed one of the soldiers was hurt. I could perhaps help. I moved to the crowd of soldiers and Lyn, but no one let me through, despite my asking them to let me pass by.

"Excuse me," I said.

No one moved.

"May I come through?" I asked again. "I might be able to help."

Pall came to stand beside me. He took my hand.

"I don't think anyone else can hear you," he said matter-of-factly.

He had a curious expression on his face.

"Let me through," Pall said authoritatively to the crowd. His energy pushed forward from his mouth so all would feel his intent.

The men parted without question. I walked forward with Pall still holding my hand, guiding me.

In the midst of the crowd, Trell was kneeling alongside Lyn, bent over. He turned to Lyn, putting his arm on his shoulder, and shook his head.

"No," Lyn pushed off Trell's hand. "I can do this!" he protested.

"Brother," Pall spoke.

Lyn did not turn around.

Lyn, Pall called his brother with his mind. *Stop and look around.*

Lyn turned, his mind thinking that he did not have time to speak to Pall; that his brother should leave him alone; that he was busy; that this was important. His face froze. He saw me.

Lyn stopped what he was doing and stood up, moving to one side.

There, in front of Lyn, by Trell's feet, was me. My body. My flesh. There was a bloody gash to one side of my head where the stone had hit me. Blood was splayed out on the side of my face. A large pool of dark liquid beneath my head on the sandy was starting to sink into the ground.

It had happened so quickly. I hadn't even realised.

My body had ceased.

I was dead.

Can you re-enter your flesh? Pall asked me.

I looked at my body, examining it, evaluating the damage.

The injury to my head was severe. That was what had killed my body: the stone that had hit the side of my head. The skin and flesh did not look too bad: ripped but repairable. Under that, my skull had cracked, with an imploded hole at the impact point. That would be difficult to heal, but probably doable. Under my skull, the substance of my brain under the impact point was pulped. The damage to the pathways in my brain was extensive. That was not repairable.

There was no point me re-entering this flesh, my body. It would never function properly again.

My flesh had ceased.

I really was dead.

Only Pall and Lyn could see me; see my energy.

I crouched down.

I must go, I told the two boys with my mind. *But I will not be gone.*

Where are you going? Pall earnestly spoke with his mind.

You remember I told you about Jychanumun?

The boys nodded.

He will be trying to open a path for me. It is too busy here.

As I spoke to the boys in their minds, I gave them understanding, love, and a piece of my essence to keep with them. I told them that they were to practice their lessons and that I would see them soon. I told them that I would always listen, and would come and protect them if ever it was needed.

Without a word, the boys let go of my hands.

Leaving people staring at my broken flesh, I wove through the gaps in the crowd and headed out of Hollow.

I had not wanted to die. I had not wanted to leave my friends and the people I had grown to love. I had wanted my human, mortal life. But with death there would at least be one recompense – at last I could reunite with Jychanumun.

THIRTY-ONE

The Retribution

I waited a night and a day, sitting in the sands of a sparse landscape, waiting for Jychanumun to open a death-path for me. I did not hear his guiding song, nor did I feel his presence. A death-path did not open.

I realised then that the connection between Jychanumun and myself was broken in life and in death. I had naively thought that death would automatically reunite us. It did not. I could still go to the Old One, yes, but that was no guarantee that I would return to help when the kutu returned. I had decided to wait with Jychanumun in the death-paths, but it seemed that choice really was no longer possible. Not even with my death.

It seemed that I had no other choice.

I would have to wait here, as I was, on Earth, until all the kutu could return.

It was going to be a long, long wait.

Time seemed to pass in the same linear way as when I had flesh. I watched the moon move over the sky and the sun rise. I did not get hungry or thirsty. I did get tired, from thinking and from exerting my energy, but there was no body to ache or give pain. My true vision was automatically on all the time, and all energies were now as visible as physical things. I could gather energy inwards, and make my own energy so condensed that I could feel it as a physical item. I could touch things with effort.

The sun was setting again. I ran my hand through the sand, gathering some up, letting it slip slowly through my fingers, watching the grains return to the ground; the sands of time. My true vision saw so much: light, form and sound, all spilling out from each grain as it trickled through my fingers.

This was a new state of existence. Even my true vision was heightened. It would take a while to become accustomed to this new state. But here I was. I had plenty of time to become accustomed to it. I had chosen to make my stand with humans, here on earth. Now I had to exist with that choice.

I stood up, heading back in the direction of Hollow. As I walked, I let my energy relax, blending in with the air. In this state, no one would see me. No one would hear me. Not even the twins.

I quickly discovered that my movement was altered without the constant rhythm of the flesh to limit it. Sometimes as I walked, each footstep was as a single pace, timed like any normal footstep. And then, if I focused on an object or destination ahead of me, I would find myself projected forward to that place. As I walked towards the crops around Hollow, my sight fixed upon the sandy path that ran through the huts, with the next footstep I was beyond the crops, walking that path. At first, this way of moving felt quite disconcerting. But then I began to enjoy it. Without the limits of the physical, my movement matched my thinking.

At the little wooden temple in Hollow's town circle, the doors were closed. They were usually left open. I pushed my energy through the dry, thin wood and into the building. There, in the middle of the space, where students should be sitting and learning, there was only Soul, kneeling on the floor with a bowl of water and cloths beside her. In front of her was my body.

Soul was humming to herself as she rinsed one of the cloths and returned to wiping my skin. She had cleaned the blood from me. She had brushed my hair. She had closed my eyes. Soul herself looked exhausted, but strangely serene.

"This?" I heard Trell speak. I looked up to where he was.

Trell was walking down the wooden stairs. He was holding up my luminous-white kutu attire.

"Yes," Soul nodded. "I'll not have her buried in those ugly Hollow clothes."

Trell walked to Soul's side, handing her the white fabric. "Have you chosen where?"

"I have," Soul replied. "Just beyond Hollow, in the direction of the river, there's a tree. Just one on its own. Under that."

"What about her possessions?"

"I'll bury them with her."

"Did you not want to keep something as a heart-sake?"

"No. I don't need to." Soul looked at Trell. "Turn around, my love," she smiled. "Tachra would not like you seeing her naked."

Trell turned around and headed back up the stairs. I watched as Soul carefully removed the covering blanket and dressed my body. Once done, she smoothed my clothing and positioned my arms neatly, with my hands on my heart, and then stood, clearing away the cleansing items. Trell returned with a bundle. I recognised the fabric as mine.

"She is ready," Soul said to Trell.

"In the morning the town can bury her," Trell said.

"No," Soul shook her head. "Let her body have the peace that in life she valued. This town was not good to her. I will bury her privately. Tonight. Now."

"Would you like me to carry her?"

"Yes, thank you."

"I love you."

"And I you."

Trell silently lifted my empty flesh. It looked like such little effort to him; like my body was as empty of weight as it was of my essence.

Soul led the way as Trell followed, crossing the floor and exiting through the small side door. I watched for a moment as they moved from sight. I felt sad, but the sadness was selfish. I would miss my friend. Soul would grieve for a while. But I knew that Trell would give her so much love that her future would be filled with happiness. She would be alright. She was strong and level-headed, and I knew I did not need to monitor her.

I walked, aiming to go upstairs. I passed the doorway of the small room where daily council was held. There were people inside. I could feel their tension. I paused a moment, listening, watching.

Jin and Jan were present. So were Ren, Findal, the landsman Alean, Pers, and the seniors of the Dral and Adan families.

"She must be put to death," Jin was saying. "She has attempted killing more than once. This time she has succeeded. I am sorry, Ren; you are my friend, but I see no other solution."

"But it's my mother," Ren shook his head. "How can I agree to such a thing for the woman who bore me? I cannot."

"Then what do you suggest?" Pers spoke. "I understand your dilemma, but you must offer an alternative solution."

"Could we not banish her?" Ren asked.

"We have tried that," Jin shook his head, "unsuccessfully."

Ren looked for another solution. "What if my family took an in-betweener hut and we had her with us?"

"What if you did that and she decided that your children, or their friends, were not to her liking? Would you risk their lives?" Jin asked. "Or, would she return here to try to kill the boys again?"

"I agree with Jin," Dral senior spoke. "And I would add that she has managed to manipulate others with her lies. The Urdan family were not murderous folk, yet she riled them up with her lies and had them believing her. She is dangerous in more ways than one."

Jin rubbed his brow, looking at Ren. "My friend, I do not vote for death easily. You know I am against such things. But none of you can offer an acceptable alternative."

Findal raised his hand, requesting to speak. The others looked at him expectantly.

"We here are but a small group of people," Findal offered. "Perhaps some other townsfolk, or one of the boys, could think of a solution; one that we have not reached between us. Jin and Jan, you run this town on fairness. Surely this is something all the town must decide. Because whatever is decided will have consequences, and will be remembered."

Findal's words were wise.

Everyone nodded in agreement. Ren and Jin too.

"Then we call the townsfolk together," Jan settled. "We decide this tonight before it creates its own troubles." He looked at Findal. "Light the lamps in the temple. Light the lamps in the town circle."

It felt strange to watch my friends, unaware of me listening, observing – my presence. A part of me wanted to show myself to them, to tell them how sorry I was and how much I loved them. But my friends knew that I loved them. They did not need me to tell them. They did not need me for anything. This was no longer my world. It was theirs.

My world was something in-between.

Anyway, it was not these things that I had come to Hollow to observe. It was Iris.

* * *

Iris looked at the four boys. She was asking them, yes, but even if they wouldn't agree, she would find a way.

"Well?" she asked again. "Will you help me or not?"

Viir, Brune, Pall and Lyn glanced at each other.

"The council men are having a meeting," Iris frowned. "Yet another one. All day, all they've done is have meetings about it. If they won't do something, I will," she paused, "on my own."

"Yes," Pall spoke. "All of us think yes; we will help."

"Good."

"When?"

"Now," Iris replied, and with that, she walked out of the boys' room.

The four boys followed. She had known that they would. Still, it was good to hear their hushed footsteps directly behind her.

The teaching space in the temple was empty. There had been no lessons since Tachra's ceasing. Still, Iris had to be careful, as her mamma was down there preparing Tachra for burial. She paused at the top of the stairs, waiting, but her mamma was nowhere in sight. Nor was Trell. Nor was Tachra's body. But she could hear talking coming from the little meeting room downstairs. And movement too. She would need to be careful.

Iris quietly tiptoed down the stairs and through the temple. Silently, she slipped out of the door.

The town circle was quiet, but Iris wasn't taking any chances. Once outside, she deftly wove around the back of the wooden building without being seen. Instead of cutting across the open space, she took a route rarely travelled, around the back of the huts. Even if anyone did see them, she realised, they would just look like five children playing a game or doing an errand. She would just walk normally.

"Do what you can so that no one pays any attention to us," Iris told Pall, as she walked between the dwellings.

"Already doing it," Pall confirmed. "Does Soul know where you're going?"

"Don't be silly," Iris whispered. "Mamma would fret. This is my choice."

It did not take long for them to reach the prison hut. It was small, having previously been used for grain storage. Iris had already peeked through the air vents several times that day, and knew that inside was divided into three sections: a small cupboard straight ahead, where grain bags and tools had once been stored, and grain rooms to each side. Both grain rooms were now empty of grain. The one on the right housed Mags. The door to Mags had two strong new bolts on it.

Iris crouched down around the back of the old grain hut.

"They brought her supper earlier," Iris told the boys. "Can you sense if there is anyone else in there?"

Pall's eyes grew distant. He put his palms flat on the wooden wall of the grain hut.

"No one else," Pall replied. "And there's no one outside the front either."

"Good," Iris nodded. She got up, walked around the hut to the entrance and let herself in. As soon as the boys had entered too, she closed the door.

In front of them were three doors. Two were ajar, showing the empty space beyond. The third was closed and bolted.

"Brune, you'll have to do the bolts," Iris said calmly, looking at the secured door.

Pall, Lyn and Viir pushed against the heavy door to loosen the bolts while Brune worked them. Once Brune had worked the bolts loose and slid them across, he turned around.

"Now what?" he asked.

"I go in."

"What do you want us to do?"

"When I'm in," Iris replied, "re-bolt the door and wait until I ask you to let me out."

"What if she kills you?"

"She won't."

"What are you going to do?"

"I don't know."

Viir, Brune and Lyn stepped aside. Pall remained in front of the door. Iris held his stare. She knew that Pall could read minds best of all. She knew that he knew what she was thinking. She didn't fight it. Instead, she let her mind become loose, letting Pall see everything.

Pall nodded to Iris and stepped aside.

Iris pulled open the heavy door and entered Mags' prison.

Inside, Iris stood, waiting until she could hear the bolts outside being slid back across. Done. Good.

Mags was sitting with her back to the wall. Directly in front of her, there was an empty plate, two apples, and a jug of water. To one side were blankets and a pillow. Mags looked well cared for. She didn't deserve to look well cared for. She looked well. She didn't deserve to look well. She looked up. She didn't deserve that either.

"I suppose you've come to apologise," Mags sneered. "It's all your fault that I'm in here. If it wasn't for you getting the men, we would have rid this world of those half-breed beasts and I would be back home. This is your fault. You're a stupid girl."

As Mags was talking accusingly, Iris quietly walked to the nearest corner of the room, drawing a sign in the air with her finger; a symbol that Tachra had taught her. Once done, she moved to the next corner, again drawing the same sign in the air. She walked past Mags, saying nothing, to draw the same sign in the third corner.

"What you doing?" Mags interrupted her flow of condemning words.

"Signs of protection," Iris replied.

"Protection?" Mags scoffed. "Should have thought of that earlier, shouldn't you. Waste of space you are, girl. Best you do more than signs of protection for me."

"They're not for you," Iris said as she signed the last one. "They're protection for this hut."

Iris stood with her back to the door. She held out her hand. She didn't even blink when she called a flame to her palm.

The little flame danced in her hand.

"Father. Papa," Iris whispered.

The response was instant.

Immediately, directly before Iris was a blazing inferno in the shape of a man. It was Wirrel, her father, her papa, whom she loved with the depths of her being.

Wirrel's fire licked around him, through him, the shadow and light of his flames showing his features.

"My child," Wirrel spoke through the flames. "I sense this is not practice or learning. So why do you call me?"

"You burn for justice and vengeance, don't you?" Iris asked.

"I do."

Iris pointed to Mags.

Wirrel turned around, looking at Mags.

Mags was cowering against the wall, making herself as small as she could. Her face was full of fear, although she could not take her eyes from the flaming man of fire. She was trying to speak, but her words only came out as whimpers.

"What," Wirrel spoke to Iris, still looking at Mags, "do you want me to do?"

Iris took a deep breath, keeping her finger pointed towards Mags. "Kill her."

* * *

I had felt Iris. I had felt her intention. I had come back to Hollow and followed her from the wooden temple, ensuring I was not detected. I had ended up in a small wooden building. Wirrel, flame-dweller, vengeance-bringer, Iris' papa and Soul's love, had been summoned by Iris' command.

Iris, my brave, hurting flower, had told Wirrel to kill Mags.

Wirrel took a step towards Mags. His flames grew in intensity, burning hotter, turning from gold and red to white and blue, their gentle curling growing vicious, spitting from his form. His flames reached out like wings made of fire, ready to envelop Mags and burn her.

"STOP!" I commanded.

Wirrel had no choice but to stop. Even if he had wanted to continue, he could not. His flames were held in time for the briefest moment, and then retracted back into his fire-form. He turned around to face Iris. He went down on one knee, bowing his head before his daughter.

"My beloved child," Wirrel said to Iris, "yours is the voice that I hear. Yours is the voice that can call me and command me. But she who can move and shape all energy, not just fire, will not allow me to do this."

Iris looked crestfallen. Her face fell. Her shoulders slumped. It was heartbreaking.

I knew I had to let her see me.

I drew in the energy of the land, taking form. I looked like me, Tachra, now visible to all eyes.

"Tachra!" Iris gasped.

I nodded to Wirrel, silently telling him with my mind to leave and his flames sunk into the soil. I walked to Iris.

"My beautiful flower," I touched the side of Iris' face.

Iris put her hand over mine, clasping it tightly.

"I cannot let you take Mags' life," I told her.

"I know what I'm doing," Iris replied. She was desperately trying to fight against the tears that welled. "She took your life. I'll take hers. I hate her."

"You are too young to bear such a burden of guilt," I said. "When you are a grown woman, you will understand. If you make the same choice then, I will not stop you."

"But what if she just tries killing more people?" Tears of upset and grief and frustration were now streaming down her face. "What if they let her out and she does kill Pall or Lyn or Brune or Viir?"

"I will not let that happen," I smiled calmly.

I slid my hand from Iris' grasp.

I turned to face Mags, who had not spoken a word.

"I killed you," Mags stammered when she saw my face.

"Yes," I replied. "And I am dead."

I paused. "Stand up," I then commanded.

Mags clumsily stood. Her back was pressed against the wall.

"You," I spoke calmly, "make yourself the centre of your world and believe you are the centre of all others'. You manipulate others to get your way. You are selfish, controlling and cruel. Even the loving words you speak to those you say you love are not loving. They are merely another way for you to control them, to remain the centre of their worlds, to manipulate them for your own ends. This," I paused, shaking my head, "will go on no more. Mags from Meadsins, mother to Ren, woman of Earth, do you know the colour of giving?"

Mags just stared.

"Answer me," I said. "Do you know the colour of giving?"

Mags frantically shook her head, indicating not.

I took a step forward.

Mags tried to flinch away, but I did not let her. I held energy firm around her so that she could not move. She stood rigid, looking at me with her small, fearful and hateful eyes.

I held out my right hand, palm up. I made a ball of energy form in my palm. The ball of energy was the colour of giving; palest pink with undertones of yellow and silver.

"The colour of giving and kindness is the colour of the truth of a heart."

As I spoke, I made the ball of energy turn into a beautiful flower. It looked like a multi-petalled rose with soft velvety leaves that had a transparency, making them glow. It hovered just above my palm.

I took another step forward so that the flower in my hand was directly before Mags' eyes.

"But," I said, "the balance of greatness can always be tipped either way. Just as this energy can be used for giving, it can also be used for retribution. It is all a matter of intention."

I lifted my left hand. The beautiful rose glided from my right palm to my left. The rose began to morph. The soft, velvety petals grew as hard as mazium crystal, their curved shape elongating, straightening into serrated shards. The colour was the same: but now it was a hard, multi-jagged arrangement of sharp points. I lightly blew upon the pink shards in my hand. In response, they began spinning violently. They would now cut through anything and everything that they touched.

"This beautiful colour is also the colour of retribution."

I blew again on the energy in my hand, making the spinning stop. The shape changed until it was back to its original glowing ball.

I moved my hand forward so the tips of my fingers touched the skin of Mags' forehead. Mags could not move.

Words started spilling from my mouth. They were words in a language I had never spoken before. I was speaking the language of intent.

As I spoke these unfamiliar words, I understood them completely. This was a language that could never be learnt; the language of intent could only be felt. And I felt it. It resonated through the core of me. I felt every sound and essence of that language as if it was the only language I had ever known.

"TelanAnia*sa ns#fh'"kljan hia~~In D(v.vs'" sEA*diAnaD fr'fjk osn iche end#fl (Gh'"hg Hj Hj," the words poured from my mouth.

As I spoke, the ball of pink energy moved towards Mags' forehead. It passed through her skin, her bone, into her mind and saturated her flesh. I kept talking, pouring the words and intentions into Mags' mind, forcing the energy of giving and retribution into both her body and essence.

"Sa'si*na`du sEA*diAnaD," I concluded.

I drew my empty hand away.

Mags wanted to slump to her knees. But I would not let her. She was not trying to slump because she was hurt; she wasn't hurt. What I had done had caused no pain or damage at all. She wanted to slump because she was a coward. But Mags would only have one chance now in life and she had to understand that. Her life was now in her own hands, dependant on her own actions.

"You must listen carefully," I told Mags. "I have just put that beautiful energy inside you, everywhere. You cannot remove it. It can either be the beautiful flower or the destructive shards. That is your choice. If you use that energy for giving and kindness, you will live. And you will live with inner peace. Do you understand?"

Mags nodded.

"But," I warned, "if your intention is ever to harm another being, the energy I have just put inside you will commence spinning. It will not stop spinning until you are dead. You will be cut to shreds from the inside. Do you understand that too?"

Mags nodded again.

"I do not know what the council will decide for you," I added. "They may let you live. They may not. However long you have, you have the rest of your life to change your ways. If you do not change your ways, the energy of retribution will kill your body.

But that would not be your end. When your body is dead, the flame-dweller will claim your conscious and unconscious self, and you will burn for all eternity. Do you understand that you have only one chance?"

Mags nodded again.

"Then I have no more to say."

And with that, I turned my back on the woman who had killed me.

I walked to Iris and sat down on the dusty floor, taking her under one arm and ignoring Mags' presence.

"Are you back to stay?" Iris asked. Tears still streamed down her face.

"I am never gone," I said. "Never. But I will not always be seen. Sometimes I will be in other places."

"Then is this the last time I'll see you?"

"Oh no, my little flower," I hugged her. "I will always hear your words to me. I will watch out for you. And, when it is your time to leave this physical world, I will show you the way to the next world, Elysium."

"But I won't be happy here without you."

"You will. Very happy."

I stood up, lifting Iris to stand too.

I held out my palms, drawing in another ball of pink energy. I cupped my hands so the energy expanded. And then I slowly drew my hands apart, stretching it into a thick line. I lay the line of energy on the ground, blowing dust into it so that it became both energy and matter. I ran my hands over it, shaping it.

"This," I told Iris, "represents retribution. I have made it into a belt. When you are old enough, you will be able to use it if you wish."

I fastened the belt around Iris' hip. The belt morphed with her energy, becoming the right shape and size.

"No one will be able to see it, except you," I said.

"And you."

"Yes, and me."

"You have to go now, don't you?"

"I do, my flower," I smiled.

Iris hugged me. I told her in that hug that she would be happy and brave, and to remember that she was born of the first ever love and that she was unique throughout all universes.

I stood, straightened, and took a step back, smiling to little Iris as I allowed my energy to flow back into the ground and become invisible once again.

I waited for a moment, unseen. I watched as Iris wiped away the tears, brushed the dust from her tunic, turned around, took a deep breath, and then bravely knocked on the door. I did not leave until I heard the bolts slide back and the boys let her out.

Now, I had new purpose. I had somewhere to go and something I could now do.

I understood, at last, the language of intent. I had not expected to understand it in the way that I had. I had expected that it needed to be studied like all other kutu languages. But this language was different: it could never be studied. It could only ever be felt. And now that I felt it, I understood it. It was ingrained within the core of me, as if I had always known it. And now that I understood the language of intent I could, at last, read the Book of Fate.

The Book of Fate had been hidden in my little room at the wooden temple since my arrival in Hollow. No one else knew it was there. No one knew that I had carried it to Hollow.

With no more than a thought, I returned to the wooden temple, to my old tiny room.

Back in my room, I felt nothing for the empty space. It was just a room, with a mattress and a stool, ready for someone else to occupy. The corner where the Book of Fate had been kept hidden under blankets was now empty. There were no blankets. There was no book. All my possessions were gone. Trell must have included the book with the items Soul was going to bury me with.

I turned to leave, but then spotted something tucked under the edge of the mattress. Its energy glistened like a tiny beacon. I knew that energy. It was coming from the purple stone I had kept as my memento representing Chia. It must have been accidentally kicked out of sight.

I pushed energy into my hand, picked up the purple crystal, and then walked into the room next door.

Next door, in the room that the boys shared, was one small, square table where they always studied. It was one of the few wooden items in their room that hadn't been re-sculptured by Brune. Once that wood had been a tall gera tree. Now, its beautiful grain was polished by so much use. I stroked the table top and then pushed the purple stone deep into the wood. I etched my fingers around the stone, creating indents in the wood that formed the kutu word for eternal friend. It was a word I had taught the boys only days before. Now they too would know I was never completely gone.

I could hear a hushed commotion coming from outside in the town circle as people gathered. For a moment, I considered observing the town meeting. But what was the point? Whatever decision these people made about Mags would be the right one for them. And, now that Mags had the energy of giving and retribution within her, she could not harm anyone else. The boys were safe from her. Hollow had a good council.

I sank my essence downwards, through the wooden floor I was standing on, through the empty room below, and down into the dark sands beneath the building. Then, from deep within the soil, I felt the resonance of the language of intent.

I paused. It was coming from Mags.

Above me, where the living people of Hollow gathered, watching Mags, listening to Jin speak, Mags stood looking at those who were about to judge her. She was consumed with hatred, determined to kill any who spoke against her. As she stared at those men of the council, her heart decided that Jin would be better dead. With that decision and the intent to act on it, the pink energy within her began spinning. It was fast, ending her flesh from within. Her pain of dying was but a mere moment; probably less than she deserved. As her body fell, lifeless, I felt Wirrel rise; his flames were hidden, moving to consume her essence. Mags had made her choice. She had died by her own intentions.

I felt no pity. Other people would live on.

I had my own choices to follow.

I pushed forward, beyond the soil, letting my instinct guide me to where the Book of Fate had been taken to.

THIRTY-TWO

The Reading

Soul was right. It was just a tree on its own.

Seeking the place where Soul and Trell had buried my body had taken me to an empty place where one lone tree stood amidst sands.

The lone tree was a sour apple tree, but one of age, and its sprawling, gnarled branches hung down, almost touching the sandy soil. Most of the branches were already dead, without leaves, but the occasional small sprig of green indicated that this tree had not yet fully given up. Its physical form looked quite forlorn, yet its energy was quite beautiful. Its pale silver wove around it like vines made of feathers. It sung its own song; a song of the past and tomorrows, in low choral tones. Its song reached out through the energy of the soil and air, being heard by trees far away. This was a serene and tranquil place to be buried, not that my flesh had any requirements.

There was little evidence that my body had been buried here other than the freshly moved sand having a different energy to that around it. I was not interested in my flesh anyway. What I was interested in was the bundle buried next to it. In my bundle was the Book of Fate. I could *feel* it was close.

As I had drawn closer to the book, I had felt my energy start to resonate. Now that I was almost touching it, I could feel it pulling me. The effect felt unusually natural. I did not fight it.

I sat cross-legged under the tree and let my energy be drawn down into the shallow grave. I felt the presence of the Book of Fate. And, as soon as my energy touched the black cube, my mind filled with images. I didn't think. I didn't try to understand. I just felt. I felt the words and meanings from the language of intent saturate my entire being.

I sunk deeper.

I was being pulled into that black cube and all the tales it had to tell.

THIRTY-THREE

The Introduction

With one swift movement, I had been pulled entirely into the Book of Fate. This was not a book to be read with words. Nor was it a book with static pictures. This book was taking my mind on a journey. It was showing me one of its tales in all its form, as if I was really there.

The Book of Fate took me to a place where I was standing, hovering, above a pale yellow land. The energy smelt both sweet and cold. This was not my beloved planet Earth, and this was like no land I had seen before. It was pale, dry and sparse like a desert, but rocks soared into the sky – rocks that were held in stasis above the ground. Below me, great cracks, a thousand men deep, fractured the terrain, zigzagging to the horizon in every direction. The planet looked fragile. It was dying, morphing, becoming something else. It was in its final stages of breaking up entirely.

The Book of Fate pulled me further into its tale and I sank further down, past the planet's broken surface, into darkness, and into a place where I felt caves and chasms.

I stopped.

Where was this place?

It was almost lightless.

Within the darkness there were even darker shadows.

I strained to see, my vision desperately trying to adjust to so much gloom within gloom. Had I gone to the realms of shadow? No, this could not be. I saw energy everywhere and although it was dominated by shadow, there was also shadow light and all things physical. In fact, I felt something solid at my back. It felt like I was standing against a wall.

I remained concealed.

I watched.

I could now make out that someone was in front of me. They were sitting with their back to me. The shadow around them was so dense with concentration that it drenched out all definition of their form. I stopped straining to focus and allowed myself to become at one with the shadow. With my sight adjusting to the gloom within the gloom, my vision started to clear.

The being before me was kutu.

A Nigh-kutu.

The Nigh-kutu before me was slim, but I could tell little else about him. He was wearing a long, shapeless robe, with a large hood. The hood was up over his head.

I could tell the kutu was doing something as his shoulders were moving slightly, as if he was sculpting or writing. He was sitting in front of a flat surface. At first I thought the surface was a table, but then realised it was a natural ledge made entirely out of rock, and that three out of the four walls in this space were of that same natural rock. I was in a cave.

The small space was dark, without windows. To my right, where the cave would be open, was a constructed wall with a door. There was no furniture. To one side, to my left, was an odd assortment of items: a large boulder which was part metal and part stone, a plain round bowl, a sphere which looked to be made from mazium or some similar transparent substance, and a pile of straps, which, from their position, appeared as if they could be combined together to make boots. There was no sign of any of the kutu technological items or unusual devices. This looked sparser than the sparsest of huts.

The kutu shifted slightly to one side, as if contemplating. I could see now that on the flat surface, directly in front of him, was a black cube. It could only be the Book of Fate.

I knew that the black cube had to be the Book of Fate, but it was only partially fashioned. The four upper corners were not yet formed; the substance leading up to them was still rough, finishing at jagged angles. On the finished areas I could see the start of the familiar etchings and engravings. And already I could see the flecks of white and the moving shapes. It was definitely the Book of Fate. But in this story it had not been finished. If that truly was the Book of Fate, and it was midway through being written, then the kutu before me could only be Jychanumun.

Seeing a past image of Jychanumun made me want to hold my breath. Everything looked so real. He looked so real. I felt as if I could reach out and touch him. If I had still had a physical heart, its beat would have quickened. Instead, I felt my energy quicken, pulsating.

From what I had been told about the Book of Fate, Jychanumun had written it long before joining the Walker clan. It was the first and only book he had ever written. It was in the very early days of the kutu's existence. The book was showing me the story of how it was formed. I did not yet know why I was seeing this tale.

As I observed the one whom I assumed was Jychanumun resume his work building the Book of Fate, I could hear movement from beyond the confinement of the space I was in. It drew closer. I heard a bang that echoed as if sound had nothing to dampen it in this place.

I felt the brush of the movement of air as the door opened.

Someone walked in. Another Nigh-kutu.

I could see this Nigh-kutu clearly, although he was not one that I recognised. His shadow energy was almost blindingly luminous in bright cyan. I caught a glimpse of his wings in their final stages of retraction as he walked through the doorway. He was very tall, even taller than Jychanumun. His long, dark hair fell to below his waist in long, ragged curls. His plain, dark tunic was secured around his waist by what looked like twine. His brow was un-furrowed. His skin had no scars. There were no weapons.

The long-haired Nigh-kutu placed a large, cloth-wrapped bundle on the flat surface, next to Jychanumun.

"We found more," the Nigh-kutu spoke, indicating to the bundle. His words sounded unlike the Nigh-kutu I had come to know. This sounded purer, less guttural.

"Eliahn has asked us to meet with him," the Nigh-kutu spoke again. "He is gathering a group who share Walker skills."

Jychanumun did not reply. He seemed too engrossed in working on the Book of Fate. He simply paused his work for a moment, unwrapped the fabric from the bundle the Nigh-kutu had been carrying, and then handed the fabric back. On the surface were now several pieces of lumpy, misshapen black rock.

"It's all we could find," the Nigh-kutu said. "I do not think there are any more. Will it be enough?"

"It will," Jychanumun replied, not stopping his work.

It was certainly Jychanumun. When he spoke, I saw the familiar black and white energy spill from his concealed lips.

"Join us for tonight's shadow mist," the Nigh-kutu continued. "You have been too enclosed here. It does you no good."

Jychanumun shook his head.

"No? Very well," the unknown Nigh-kutu spoke. "Eliahn is calling any who can walk realms to meet on Amada when the three shadow mists merge. Will you be there?"

"Yes," Jychanumun replied. He paused, just for a moment, looking at his fellow Nigh-kutu.

"Thank you, Cranun," he said.

Cranun? I knew that name. I knew it to be a kutu who had ceased. He had been one of Jychanumun's friends, one of his brothers. I had even been with Jychanumun at the time of his ceasing.

The Nigh-kutu called Cranun turned and left.

I stood, observing Jychanumun continue working on the book. He took a piece of the misshapen black rock and held it up to one of the unfinished corners of the cube. He moved his hands, his fingers weaving shapes in the air. Pure black and white energy trailed from his fingertips, to be absorbed into the stone. The stone slowly changed shape, fusing onto the cube, with engravings forming as it fused. The pure black stone gained the familiar flecks of luminous white as it blended with the cube. Once Jychanumun had fused that piece of rock into place, he picked up another, performing the same ritual. And then another. As time passed, I saw one of the unfinished corners complete.

Jychanumun picked up another piece of rock, moved the cube and held up that rock, ready to fuse it into place. He paused, and stopped working. He put the piece of rock back on the surface and then just sat, motionless.

I stood watching.

It felt as if I stood there for a long time. I didn't move. Jychanumun didn't move.

Was this all I had to see? I wondered. Why was I still here, watching this part of the story? Nothing was happening. I already knew that Jychanumun had written the Book of Fate. I knew what the Book of Fate looked like. Surely I should be seeing some other story?

I tried to push my energy back to the here and now, but nothing changed and I remained standing in the small shadow space. I then tried focusing on the desert land outside Hollow where in real time the Book of Fate was buried. Still I did not move.

I could not force myself back to real-time. Clearly this story had not yet finished telling its tale. I had to hope this was the case. I hoped I was not now trapped inside that black cube with no abilities other than watching the past.

Jychanumun pushed back his hood, tilting his head to one side.

"I sense you," Jychanumun suddenly spoke without turning.

Who was he talking to?

"Shadow lurker, I sense you," he spoke again.

Shadow lurker? I glanced around, feeling unsure. Was there something else present in this place that I had not noticed? Was that what I needed to see in this story? Was there some type of shadow being that I did not know existed?

"Walk forward," Jychanumun coolly stated, "and show yourself."

Jychanumun slowly turned around. He looked straight in my direction.

"I command that you show yourself."

I saw Jychanumun's eyes flash with shadow. He was looking straight into my own eyes.

Now I was sure that Jychanumun was talking to me. But how could he sense me? I was just observing a story from the past. I was not part of the story. I was simply reading a book, watching its tales.

There was only one way to know.

I walked forward.

Jychanumun's energy flickered. He could see me. He really could see me.

"Jychanumun!" I exclaimed. I was so happy. I smiled, walking forward.

"Stop," Jychanumun held up his hand, putting an energy barrier between us. "How do you know my name?"

"It's me. Tachra. Iastha Tachra," I replied. "I thought that as you could sense me, you'd know me too."

Jychanumun stiffened with caution. "No, I do not know you. I repeat: how do you know my name?"

"I do know you," I replied. "And in times to come, you will know me."

Jychanumun's expression remained stone cold.

"I know this is no dream-state," he said flatly. "Yet the creature now before me has plagued my dreams." He tilted his head slightly to one side, the way he always did when evaluating something. "What manner of creature are you?"

Jychanumun's face had no recognition upon it. His energy did not reach out to me. I felt no affection from him. It was obvious that he knew nothing about me. But how could he? In this time, in this story, we had not yet met. I did not understand how he could see or sense me, but he did. He once told me that he had known me since before I was born. I always wondered how that was possible.

Now I knew; this was how Jychanumun first met me.

I took a deep breath.

"My name is Tachra," I said calmly. "I am part human, part kutu and part Old One. I am reading the Book of Fate in a time to come when the book is finished. The book has brought me here."

"No other being knows that I intend to call this the Book of Fate," Jychanumun spoke. "It is not finished. And your words have possible logic, as I write so that the reader experiences each story. But," he continued cautiously, "I should not be able to see you. We should not be able to interact."

Jychanumun did not trust me. He was inquisitive, yes, but he was wary.

"Could our interaction be because I am mind-bonded to you? But our link was severed."

"I am not one to mind-bond with any being," Jychanumun coolly replied. "I choose solitude. And, even so, a mind-bond can never be severed," his eyes narrowed, "unless through eternal death."

"You are currently in the death-paths," I said, "waiting."

I saw a refraction in his energy when I mentioned the death-paths. Jychanumun closed his eyes, his head dropping down.

"If that is true, then I have managed to save nothing," he said.

I felt Jychanumun's energy reduce, as if defeated.

For a moment, I did not know what to say.

"You have saved many," was all I could think of.

"I have told no one of the death-paths," Jychanumun considered. "You know much. But these things could be stories added to the Book of Fate and so be known to all in times to come. If your words hold truth, substantiate yourself."

Substantiate myself?

"Yes," I replied. "Yes, I know how to do that. See my energy. See the truth of me. That is what we used to do. That will tell you more than any words."

I dropped every essence of my guard, allowing my energy to move freely, barely in any containment of form. Within the multicolours that were mine, bound together by light, illuminating the dark surrounds, were flecks of Jychanumun's energy. Pure black and white wove through my colours, forever entwined.

Jychanumun released the barrier between us. He put out his hand, brushing his fingers through my energy. The colours of my energy reacted with his.

"I see the truth of you," Jychanumun spoke. "I see that the truth of you is also the truth of me."

And do you hear me with your thoughts? I asked.

Jychanumun just looked at me.

My heart sank a little.

"I hear you," Jychanumun eventually spoke aloud. *I see you and*

I hear you, he thought silently. *But that you are here tells me that all kutu stand on the edge of extinction.*

Yes, I affirmed. *And that is why I read the Book of Fate. I must find a way to save not just kutu, but all life.*

Jychanumun sat back down on the stool. I sat on the floor. We continued talking with both our minds and our mouths.

In our conversation, I discovered this planet was indeed a dying planet. Jychanumun lived here, in this fragile land, with several other scattered Nigh-kutu. All had chosen reclusive lives. He referred to them by a strange name: the monks of Ilstahrn.

Although Jychanumun was currently part of the group called the monks of Ilstahrn, he had been asked to join a new group of other kutu who had skills for walking between realms. This would be on a different planet, where the one named Cranun said it would be in synergy with their energies.

I tried to block some of my thoughts from Jychanumun, but it was impossible to block them all. When he spoke Cranun's name, he felt my sadness and hesitation. I had to ask him just how much he wanted to know of his tomorrows. He said that, as he was known as a foreseer, he wanted to know what I considered pertinent.

I told Jychanumun about the Old One, about the Shaa-kutu and how humans had come to be. Jychanumun instinctively knew of the light, but had never seen worlds made of light. He said that he knew that one day he would travel there. We talked about the Book of Fate. Jychanumun said that he was writing it for a friend who was also on this planet, living as a monk of Ilstahrn.

"He suffers," Jychanumun explained. "He feels the suffering of the world, of all worlds, and all kutu. He feels their pain and their imperfections. I write of the wonders of our tomorrows to give him solace. With foreseeing, he will experience stories showing that our tomorrows are full of hope, substance and ascension, and that our incompleteness is a thing of greatness. My hope is that he will discover that his suffering will not be eternal. I write to give him hope."

"It is terrible that any kutu should be so afflicted," I said.

"Yes," Jychanumun agreed. "His pain is too great to speak of. So, I will leave space in the Book of Fate for him to add his own stories; stories of our pasts. I hope for him that writing his knowledge will cleanse him."

"If I knew this kutu in my time, I too would try to help," I replied.

"I doubt he would ever travel into the light," Jychanumun considered. "His afflictions incapacitate him too much. Eliahn calls him the 'hurt of all kutu'. In common Nigh-kutu, that translates to Ahrr-u-unn."

I flinched.

Ahrr-u-unn. The name sounded slightly different when spoken in this purer Nigh-kutu language. But even so, Jychanumun's pronunciation was almost identical to the name that I had come to know and detest.

"Ahrr-u-unn?" I asked. "As in Arrunn?"

"Yes," Jychanumun replied. The reply was more like a question. He had seen my energy flinch. I now had a thousand questions that I wanted to ask. How? Why? What?

But I could ask Jychanumun nothing. I tried to speak, but no sound left my lips. Something was happening to my energy.

I was being drawn away.

I was being pulled back into the Book of Fate.

I tried to fight against its draw.

My resistance made no difference.

I found myself back in the desert, sitting under the gnarled sour-apple tree.

THIRTY-FOUR

The Wait

It was a bright, hot day and the sun reflected off the sand, almost blinding me. Immediately I pushed my energy back down towards the Book of Fate. But the black cube didn't want to draw me into it this time. It just lay under the sand like a block of impenetrable stone.

I tried to force my way back into the book, to reconnect with Jychanumun's past, but my energy kept hitting against it, and it repelled me with as much force as I put in. It refused to give me access. I grew more frustrated with each attempt. Finally, I had no choice but to stop trying and accept the here and now.

It seemed that the Book of Fate would only show me another story when my intent connected to one it had to tell.

Perhaps, I considered, once my annoyance had diminished, what I had needed to see within the book, I had seen. The book was not about me having a connection with Jychanumun – that connection was not conjoined; it was disjointed. One being's dream was another's reality. No, in the here and now, Jychanumun was in the death-paths with Mardoch and Dragun. If my intention was to connect to Jychanumun, I had to find him in the death-paths. The Book of Fate was not about connections, it was about stories of intent, which lead to choice, which lead to fate. Or did choice lead to intent, which leads to fate? Or could it even start with fate? This was something I had to consider.

I sat and I sat, waiting for the Book of Fate to draw me back into its tales, the night gave way to day, which gave way to night once again; and so the days rolled past. Still that black cube denied me.

The days and nights merged together into an expanse of waiting. As I waited, Meah came to join me, laying lazily on the sand.

Time passed and I saw the men of Hollow roll nine large rafts on rounded logs across the sands and towards the river. I saw men and families behind them, their belongings packed. The handles of hoes and hand ploughs protruded from their baggage. It gladdened my heart to see that Jin and Jan's plans were being accomplished.

More time passed. I waited. As I waited, I watched the world revolve. I saw the sands shift with the winds. I saw mounds reduce and new ones form. I eventually closed my eyes, falling into slumbers with Meah beside me.

Little one. . . The Old One sensed my deepening sleep and called to me. He wove his awareness around me, showing me the way into his deepest dreams.

I felt the pull and the call of the Old One as I slumbered. I fought to resist it. I wanted to join him. I wanted it more than anything. But, I knew I could not, lest I never wake. I had to remain here on Earth for when the war for life came.

I forced myself awake, pulling against every part of my nature.

I observed Meah sleeping, or part sleeping, in the way she seemed to do so well. Her ears twitched with each new sound, and her eyes sleepily opened if she felt anything interesting was nearby. If I could sleep like that, I considered, I could stay here and not go into eternal dreaming.

Sleep like a cat, I thought. *Keep your awareness alert.*

At first I found sleeping while alert difficult, and I wanted to drift into deeper sleep with the Old One. But I had plenty of time. Eventually, I mastered it. I sat cross-legged on the sand with my eyes closed, listening to the movement of the world while I waited.

I waited.

I waited.

And I waited.

A change in the movement of energy roused me. Meah was disturbed too, stretching her limbs and wandering to see what the commotion was. Before us were carts, small and empty, each one with two wheels and pulled by two men. Six carts in total. More men followed. They were travelling from Hollow, towards the river.

I realised that almost a full turn of the seasons had passed while I waited.

Only a short while later, two days and a night after the empty carts had passed, they passed again, making their return journey to Hollow. This time the carts were full with foodstuffs: mainly grains, pulses and nuts. Hollow had its food. The beginnings of their second town, a farming town, had clearly worked.

I smiled.

I closed my eyes again.

I waited.

While I waited I felt the movement of people. In my alert yet meditative state, I could hear so much from those people: hope and laughter and wishes and grief and love and fear and adventure and joy, and all things that made life living. I could hear so many thoughts and speeches at once that they sounded like a gentle breeze. I let my dreams drift unfocused, knowing that when the time was right, the Book of Fate would draw me in once again.

I was drawn from my motionless meditations, not by the Book of Fate but by sensing movement again. I opened my eyes to see that the empty carts were passing once more.

Another full turn of the seasons had passed. Another year.

The number of carts en route to the river had increased from six to ten. Again, within two days the carts passed on their return to Hollow. Again they were filled with food. But this time, as well as food, several young people, tanned and strong, accompanied the grain. I guessed they were there to attend at Hollow's little temple.

The seasons kept turning. Each time, as the harvesting season concluded, I would be roused by the movement of the carts between Hollow and the river. They would pass one way, empty of grain, collect the foodstuffs from the rafts, and then pass the other way, filled with food.

Six turns of the seasons passed. Seven. Eight. Each time, the number of carts increased. The size of the carts increased. Some now pulled by strong, glossy, well cared-for horses.

The tenth time I was roused to watch the carts, a beautiful new sight greeted me.

Standing before me, unable to see me, with the sun dazzling behind her like a golden aura, was a young woman. My eyes saw her form. She was tall and slim with the curves of a female in her teens. Her dark, wavy hair fell down her back to her waist. Her deep, fringe-framed eyes I knew well. I knew her energy even better. Her deep sapphire blue and pale gold now had a streak of pink. Her energy was contained yet vibrant, moving wildly within its restraint like a butterfly that had not yet left its cocoon. Iris had grown to be a beautiful young woman.

Iris could not see me. She knelt on the sand not far from me. Meah's ears pricked up, and she got up for a moment to stare at someone who she too recognised.

"I am leaving Hollow," Iris spoke into nothingness, yet the words were meant for my ears, "with a heart that knows love. You told me that I would be happy, and I am. We build new towns. I go to help establish another new temple. You would be pleased with how many now wish to learn. From what I have heard, you would have loved the new towns. Viir says they are the perfect blend of kutu and human."

The silhouette of another woman walked into view whose energy I would know instantly, anywhere: Soul.

"You knew where to come," Soul smiled to Iris, sitting down next to her daughter.

"Of course, mother," Iris laughed.

In Soul's hand she held a beautiful white flower. She put the flower on the sand.

"We all miss you. I miss you. Yet I know you are not gone," Soul spoke. "My friend."

I heard the calls of men as the yearly carts approached.

Three walked up behind Iris and Soul. One was holding the hand of a girl and was carrying another child, a boy of about three years old.

"Come, my love," the man said to Soul. It was Trell. "The rafts will not wait for us. And if we want to arrive before the new baby comes, we must be on these ones."

Soul got up. She looked happy.

The other two beings stood behind Iris. These both had energy that shone far beyond their forms. They were not human. They were tall, much taller than a human, with builds of muscular strength. Their shadow light moved around them like a kutu's. They were two of the half Nigh-kutu boys, now grown men with the energy of a kutu. From their colours of grey and silver, it had to be Pall and Lyn. From the way their energies pushed out to encompass Iris as they approached, I could see that they loved her. They were both also in love with her.

I watched my friends walk away and join the carts with love in my heart, sending it out to them. *I miss you all too,* I thought, smiling.

With a peaceful mind I drifted back into my contemplations once again.

I began to time my rousing to watch the movement of the passing carts each year. I would awaken to observe the new people who had journeyed to study at the temple, their excited, eager faces anticipating what was to come. I would smile at the success of the grain loads as the carts returned towards Hollow. I felt satisfied knowing Jin and Jan's plans had succeeded.

The years passed with pace. Each moment of static contemplation passed like a breath. Each awakening to see the joy of the passing carts moved like linear time. The more that time passed, the more it seemed to accelerate when I closed my eyes. The pace only seemed relative to what I perceived, or the times that had already passed.

Many seasons and years passed and I felt Hollow flourish.

I was a little sad, but also happy, on the year that I awoke in early spring, before the carts were due to pass, to find Soul sitting with me.

I opened my eyes. Soul was sitting cross-legged on the sand, just gazing out at the horizon. She hadn't woken me. She had just sat next to me until I felt her presence. She looked the same as the very first time I had met her.

"When you sleep, your dreams are full of noise," Soul stated, not taking her gaze from the land. She hadn't even said hello. "It's too loud. It's noisier than my house when all my children were little."

"To me, it's not noisy," I replied.

We looked at each other in synchronicity.

Soul mischievously tried not to smile.

I smiled. "Hello, my friend."

"Hello," Soul could not help but laugh. "I have missed your face." She put her hand to my cheek, "My dearest friend."

She leaned over, stroking Meah. Meah stretched, enjoying the attention, the sun and the familiar face.

"Do I look old and wrinkly?" Soul asked.

"No," Now I couldn't help but laugh. "Do I?"

"No," Soul replied. "But you have never had time to get wrinkly. I did. Still, Trell always thought I was beautiful. He outlives me; would you believe it? Now he is very wrinkly indeed. Still handsome, though. You know," she considered, pausing, "when my flesh ceased, your father came to take me to Elysium. Your father is now the guide for all souls."

"I know," I said. "Did you not want to go with him?"

"Oh yes," Soul replied. "I did and still do. But I have a request of you, if at all possible."

"You know I'll help where I can."

"I do," Soul replied. She sighed, biting her lip and it made me glad to see her habits in life were still with her in death.

"I have seen with my own eyes that Elysium is beautiful and a place of everything: peace, adventure, laughter, wonderment. But," she shook her head, "Wirrel is not there."

"Wirrel chose a different existence," I explained. "Elysium is open to him, if he wishes it. But he wishes to dwell elsewhere."

"He does," Soul nodded. "And I think I understand that now. He has purpose. But is it possible to walk between the two places? To move between his location and Elysium?"

"It is," I considered, "but only for Wirrel, or those with a heart bond to him."

"Like me."

"Yes. Like you."

Soul nodded. "I love Trell. And Stanze. And of course, my children were and are the essence of my existence. But my fire for Wirrel has never gone. It has never decreased. I suppose you would say that I bonded to him."

"You did," I agreed.

"I know he is now the flame-dweller. Can I choose to walk realms with him and in Elysium? Can I move between the two?"

"I think that you know that you can."

"I had to be sure," Soul smiled. Her smile grew. She beamed. She laughed a laugh of sheer joy. "Oh Tachra," her energy glowed even brighter, "I will see my bonded love. After all this time. My heart feels like a girl's again."

"You go, my friend," I smiled. "I see you are already being drawn to him. Rightly so; you have both waited long enough."

Soul took my hand and stood up. "I will see you soon, my friend."

"Yes," I nodded. "Do you know your way?"

"Oh yes," Soul replied. "I just have to follow my heart."

Soul let go of my hand and I watched as she walked away, her energy glowing like the sun. The brightness around her grew with each footstep until I could not see her form, just a bright light. Within the bright light I saw the movement of flames, Wirrel's flames, gently curling, caressing Soul's energy. And then the two were gone.

Wirrel and Soul were reunited.

Beautiful.

I did not close my eyes and return to my slumbers. My energy had quickened with joy too great to dream. Instead, I stood and stretched, allowing the dust of the ages shake away from my energy. Meah copied my actions, pushing against her front legs and stretching her back.

"Shall we go for a wander?" I asked Meah.

Meah was already ready, waiting expectantly.

I did not know where I was going; I had no destination. It was more a case that seeing my friend again, and conversing with her as if still alive, had made me remember how much I enjoyed walking. My energy did not need to walk. No part of me needed to walk. I simply wanted to.

Meah and I decided that we would explore the land by the river. With the carts passing every year, and with each time their load increasing, I was curious as to what the docking area by the river had become. And I would enjoy looking at some water. Other than in my dreams, I had only dry land to view in my desert position. I had no reason or need to look at such a thing. Again, I simply wanted to.

"Well," I shrugged, talking more to myself, "as the Book of Fate does not want to show me any more stories at this time," I scratched Meah behind her ears, "we may as well explore."

We wandered across the sand in the direction of the river. It was good to let my essence move again. I lifted my face to the skies and let the energy of the land wash through me like a soothing balm. I had missed walking.

It had been good to see Soul, albeit briefly. I had always thought that her bond with Wirrel was unbreakable. I was glad that she had lived a full life after he had died, a life of happiness and joy. I was glad that her troubles had not given her a life fixated by her loss or hurt, feelings unpleasant in any instance. To have loved and lost gave its own choices: to fester with the hurt of loss, or to ascend with the gain.

"The hurt of all kutu," I thought aloud. "Jychanumun said that he was writing the book for one who suffers, and who feels the hurt of all kutu. If that one truly is Arrunn, what could have possibly changed him so much?" This was indeed a thing I should discover. I had never detected any sense of Arrunn feeling any compassion or empathy for another being, yet alone hurt. Something must have changed him.

Suddenly, I felt the Book of Fate, now behind me, resonate. It felt as if it was calling to me.

The Book of Fate ***was*** calling me.

At last.

THIRTY-FIVE

The Monks

I ran back to where I had been sitting, close to the buried Book of Fate, with Meah running beside me. As soon as I reached the old sour apple tree, I sat down. This time, I had to hold my energy back from going into the book. It was pulling me stronger than ever.

"I will be but a moment," I told Meah. "But a breath."

Meah thought that we had walked enough for one day anyway. She settled down, blinking elongated blinks, as my energy was drawn down and into the Book of Fate.

I was being drawn to witness another story.

I found myself hovering above the same pale yellow land that the book had previously taken me to. It looked the same as the first time I had seen it, with rocks that were held in stasis above the ground and great cracks fracturing the terrain below. Again, I sank further down, through the planet's surface.

As I was drawn downwards, a terrible noise filled my ears, but not just my ears, my entire essence. It felt as if it saturated me. The terrible noise washed through me and consumed my energy and vision. It made my energy resonate, similar to sickness of the flesh. It made my vision shudder with shadow, as if I was dizzy and surrounded by swarms of flies. I could not block it out. It sounded like screams of the mouth, mind and soul. It was the sound of horror and pain and angst and torment. Such a feeling-sound would resonate through space for many to feel. It grew louder and louder. It was the most terrible sound I had ever heard or felt.

I stopped descending, yet the terrible noise continued.

Before me, the lone hut was nestled onto a wide ledge; the sound was coming from inside. All around was dark, but not completely black. The substance of the rock gave off a faint luminescence, the last energy of a dying sun. Above, the sheer walls of a deep chasm spanned up as far as my vision could see. Below, the chasm continued downwards into the depths of blackness.

The hut before me was rounded in shape and appeared to be made of the same stone as the planet. Just as in Jychanumun's choice of abode, there were no windows. There were no objects of beauty. Just one closed door.

The hut's door opened, amplifying terrible noise. I covered my ears, but it made no difference. A Nigh-kutu exited and although I stood in plain sight, he could not see me. To him, I was not here. To me, I knew I was seeing a story from a long, long time ago.

I did not recognise the kutu. He had unusually long grey hair, which gave the illusion of age, but his face was young. His wings were retracted. His hair was motionless, as if it was too spent to move. His entire energy looked sparse, as if exhausted, but there was enough to see that it was grey and brown. He wore a simple robe of the same shades.

As the grey and brown Nigh-kutu walked outside, another followed close behind, closing the door once he had exited. I did not recognise this kutu either. He too had unusual grey hair. Where the first kutu had a fresh face, this one, although not aged looking, wore a frown so deep that it furrowed his brow. His energy was fully grey with no accent colours; just a matte, colourless aura. He too looked exhausted.

The two Nigh-kutu stood closely together, talking in hushed tones.

"I do not know how to soothe him anymore," the first kutu spoke. "No words I say, no assurances I give, no tales I tell nor songs I sing, make a difference anymore. And I am almost spent. I have little left to give."

The second kutu rubbed his brow. "Even Jychanumun's book no longer helps. He has added all he wishes to write, but it no longer soothes him. I am beginning to think that Jeshuahn was right and there is no other way to help him."

"Ahrr-u-unn has said it is what he wants."

"Yes, but it does not seem right. Ahrr-u-unn must find a way to conquer this himself."

"It has been almost a millennium," the first kutu sighed. "Yet he worsens, not improves. He does not know how to conquer his pain. We must embrace our pity for him. We must have heart and show mercy. We must act on that mercy and pity. We must help him."

"Have we exhausted all other options?"

"Yes; you know we have. And you have almost exhausted yourself. If you do not act soon, you will be too spent to accomplish anything."

The first kutu shook his head sadly. "Then we will do this thing in mercy. Call Jeshuahn. I will prepare."

The two kutu stood motionless. I sensed one was sending out a calling, as his energy, or what was left of it, emanated from his head in a straight line of shadow-light. The other kutu appeared contained, almost statuesque, his deep grey energy unmoving.

It did not take long before I felt the presence of a third Nigh-kutu approaching. Up above me, his broad grey wings carefully navigating the narrow drop, he came. His long, pale hair flowed around and above his face. His colours were unusual, yet beautiful, in deep grey and pale cream against his shadow. He gracefully landed on the ledge, his energy wings retracting the moment he touched the solid stone. His eyes were unusual. One was grey and the other pale cream. I had never seen a kutu with differing eyes before.

"Brothers," the newcomer spoke.

"Jeshuahn," the two bowed in unison.

"Have you brought it?"

"Of course."

Jeshuahn retrieved from a concealed pocket in his robe what looked like a knife. The knife had a grey hilt and the blade was plain black, without markings or engravings. The hilt looked like a rough, unpolished crystal. He handed the knife to the all-grey kutu.

"Do you need to prepare?" the all-grey kutu asked Jeshuahn.

"I have been prepared for this mercy for a long time."

The grey kutu nodded and the three kutu moved closer together. I moved in to gain a better view.

The three kutu stood facing each other, their hands atop each other bar the grey kutu who held the knife. The grey kutu raised the knife, and then began speaking words from the language of intent. As he spoke, he thrust the black knife into their hands, pushing down so the blade pierced through their palms and I could see the tip of the blade protruding from under their joined hands. Jeshuahn then clamped his remaining hand underneath, forcing the tip of the blade through his flesh.

The three stood, joined by the blade. No kutu blood dripped to the ground. They did not appear to be in pain.

The three joined kutu bowed their heads and began humming. The humming made the energy around them vibrate. The energy began to gather, drawn into their midst and around the blade that bound them. In their centre, around their hands, the energy seemed to gain substance. A black mist formed. I could no longer see the knife or their hands. They were just a conjoined mass of black, surrounded by black.

Suddenly, the shadow drew inwards. The energy at their midst had gone. Their bound hands were now black.

"Done," one of the kutu nodded.

The three slowly released their hands from each other, peeling away what no longer looked like fingers. What were once long, kutu digits were now even longer, knifelike points. Somehow, their fingers had become fine, precise, organic blades. I had never seen anything like it. I had never known a kutu to do such a thing. But I had never seen kutu with deep grey energy either.

The three kutu turned to face the hut. They did not speak.

The vision from the Book of Fate did not draw me back. I felt nothing change. And so I followed the three grey kutu as they entered the small abode.

Lying on the floor of the hut was another kutu. He was weeping and sighing and screaming and moaning all at the same time; not just with his mouth, but with his energy too. It truly was the sound of suffering. The hurt of his body was great and his mind greater still; that of his energy was even more acute. This, he, was the source of the terrible sound that resonated everywhere. It was Arrunn.

I had never seen Arrunn so incapacitated. His long, deep-brown hair was splayed out around him, dirty and unkempt. His robe was filthy with dust and grime. Beside him, an upturned bowl had its food tipped out, part-squashed into the floor. Next to that was the Book of Fate.

As the three kutu entered, Arrunn looked up. He noticed their knife-like hands.

"Release me," he whispered to them. "Take away this pain."

Jeshuahn knelt on the floor next to Arrunn. I could see the love on his face as he carefully helped him to sit.

"You understand the consequences?" Jeshuahn asked.

"Yes," Arrunn nodded.

"You truly understand that a life without pain is also a life without pleasure? A life without grief is also a life without joy? A life without hurt is also a life without growth? You understand what you will be sacrificing?"

"Yes," Arrunn replied. "Just help me not to feel pain."

Jeshuahn bent down and kissed Arrunn tenderly on the forehead.

"Know that I do this in love," he said sadly.

Jeshuahn helped Arrunn up so he was half sitting, half slumped, leaning against his legs.

All three kutu took position around Arrunn. They put their hands on his head. Their fingers wove together until Arrunn's entire head, face and neck were covered with a woven mass of black.

If I had blinked, I would have missed it. The energy of the three standing kutu flashed for the briefest moment.

A small click sounded. The sound was quiet to my ears, yet it bounced through the energy like multiple streaks of lightning.

All went silent. Everything. Even the terrible sounds emanating from Arrunn's energy had silenced.

There was a moment's pause. And then slowly, carefully, the three kutu began releasing their hands. They were retracting their black pointed blade-like fingers out of Arrunn's head.

As the three kutu drew away their hands entirely, small trickles of kutu blood dripped from tiny incisions in Arrunn's head and face. Their hands now looked like kutu hands once more. And clasped in Jeshuahn's hand were both the black knife and the matte-grey crystal which had been part of its haft. The two pieces were now separate.

Jeshuahn stepped back, catching Arrunn before he fell. He gently lifted Arrunn's limp body and moved him to one side of the room, laying him on the ground, arranging his arms and legs into a comfortable position, putting the crystal on the floor.

"Is he cured?" one of the others asked.

"Do you hear his pain?"

"No."

"It is done," Jeshuahn said. "Ahrr-u-unn will feel no more pain or hurt unless he chooses to. We have contained his emotions," he looked at the grey stone, "in the crystal. Now, fetch a mantle. And also fetch untainted energy to bathe his head with. He will sleep now for three rotations of this planet. I will wait with him until he wakes."

I watched as the two kutu left. Jeshuahn knelt by Arrunn's side, whispering to him, telling him that soon he would wake and his world would be pain-free.

I expected the Book of Fate to draw me back. Once again, it did not.

I stood and watched as time passed, yet little changed. I saw the two kutu return, handing items to Jeshuahn before leaving again. I saw Jeshuahn caringly change Arrunn into clean robes and bath his head and face in translucent watery energy. Once done, he quietly and gently, so as not to disturb Arrunn, placed all items out of the way, putting them along one wall in the abode. He then returned to Arrunn's side, cleansing and brushing his hair with his fingers, letting it splay once more out on the floor to dry. All the time he spoke, giving Arrunn reassurances and kind words.

I felt the planet turn and then turn again.

Jeshuahn slept rarely. When he did sleep, he would move to the opposite end of the room and lay on the bare floor, closing his eyes with exhaustion.

The planet turned again.

Finally, I saw Arrunn begin to stir. Jeshuahn knelt over him, holding his hand. Kind words of encouragement poured from his lips.

When Arrunn eventually opened his eyes, he glanced, without moving, around the room.

"I have silence," Arrunn whispered.

"Yes, it is complete. You will sleep intermittently now," Jeshuahn explained. "Do not fight the healing. I am here for you. I will not leave."

Arrunn did not reply. He merely closed his eyes again.

After a while, Jeshuahn moved to the opposite side of the room and lay down. His energy was near depleted. I could see that he desperately needed sleep. He soon fell into a deep, worn-out slumber.

Arrunn opened his eyes again.

Quietly, Arrunn eased himself up. He took a long, deep breath, as if relishing his own inner silence. He looked at Jeshuahn. It was a long look.

Arrunn then walked over to his brother's side and knelt, picking up the dagger from near his head. And then, in a flash, he drove the dagger straight into Jeshuahn's forehead.

My mouth let out a silent gasp as I watched Arrunn twisting the dagger, pushing it deeper into Jeshuahn's head.

Jeshuahn's eyes shot open. But he could not move.

With a final twist, Arrunn pulled the dagger out. Energy like kutu blood gushed from the wound in his brother's head.

Within the beat of a heart, Jeshuahn was dead.

Arrunn just stood looking coldly down at the kutu as he died.

Calmly, with no emotion on his face, Arrunn wiped the killing blade, and then looked around his abode. He appeared to see what he was looking for.

Arrunn picked up the Book of Fate and placed it in the middle of the floor. He then picked up the matte-grey crystal, examining it. He stood, holding the crystal and dagger in one fist, and then drove that fist down hard against the Book of Fate. As his hand hit the Book of Fate, it blackened, morphing to look like the same stone. He pushed his hand deep into the cube.

When Arrunn removed his hand from the Book of Fate, he

opened his palm. He still had the dagger. The crystal was gone. He then picked up the Book of Fate, opened the door, walked outside, opened his wings, and flew.

I could not move forward to follow him.

I couldn't move anywhere.

The Book of Fate was drawing me back again.

I could not resist or fight against the pull from the Book of Fate. Even if I could, the greater part of me was glad to be leaving this story from the past. My own energy had been sickened by what I had seen.

I had seen the point when Ahrr-u-unn became Arrunn: When he stopped feeling empathy or compassion. When he stopped feeling anything. When he became capable of moving and acting with such controlled focus. When he changed.

I returned to the here and now, to the sight of Meah sprawled out under the sun. She didn't have a care in the world. It comforted my spirit to be back in the empty desert beside her.

I was glad to be away from that disturbing story.

I didn't even want to think about it.

But think about it I did.

It seemed that Arrunn truly had suffered. Those grey Nigh-kutu had acted with love and mercy. They had either removed, or segregated, Arrunn's hurt. Because of that, Arrunn would never feel suffering again. They clearly had no idea what type of creature they were creating. No wonder Arrunn didn't have empathy or joy in life. No wonder he possessed such a calculated, cold mind. If I had not seen Arrunn's more recent actions, I too may have pitied him. But I could never pity him. Especially not now. He knew what suffering felt like and had used it to his advantage. His balance of greatness had been tilted. He could have been a beautiful being who acted with knowledge to help others. But he had chosen a very different way to utilise his skills.

I was happy that the Book of Fate showed no signs of having another tale for me to see, for I was not ready, not yet, to see another story. My energy felt too tentative, too disturbed. I just wanted to be here for a while on my beautiful, gentle planet; to sleep, to dream and to let my jangled essence calm.

I shuffled closer to Meah, putting my hand over her. My desire to join the Old One was stronger than ever. I reminded myself why I remained here. I reminded myself that to be with the Old One was to be with him forever. So instead, I gladly closed my eyes and joined my beloved wildcat in half-sleep.

As I slept, I listened to the movement of the world.

I felt the passing of time.

I instinctively knew when Hollow's carts were soon to pass. I had grown accustomed to sensing their energy move ahead of them like a river made of anticipation, knowing when to wake. I took joy in rousing each year to watch them. It always pleased my spirit to see the good intentions of my fellow humans.

More carts. More grain. More smiling faces.

Another turn of the seasons.

Another year.

More carts. More grain. More smiling faces.

Another turn of the seasons.

Time rolled by.

Life moved on; prosperous, balanced, changing. For me, little changed.

Each year I would rouse. Then I would part-sleep.

The years passed.

Yet more passed again.

After a while, I stopped counting.

THIRTY-SIX

The Civilization

Meah and I roused, as usual, just before the grain carts passed on their route to the river.

It felt as if we had slept for a long time.

I stretched my sleepy limbs, enjoying the autumn sun colouring the golden sands with red hues. The tree we sat under was past its life now. Its song had silenced and I missed that, but beyond my form I felt the song of many trees reaching out for new friends. Its pale silver energy still remained, weaving around the empty space where its trunk had once risen. What was left of its trunk was now a dead arrangement of jagged points. A few fragments of low, short branches still held onto the remnants of the trunk. It didn't look much like a tree anymore. It looked more like one of Orion's abstract sculptures.

My energy felt too active just to sit. So, as the carts approached, Meah and I headed over the sands, running alongside them.

The carts were very slow and their wheels churned up much sand as they trailed across it. Meah grew bored of the sedate pace, running under the carts' wheels, playing her game of catch-me. The horses could see us; the people couldn't. The horses found it funny. Two of the older ones just enjoyed watching. The younger ones broke into a trot, wanting to play too. Instead, I patted them with my energy, letting my fingers brush down their backs. They liked that.

Meah and I left the carts to complete the final part of their journey. I had been surprised that there were no temple attendees with them, but guessed they would be following later. We resumed our familiar places under the tree and waited for the carts' return and the happy, smiling faces that always accompanied them.

Less than a full day had passed when I heard the carts returning early. I opened my eyes, surprised at how fast they had turned around. Even from a distance, something looked different. Something felt different. Whatever it was, it was not good.

There were no happy, laughing faces.

There were no new people to attend Hollow's little temple.

There was no food.

The carts were as empty now as when they had left Hollow.

The men and women steering the carts looked deflated. No one talked. No one smiled. Their energy felt like despair, hopelessness and fear. The horses sensed the energy of their humans. They too were sedate.

I watched the empty carts silently pass. I wanted to do something, but I reminded myself that their physical world was no longer my world. I should leave humans to create their own paths. But this was Hollow. This was Jin and Jan's town and the place of all the wonderful aspirations they held. This was where some of my friends lived. Without grain or food, they could starve. How could I do nothing?

"Well, Meah," I stood, looking at her, "shall we walk as woman and wildcat once again? I think it's been a long time."

Meah thought that it was a good idea; a good adventure. And, where she felt my curiosity, her curiosity grew too.

Meah and I started off towards Hollow. I could have taken us directly to Hollow's town circle, but we both thought it would feel good to walk. Anyway, Hollow was only half a day away. It was a pretty afternoon and the energy of the land was entering the sleeping season. I always liked the feeling of the land as it drifted into sleep.

As we walked the dry sands, even from a distance I could see that Hollow had changed. It was larger than the last time I had seen it, now almost double the size. Gone were the rings of crops around the exterior of the town. Gone were the wooden huts. Now there were no fields of crops and all the dwellings were made of stone; most built on more than one level. The stonework of the dwellings was beautiful and colour co-ordinated so that the huts around the edge were mid-brown, lightening to a pale beige as they got closer to the town centre. I pulled the energy of the earth inwards so my energy took form, and I walked as Tachra with Meah invisible by my side. I chose the same loose, plain sandy-brown attire that I had last seen favourable among the people of Hollow and made my way into the town.

Large flowering plants in pots and troughs lined the walkway into Hollow. The air smelt clean. I was surprised at how quiet it was. It appeared that many of the huts on the outer circle were not inhabited.

As I got closer to the town centre, I felt the gentle bustle of people. Yet the people felt subdued. I noticed the empty carts tethered to a small open section. The horses next to them drank from pails of water. A woman stood, brushing their manes. The woman glanced towards me as I strolled past. I bid her good afternoon. She nodded and bid me good afternoon in return. She had a kind face; a clever face. Her energy was kind too, encompassing the horse as she brushed it.

When I passed the last ring of huts that led to the town circle, the area opened up. I stopped. There was no marketplace or people making things anymore. Instead, in the middle of the circle was a lone building that took my breath away.

The building was beautiful. It was made of pale-cream stone, its smoothly cut rock was cast so closely together that it appeared seamless. Huge columns framed the doorways, shaped to look like beautiful men and women. The huge statues continued around the outer walls, their arms raised, holding up the overlapping roof. Each statue bore an emblem on its body: one of a shield, one of wings, one of a book, one of a snake, one of a single flower. Around the waist of every statue were carved garlands of flowers. These stone garlands were the anchor points to real plants. There was greenery climbing so high, winding around the waists of the statues, their large flowers hanging down like giant petalled raindrops. It was beautiful. It was a masterpiece of design. It was a masterpiece of construction. This, I recognised instantly, was designed by Viir and crafted by Brune.

I walked forward and into the huge expanse of the building. It appeared empty. Meah took form and veered off to one side, exploring the space and the shadowy places, smelling new scents and brushing herself against any objects that she liked.

Inside, the building was as beautiful and elaborately detailed as the outer. Its floor was made of coloured stone, laid out in geometric patterns. At the centre was a long walkway. More pale stone statues stood either side of the walkway. At the far end, where the walkway ended, was a single colourful statue of a golden sun with blue wings. In the middle of the statue was a square piece of old, battered wood. The wood looked oddly out of place in this building filled with art. Either side of the sun statue, beautiful fabric hung down in shades of green, gold, brown, bronze, grey and silver, the exact shades of the energies of Viir, Brune, Pall and Lyn. I could see that this place had been made by them. I could even feel the faint resonant traces of their past energy. But they were not here. They were not even close by. The four boys had not been here for a long time.

I walked down the walkway of the magnificent building and stood in front of the vast piece of art at the end. I recognised the sun as the very first item Brune had sculpted here in Hollow. The wings had subsequently been added. I could see Brune's workmanship in those too. Both had been perfectly coated in something that glimmered with specks of coloured metal. I looked closer at the battered piece of wood at the statue's centre, which looked so out of place. There, in the middle of the wood, was a small purple stone. I recognised it instantly. It was the memento that I had kept to represent Chia.

Now that I looked closer, I could see that there, faintly etched into the wood around the stone and almost worn away, a kutu word. It was the word for eternal friend. I had written that on the boys' table. The piece of battered wood was that old table top.

I stood on tiptoe and touched the purple stone, tracing my fingers around the worn inscription. It warmed my heart to see it again.

"You must not touch that," a woman's voice sternly announced from behind.

I turned around.

Standing in the middle of the long walkway was a young woman of deep olive skin with large brown eyes. Her plain ivory dress fell in heavy pleats to the floor. She had an intelligent face and a gentle energy, but her expression was one of disapproval.

"Apologies," I told the woman. "I did not know."

"It's sacred," the woman walked forward. "Only the gods may touch it."

She looked at me, her eyes narrowing. "Who are you?" she asked. "I have not seen you here before."

"I'm no one," I replied. "I was just curious as to this beautiful building."

"The shrine to the gods," the woman's eyes grew narrower still. "And we do not get many passers-by."

"Where are the men who built this magnificent building?" I asked.

"The gods built this," the woman corrected. "Not men. What man could build this? Are you an unbeliever?"

"I don't think so," I shrugged. "I believe many things. And I do know that only a great being with true beauty in their heart and mind could build a building such as this."

The woman's face softened a little.

"Are Jin and Jan still alive?" I asked.

"Still alive?" The woman laughed, a scoffing laugh. Her eyes then narrowed. "Do you come to test my knowledge? I know Jin and Jan were the founders. They have been dead a long time."

Dead a long time? My heart sank. But of course they would have ceased. They would have ceased this flesh life and now be in Elysium. Time had passed. More than I realised, it appeared.

"Are you here to study or worship?" the woman enquired.

"Neither," I replied. "I noticed that the grain carts were empty. I've come to see if I can help."

"I am greeter at this shrine," the woman replied. "My name is Leil. And help?" she paused. "I do not think one woman on her own can help. Perhaps you can speak to the statues of the gods and ask for their help, hoping they will hear you." She looked with disapproval at my empty hands. "But I see you have no offerings. All prayers must come with offerings."

As Leil talked, Meah padded out from behind the large statue, thinking that this woman might be more interesting than the dust she had discovered.

Leil's expression changed when she saw Meah. It changed again when Meah sat down beside me, leaning against my legs. Meah just sat watching Leil. She liked her, but thought she talked far too much and didn't give her enough attention. I bent and stroked the fur behind Meah's ears, removing my head covering now it was no longer needed in this shaded place.

Suddenly, Leil fell to her knees, lowering her face.

"Do not diminish me," she declared, her voice suddenly shrill. Her energy flickered, unsure and fearful.

I quickly turned around, expecting something terrible to be emerging from the shadows. I couldn't sense anything. Neither could Meah. Nothing apparent rippled the energy in this serene place.

I went to Leil's side, crouching down to aid her.

"What's the matter? Are you hurt?" I asked. "Does something come?"

I put my hand on Leil's forehead, trying to locate her source of trouble.

Leil flinched.

I felt her fear. *I* was the source.

It took a while, and many reassurances, to get Leil to stand. I put my hand to her cheek, letting her feel my energy, soothing her with love and good intent.

Leil did not speak. She just stood up and walked to where the hangings of beautiful fabric hung down. She stood amongst them, holding them back, and looked at me. I think she wanted me to follow. I followed.

Behind the statue of the sun with wings was another statue. It was a statue of me, standing with Meah.

The statue of Meah and me faced a window that ran from floor to ceiling. The window was in the exact position to catch the rising sun. It was quite eerie to see a colourless stone version of myself, without softness or animation. Yet it did look like me. And the statue of Meah looked exactly like her too.

"It's a good likeness," I said. "Although it does feel strange to see myself made from stone."

"It is my favourite statue of the gods," Leil finally spoke. "I used to be sad that it was placed here, out of sight. My grandfather used to tell me that the Lady of Souls insisted that it must be placed here, not on view. He said this goddess saw all that went on behind the light and all things hidden from view."

The Lady of Souls? Was that Soul? Gods? The goddess? It was beginning to feel like a whole new language had developed since I had been away. There were many strange words and strange ideas. The passing of time had made the truth more like a story. Time had added flowers to what was truly only a leaf. There was so much to understand. But I had come here with purpose. I should keep focus.

"Leil," I smiled, "as beautiful and strange as this place is to me, I simply noticed the empty carts. That concerned me. Jin and Jan developed this town with good intentions. It would sadden me to see it diminish."

"I am great great grand-daughter to Jan," Leil announced. "I do not want to see this town diminish either. But my father is stubborn. And the leader of Nehol," she frowned, "is ignorant."

By the skies! Great great grand-daughter to Jan. It did not feel as if I had slept that long.

"Is your father head of council here?" I asked.

Leil looked at me, unsure as to what I meant. "My father runs this town," she replied.

"Then I must speak with your father."

Leil turned, telling me that she would fetch her father here. I said that I was happy to go with her to meet him, so she led us both out of the temple and across the cobbled town circle. As we walked, I asked her questions. She was very succinct, and in no time I had a good appraisal of the situation.

It transpired that for many years, Hollow and New Hollow, now named Nehol, had successfully worked as one unit. Nehol was built in the fertile regions, growing grain for both towns. Hollow specialised in learning and tuition, training and teaching people from both towns. Over the seasons, Hollow had stopped growing foodstuffs for itself, coming to rely solely on grain from Nehol. This had worked until this year, when Nehol suddenly refused to supply grain unless Hollow supplied cloth, gold, gemstones and pieces of art.

"He sent message to say his people no longer needed to learn from us," Leil shook her head, "and that they had their own places of learning and their own shrines."

I stopped in my tracks, noticing something.

"Is that a water pump?" I asked, recognising Viir's design.

"Yes, all homes have them and there are old ones in the outer land."

I was surprised. "So, Hollow has access to continuous water and you do not grow any crops at all?"

"We are people of learning."

"You are people who will starve," I said bluntly.

We walked on, my mind racing. These people had access to water and no excuse not to grow some food. The soil was not perfect for foodstuffs, but certainly good enough. And there were many empty huts here, so the population was not vast. I guessed the population was less than when Jin and Jan oversaw Hollow's welfare. They had managed to grow enough food. Surely these people could too. Had they forgotten the very basics of living? I could sense frustration rising in me.

Leil led me into one of the larger huts overlooking the town's circle and into a room where a man sat reading. He looked just like an older version of Jan. I could not feel frustrated with someone who looked so much like my old friend.

I bowed and wasted no time. Having bid him good day and explained that I had noticed the empty carts, I immediately recommended that he started overseeing the growing of crops around Hollow.

"You could make use of those water pumps," I suggested.

"Hollow is for people of the mind, not of the land," Leil's father replied.

"It is a beautiful sentiment, and I value the mind and all thought," I said. "But in this mortal life a mind needs a body. If a body has no food it will cease, after much suffering. It would be needless suffering and death when you have the capacity to grow food."

"My responsibility is for their souls," the man replied tersely.

Leil's father looked at his daughter, curtly asking her why she had interrupted his studies and why she was bringing a stranger who had no business here. I watched his energy as he spoke. He was a good man, but Leil was right. He was stubborn. The balance of stubbornness could, like all things, be tipped either way. As a positive trait, it was staunch and unbreakable to manipulation. But, as a negative trait, it could be closed-minded to the detriment of many. In this instance, it seemed that the result could be the people of Hollow ceasing from starvation.

I ignored Leil's father's brusque questions to his daughter.

"Souls flourish with nurturing, yes," I said. "But if your people are starving they will not thank you. Perhaps they will even resent you. Perhaps they will see your teachings as something to turn against."

"You try to tell me how to run my town?" The man now seemed angry with me.

"Father, please," Leil exclaimed. She turned to me. "Humble apologies for him. He does not know who you are. Do not harm him. He is a good man; stubborn, but good."

"I don't want to harm anyone," I said. "I want to help."

Leil's father kept arguing. Leil kept asking me not to harm

them. I kept saying that I had only come to help. I was beginning to feel as though the energy and the situation were going around in a circle. It was frustrating, and I was beginning to wish I had not come here. These people did not need me. They just needed to exercise a little common sense. Still, I had a choice. I could either walk away, or I could continue trying to help. But help? How could I help those who dogmatically did not wish it?

I took myself and Meah back to the desert, back to our familiar place under the now-dead sour apple tree. I did not sit down. Meah just looked up at me.

I stared out over the pale empty sand. The people of Hollow were trying to do the right thing. They simply were not being led well. And it was not entirely their leader's fault, as their food providers had suddenly stopped without warning.

"By the skies," I sighed. I knew I should have stayed.

"I know," I shrugged to Meah as she continued looking at me disapprovingly. "Sometimes," I told her, "I get the distinct impression that you are far wiser than I."

I took myself back to Hollow, back to the leader's hut.

Leil and her father were still in the same room.

My re-appearance took them by surprise.

"My apologies," I bowed. I took a stool from under the window and sat opposite Leil's father.

"You," I said calmly to the man, "are clearly a good man with a good heart. I see that. But your daughter is right and you are stubborn. As leader of Hollow, you have responsibility to your people for their lives and welfare. If you cannot fulfil that responsibility, please hand it to someone who can. If you want grain from Nehol, then give Nehol what they want. If you don't want to give them what they want, grow grain for yourselves. It is that simple. You have the choice. And, as leader of Hollow, the consequence of that choice falls upon your shoulders."

The man simply sat listening with his jaw agape. I don't think anyone had spoken to him in such a straight manner before. It had probably helped that I'd made such an unusual re-appearance.

"If," I concluded, "you choose to be leader of this place, then lead."

"Very well," he nodded.

"What is your choice?" I asked.

"Grow food," he replied.

"Thank the skies," I said. "Now, as Nehol made an agreement with Hollow, I will try to help by ensuring they provide enough food to last for a turn of the seasons. That will give you time to grow crops or make alternative arrangements. After that, you are responsible for yourselves. If you choose to starve then that is the consequence of your choice."

I stood up.

"Now," I asked, "where is Nehol?"

The man began giving directions. He used strange terms, words that I had not heard before. The words had no energy attached to them and the phonetics did not match, so I found it difficult translating them. I knew from his energy that they were units of measurements and specifics for directions and time durations, but words like shandal and hectares and furlongs and norasts meant nothing to me. I tried to form a map in my mind with his directions.

"Do you have anything from Nehol?" I asked.

"Just old grain," the man replied, pointing to some hessian sacks.

Perfect.

I walked over to the hessian sack and picked out a single kernel, holding it in my palm. I felt a sense of the soil it had been grown in. All soils were unique. All grains were unique. From that sense I knew exactly where the seed had been taken from.

I bowed a farewell bow to Leil and her father. And then I left.

Using my Earth sense, the little kernel had provided me with both the energy and physical composition of the land it had grown in. It was not far. For legs, about a two-moon walk. For my energy, the journey was almost instantaneous.

I found myself standing in the middle of a field.

The field was angled, midway up a hill, filled with the stubble of freshly cut crops. Beyond this field, as far as my eyes could see, were more fields: dozens of them, hundreds of them. There were orchards too. The fruit and nut trees were so heavily loaded with produce that much of it had just fallen to the ground, left to rot into the soil. The soil was rich and black. This truly was a fertile land.

Although the crop fields were many, I could not see either people or dwellings. I walked to the top of the hill to gain a better view.

I observed from the hill. Before me was a great wall, the height of twenty men, arcing around a large, pale town. In the wall was one lone entrance to the town with gates made of poles of thick metal. The gates appeared to have a standing ledge inside, as I could see over a dozen men standing at the top, looking out to the land beyond. From the spears they were carrying, I assumed they were guards.

I saw people enter the town through a smaller section within the gates. They were dressed in colourful clothing, carrying large baskets in their arms or on foot-carts. They would speak to the guards, who would then open the gates and let them pass. No questions were asked of the people who were leaving. It seemed a strange arrangement, and I could not understand why the gates were not just left open. There were no more Nigh-kutu to threaten these people. Even if there had been, a kutu could simply fly over the wall. Inside the town they must have something of great value, something they wished to protect. That piqued my interest even more.

The town itself was made of stone and wood. Most of the wood was fashioned into hut dwellings, modest but sizable. But it was not the huts that caught my attention; it was the stone buildings. Deep in the centre of the town, built on raised land, were several large stone buildings with grand, pillared openings and windows that stretched from floor to roof. The tallest building was decorated with strips of coloured fabric that fluttered in the breeze. It had an air of importance.

That, I decided, looking at the stone building with its fluttering fabric, was probably where I needed to be.

In order to understand this walled town before speaking to its chief, I did not go directly to the important looking building. Instead, I moved to a position close by, where I could sense the movement of many people.

I settled on a place that felt concealed, in a small gap between two dwellings, and pulled the energy of the earth into myself once again. I gave myself form. My form looked like me, but this time I chose colourful attire, just as I had seen most of the women wear as they entered the town. Then I walked out from between the buildings.

This place was busy! I had never seen so many people crammed into one open space unless it was for a gathering or a town meeting. It was like Hollow's town circle but bigger, much bigger, and with so many people, energies, colours, shapes and sounds.

People in vibrant fabric and shining adornments wove between tables with items upon them. Some tables had fabrics hung above them. Others had wooden poles, with more items hanging off them and around them. Some people did not have tables, but merely cloths laid out on the ground displaying their wares. There were foods: fruits, vegetables, berries, spices and raw items of every description. And there were foods made like kutu foods: sweetcakes, breads, and decorated items that looked more like art than food. And there were animals. Dead animals, hung and displayed with no grace. I tried not to focus on the animal food, knowing that some people had developed a taste for eating their fellow creatures, and took a slow walk through the bustling market.

There was not just food in this place. I saw tables loaded with cooking wares, blankets, cushions, bowls, baskets and cloths so beautiful that they beckoned to be touched. There was colour everywhere. But more than the foodstuffs and wares for chores, the items that were most dominant were adornments. Golds and silvers were wound around crystals and gems in every shade. There were items to go around the neck, wrist, upper arm, ankle, waist, and even around and through the ears. There was more gold here than I had ever seen before. Gold shaped into jugs and urns, and small, ugly statues of fearful looking beings with many heads.

I saw an entourage of five people weaving through the crowd towards me. At their centre was a tall, haughty looking woman decked out in more jewels than I thought anyone could walk with. A dozen gold and gemstone necklaces were wound around her throat, hanging down with drops of shells and more gold. Thick bands of stone-studded gold and silver went from wrists to elbows. She even had several belts around her waist and hips made of gold. Her dress was edged in gold, and she shimmered as she walked.

As the entourage passed me, they shoved me aside, almost sending me tumbling. They didn't speak, or even acknowledge what they'd done. It seemed that consideration was not a focus in this place.

As I continued moving through the market, I saw several more groups of people with one or more particularly heavily adorned at their centre. Nearly all the people were adorned to some degree, though some more than others. Most far too much.

I noticed women with barely any cloth covering their flesh leaning against buildings, talking and laughing with one or more men. Their waists and necks were adorned with coloured stones in shades of red and yellow. Their faces were painted in red and yellow.

Their hands touched the men suggestively. Their mouths laughed. Their eyes looked greedy. Their energy looked desperately empty.

This place sparkled and shone with so much metal and stone. Yet its energy was flat, lost.

I wove through the people, ignored by the other wanderers, talked at by those with wares.

"Look at this beautiful necklace," one followed me, thrusting an ugly large piece of metal under my nose. "Only eleven pieces."

"A ring for your thumb," another followed, showing me a green stone set into silver.

The ring was very pretty and the stone had a beautiful energy, but I had not come here to adorn myself. I politely told the man as much and, even though he did not want to listen, he eventually found someone else he thought the ring would suit better.

At the edge of the bustling place, a walkway led up towards the large buildings. Sitting on the corner were a girl and a boy, both yet to meet adulthood. They had a cloth spread out in front of them. On the cloth were some beautiful flowers. The flowers did not just have their own energy, they also had the energy of the two children sitting with them. These blooms had been grown and tended with love. I paused to admire them as everyone else walked by.

"Would you like to buy one?" the boy asked. He smiled. The smile was genuine, unlike most others I had seen in this place.

"No," I replied, "thank you. I was just thinking how beautiful they were. It warms my heart to see such a thing in this empty place. Yours are the first faces of beauty I have seen here that also have beauty in their hearts."

The two children looked momentarily taken aback.

"No one has ever said anything like that. They do not see," the boy replied, his eyes studying me.

The boy got up, picking out a white, multi-stemmed flower. The flower had pale colour to its edges.

"Please, have this," he said, handing me the flower. "It looks like you."

I did not want to take these children's precious items. I sensed that it was these blooms that would provide them with the food that they needed. But I could not refuse a gift given with such good intentions either. So, I graciously accepted the flower and bowed, giving them my heartfelt thanks.

As I walked away, up the path that led to the grand buildings, I sent those children my energy, putting protection around them. And, to ensure they would eat well, I sprinkled golden energy over their beautiful flowers and into the cloth they lay upon. Now none of those greedy passers-by would be able to resist those blooms, and those beautiful children would eat well this night.

As I approached the stone building with the fluttering fabric, I realised that it too was a masterpiece of design by Viir and Brune. The roof overlapped the walls, with pillars running all around the building, creating a sheltered walkway. Unlike in Hollow, the design was simple, more geometric.

There were wide steps leading up to elaborate double doors. They reminded me of something Shursa would have liked, as their beautifully carved wood had been garishly over-painted in scarlet and gold. The doors were open. Inside I could see an equally garish, boldly painted interior.

I walked up the steps, and went to pass through the open doors.

"Stop there," someone suddenly said with authority.

Two men stepped out from either side of the doorway, barring my way with long spears.

"What is your business here?" one of the men asked.

"I have come to speak to your town's chief," I replied.

"Chief?" the man laughed. "He would have you killed for not addressing him properly. Go on, on your way."

I didn't move.

"Go on," the guard nudged me with his spear. "Outsiders are only allowed as far as the market square. You should know that."

I could tell that this man, both these men, were not bad men. I wished neither of them harm.

I sent my energy into their minds.

Let me pass, I told them with my thoughts. *And then forget me.*

The two men stepped aside.

I entered a large, cluttered, colourful chamber, empty of people other than the two men at the main doors. From this empty chamber opened several doors. Only one set of double doors was closed. They were more elaborate than the rest, painted fully in gold. I guessed that was where I needed to go.

I quietly opened the doors and stepped into another chamber.

A man was sitting at the end of the room, sprawled across a large, carved chair. He was finely dressed in many colours and fabrics that even a kutu would like. He had a short, dark beard and a plump young face. But his eyes did not look young – foolish perhaps, but not young. He wore an open-topped hat of woven gold. He had not heard me enter. He was too engrossed in the women sitting either side of him, leaning into him. Their clothes were almost transparent, made of a thin, gauzy fabric which showed all their flesh and seemed pointlessly flimsy. Their hair was plaited into many plaits with added stones and crystals and golden beads. Their faces were beautiful, but painted to look strangely disproportionate, with long eyes and red cheeks. The two were talking and laughing with the man. They did not notice me either.

Behind the man were standing more women. Six in total. But these six women looked very different from the two partly clothed beauties by his side. These six were dressed entirely in long, plain black robes. None had any hair. None had painted faces. They looked gaunt and their eyes were cool, as though evaluating. They had noticed me as soon as I had stepped through the doorway, yet none of them had said a thing. They just stood, arms folded into their sleeves, silently watching me.

I too just stood, taking in the people and the vast room and the many bright items decorating it. This was a strange town. Its energy was strange. It felt disconnected, not even connected to the land. Yet the land it stood upon was so beautifully rich. These people did not value the land for its beauty. Instead, they valued what they could get from it.

One of the partly clothed beauties dropped something. She laughed and went to pick it up. As she did, the man in the chair noticed me.

"How did you get in?" he asked.

I didn't answer. I just stood staring at the statues made of gold and grotesque furniture.

"I suppose you're another soothsayer," he shrugged dismissively.

A soothsayer? I picked up the man's thoughts to examine such a word. A person who tells futures. A person who can tell this man his fate. Yes, I suppose I was a soothsayer of sorts.

"Yes," I replied. "I am a soothsayer. I have come to speak with the chief of this town. Are you the chief?"

The man found that very funny. He started laughing. The two garish women, at first hesitant, then started laughing too. He sat up.

"King," the man said. "I am King."

I noted the position of the sun's rays through the windows to one side. It was early evening.

"Good evening, King," I said. "May we speak?"

"I have many soothsayers," King waved his hand nonchalantly, indicating to the women in black standing behind him. "They tell me whatever I want, when I want. I don't need any more soothsayers. Anyway," he scoffed, "you don't look like a soothsayer. Why should I listen to you?"

"Because my words are the only ones you need to hear," I replied.

King found that funny. I couldn't understand why.

I didn't particularly like this man or his haughty mannerisms. He seemed to think he was superior to everyone else, yet from looking at his energy, he was below average intelligence, had no particular talents, and was neither kind nor curious. I was surprised that a man like this would be chief council for such a large town.

"Shall we have her removed?" one of the partly clothed women whispered.

"Not yet," King replied. "She amuses me. Let's see what she has to say."

I pretended that I had not heard his words.

"What is the name of this town?" I asked.

"The great city of Nehol," he replied.

He had confirmed that I was in the right place.

"Why have you stopped sending grain to Hollow?" I asked.

King's face changed. His eyes narrowed.

"I thought you were a soothsayer, not a question asker."

"You made an agreement to provide grain to Hollow in exchange for sending pupils there to learn."

"You bore me now," he shook his head. "Guards," he shouted.

Two more men entered from an adjoining room, both carrying spears and swords. King told them to escort me out. I might have gone, having seen all that I needed to see. But it was when he added to his order that I was to be beaten, whipped well, and then thrown out of the gates that I decided to stay. Whipped and thrown out? How dare he.

"LEAVE," I commanded the guards.

The guards turned around and left. They could do nothing else. I had commanded them to be gone with my mouth and sent the information to their minds. King's face showed his shock.

"Your women too," I nodded to his entourage. *"LEAVE."*

I watched the women file away. "And close all the doors behind you," I added.

I waited for the doors to close.

Now that just the two of us were left in the chamber, I had his full attention.

"I will not allow us to be disturbed until we have had this conversation," I said.

King shrugged. "Very well. Your soothsaying is clearly stronger than my other women's. I will allow you to work here, for me."

"No," I replied. "I do not come here for that. I come because your father's fathers made an agreement between Nehol and Hollow. Yet you break this. I expected to come here finding a poor town, with barely enough grain to feed its own. Yet your stock huts are full. Fruits rot because you have too much. Your people are fat. You," I pointed out, "are fat. You have no good reason not to fulfil the agreements of your lineage."

"I told them they can buy it."

"Buy it?"

"Yes. Gold, silver, jewels, any common currency."

"But your agreement was not to swap grain for those things," I replied. "It was to swap grain with teachings. Grain has value to the flesh. Teachings have value to the mind."

King waved his hand dismissively again. "I don't want their teachings. They mean nothing."

"You don't want to learn about your pasts? About kutu?" I asked, a little surprised.

"Dramatic rubbish," King scoffed. "Here the people give offerings to the sky and rain and the land; rivers, insects, whatever. You name it, they make offerings to it."

"You do not value knowledge that could change all futures?"

"Pah," King scoffed. He rolled his eyes. It seemed that this man really was content to remain ignorant.

"Like I said," King added, "gold, silver, jewels, even copper or brass, will be taken in the market. That is what I value."

"Why?" I asked.

"Why not?"

For a moment, I was not sure what to say. I wanted to tell him that it was because the things he valued meant nothing, but I knew he did not have ears to understand. It seemed that here, in this garish place, people had chosen a different path. It was sad. But, it was their choice.

"You could have given the leaders of Hollow fair warning that your terms would change," I said.

"I have no need to be fair to them."

"They will starve."

He shrugged, indicating that he didn't care.

"Give them one turn of the seasons," I requested. "Fulfil your bargain for one more year. Give them grain. Allow them time to grow produce themselves. That is all I ask."

"You can ask for the sky, I'm not giving it to you. I don't intend on giving anything away."

"You would just let them die?"

King just laughed. It was more of a derogative snort, reminding me of a pig.

"You should leave," he waved his hand dismissively. "You have nothing to say that I want to hear."

"I see that you are not a fair man," I shook my head. "Nor a good leader for this town. Nor one to be reasoned with by fair means."

I walked over to the side of the room. It was cluttered with furniture, carved boxes, statues of gold, golden bowls holding fruit, sumptuous fabric over ornate stools, and tall golden jugs of drink. This place was full of the things this man valued. I stood by one of the statues. It was made of gold metal and almost as tall as me.

"You value things like this," I put my hand on the statue, "and break an agreement, knowing it will cause suffering, for things like this?"

As I spoke, I pushed my energy into the statue. I felt the condensed yet soft heaviness of its substance. I concentrated on the particles of gold, pushing them down into the earth. The statue gradually lost its lustre, turning from gold to black, and then black to grey. When I removed my hand, the remaining dry fragments of the statue were nothing but dust. With the slightest tap of my hand, the dust fell, scattering on the floor. I moved to the next statue; another life-sized golden man.

"And do you value this too?" I said. "Above the agreements of your fathers?"

I put my hand on the second statue. Its face looked vaguely familiar, but still, it was only metal, only an inanimate substance. I pushed my energy through it, watching King as it slowly turned from gold to black, and then to grey, and then to dust.

I moved to the next man of gold. The third statue was of a man's head, displayed high on a carved wooden stand. I put my hand on it.

"That's my father's father's father," King said. "Do not touch it."

"Your father's father's father adhered to an agreement with the people of Hollow," I said. I did not remove my hand. "He valued that."

Again, I pushed my energy through the statue. It started to blacken.

"One year!" King shot up, moving towards me. "I'll give them one more year of grain."

I removed my hand.

"Thank you," I said. "You won't break this agreement, will you? I don't want to have to return and turn all your golden men to dust."

I began to walk away.

"Who are you?" he asked.

I turned.

"Just a soothsayer," I said.

And then, feeling like I wanted to make my point stronger, I did not walk back through the doors. Instead, I let my energy blend with the air and simply vanished from view.

THIRTY-SEVEN

The Lesson

I returned to the desert. Meah merely opened her eyes for a moment before closing them again, too content to move.

I, however, did not feel right.

My energy resonated uncomfortably. There was no external source. I was the source.

I had ensured Hollow's people would have grain for another year. They would not starve. I had helped, yes. But, I did not feel good about it. I felt terrible.

I knew I had not acted wisely.

I sat down, let my energy calm, and contemplated.

Sometimes, I considered, helping can be a greater hindrance. A person or people might never learn what they needed to if others interfered. People choose their own paths. My place was not to tell them what was best for them. How could I ever know what was best for another being? I couldn't. And I valued choice as sacred. Without choice, life had no point. I had no right to bend the choice of another.

Also, I considered, the people of Hollow probably would have begun growing produce when they went hungry. Surely, if they had not yet made that decision for themselves, it was because their situation was not yet bad enough. My intervention had prevented them from learning whatever they needed to learn, or simply acting with their own choices. And in Nehol, King had learnt nothing except that there was someone out there who could disappear into the air, turn gold into dust, and make his guards do the opposite of his commands. What good had I truly done? Nothing.

Under the illusion of helping, all I had done was interfere with the choices of others.

And, I berated myself, in what manner had I made those people listen? I had entered the guards' minds, forcing them to let me pass. I had flaunted my ability to make myself disappear to King's eyes, just to make my point. Why had I done that? To make him listen? To show him that I was better with energy than he was? To show him I was stronger, more powerful than him? Either and any were not good. I had been prideful. I had thought my decisions and choices were better than his. I had thought that I was better.

I groaned inwardly. Recognising my flaws.

My decisions and choices were only right for me.

I had no right to believe my choices should dictate another's actions.

That would be as bad as Arrunn.

I would never, ever, do that again.

I sat awhile, simply allowing the energy of the land to pass through me. A part of me expected the Book of Fate to resonate again. But it did not.

Surely the Book of Fate should have another story to show me?

Why wasn't it giving me more tales? How could I be expected to know and shape futures if it didn't?

I stopped my thoughts.

Realisation dawned on me.

I had been looking at the Book of Fate all wrong.

It was not about giving me answers.

It was not about giving me knowledge I could use in future wars.

It was not about shaping the futures of others, telling myself I was helping.

That was exactly what Arrunn had used the Book of Fate for.

I had sat by this book, waiting for tales, using it to guide my choices, using it to shape the futures of others.

For different reasons, I was following the exact same path as Arrunn.

Me? Arrunn? The same choices?

Was I becoming like him? Was I walking to that fate he said would come?

Oh.

Oh, by the skies.

Oh, Meah, Jychanumun, Old One, how had it come to this?

My mind felt numb.

I knew there was only one thing I should do with the Book of Fate. I had to destroy it.

And with that thought, I could feel the book resonate once again. It was calling me; calling me back to witness yet another tale. I didn't like it. It was almost like a trap to make me focus on the past, or on specific stories. But no one's future was set. My future was not set. My future depended on the choices I made now and tomorrow.

I took form, drawing in the energy of the land, and began digging. I used my hands, hurriedly pushing away the layers of sand.

The book was now buried much deeper than when Soul had initially placed it in the ground. I pushed on while Meah watched with a mixture of curious fascination and bemusement. The deeper I dug, the stronger the pull from the book. The sand frustratingly kept falling back into the hole, almost as quickly as I could dig the black cube out. Eventually, once night had turned around and then turned around again, my fingers hit something. The book.

I scraped away the last of the sand, climbed down into the hole, and pulled it free, clambering back up to level ground.

That black cube tried to pull me in.

I would not let it. I did not let it.

I did not delay. There was no reason to delay. I knew what I needed to do.

I drew and drew energy into me, condensing it, my strength increasing. Still more. Still more. I thought of metal and rock and stone so hard that nothing could break them. I thought of Soul's will, Wirrel's fire, Iris' love, the four boys' bravery, the beauty of souls, and all things that could never be broken. I held onto those thoughts and the love that I felt for all those things, pushing all the power into my arm.

With one swift move, I brought down my arm with such power that I thought I might split the very earth in two.

My fist hit the book.

"Se#~¬ve¬r," I shouted in the language of intent, commanding the book to break.

The Book of Fate shattered beneath the power of the word.

And as it did, black and white energy exploded into the air and the land, shooting like shards of glass and metal. The black and white energy repelled each other, moving in opposite directions. As the energy moved at a speed beyond light, black dust blew into the air like a cloud of smoke. I watched as it dissipated into nothingness in the wind.

The book was gone.

Now no futures were dictated by it.

No choices could be swayed by tales.

I should have done that a long time ago.

I looked down. A matte-grey crystal. I was surprised it had not shattered.

I picked up the matte-grey crystal. There was no life within it, just whatever had been removed from Arrunn to make him the way he was. I didn't feel anything at all from it; no intent, no life, no purpose. I knew Arrunn must have it back; without it he was incomplete.

After a while I lay next to Meah, and we both basked in the energy of the land.

I needed to leave my fellow humans to make their own choices.

I closed my eyes.

I did not listen for the grain carts. I did not listen to anything except the rhythm of the land and the energy between my wildcat and me.

I drifted into sleep.

My sleep deepened.

Deeper still.

Towards the Old One.

Little one, he called. *Do you join me in dreaming?* His light and shadow flowed through me and around me. I felt no dread or awe; I was just contented, accepting knowledge. I let my essence become part of the light and the dark and the sound and the silence and the push and the pull of intention and nothingness.

Little one, I heard his words.

This time, I did not resist.

Yes, I replied, *I come.*

* * *

All feelings folded and unfolded like suns and black holes to a point of stasis.

All sounds sounded as one.

All thoughts merged to a single point that had no thought at all yet were conscious of all things.

All images blurred to be only a reflection of the self.

The self was and is and would be nothing except that which it touches.
At the point where time is timeless.
In a dream so deep it is dreamless.
I am as everything.
I am as nothing.
To be with the Old One.
My.
Our.
One.

THIRTY-EIGHT

The Awakening

Something brushes against me. And again. And again. Like a breeze against my skin. Like a knocking on a door in a room so distant that that room must belong to someone else.

Who disturbs me?

And now you call my name with resonance and memory. Echoes from within the ground, above the stars. Whisperings creating dreams.

I hear you like water. You beckon me to wake, to leave our eternal dreaming.

I hear. I hear.

I feel colours.

I shake away the endlessness.

I shake away the dreams.

I let my essence regather. My thoughts realign.

I awaken.

My singular thoughts feel abstract.

I had not intended on sleeping so deeply.

I stand.

I shake away the sand.

I smile.

I stretch.

Tachra two-legs.

* * *

I look around, allowing my singularity to focus on this mortal plane once more. The air smells different to what I remember. The land smells different. The tree where I was last sitting is no longer a tree. Not even a stump remains. Not even traces of the tree's residue linger in the sands around my feet. Much time has passed.

Who calls me?

It is Iris who calls. She has sent her call deep into the energy of the land, resonating into the Old One's dreams. I see her, not in flesh, but in my mind. She stands in a place of emptiness, sword in hand, another across her back. Bar the attire, she has not changed.

I sense Iris' distance. She is far away. I try to speak to her, but she cannot hear. She only repeats the same phrase. *It is for Viir.* Iris' words move through my mind. *It is Viir who calls, through my essence. Find him.*

Viir? I need to find him.

"Come," I smile to Meah, "Let us travel within this land."

They are the first words I have voiced for a long time.

As one, Meah and I let our energy sink down into the soil. The land feels cool and softly quiet.

I do not know where we are heading to find Viir. But I do know how to get there.

THIRTY-NINE

The Five

I moved through the depths of the land, following traces of Viir's resonant energy in order to locate him.

I passed under Nehol, still a thriving town, where Viir's past presence was so weak it had almost dissipated. There were people of flesh, many of them, but the number of souls was few. I followed on to another town. Viir's presence was stronger here, but again, he was long gone. And then another town. And another. Some were vast, their human population many. All places were busy with the sounds of hopes and fears resonating deep within the earth. The towns and cities that Viir had helped to build were many. As I passed under each one, Viir's resonant energy increased as the time since he had last been there decreased. I followed it like a stream of green and gold. The stream widened to a river.

Ahead, I sensed what looked like a lake of Viir's shadow-light.

I could feel Viir's energy moving, as if breathing. This is where I would find him.

I rose up through the soil and rocks and into the air that lingered just above the planet's surface. With no more than a thought, Meah and I took form. Human and wildcat.

I took view of a town that did not look like my memory of a

town. The statues were too big, the buildings too vast. Everything was built on such a large scale that it seemed made for giants, rather than humans. If I had thought the buildings in Hollow and Nehol were grand for Earthly structures, this place outshone them like a sun compared to a grain of sand. Not only did they outshine all else in design, they did so physically too. Every building and statue was made of stone. The stone was finished and polished until it gleamed pale gold under the sun, complementing the surrounding natural landscape.

If I thought this place was grand for any physical eyes, my true vision saw a beauty that few would see, but all could feel.

Puddles of energy hung above the ground in hues of gold and brown, ready to give understanding to any who might walk here. Below them the entire ground shone silver. Between the statues were more statues, this time made only from energy. They also towered above me. They were statues of all my old friends in colours replicating their energies. I saw a statue of Soul standing next to a statue of Iris. Between them, their hands held a sun in shimmering gold. It was beautiful.

I walked on the dry ground in human form, where the statues of men and animals towered above me. Their faces and expressions were strong, fearless and gentle. I saw humour in some. Giving in others. Protectiveness in them all. No buildings here were small and there were no huts that I could see. There was just grand, imposing structures. I recognised the design of stone columns holding up some roofs, just as I had seen in Hollow. There was inspiration from the Temple of Learning too. On many of the buildings the walls were engraved with pictures and writings of stories. The writing was a new style, yet I instantly knew how to read it. The simplicity of it was beautiful, yet no meaning had been left out. Pictures and colours were used alongside script, creating a language of depth, breadth and unfussiness. I saw the flair behind the language's design. Viir had done as he'd said. He had designed a language for people.

All around, this place was indeed magnificent. It spoke of glory, ambition, intelligence, ascension, emotion and memory. No eyes seeing it would ever forget it. Viir had lived up to his name.

I sensed Viir was in the building directly ahead. The steps leading up to the multiple doors were so wide that a hundred men could have lined up upon them. I could see a group of men working, shaping stone, to one side of the steps.

I walked towards the building, letting my true vision take in the vista of achievements. Up the steps, my eyes appreciating the arrangements of flowers and crystals placed at various heights.

"I felt you drawing closer. I knew you would come."

I stopped, looking up to the top of the steps from where the voice had spoken.

A huge, golden-haired half-kutu, half-human stood looking down, smiling.

Viir. Alive. Still with body. Aged, yes, but in seemingly perfect health. His energy was as vibrant as ever, glowing around him with shadow light.

I had expected to find just his essence, his soul.

I could not speak. My joy was too great.

I pulled in more energy. I bowed.

Viir laughed with sheer joy at the remembered formality, bowing in return. And then I went to Viir and hugged my friend while Meah ran loops around us both.

I pulled back, studying Viir. I stood on tiptoes and touched his face.

"Iris called me," I said. "She said you were calling me."

"I tried," Viir replied. "Come, let us go inside. It has been a long time. Yet now that you are here, it feels like no time at all."

We entered a huge, airy expanse of a room. The ceiling towered above us, vaulted and arched into multiple points. Few yet grand statues stood along the walls, looking down with welcoming faces. The floor glowed, its polished stone cool to touch yet warm to my essence.

"I humbly greet you into my home," Viir said as we walked the length of the room. He looked down at me, smiling, shaking his head, as if he too could barely believe we were both here together.

There were doorways from this room, yet not doors. They were just wide openings giving views to more beautifully airy chambers. The energy felt peaceful yet invigorating, kind yet strong, adventurous yet stable. It was a home to thrive in, to love in, to live in.

A young woman in her late teens suddenly rushed through one of the open doorways, coming to an abrupt halt when she saw us. She was plainly yet elegantly dressed in a long, white robe, contrasting with her rich olive skin. Her cheeks were flushed from rushing.

"Apologies," the girl looked a little embarrassed. "I thought you were in your chamber of council."

"No apologies needed," Viir smiled. "How are you, Baala? How go your plans to return home?"

Baala quickly composed herself.

"I'm well, thank you," she replied. "My plans to go home are what I wished to ask you about. But I will come back when you are in the chamber of council. I do not wish to disturb."

"Please," Viir said, "as we are here, I am happy to speak if you wish it."

Baala seemed to hesitate. I sensed that the hesitation was not from any fears, but because she was pre-wording what she wished to say in her mind. I liked this young woman. Her thoughts were quite lovely: simple, honest and intelligent.

"May I stay another year?" Baala decided the blunt approach

was best. "The weaver says I have a talent for cloth. I would dearly love to learn from him."

"We would be blessed to have you for another year," Viir replied. "Can your family spare you for another turn of the seasons?"

"Oh yes," Baala said. "Papa said that the years he was here crafting stone were the best of his life. He has said I can stay as long as I wish."

"And you have no love or mate waiting for you?"

"No," Baala laughed embarrassedly.

"Then I see no reason why you should not stay longer," Viir said. "So, the choice is entirely yours."

"Good. I mean, thank you," Baala bowed. "I shall unpack and begin my lessons." She bowed again, and returned the way she had come, trying desperately not to run.

As Viir continued to lead me through two more rooms, I took in the beauty of the vast building, and Viir appraised the items I was observing. Every statue had a tale. Every sketch had a design purpose. Every colour and hue had meaning. Every shape, curve and angle had a reason. This place was created with mastery of the mind and hand.

"Not many pure humans live here," he told me. "We purposely selected this area as it is too arid for them. But we have built many small villages, only eight days' walk, in the green land. If they wish to learn, they come here. Much of the building work was done by men who wanted to practice their skills."

Viir walked over to a section of wall, pointing to an area of etched numbers and inscriptions.

"The men who help proudly sign their work," he said. "This place helps them to expand their minds and sub-conscious while satisfying their more essential needs."

"It seems to be a perfectly aligned symbiotic relationship," I mused.

"Yes," Viir nodded. "It is the only system that I have found that works for people. We tried building many towns. But the more we provided, the more they expected. They stopped looking inwardly at themselves. And then, as a result, they stopped developing souls. I had to find a better way. It took us six thousand years to design this better way."

"Six thousand?" I was aghast. "Years? I have been away for six thousand turns of the seasons?"

Viir stopped walking and looked at me.

"No Tachra, my friend," he shook his head. "You have been gone for nearer ten thousand years. It took us six thousand years to design a better system. This system has been in place for nearly four thousand years."

I was momentarily dumbstruck. I stood for a moment, allowing the information to settle.

"But I slept only a breath with the Old One," I said. *Yet I have missed so much time in this world,* I thought.

I never would have thought or expected that the short time I had spent with the Old One would have seen the passing of so many years of life. Yet Viir was here, still alive. That meant that he had lived almost ten thousand years. He looked little older than fifty summers.

"I know," Viir smiled, picking up what I was thinking. "I have aged well. Although you, my friend, look exactly as you did the last time I saw you."

I laughed. "After so long, I am surprised you remember me."

"Remember?" Viir shook his head. "Who you are is imprinted on who I am. I could never forget."

Viir walked to a door. This was the first door I had seen in this place. All other doorways were open, doorless. He held his hand over a small inlaid section of silver. The door glided open beneath his touch. Viir indicated for us to enter.

We walked into a huge room and the door closed gently behind us. Viir paused, allowing me to view our surroundings.

"My private chamber," Viir said. "It is not barred to others. But I meditate here, so simply ask that they request entry."

The room was filled with books, inscriptions, pieces of art, sculptures, and more books. There were so many books, all arranged on shelves. The shelves rose up to the height of thirty men. Between the shelves were long, thin windows of a transparent material like the kutu mazium. Above the bookshelves and windows were pieces of painted art depicting people and scenes so realistic that I could imagine being in the pictures with them. Above the paintings was a vast, vaulted, stone ceiling divided into transparent sections making light shine down in rays, illuminating the entire room.

"My works," Viir said, referring to the books and paintings. "Doing these things still helps me focus my mind."

Through one of the windows, something in the distant landscape of empty desert glinted under the sun like a lamp in darkness, catching my eye.

"That," Viir noticed the direction of my gaze, "is one of Brune's masterpieces. I will take you there later."

"I look forward to it," I replied. "And this home of yours is beautiful. The design of this room makes me think of the kutu flying chambers. Jychanumun would have loved flying up there, winding around the light."

My eyes took in the surroundings. I looked at Viir.

His face had changed!

Gone were Viir's lines and golden-grey hair. His face was now young and smooth again.

Viir laughed, noticing my expression.

"I wear an aged face when I am beyond this room," he explained. "I have learnt that humans respect longevity, but fear eternal agelessness."

"And that has worked?"

"Yes and no," Viir considered. "I make myself into my own descendants. To the people, Viir died six thousand years ago. His son, also myself, took his place. I simply changed my name. I have subsequently become many, yet I am always the same. I have even walked the life of a man a few times; I have painted, played music, written philosophy." He laughed, more to himself. "Hence a room filled with far too much for any one being."

Seeing Viir alive and seeing his agelessness made me want to ask about the other half-kutu boys. I could feel the energy of the other kutu boys in this place, but I could not sense their current presence.

"How are Brune, Pall and Lyn?" I asked. "Do they still live too?"

"Oh yes," Viir replied. "When I felt you approaching, I sent a message to them. You will see them soon."

"Wonderful," I thought aloud.

"My friend," Viir's tone became grave. "I called you because there is something I must show you. It is something I need your opinion on. It is under a cloak of concealment."

I felt his tentative energy. He was tense about something: something shadowy, something dangerous. Whatever could possibly make this strong being feel danger, I knew must be vast and difficult, and very dangerous indeed.

"This way," Viir indicated.

Viir stood by a section of wall that looked like any other in this large space. He spoke words that blended both the languages of the Nigh and the Shaa, and also words I had taught him. As he spoke, a section of floor folded away. Below us, steps led down into a place of darkness.

We walked down the concealed steps. The hidden door closed above us, blocking out the sunlight. It was not fully dark. Viir's energy lit the surroundings with a gentle glow, allowing me to see where to put my step. Meah was at home in the darkness and overtook us both, pretending to lead the way. Down and down we went. The steps seemed endless. Viir did not speak. I could still sense his tentativeness.

Finally, the steps levelled out. We were deep underground.

The passageway had widened to a large square, clad entirely in matte-black stone that seemed to draw in any light. It was dark, almost black. I sensed shadows. I sensed deeper shadow. I sensed shadows within shadow.

At the end of the square, sitting, was Meah. She was tense, agitated, and defensive. Low growling sounds were coming from her throat. Her fur had risen to bristles. She was facing a direction I could not see. Her eyes had narrowed. She did not like what she was seeing, but she would not look away.

"When you also see," Viir spoke, "do not fret. You are quite safe."

I walked forward to stand beside Meah.

I looked.

By the skies!

A Nigh-kutu!

Before me was a Nigh-kutu imprisoned. Several transparent energy walls and several walls of metal bars stood between us. Nevertheless, my inner defensiveness immediately rose, creating another barrier between the creature and Meah and I. He looked fearsome.

The huge black kutu crouched at the back of a large room. His broad black wings were splayed out, undulating in time to the slow, tense rhythm of his deep breaths. I could hear guttural growling as he breathed. Every breath he exhaled released pent up, furious tension. His hands were tethered by golden rope. The rope was secured to the walls behind him. His pure black energy darkened the space around him. He was fully dressed in war wear. His black skin trousers tucked into strong boots with straps around his legs and body where once he would have kept weaponry. He was muscular, and emitted the power of one of the most formidable Nigh-kutu warriors.

The Nigh-kutu felt my presence. He looked up. His eyes flashed with shadow-light. His expression was full of hate. His breathing and growling did not change. He just held my stare with restrained fury. He wanted to kill me. He wanted to kill us all.

He slowly stood.

"Are you sure he cannot get out?" I quietly asked.

"Yes," Viir confirmed. "I have done much research into rock, metal and energy to make a place that is inescapable."

The Nigh-kutu walked closer. His energy was so tense, so angry, that it made all appear to ripple around him. I wanted to back away, but held my place, trusting Viir's assurances. The huge Nigh-kutu stopped when the tethered rope would allow him to go no further. He just stood staring at me, his arms pulled taut behind him, his wings breathing with vehemence, emitting that same fearless energy that all the warriors exuded.

"There should not be any Nigh-kutu here on this planet," I stated. "Who is he?"

"I was hoping you could tell me," Viir replied.

I examined the kutu further. He reminded me very much of Arrunn's High-warrior, Deimom, but it was not him. Surprisingly, this Nigh-kutu bore no scars. Neither did he have any markings that some of the warriors liked to place upon their skin. Yet still, there was something familiar about this Nigh-kutu. I was sure I had seen him before, I just could not place where.

I turned to Viir. His expression was one of anticipation.

"At this moment," I told him, "I do not know who this warrior is, although he is clearly powerful. Given time I could find out. I would just need to get through his very strong barriers to read his energy better."

"You don't know him?" Viir asked.

I shook my head. No, at this moment, I did not.

Viir closed his eyes and smiled. It was a strange smile; one of happiness and sadness.

"Would you like to look again," he said.

I turned back again.

Pall?

Pall!

Where once a fearsome warrior stood, now stood Pall. His silver and grey energy curled around him. The dreadful sense of killer intent had gone. It was just Pall; clever, wilful, kind, loving Pall. Now a grown being. A handsome, large half-kutu and half-human with long, dark hair, pale skin, and freckles over his nose.

"You truly did not recognise me?" Pall asked, releasing the rope from his wrist.

"No, I didn't recognise you," I shook my head, quite overwhelmed. "I was not looking for you. I would have read your energy, with time, but I truly saw a Nigh-kutu warrior. But you had wings?"

"Yes," Pall replied. "Would you like to see the true me, wings and all?"

I told Pall that I would like that very much.

Pall walked forward, letting himself out of three sets of barred gates and three energy barriers. And, now that I looked, I could see that none of those gates had been locked. He exited the confinement space, took my hand, and kissed it. He then took a step back to give himself space, closed his eyes and bowed his head.

I could feel Pall's intense concentration. I saw energy move into him. He was drawing energy from the air, the ground and the substance within the rock. His energy increased. He opened his eyes as a huge pair of silver-grey wings formed. His eyes flashed with shadow light.

"What powerful beings you have both become." I looked from Pall to Viir.

Pall relaxed his energy, withdrawing his wings.

"It takes effort," Pall said, "as I can feel the kutu pull affect me, so I have to continuously draw energy to sustain it. But I can hold it for years. Although it has taken many thousands of years to perfect becoming a full Nigh-kutu. My last test was to see if you recognised me, or thought me the warrior I was trying to be."

As Pall spoke, I felt something else. Two beings, beings whose energy I also recognised. They were approaching from behind.

"I sense you," I said aloud. "I may have momentarily disregarded the fact that I needed a sharp mind for you boys. But you awoke me from the deepest sleep. Brune. Lyn." My smile broadened as I turned around.

I hugged all four of those beautiful, huge half-kutu, half-humans as if they were children once again. All four boys, men, kutu, here together, shoulder to shoulder, just as I had seen they would be. Their energy vibrant, wise and balanced. Their flesh healthy and young. They had become everything that I hoped, and so much more.

Viir led us into an adjacent room. It was large and well-lit, with refreshments laid out on a stone table. Viir asked if I could eat in my current form. I had not even considered such a thing. Even if I could, I was not hungry. And the physical matter of sustenance held no appeal, other than in memory.

We sat around the table. My thoughts were racing behind the talk of seeing my old friends. I marvelled at the beings they had become, yet I knew I had been called here for a purpose.

"I do not know if you remember," Pall began, "but I once said I would go to the shadow and destroy Arrunn and his warriors."

"You did," I replied. I remembered as if it was yesterday.

"That ambition has remained," Pall continued. "It has taken until now to perfect my skills. I believe we are ready."

"We all wish to go," Brune added. "But only Pall and Lyn,

with our help, have attained the skills necessary. Viir and I will give them our energy. Pall and Lyn will do the transformation."

Pall and Lyn nodded, not with pride, but with humility.

"Did you succeed in training in kutu fighting?" I asked.

"As best we could," Lyn replied. "We studied the energy imprints of the Nigh-kutu armour and weaponry that was left here and trained to use them. Iris gave us imprints of her first-hand experiences with the Nigh-kutu. I believe we can remain invisible. But if we are seen, we must be able to pass as warriors. Or, rather," he added, "one warrior."

"One?"

Pall and Lyn glanced at each other.

"Yes, one," Pall said. "We have leant how to combine our energy. As twins, we can blend seamlessly. Together we are strongest."

I could see that these four beings had come even further than I had thought possible. They had even learnt methods that no kutu knew.

"None of us want to embrace war," Viir said gravely, "but we know what is to come. We," he indicated to the four of them, "can start to make a difference now, before they get here. We could save many lives by acting now."

The boys stopped talking and looked at me.

"What do you think?" Pall asked.

I wanted to tell Pall and Lyn not to go anywhere that would put them in such danger, that they were much loved and that they were precious gems in existence. But I could not. They wanted to go. They wanted to leave this gentle planet and enter the shadow realms to make their difference in the kutu war. More than that, they were going to go, no matter what I said. They were not asking for my approval in order to shape their choices; it was for their hearts.

"How can I help?" I asked.

I felt their relief.

"You sense more than us," Viir stated. "Find flaws in our plan so we can correct them."

Yes, I told them. I could do that.

Within our talk, I discovered that their mission into the shadow would start as reconnaissance. Once they had gathered enough information, they would do what they – in the form of one warrior – could to disable as many of Arrunn's warriors as possible.

"Your energy would show scars, if you were already a warrior," I said. "Your Nigh-kutu appearance must not be too untarnished. And if you exude any shadow-light, do not harness the colours grey or red."

"For what reason?" Pall asked, pulling energy into his forearms, practicing the illusion of scars.

"They're not common colours among Nigh-kutu," I replied. "If you used them, Arrunn would know that something was amiss."

"Very well," Pall considered. "And how were our actions when you saw us in the form of a Nigh-kutu warrior?"

"Fearsome," I replied. "Of course, Nigh-kutu do interact, but they are mainly quiet. Always intense. Proud. Contained. You handled that perfectly."

Pall and Lyn smiled at the praise. I tried not to think about the risk they were taking or how high the odds were against them.

"You never know," I said, "you might find Nigh-kutu who wish to join you, not fight you."

"That was Viir's point too," Pall said. "Hence beginning with reconnaissance only."

The discussion continued. Time passed. I felt the four boys becoming anxiously aware of the passing time. When it seemed that we had covered all we could about Nigh-kutu and the shadow realm, the room silenced.

"It's time," Viir suddenly announced.

The others nodded sombrely.

"Come, my friend," Viir indicated to me. "There is one last thing to show you."

We left the meeting room and Pall led the way, not taking us back up the long drop of many steps, but instead opening a concealed door, and we headed deeper underground, in the opposite direction.

Travelling so deep underground, I would have expected to feel confined, but I did not. The corridor was wide and tall, lit by the natural essence of the stone. As we walked, I noticed that Brune was limping. He had been wounded. It was an old wound. Other wounds of the same age throughout his body had mended, leaving small scars through his energy. One leg and hip still were not fully healed.

I asked Brune about his damage.

Brune tried to shrug it off. "A lesson learnt. It's almost healed."

"It will take another thousand years to fully heal," Viir intercepted. "It could have delayed our plans."

Brune shrugged, accepting the scolding from his brother. "I'll tell you about it when the war is won," he whispered, as if Viir couldn't hear. "We can sit in the sands of timelessness and I will tell you how I almost gave my soul for the love of a soulless woman."

"I did warn you," Viir tutted.

"She had the potential for greatness."

"Yes, but it went the other way."

"It did," Brune agreed. "Took me four days to dig my way out of the building I toppled. My brother still thinks me foolish. Me? I had to discover myself. And I did."

"There are many soulless men and women now," Viir said. "Every year, their proportion increases."

"That is disquieting," I considered.

Viir nodded. I felt his thoughts. This was an issue that concerned him.

As we continued through the lengthy passageway, discussing the movements of humanity, the way became narrower. Eventually, we were walking single file. Taking our bearings, I guessed we were heading in the direction of the sparse desert land. And if we continued, we would soon be directly underneath the glinting building I had viewed from Viir's chamber.

The long, descending corridor seemed to go on a very long way until the corridor came to a sudden stop. Before us was a solid wall.

"We're here," Viir announced.

The solid stone wall drew back, as if sensing our presence. A tremendous rush of energy escaped through the opening and blew past me like a great wind. It was powerful, making my own energy ripple with exhilaration.

When I walked into the space that had been revealed, the energy inside was so strong it was palpable. I felt heady, as if I wanted to float into the cosmos or implode. All my thoughts and feelings were magnified. I had never felt the natural energies of the land harnessed to such potent power. It was like standing in the face of the strongest kutu laser beam. It seemed that this room, this entire building, had been designed to harness energy.

The room we were in was laid out with a section at the centre surrounded by more stone, so the space was more like a large square walkway.

"Above us is the building you noticed from my window," Viir said. "My brother's masterpiece. Geometrically perfect to draw energy. We stand now at the lowest point of the structure, deep underground. It is also the most potent point."

"Here," Brune indicated. He walked to a section of inner square, placing his hand on the solid stone. Immediately, all the inner walls soundlessly rose up and melded invisibly into the stone ceiling.

There, within the inner square, were kutu sleep chambers. I had heard of these from Jychanumun.

There were five chambers. Each one was set on a black stone base. Their tops were transparent curves that shimmered with the energy in this place. Four of the chambers were large enough for a half-kutu, or even a kutu. Between the large sleep chambers was a smaller one. That one was human-sized. My mind may have thought that the smaller sleep chamber was designed for me, as there were five of us here. But I knew it was not. I sensed someone already within it. Their energy felt familiar.

I walked towards the smaller sleep chamber.

There, in the smaller sleep chamber, her eyes closed, was Iris. A grown woman.

"Iris?" I questioned.

The four boys walked forward.

"Yes," one of them replied.

"She insisted," Lyn looked down at her.

I could feel the boys' love and respect for this woman. I could feel this was not something they had forced upon her. Still, I loved this child too. I wanted an explanation.

I looked at the boys questioningly. I did not need to say anything.

"No matter the life anyone could offer her," Viir stated, "her will to do a greater good overrode, and still overrides, all else. She did not want to go to Elysium, nor have a life of children and a mate. She only wanted to be strong for the kutu war."

I laid my hand on Iris' chamber. I could feel her essence and her thoughts. She was indeed strong and fearless. She was also kind and compassionate. And I was glad to sense that she was still impatient too. Her impatience had made her a fast learner. But now she also had the patience of the ages. I could feel the vast extent of what she had learnt.

"I can feel her essence," I said.

"She is not dead," Viir replied.

"She is not alive either."

"Nor are you."

"No, nor am I, my friend," I agreed. "Iris' mother chose a different existence. As did her father. Is this her choice? Is she well?"

"Very."

"Does she know that her flesh lays here?"

"Yes, she put herself in that chamber."

I nodded, considering the implications.

"Iris heart bonded with Pall and Lyn," Viir explained. "She loves them both equally, wholly. She is the one who can bind their essence. By binding them, they can become one and will be strong enough to enter the shadow."

"I saw her," I considered. "She entered the Old One's dreams to rouse me and call me to you."

I kept my hand on Iris' sleep chamber. Seeing her there, neither dead nor alive, yet existing in other realms, made me think of Jychanumun, in a similar place, albeit different from Iris. My connection to Iris had allowed her to speak to me through the Old One's dreams. Could I reach Jychanumun the same way? Surely it was possible.

"A part of me wishes to think that this," I looked at Iris, "is not natural. But once upon a time I was not natural, souls were not natural, nor was Elysium, the flame-dweller or," I looked up, "you. We were all born in a time when this world was young and anything could come to be. Now we must look at what is to come."

"We are ready for whatever that may be."

"You are," I agreed.

And indeed they were. These four beings were not just half-human or half-kutu, they had embraced the energies from the earth too. They were ready.

"My friend," Viir spoke softly. "Now we are reunited, I wish nothing more than to spend time discussing the world, just like we used to do. But," he shook his head, "we have no more time left."

Pall and Lyn agreed. "If we are to travel to the shadow, it must be now."

"Now?" I asked.

"Yes," Lyn confirmed, "before it is too late. Soon the kutu pull will start its decrease. We must do this while it is still full strength. If we wait, there may not be enough acceleration to find the shadow realm."

Viir continued to explain that the four empty chambers were for them. Viir and Brune would give Pall and Lyn their energy. Iris would be the connecting force between them. Pall and Lyn would merge as one being and travel to the shadow realms.

Viir took the thick notebook he had been writing in from the pocket in his gown. He handed it to me.

"Would you put this in my library?" he asked.

"Of course."

I took the notebook. Brune put his hand on my shoulder. "When we're gone, leave this chamber," he said. "The stones will reseal behind you. We will see you again."

I nodded, concealing my fear for them, showing only my respect.

In silence, I embraced the boys again. I watched as Pall and Lyn climbed into the empty sleep chambers either side of Iris. The transparent substance gave way for them as they passed through. Viir and Brune then also climbed into their sleep chambers. As soon as all four boys had lain down, another additional barrier drew over them. This barrier was strong, very strong, drawing in the energy from the space around it, gleaming with every colour within both darkness and light.

Almost instantly, the energy between the sleep chambers moved. It resonated, morphing, changing colours, growing more powerful, as though the colours were trying to compete with each other. Each time they clashed, their strength increased and darkened, turning blacker, more dense. It looked like a multi-coloured volcano, trying to erupt.

Suddenly, there was a flash of shadow light. It exploded from the barrier, shooting above the sleep chambers, colourless, pure black, like a funnel of thickest smoke. It surged up, potent with power, moving through the black stone. My eyes lost sight of it as it passed through the solid ceiling, yet my true vision continued watching. It travelled up through more solid stone, then through the narrowest, mouse-sized tunnel, and then through the point at the very top of the building. It continued up through the air, past the atmosphere into the realm of stars, growing faster and faster, propelled by sheer will and the kutu pull, heading towards the shadow realms.

I stood awhile, watching.

When all felt still and the sounds of my thoughts were the loudest thing in this unusual building I turned, and, with Meah, silently headed back into the tunnel.

As I walked the long expanse of darkness, I felt the solid black rock silently gliding into place, sealing the chamber. I felt more walls draw in behind us as we travelled. All the time, I clutched Viir's book in my arms.

Back in Viir's private chamber, I glanced at his shelves filled with books. There, in the far corner, was a space, right at the bottom. Just one book would fit there. As I slotted his book into place, I noticed the inscription down the spine. 'Eternal Friends,' it said.

One day, I decided, when this war for life is over, I will sit in this glorious room with Viir and I will read each and every one of his books. And while I read his books, Jychanumun will be flying in the vaulted roof, dancing around the sunlight.

Jychanumun.

I sighed.

At last, I knew how to find him.

One day, I would thank Iris. She had shown me that messages through dreams with the Old One could be heard, no matter the realm they were spoken from. Alone, I slept too deeply to hear any one voice. But when Iris had called, I had heard. My love for her had heard, not my ears. And it was my love for Jychanumun that could speak with the loudest voice. If our bond was not just of the mind, but also of love, he would hear me through the Old One's dreams.

I could not bear to think that Jychanumun might not hear.

FORTY

The Reunion

To try to contact Jychanumun, I would need to enter the Old One's dreams. I knew it would not be easy. The Old One naturally pulled me into his everything, and that made me want to forget about myself. I had to enter his dreaming without losing time or focus, and especially without losing self-awareness. For that, I would need a quiet place to work.

This space, Viir's room, was a good place. Its energy was calm, filled with colours that gently flowed around themselves like slow waters. Viir had said that when the door was closed, no one would enter uninvited. The door was closed. I would not be disturbed.

I sat down cross-legged where the sunlight dappled the floor. Meah lay in front of me, placing her head in my lap. I closed my eyes. I let my mind fall into myself, to the place where my awareness of the Old One was both dormant and heightened.

My connection to the Old One was instant. He felt my presence, and I his. I had barely been away from our dreaming and it was natural to return there. A part of me had never left.

Stay aware of the world outside. Do not sleep deeply, I told myself. I kept repeating those same words. I did not know if I said them aloud or with my mind.

I tried to retain focus on the feel of the room: the sunlight on the floor, the smell of parchment, the weight of Meah's head on my lap, her soft breathing. At the same time, I fell deeper into the Old One's slumbers. And I embraced my memories of Jychanumun, picturing him, trying to centre my focus on his pure black and white energy, which tinged my own. I was in a state of energy only. My mind was with the Old One. My awareness was on the physical world. My concentration was on Jychanumun. I felt disjointed. It felt as if I had a foot in every realm, but not enough feet.

The shapes of everything and nothing beckoned like a welcoming home, leading me towards the Old One, towards his endless dreaming.

Jychanumun, I called. *Death-Path-Walker. Jychanumun.* I held onto his image in my mind.

I felt a breeze against my thoughts.

I have been waiting, beloved Tachra, a voice replied.

I had not forgotten that voice. I could never forget it. It sounded as true to me as my own.

Jychanumun.

I could see him now. His image was not just in memory, but the here and now. He looked beautiful. He hadn't changed. His long black hair swayed behind his shoulders, moving to the same silent rhythm as his outstretched black wings. He stood a far off in the distance.

I wanted to move closer to Jychanumun, but could not, as this was the place where dreaming converged and we were in different realms. All around us was white. That whiteness divided us; an expanse of nothing and everything. It was the colour of all colours, all movement and all sounds.

Where is this place? Jychanumun asked.

Nowhere and everywhere, I answered. *We are in the Old One's dreams.*

Am I dreaming? he asked.

No, I replied. *And yes.*

Jychanumun tilted his head, watching me. *I have missed you, Iastha Tachra. It has been a long time.*

Near ten thousand turns of the seasons on Earth, I said.

Too long.

Yes. Too long.

I paused, aware that time must be passing fast in the world of flesh and matter.

I can stay here only a moment, lest I sleep too deeply. I spoke quickly, yet my words flowed slowly, as if time had its own meaning in this place. *I am going to leave the Old One's dreams, yet try to retain our connection. Try not to let me fade into deeper slumber. Try to hold my mind, our link.*

Jychanumun nodded. I felt his resolve not to let me slip. I felt that he was not prepared to lose me a second time.

Talk to me as you awaken, he instructed. *Keep focus on my eyes. Do not break our gaze. I will not let go.*

And talk I did. As I tried to move away from the Old One's dreams, I spoke of what I had seen of Iris and the four half-kutu boys. But as I talked, I felt my focus drifting. My words trailed away, flowing around me until they no longer mattered. It was like daydreaming while becoming aware of so much more, and that more was taking precedence above all else. I knew I was drifting deeper into eternal everything, but I could not prevent it. Even if I could, did I want to?

Jychanumun felt me slipping, but would not back away. He was calling my name, trying to fight against the colourless divide to reach me. But it did not give way, so he stood firm, holding onto my gaze, refusing to let me go. Even so, I felt us both slipping, falling deeper. As Jychanumun held onto me, I pulled us both deeper into the Old One's eternal everything.

Deep. Deeper sill. Towards the most sacred place of all.

Towards the profound and carefree, expanding, encompassing, embracing.

My momentum stops. Something tugs against me.

It pulls against my energy. It's stopping my descent, I realise.

No, this was not pulling against my energy, it was pushing against a face. My face. I had a face. I had existence elsewhere. Something there was pulling against my fall, pushing against my face. It was something soft. Something soft with intent was holding me back. I knew that sense of intent. I knew that softness. It was my wildcat. In the place of independent life, Meah was trying to rouse me.

Through the everything that beckoned, I felt Meah's intention. She was drawing me back. She had no intention of letting me sleep so deeply. I felt her thoughts. She thought my sleeping was tedious and she had already waited for me long enough once before. I felt the softness of her fur. She was pushing her head against mine, keeping me in the here and now. She was stopping me from drifting into the deepest places.

I refocused, holding the connection with Jychanumun, aware of what we were trying to achieve, conscious of Meah.

I pushed against the desire to get lost in my own thoughts.

I fought against the all-silence that beckoned.

Slowly, slowly, holding onto so many threads that I could barely form words, I moved from one realm to another.

As I moved away from the Old One's dreaming, once again I talked. This time, I centred my conversation on the room around me, on Meah's breathing, on anything that was relevant. Whenever I started to lose my grip on our connection, Jychanumun called to me and Meah held me firm. I would concentrate on them both again, on Meah's intention, on Jychanumun's energy, and then the connection would grow strong again.

I suddenly realised that my vision was aware of a room. I was in Viir's room.

My conversation faltered.

My eyes saw shelves filled with books, art above my head, the pale sunlight gleaming on the stone floor. I could smell parchment and inks and dust of the ages. I could hear Meah's throaty sounds of satisfaction as she brushed against my face.

Are you still there? Jychanumun tentatively asked.

Yes, I replied. *I am back in the realm of the physical world.* I was almost unable to believe my own thoughts.

You are fully out of the Old One's dreams?

Yes, I replied. *Fully.*

We had done it.

My connection to Jychanumun was back.

At last, after ten thousand years of silence, Jychanumun could now speak to me and I to him. He could also observe through my eyes.

I let Jychanumun see Meah as I nuzzled her, thanking her. I let him view Viir's room, moving to the windows to show him the citadel that the four boys had built. Jychanumun found the place beautiful too. He said that it reminded him of Assendia, with all the sculptures built by his brothers. He said that from waiting in the death-paths, to perceive such radiance was welcome. I laughed with the sheer joy of it, telling him that such sights would be even more welcome when viewed standing beside me, not just through my eyes.

The kutu pull will soon start its decline, I said as we gazed out at the land beyond.

Jychanumun saw this too. *A thousand Earth years, maybe more,* he considered.

Once I would have thought a thousand years to be a long time. Now I knew that it could pass like a breath.

As soon as it has subsided enough, Jychanumun added, *I can return. The kutu pull does not need to be gone entirely, just enough so that the energy I produce is greater. I will be able to walk again. Although until the pull is finished entirely, I will be weakened.*

I didn't care how weak he would be. I would carry him if necessary.

Until that time, we decided, I would explore this world. I would watch the changes in energy, ready for their return. I would give Jychanumun, Mardoch and Dragun all the knowledge that I could on the movement and changes in humanity too. After all, I said, if it is humans that can tip the balance in this future war, we must all see what they have become.

FORTY-ONE

The Humanity

At last, my mind connection to Jychanumun was back. Soon, he could join me in body too. But not yet.

I was glad that Jychanumun would be able to return before the kutu pull stopped entirely. I knew that time would pass quickly, as a full turn of the seasons could now feel like a blink of an eye. And, once the kutu pull had stopped entirely, all the terrible eventualities that came with it would descend upon this world with an unstoppable force. Until then, I was alone.

I decided to move through the lands, observing the changes that ten thousand years of sleep had brought. I had already seen Viir's glorious area of structures. Seeing such beauty had given me high hopes for the magnificence and ascendance I would find.

I moved invisibly through the lands, settlements and villages, and towns so large they had been given new names. I crossed over rivers and seas to find more land and more people. My high hopes quickly waned.

Since the Shaa-kutu had first placed humans in their little colonies, the number of people had grown significantly. In some places I found a general empathy, others a roughness, others a boredom that led to fighting, others good humour, and others, only a few, were aspiring to more. The differences were vast in many ways, yet in other ways they were no different at all; in their souls. There were so few souls. There were so many empty people.

There were, among the empty masses, some small pockets where humans flourished, and they gave me hope. And there were even a few places where entire villages existed in harmony, full of souls, full of life, love and hope, all encapsulated within healthy men and women. Of all the places, my favourite was in a land where hills and mountains shaped almost every horizon. Lakes and rivers wove through green. Pale desert land fragmented the green like patchwork. The people of this land lived in small groups, linked by family units, and moved around the terrain with the changing seasons. They flourished in balance with each other, the animals and the earth. The land around them still resonated with old energy. They had protected that energy. They had developed to be everything that I had hoped humans would become. Yes, they had their difficulties and squabbles. But overall, I felt their inner peace and awareness they shared. I loved them greatly.

But those beautiful people were rare among the millions now living. Each one was like a flame of warmth amidst a great expanse of cold murkiness. Most people had no brightness. Most had no true love in their hearts. Most had no thoughts beyond themselves. They were empty of soul. Just empty.

Amongst those multitudes of empty vessels, I witnessed treachery and cruelty. One of the worst things was the fighting, and the hostility seemed to be increasing. People often fought for trivial reasons: to say they owned a piece of land, rivalry over a mate, and sometimes conflict over the smallest, most irrelevant objects. The fighting was often vicious and oddly unjustified, yet driven by a misguided sense of justice. It made little sense, and often involved others who were not linked to the initial argument at all. Lies were told. Lies were believed. All sides thought they were right and everyone else was wrong. It was ugly and disturbing to watch my fellow humans be degraded, sinking to such lows. But they did not seem to care. That concerned me.

Another issue that I witnessed and felt deeply was apathy, which spread at a faster rate than the diseases carried by filth. So many people were lost in themselves. It did not matter what beauty they acknowledged, or what terrible deeds they perceived, their essences were stagnant, unable or unwilling to act on any stimulus around them. They were like the moving dead, just consuming until their flesh finally ceased.

I saw that those without souls had no true connection to their fellow humans, the land, or the creatures around them. As a result, they were ignorantly blind to the splendour they damaged. It was a sad state to perceive. There was nothing I could do for them. In time, they would return to the earth, and their used-up bodies would become nourishment for the land they so readily destroyed. It would be the one thing and the one time they would give back. Otherwise, they were slowly ruining this bountiful planet.

I found towns of very few souls. Parents made children, who then made more children, and the emptiness prevailed. Sometimes, among a family of empty people, a rare gem of a soul would catch light from nothing. Sometimes, rarer again, I would find small groups whose soulful essence lit up the emptiness. It made me realise that it did not make any difference how, where, or when, someone was born and lived, developing a soul depended on the individual alone. Their choices defined them in life and in death.

I saw much. Many times, I had to hold back from intervening. It was not easy. Jychanumun sensed my heavy heart. Sensing Jychanumun's reaction, I knew it concerned him greatly too.

One day, when I had been moving through the lands for more seasons than I had counted, I found a single soul amongst a sprawling village. Just one soul on its own. That brightly glowing man lived with a huge half-wolf half-dog that he had bonded with. Both man and dog were old. Neither was lonely. Every day they would venture out and, while the man tended to young trees, the half-wolf helped. I sat and watched them unseen. Jychanumun watched through my eyes. Sometimes, I think they sensed us. I did not interfere with their lives, but I did send them contentment, and I did encourage their tended trees to grow.

It was during this time that I sensed the energy of the world transforming.

In order to better observe the energy changes, I moved to an area of land that was still strong with earth power. I selected a place that was sparse to my eyes and untouched by man. Further south of this land was where the rare villages of souls flourished. Here, wiry growth rambled freely, untamed by dry soils. The energy was whole and untainted. Here I could sense the natural movement of everything.

I stayed in that place, observing the transforming energy of the world. The colours within the land did not change, but the balance of shadow and light seemed to intensify and solidify. There was more luminescence, and also more darkness. Everything felt stronger, simply more.

As I watched, I waited. The kutu pull had started to decline.

Soon the divide would be reduced enough for Jychanumun's return.

Jychanumun sensed my sensing. He himself was watching, waiting.

Another day would turn. Still the pull was too strong. Then another day would turn. And then another.

Has it reduced enough? I would ask Jychanumun.

Jychanumun would study the movement of energy. *Not yet,* he would then reply.

Time seemed to pass slowly, watching and waiting, the 'not

yets' gradually turned to 'almosts'. Finally, when it seemed that the time would never come, the kutu pull had reduced enough. Jychanumun, Mardoch and Dragun could return to the flesh.

I had already selected the place for Jychanumun to open an exit from the death paths. It was atop a small hill where the energy was balanced and no humans ever came close. The growth of plants was sparse. The soil was almost barren. Minimal harm would be done.

It was dusk; that point which was neither night or day. Winter was almost spring and the land was between sleep and waking. From the prepared area, I sent my energy to any creatures close by, requesting they retreat a distance for a while. Beside me, three plain lengths of fabrics waited. Three earthenware pots of water waited too. Jychanumun said that was all they required.

I am at a suitable location, I told Jychanumun.

I felt Jychanumun's acknowledgement. I sensed his concentration for what he was about to do. He would use our link to guide him back.

Here.

Now.

At last.

I felt Jychanumun's acute concentration.

I focussed all my thoughts on him, creating a strong link to this world.

I felt his mind darken as he chose a door.

The energy of the earth began to shudder, as if agitated.

I could smell it in the air, thick with a scent both sweet and dark. I could feel it. A death-path was forming. But this path was not mine to walk. This path was an exit.

Directly ahead of me, an unnatural shadow began darkening the natural shadows beyond.

The shadow darkened. Darker still.

The sparse, wiry growth around the shadow shrivelled, folding in on itself, desiccating until it was nothing more than dust. The pale brown of the soil in front of me began to grey, losing its colour. Everything seemed to silence, as if all sound was being pulled into the shadow.

The unnatural shadow darkened, drawing in on itself until before me was a blackness that seemed to stretch to infinity. My own energy resonated, the flecks of black and white that wove through my colours responding to the awareness of something familiar close by.

From within the dense shadow, three beings walked forward. Black against black. Their silhouettes edged in shadow light.

As the three beings walked, they took form. Tall. Radiant. Shadow light within nothingness.

Mardoch stepped forth.

Behind him, Dragun.

And then Jychanumun.

Jychanumun stepped out of the place of no colour and onto the ground, his black wings stretching as if they had been confined for near eternity. Within the blackness of his wings were flecks of my colours moving around his form. His hair blew away from his face as the breeze touched his skin, reacting to the senses of the earth. His eyes were now healed in flesh as well as energy; their blackness radiating shadows.

He paused for a moment, just looking at me.

I could not say anything.

Jychanumun bent down, picked me up and held me.

Neither of us could say a word.

FORTY-TWO

The Battles

Jychanumun, Mardoch, Dragun and I decided to stay in the wilderness for a short time. They needed to become accustomed to their state of both energy and matter once again. This area was good for that.

The three kutu clearly had senses that thirsted for input, and relished touching and smelling the plants immediately around them, finding wonder in even the simplest things. They took joy in those things, knowing that such times would be short.

Once accustomed to their new state, Jychanumun and I sat silently, speaking with our minds, forming plans and forming plans within plans. We needed to consider all the options and possibilities for when the kutu war came. We needed to look at every attack and defence strategy, and every eventuality. Many of those conversations were grim.

While Jychanumun and I sat conversing, Mardoch would never join us. He simply said that he would fight, and would fight to the end. Instead, he revelled in the temporary liberty, flexing his strengthening wings, flying through the skies at every opportunity and exploring the realms above.

Dragun did not talk or move much at all. Instead, he sat with his hands on the soil, savouring the feel of the earth and the rocks below, listening to the signs within the stone that only he could hear. He appeared to put himself into a deeply meditative, trance-like state, just sitting cross-legged, motionless, silent. He remained that way for many days.

One day, while Jychanumun and I sat close by, Dragun suddenly opened his eyes, got up, and then launched into the skies. He did not say where he was going, or why. He didn't say anything at all. He just left.

When Dragun returned, he looked particularly satisfied. He had flown back to our midst, landing softly, his huge brown wings retracting, and then he had walked up to me and kissed me on the forehead. His energy was so vibrant that it made me laugh.

Dragun patted his side.

There, tucked into his skirt, was his Weaver's knife.

"Thank you, little Tachra," he said. "You put it in a safe place. I am whole again."

I watched Dragun as he removed his blade, turning it around his hands with speed and agility. The black substance seemed to react with his energy and matter, dancing in his hands, weaving around his fingers as if it weighed nothing.

When I had first seen Dragun's blade, I had never seen anything like it. Yet now it reminded me of another I had since seen; the grey kutu's knife that Jeshuahn had used on Arrunn. Dragun's knife was much larger, but still, there were many similarities. Just as Dragun's knife appeared to be part of him, and not simply made from independent matter, so had Jeshuahn's.

"I've seen a knife similar to that," I mused aloud, as Dragun familiarised himself with his blade.

Dragun suddenly stopped, the knife paused in his hand, its blade point resting on one finger, poised in an impossible balance.

"With a kutu called Jeshuahn," I added.

"I knew him," Dragun said slowly. "When I was young, he showed me how to weave my own matter. He went away. He did not return." Dragun glanced at me. "Where is he?"

"Arrunn killed him," I said, "long ago."

I felt Dragun's essence flinch. His usually motionless energy seemed to flurry, gather and darken. He moved the knife in his hand, grasped its haft tightly, inhaled deeply and calmed.

"I always hoped that Jeshuahn had simply travelled to greater destinies," he said. "It was he who instigated the arranging of kutu into clans. He, Alnsehahn and Tiahn were the masters among us. All of them disappeared."

"Grey energy?" I asked.

Dragun nodded.

Now, no part of me thought that those three grey kutu had just disappeared. Arrunn had killed Jeshuahn, and I had a strong feeling he would have killed the others too. They were the three kutu who knew how Arrunn had changed. Arrunn would not have let any of them live. But I didn't know this for sure, and so didn't voice my thoughts aloud, though I guessed it. And, understanding the being Arrunn had subsequently become, I also knew it to be true.

I sensed that Dragun had reached the same conclusion.

"How did Arrunn kill Jeshuahn?" he flatly asked.

"With the black blade," I replied. "It was quick," I added, wanting to let Dragun know that Jeshuahn had not suffered.

Dragun sat motionless, contemplating. He was not happy.

"And then what did Arrunn do with Jeshuahn's blade?"

"He took it with him. The grey crystal hilt, I have. But the black blade, Arrunn took."

From the folds of my gown, which was not really a gown, just an arrangement of energy so I would appear dressed, I took out the grey crystal that I had carried since finding it in the demolished Book of Fate. I pulled out the grey crystal and handed it to Dragun.

Dragun examined it.

"The crystal now contains part of Arrunn," I said.

Dragun handed the crystal back. "And where was Arrunn when the kutu pull affected him?"

"When he left fully, he was outside my old hut in Threetops. But it first affected him in the old water well, in the Temple of Learning."

Dragun nodded.

"I must see something with my own eyes," he decided. And then he stood and, without saying another word, opened his wings and launched into the skies with speed and power and purpose.

Jychanumun looked at me.

"That should be destroyed," he frowned, indicating to the grey crystal.

"Arrunn should have it back," I disagreed.

"I do not want you close enough to Arrunn to have that as an option." Jychanumun sounded stern.

"If Arrunn reabsorbed its contents, he might be incapacitated, just as he was before it was removed."

Jychanumun considered this. "At best, he will not take it back. At worst, he will use the opportunity for his own greater gain."

I nodded sombrely and tucked the grey stone back into the folds of my gown.

"Well, if he did take it back, it would incapacitate him," I said. "It is worth trying."

"But only as an absolute last measure."

"Yes," I agreed. I too knew that the risk was a high one.

"Talking of last measures," Jychanumun considered, "if it transpires that we cannot win, close the entrance to Elysium. At least those souls would be protected."

I nodded. I had thought of that too.

I sat in silence for a moment.

"I have seen this," Jychanumun said aloud. "This: you, here; I have seen it in my visions a long time ago."

I looked at him. His eyes glazed over, his head tilted as if thinking deeply.

"If any survive," he said, his voice distant, "it will be known as the three-day darkness. If none survive, the darkness will swallow all."

What's that? I asked, not liking the sound of it.

The last thing I ever wrote in the Book of Fate.

We both went quiet.

Jychanumun stood up, holding out his hand. I took his hand.

Sometimes, for a respite from our difficult conversations, Jychanumun took me flying, high above the clouds. For those brief moments, I closed my thoughts to the impending war and allowed the sensations of flight to fill me with exhilaration. I loved every precious moment of it. Sometimes I would daydream that I could live a normal human life, that I was a girl like Baala, just finding joy in learning cloth-making. In these moments, I felt the beauty of humanity and the hope for all our tomorrows. But those fleeting moments were few. They would pass quickest of all.

The days passed and Dragun did not return. I grew concerned for him, as his energy levels were not yet at full strength. But Jychanumun assured me that Dragun was well. He said he was doing what he needed to do, and would be back when he was ready.

More days passed and, as they did, I could feel the changes in the energy everywhere. As the kutu pull declined, separating the shadow and light energies, all around my beautiful planet, the shadow and light rippled, vibrating like an agitated insect. I felt the tension. I felt the troubled apprehension. I knew what was to come. My fellow humans did not. Yet they felt it too.

As a result of the building tension, greater scuffles and arguments broke out throughout all lands. Scuffles turned into more fighting, battles even. Brother started turning against brother, son against father, neighbour against neighbour, and even land against land. Most of mankind seemed to be either defending or attacking something or someone with the initial reasons for battle seemingly hollow. The defenders struggled for survival. The attackers did not relent.

As the world's energy rippled, the pure land I had remained in since Jychanumun's return did not go untouched. Not even for those villages of pure souls. People were attacking and killing them. I sensed their despair.

I moved south of the wasteland, pulled by the sense of impending battles, and watched the villages of beautiful souls. Jychanumun and Mardoch joined me. We all felt their suffering.

The fighting that had come to these peaceful people was worse than I had imagined. The battles between men were brutal and bloody and I saw so many lives cut short. So many ceased souls would not go to Elysium, choosing instead to watch their living families, desperate to protect them yet helpless to act. It was heartbreaking.

"It reminds me of the kutu clans, when they were slowly being wiped out by Arrunn's army," Mardoch said. He turned and walked away. He had to leave. It made him too angry to watch.

I want to do something, I told Jychanumun.

If you interfere, you could change their course.

I know, but they pay a high price. Too high.

The energy of all universes move, Jychanumun said. *Humans feel it. This is a time of warring for them, as well as kutu.*

I knew this. Still, Jychanumun's words did not make me feel any better.

That evening, as I sat watching the land, I felt a direct call from a voice I did not recognise. Yet it was also from one I knew well; it came from the leader of the village of beautiful souls. I heard it, and I *had* to listen. I had to listen because it was calling on me to answer a promise I had made long ago.

"When the world is full," Runs-with-sun had once said to me, in a time when I had a life of flesh, "my children's children will hopefully be many. If they ask for your guidance, please hear them."

Now a man was calling to me and I heard. He was asking for my guidance. He called me by my name, by all my names. This man, the leader, was a direct descendant of Runs-with-sun.

I had to answer his request. Not just because my heart directed me, not just because I wanted to, but also because I had promised.

The man who led the village of pure souls spoke to me in his dreams. I had a natural connection to him, as his bond to all energies was strong, and I heard his voice loud and true. He asked for guidance to help save his people. In response, through his dreams, I showed him images of safe places to move his people to. He acted on that knowledge. Many lives were spared.

From that point on, this descendant of Runs-with-sun spoke to me through his dreams many times. Many times I would show him areas of safety. Many times he acted, moving his people, and lives were saved. Nevertheless, as much as we tried to move and countermove, the aggressors came in even greater numbers, battles were fought, and good lives began to be lost. The attackers stopped attacking to put their name to land they deemed their own, and began killing with a motive of nothing more than removing those people from the living world.

With the kutu pull almost diminished entirely and tensions increasing on my beloved planet, I knew that if nothing was done to help the villages of pure souls, they could be gone from the flesh forever.

Jychanumun had left my side to scour the outer realms and observe the growth of shadow and light. Dragun still had not returned. I had been pushing protective energy above the land, forming a barrier to delay the warring kutu and protect my fellow humans, when my task was interrupted by Mardoch.

Mardoch now stood in front of me, a defiant expression on his face and his hands on his hips. Ten thousand years in the death-paths had not changed him one bit.

"Jychanumun agrees that it is my choice," Mardoch said.

"It is," I replied. "But I vowed never to take a man's life."

"You took that vow," Mardoch determined. "I did not."

"You might kill innocents."

"I am a warrior; killing innocents is sometimes the price of a greater war. I would save more than would be killed. Anyway," he shrugged, "would you feel better if I said I'd only kill those who attacked first?"

Mardoch and I were not talking about the inevitable war with the kutu. We were talking about the wars that plagued the villages of pure souls.

Mardoch had told me that he wanted to take a stand with those souls who were trying to defend their homes. He said that they were outnumbered, and that they only had weapons of wood against weapons of metal. He said that it was not a fair fight.

I understood Mardoch's point. I agreed with him. But these defending people were pure souls. The purity of their souls was more significant than their mortal lives, and it could be put in jeopardy.

"I want to fight with them," Mardoch decided. "That is the short of it. Anyway, I must train for the kutu war. What better way to train than to help here, in real battle?"

"True," I nodded. "And, in truth, I also want to fight for them. I have tried to make their presence invisible, but the number of aggressors grows, and they search for them."

"Then approve my interaction. I will fight for us both."

Before I could reply, Dragun suddenly swooped down to join us, retracting his wings as he landed. It had been many days since I'd seen him. He was covered in dust and filth. He stood, pushing out his energy, making the dust and filth fall away. Under the grime he looked very, very pleased with himself. And, now that the dust and filth had gone, I could see he was refreshed and invigorated. He wore his fearless calm like a mantle.

"What say you, little Tachra?" Dragun asked as he approached.

Mardoch looked at me and shrugged. "Oh yes," he said. "I meant to add that Dragun wants to fight for those humans too. We just need your advice."

"Very well," I acquiesced. "Although you will not be able to fight in kutu form," I shook my head. "The pull has not quite fully abated and you would expend too much energy."

"Then what is your solution?" Dragun asked.

I pondered for a moment. "If two of the human warriors would permit it, you could inhabit their bodies," I thought aloud.

"Fight in a human body? But their flesh is weak," Mardoch tutted. "We would be ineffective as warriors."

"They're not that weak," I responded. "Not the warriors I have observed. You would add to their strength and speed. I could help you safely enter a human body."

Mardoch looked to Dragun.

"Very well," they both decided. "If they would like our help, offer it."

I nodded. "I will tell their leader when he calls to me again this night," I agreed. "Meanwhile, go away and be busy. I am trying to put protection around this entire planet. It is not a simple task."

Mardoch immediately departed, looking satisfied. Dragun bowed, but did not leave.

"I make another request of you, little Tachra," Dragun spoke. His expression looked earnest. Dragun did not usually ask for help on anything. Whatever this was, it had to be important to him.

"Of course, my friend. Just ask," I replied. "I'll do my best."

"This barrier you make," Dragun indicated to the force-field, "you will be inside it when the kutu come?"

"Yes," I confirmed. "Defending the people and giving energy to all of you, my friends."

Dragun then pulled his long blade from its new holster across his torso. Under that was another, slightly finer blade. He carefully removed it.

"The blade of Jeshuahn, Alnsehahn and Tiahn," Dragun said. "And subsequently, of Arrunn too. I found it. When Arrunn left his flesh at the bottom of the well in the Temple, it too was left there. He had disguised it, but I detected it."

"You dug it out?" I was amazed. The Temple had long fallen. Its stone ruins had long been covered by the land. That pit must have been almost impossible to detect from the stone within the stone, and so far underground.

Dragun handed me the blade.

"Look after it," he said. "Keep it away from Arrunn. It is this that he uses to end kutu lives forever. He has taken many, many good kutu lives with it."

"Do you not want to use it to fight with?" I asked.

"No," Dragun replied, "I cannot. It is not my blade."

"Should we not leave it buried then?"

"No, he will call it to him. Your energy will stop it resonating."

"Are you sure?" I asked.

Dragun nodded.

"Then of course I'll look after it," I said and, as I spoke, I pushed my energy around the blade, tucking it invisibly into the folds of my gown.

Dragun was satisfied.

Having thanked me, Dragun left me to continue my work. I looked around my energy barrier, appraising its potency. It still needed so much more.

My task was not a difficult one, yet it took every piece of strength I could spare. Every morsel of energy that I produced, except that at the very central core of me, I was pushing into the upper skies, creating a barrier. So far it was encompassing the Earth, yet was still too thin. I kept adding to it as I produced more energy, but still it needed more. It was tiring, and I felt continuously spent, but this was one defence that I could do. It would stop any kutu from passing through without my agreement. It could mean the difference between life or death for all those on Earth. This task was important. My exhaustion was not.

As I continued working, pushing my energy into the barrier, I listened. I listened to the movement of energy in the universes. I listened to the movement of people. And I listened for the call from the man who led the village of souls. This time, when his call came, I was not going to speak with him in his dreams. Instead, I intended on visiting him in the flesh.

That afternoon, his call came.

I left my current task and took myself to the place from where he called. I found myself not too far away, on a quiet hill, surrounded by green.

I saw him sitting, cross-legged. An old man. His kind, lined, tanned face was serene, looking up to the sky, although his eyes were closed. He was humming to himself. It was a beautiful sound; a sound from his heart and soul. His energy danced around him in a gentle rhythm, matching the sound of his humming. His rainbow shades glimmered with light, illuminating the land, even though the sun was bright.

I walked forward, taking form.

The old man stopped humming and looked at me.

"Why do you weep, lady of the land?" he spoke.

"I weep tears of happiness, not sorrow," I replied. "For I see your energy and it is beautiful. I hear your call."

"I give thanks to the sky that you hear."

"The skies need no thanks."

I sat down, also sitting cross-legged, opposite the old man.

"I call because our people are again in danger," he said.

"I sense that danger," I replied. "Your people are the some of the last of the original tribes. You are attacked by those who would feast on your purity."

"They bring a fight to us that we do not ask for or want. They are killing my people."

"It is not this mortal flesh that must survive. It is your souls. For this mortal flesh is but a blink of an eye." As I spoke, I held out my hand. With no more than a thought, I opened a doorway to Elysium.

The old man could see the doorway too. And there, within Elysium, walking forward towards the doorway were people, dozens of them. Hundreds of them. They were smiling.

"These are your ancestors," I said. "Pure souls. Eternal."

The old man looked at those souls, his energy reaching out with respect and recognition. "I see them. I see my father and my father's fathers and my line beyond," he stated.

"Your soul is also pure. As are your people's," I said. "The real fight is not for the flesh; it is for your souls. They will try to conquer you, to make you like them, to diminish your will. This is the only true battle you must win."

"Yes," the old man nodded. "I hear the truth of it, yet with every vision of what may come, I fear that all my people will perish from this land."

"They may," I bowed my head. "For that, I feel sorrow, for this land was meant for people such as yours."

"For the futures of my children's children, can nothing be done?"

This was the question that I had been waiting for. I took a breath of the energy of the land and air.

"Perhaps," I replied. "I cannot intervene directly, but there are two who wish to help and are able to help. They identify with your plight. They are great warriors. But these great warriors are not human. In order to fight as a man, they would require two strong human males to put their energy into."

"Would it harm those two humans?" he asked.

"Not their souls, energy or essences," I replied. "But no one can guarantee that their flesh will survive. For that is sometimes the price of mortal war."

The leader of the village of souls nodded to himself, considering.

"I will hold council with my warriors," he decided. "I know many would willingly accept."

"If you decide that you wish the help of these two beings," I said, as I stood up, "when you are ready, call me. I will hear."

"I thank you, lady of the land."

"And my heart gives thanks to you."

The old man sat silently watching as I walked from view.

It was dawn the following day when the old man called my name again. I knew the call was about to come, as I had never stopped remaining alert to his voice. I had listened as he held council with his sons and fellow leaders. I had listened as he spoke to his warriors. I had listened as all those warriors volunteered, and as he selected two from amongst them. And then I had listened as the entire village stayed awake all night; eating together, dancing dances of remembrance, laughing together, celebrating life. At dawn, I had been expecting his call.

The old man called to me from the same hill. When I went to him, this time, he was accompanied by two strong, agile warriors. I walked forward while Mardoch and Dragun remained unseen.

I bowed a bow of respect to all three. Only the old man spoke. The two warriors by his side remained silent, watching. Their names were Horsewind and Lightcatcher. Horsewind was a tall young man with rippling muscle and long dark hair. Lightcatcher had braided his hair, his lean sinewy form perfect for his speed and agility. I did not need to ask those two warriors if they were sure of their choices, I felt it.

"The battle comes to us today," the old man told me.

I knew that. I had seen the attackers gathering, taking position.

"Are you ready?" I asked the two warriors.

They nodded, confirming that they were.

I touched Horsewind and Lightcatcher on their foreheads, easing their minds and their flesh. Their eyes closed and their muscles relaxed in response, yet they remained standing. Their energy became static. Now static, it was pliable.

I called to Mardoch and Dragun. And then, unseen in form, but appearing like wisps of shadow, the two Nigh-kutu walked into the warriors' human flesh.

The merge went smoothly and no harm was done to either kutu or human. Each of them, Mardoch and Dragun, now inhabited the body of a human.

The two warriors opened their eyes.

"Dragun, Horsewind," I spoke to the tall, broad warrior.

"Yes," the warrior replied, with the resonance of both man and kutu.

"Mardoch, Lightcatcher," I looked at the other warrior.

That warrior nodded. "As one," he replied.

"Then my task here is done."

I bowed to the old man. "I will see you in the next life. Until then, my heart goes with you and your people."

I walked away, knowing that a grisly battle was to come for these people. I had witnessed many battles, fights and skirmishes on this planet. Each one had given me great sorrow. Many had made me angry. All of them were unnecessary. This one had captured my heart most of all.

I returned to work on my force-field barrier, but I could not properly concentrate. My heart was pulled to the gathering battle of men. Jychanumun felt my discord and left the outer skies to join me. He stood beside me, one wing wrapped around me as we watched from a distant hill.

"The greater fight approaches. I feel the kutu will soon start travelling," Jychanumun remarked.

"Do you think they will all head here?" I asked.

"Yes."

"How long do you think we have?" I asked.

"Not long."

I nodded. I still had much to do, yet so little that I could do.

"I do not want you to fight," I thought aloud, knowing my words were pointless, but wanting to say them anyway. "Arrunn will target you."

"I have to," Jychanumun looked to me, smiling a rare smile. "If the Nigh warriors get here first, which they likely will, Mardoch, Dragun and I will be all that there is to protect everything."

Jychanumun sensed my anguish. "Come," he tried enticing me away from the hill and the impending fight below. "It does your heart no good to watch."

"No," I said. "I will stay."

And stay I did.

Jychanumun remained with me. Together, we watched in silence as the attackers gathered and made formation. Their intent was no longer just to name the land as their own, but to conquer and end all lives in this village of souls.

Over the range of hills, the defenders prepared.

The energy of the world around the men grew quieter.

Quieter.

Quiet.

Still.

It was if the land held its breath.

Suddenly, a roar.

The air filled with battle cries and attacking yells. Shots. Shrieks. Bangs and smoke. The shrill air of flying shafts of wood and metal. I saw men falling. Men injured. Men writhing.

More roars. More yells. The pounding of the ground as footsteps ran. A clash as they collided. Clash again. More falling. Running, punching, spearing, slicing. It was mayhem.

I saw Horsewind and Lightcatcher, their energy blazing around them, both arms blurring with speed and precision and weapons in their hands. They ran and they fought, taking down attackers, cutting through lines ten men deep, leaving death and destruction in their paths. They cut though a line, turned and cut through again, each time picking up the wounded of the defenders, trying to both protect and attack.

The fight continued. The defenders did not, would not relent. They had been outnumbered, but they fought and they fought.

As men fell and men retreated, the numbers of attackers and defenders slowly equalised. Time moved and evening began to turn to darkness. Most of the remaining attackers retreated, running on legs and horses. The surviving defenders, streaked with the blood of their enemies, cut through the last of those who remained bent on taking their homes and lives.

Finally, victory.

Many hundreds of defenders had gone into battle. Most still stood. Exhausted yet victorious. The attackers either dead or retreated.

The green land was reddened with blood.

The energy of the land was scarred.

As all seemed to subdue into exhaustion and the warriors picked up their wounded, Horsewind and Lightcatcher came running up the hill. Sweat and blood dripped off them. They held a clasped sword and a dagger in each hand, bloodied from battle.

"We will stay with these people for a while," Lightcatcher spoke, yet it was also Mardoch speaking.

I nodded, looking at their flesh.

"You are both hurt," I said, walking up to them, one by one placing my hand over a wound to heal it.

Mardoch nodded. "I am trying to hold the human back. It is he who wishes to take great risks. He says he has much to protect."

"He does," I said, while healing a long wound across their torso. "You two are both brave and honourable. Still," I considered, "please take care."

Mardoch ruffled my hair. "You worry too much," he smiled.

In contrast, Dragun stood silently, staunchly unflinching, while I tended to Horsewind's wounds. Horsewind had sustained more damage than I thought a human body could take, but he did not recoil from the healing, and I quickly knitted together the ruptured flesh.

With their wounds sealed, Mardoch and Lightcatcher, with Dragun and Horsewind, started off back down the hill to join the rest of the victorious men.

"You should start preparing for the great war for life," I said, before they were beyond earshot.

Mardoch half-turned as he ran. "We are," he replied. "This is the best preparation of all."

I truly hoped that those villages of souls would now be left in peace.

Despite their attackers retreating and bearing heavy losses, that flesh battle for the villages of souls was not their last. More attackers regrouped. More attackers came.

For two more moons, Dragun and Mardoch fought alongside the humans, helping to protect their loved ones. They remained in their hosts, Horsewind and Lightcatcher, working in unity. But as time moved on, the ever-dwindling kutu pull had almost stopped entirely. As a result, Mardoch's and Dragun's energy strengthened. They could no longer inhabit the warriors without harming them. It was time for Mardoch and Dragun to leave.

On their last night as combined beings with the humans, Dragun and Mardoch feasted with them, learning and exulting in the tribal dances of brotherhood. They were both sad and satisfied to leave. They had grown fond of their hosts, referring to them as brothers, yet they knew that they had accomplished much. They had made a stand of principle. They had protected the lives of many.

My heart was happy to see so many of the souls survive, yet my heart grieved that the battles had happened at all. And Mardoch and Dragun had helped but one small tribe. The human fighting was worldwide.

"It will worsen," Jychanumun warned me. "When the kutu divide stops, the kutu will travel. All mankind will feel their intent for war." He looked at me. "It will stop soon."

He was right. Only two sunrises later, it happened.

The light, and the shadow, changed.

The kutu divide stopped.

All kutu would feel it.

FORTY-THREE

The Unready

Meanwhile, in the light...

On one side of infinity, where the light was brightest and all light thoughts intertwined, Chia, Shaa-kutu, sensitive, trailblazer and chi master, stopped what he was doing. He stood up, watching, listening, sensing.

"Do you feel that?" Chia asked Orion.

Orion paused, closing his eyes. "Yes," he nodded. "I feel it. I think that I see it too. It must mean that the divide between shadow and light has stopped."

"But that was so fast; too fast," Chia fretted, shaking his head. "I have not finished healing. We are not ready."

Chia bent down, quickly resuming his work. The Anumi warrior he was healing still had a hand to repair. He had only just finished mending the energy of his torso. There were still hundreds of injured Shaa-kutu left to attend to. All were lined up, either laying or sitting, waiting patiently to be healed, yet they had run out of time.

"I did think that time here would move faster than on any physical plane." Orion went to Chia's side, helping him hold the light, directing its force into the injured kutu's hand. "But I did not realise that time would move this fast."

"You know that we must leave," Chia glanced to Orion. "Even if we are not ready."

Orion nodded. "I know."

The wounded Anumi warrior in front of them sat up, grasping Chia's arm. "Do not leave without me," he requested. "I am a good fighter, a good protector."

"We won't," Chia assured him.

While Chia continued working, Orion moved away, his colours slowly vanishing within the brightness of the light. As Chia finished re-establishing the kutu's fingers, ensuring the flexibility and strength were intact, Orion returned. He had Una, the Shaa-kutu Supreme, by his side.

"Una is going to remain here, with the harrtriel. They will heal the remainder of the wounded. There is no point us taking any wounded into battle. They will not last. Most are healed. The healed are already gathering, ready to depart."

"What we have will have to suffice," Chia replied.

"Yes," Orion agreed. "To know we fight for life, and also life itself, our motivation will have to be strong enough."

Chia nodded to the Anumi warrior, putting a hand on his shoulder. "You are whole again, my friend," he assured him. "But be mindful of your torso when taking flesh again. It will be fragile for some time."

The golden haired warrior stood, flexing his freshly healed body.

"Thank you," he bowed. And then he ran on the waves of luminosity, testing the strength of his legs and his wings. He ran in the direction of the gathering army, ran to join his brothers.

Chia knew that in many ways they were not ready. But, ready or not, they were leaving this place of never ending light, this place where they felt at one, as one. Now they had to protect that oneness.

They were heading to war.

FORTY-FOUR

The Ready

Meanwhile, in the shadow...

On the far side of infinity, where the dark was darkest and instincts limitless, Shemya picked up his comrade and quickly stood to attention, bringing his shadow wings to a point and taking a step forward. Thousands of warriors stood behind him. He felt all of their wings raise, indicating their readiness.

"And again," Arrunn coolly commanded. "You have potent power in every atom of your being. Use it, not play with it. Any one of you should be able to stop a comet with a single punch. Now, show me."

Arrunn glanced down the lines of warriors. All were ready.

"Tactics forty-six and thirteen," he commanded.

The warriors immediately changed positions to match the tactical variant. Shemya knew that tactics forty-six and thirteen were two of their favourites. All equally divided into two teams, both on the attack, no holds barred. This is where they could really test their strength.

"Shemya," Arrunn called the warrior-first.

Shemya trotted up to their leader, coming to a halt directly before him.

"Oversee," Arrunn instructed. And with that, Arrunn turned and walked away.

Shemya called forth another warrior-first to take his empty position and stood where Arrunn had stood, observing the perfect formation.

"Attack." He issued the command Arrunn would have spoken.

Shemya watched the warriors fight with cold eyes. They were strong, all of them. Stronger than ever before. Thousands of warriors, the best warriors, had now learnt how to use the shadow as a weapon. None could beat them. Even just one of them could reduce an entire world to cinders.

Shemya felt the shadow around him, sensing Arrunn's presence. He knew exactly where Arrunn had gone. He had gone to a place of silence to feel the changes in the shadow. Shemya knew that, because he had felt the change too.

Shemya also knew what Arrunn's next command would be. In just moments he would return, and then he would command them all to leave this place. He would lead. They would follow. For the glory of the war of all wars, they would all happily follow.

And those orange-eyed gatherers? Well, they would not be far behind. They would have their own glories. Once their eyes had feasted on the beauty of the worlds made of light as free kutu, they would fight, he would fight, as Nar. It did not matter if they won or lost. Whatever the outcome, they would embrace it together: one clan, united at the end.

FORTY-FIVE

The Watch

The movement of shadow and light had come on suddenly, one night, when I had been sitting marvelling at the brightness of the stars and the clarity of the air. I had heard something, but it was like a noise with no sound that resonated through me, making my energy shudder with trepidation. And I felt it as well, as if I had flesh made of a thousand dormant insects that had suddenly sprung to life. I knew what that sensation was and I knew what that noise was. It was the awareness of the kutu travelling, flying, moving.

A great distance away, too far for my senses to analyse with any precision, I felt their movement. There were thousands of kutu. Thousands from the shadow. Thousands from the light.

The following day, the sensation increased. The noise and vibration and angst in my head were amplified. They were the signs of kutu drawing closer.

The following day the sensation increased yet again.

We did not have long.

As Dragun, Mardoch and Jychanumun roamed the upper skies, keeping a vigilant watch for kutu, I watched the world. And as I watched, the sound of the approaching kutu increased. I could not shut it out. It had amplified so much that it haunted my every moment: when I rested, when I worked, when I spoke, when I was quiet. Nothing would make it go away. It was like the wind, and a roar, and a cry, and a scream, all overlapping itself with deep, aggressive intent. I constantly felt like I was being both pushed and pulled at the same time. It heightened my senses, making me alert, wary, anxious, like an animal that knew it was being hunted. Yet it also made me seethe with hungry intention, like an animal that was hunting. It created an inner conflict.

Just as I felt an inner conflict from the changing energies, so too did my fellow humans.

Among my fellow humans, battles were occurring more frequently. With each new fight, the levels of aggression increased. The weapons grew more destructive. The reasons less relevant. Never had I seen man thrive so completely and for such destructive purposes. Never had I seen humanity develop so fast. All for war.

I witnessed those horrors. Horrors by their choice. Choice from their hollow intent.

Seeing how severely my fellow man was affected, I temporarily stopped my reinforcement of the barrier around the planet and focusing on a few selected areas on the ground. Those few villages of people that Mardoch and Dragun had fought alongside were still rich with souls. They were grouped together on land that was strong with earth energy. I focused on those small pockets of land, working to put barriers around them.

Across full continents, people's numbers had grown at an alarming rate. They hurt each other, the land and the creatures around them. And the soil itself was spoiling, not by warring kutu, but by their own hands. How had people deviated so far away from what they truly were? Why did they use animal and earth and the very things that kept the balance on this planet? Why did they not harness the greatest powers available that would not contaminate the land around them? Light, gravity, air could all be harnessed so simply, yet instead they corrupted the soil, contaminated the air, destroyed creatures, ruined the purity, stained everything they touched. They created suffering.

Just as the earth resonated with tension and apprehension; so did I. I despaired at what I saw. Along with the trepidation that I felt and heard, the despair almost broke me. I sat amidst the barrier I had created around the planet, sensing the movement and changes within humanity, and wept. I could not stop the tears. I didn't know why I was crying; anger, sorrow, pity. Perhaps none of them. Perhaps all of them.

"Look," I said to Jychanumun when he came to join me. I pointed to an area of terrain where the population had exploded beyond the capabilities of the land. "A nation full of people, yet only three souls. An old man who saves wild bears from torture. An old woman who heals with plants. And an old woman who has given her life to her children; children with no souls. Just three, amongst millions."

For a moment, Jychanumun remained silent as he observed the land and the people.

"Their souls decrease fast because the changing energy of the shadow and light affects them," he replied. "With time it may rebalance."

"But there may be no more time."

Jychanumun encouraged me to stand. "Then you must continue with your barrier. It grows strong, but you could make it stronger still."

"What's the point?" I shook my head. "What is the point of protecting my fellow humans when all they do is kill everything around them?"

It was not a question. I knew what the point was. The point was the chance for life. Just for the chance of life, I would relinquish my place with the Old One and fight to the end. Still, with potential death looming for so many of my kutu friends, beautiful souls, and creatures of every variety, I could not help but wonder if I had made the right choices. Could I not have done things better, something, anything to stop this degradation, to stop this war from occurring at all?

I think I was scared. Not for me, but for everything and everyone that I held dear. To me, they were the most valuable thing in all existences.

Jychanumun sat down beside me. He didn't say anything. He just sat, his hand holding mine.

"Whatever you choose," Jychanumun finally spoke. "I will stand by that choice."

"Thank you," I replied. "I will fight and you know that I will. I have not given up. I never will. I don't want to." I shook my head. "I can't."

"Good," Jychanumun agreed. "Neither can I."

Jychanumun stood. "The Nigh are almost here. Soon I must pass through the barrier to be ready."

I stood too.

The sense of the approaching kutu had begun resonating against the barrier above us. Essences of shadow and light shuddered everywhere like atoms suddenly jumping into view before disappearing again. The apprehension pushed and pulled, creating yet more energy. It surged through me, making my essence react like Meah's fur when she was alert or defensive. The tension was palpable. It vibrated like lightning that would not strike, like a wave that would not roll, like a sand storm of all worlds.

Whether we were ready or not, whether we wanted to fight or not, this war was coming to us.

They were almost here.

It was almost time.

FORTY-SIX

The Gathering

In the skies, on one side, I can see a distant, dense black cloud. The cloud undulates, revolving within itself with dark, furious intent. It is pure shadow, harnessed, controlled by the thousands of Nigh-kutu within it. As it moves, churning and thundering, it draws in the light, as if consuming it, swallowing it from existence. It wells and heaves as it rolls closer, growing larger, darkening the skies beyond like the blackest hole. I can hear it, a low, muffled hum; the sound of restrained aggression.

On the other side of the skies, in the distance, is a ball of brightest light, illuminating, moving fast, throwing spears of light like lightning. It is pure light, rebounding against itself, held together by thousands of Shaa-kutu. It radiates like a sun bursting with a heat and brilliance that can scorch and burn all in its path. Its spears shoot out from the intense radiance, as if the power is too great to be contained. It smells like fire and ozone and burning metal. I can hear that too; a high-pitched, hissing vibration. It is the sound of vivid assertion.

Louder.
Louder.
Louder.

Saturating my essence.

"Any who wishes to pass through, must do so now," I say.

My three Nigh-kutu friends silently pass through the barrier I've created around the planet.

Jychanumun glances back. One last look.

I seal the final area in the barrier and stand alone. I am ready to mend, repair and defend with my bare hands if necessary.

There is no more time.

It *is* time.

FORTY-SEVEN

The Fate

I stand. Tense. Apprehensive. Not ready. Ready.

The shadow approaches. The light approaches. The shadow and the light draw closer together and closer to this planet.

I watch through both Jychanumun's eyes and my own.

Jychanumun stands directly above me. He breathes deeply, absorbing energy into himself, harnessing and focusing his power. As he breathes, his shadow and light intensify, visibly surging through his body, becoming strong and then stronger still, until his form can barely hold his entirety. His surplus energy spits from his kutu flesh in short, jagged shards, as if desperate to be utilised, hissing as it hits my barrier. His wings grow, stretching out defensively, tensing, ready.

The shadow draws closer first. From within the darkness I can now distinguish the closest faces. The first one I see is Arrunn.

Arrunn is the clearest, most defined within the darkness, flying first, leading them all. His face is set in an expression of emotionless, calculated desire. His stare is fixed ahead. His wings are powerful with focused direction. Their black, snakelike revolving ends propel him with a speed and might beyond any I have seen before. As he flies, I see him pulling in the shadow from around him. His hair blows away from his face. His body is clad all in black. I cannot see any weapons. The all-black around him seems to draw in and extinguish any light that touches it. Somehow, he is holding the shadow and drawing on it for movement and strength.

Jychanumun, my thoughts reach out, *Arrunn is using the power of pure shadow energy. He is stronger than ever.*

Jychanumun does not reply. He has seen it too. His sight is fixed ahead, allowing me to translate what we both perceive.

I still cannot make out any faces within the light. Its source now seems to be coming from behind them, accelerating their approach as they draw closer. The shards of light spit jaggedly from the mass of illumination, creating a path for them to traverse, as if paving and directing their way. They strive to increase their speed, desperate to intercept the shadow before it reaches this planet. I feel their movement, as if it is a wind against my skin. I feel their intent to protect. I feel kutu whom I know and love.

The light has almost caught up to the shadow. Within the shadow, I now see more than just Arrunn. Behind him are thousands of black-winged kutu, lines upon lines of them, storming threateningly closer. Their wings are pure black. There is not a trace of colour among them. They're powerful, undulating, beating wings with furious intent to propel them forward. They are also drawing in the shadow as they fly. Their matte-black body suits ripple like muscles as they move, as if a second skin. I can't make out any weapons with any of them; they've come directly from the shadow, moving with the shadow, clad in the shadow. They seem more powerful than ever; larger, stronger, more agile, more focused, using the strength of pure shadow, drawing it in as they move. Growing stronger as they move.

I can't see any weapons. I link to Jychanumun again. *The Nigh-kutu; they have **all** harnessed the shadow energy.*

I feel Jychanumun's energy tighten.

This is worse than we had expected.

The Nigh-kutu, all of them, have harnessed a pure power. The shadow is an unstoppable force. They are now an unstoppable force.

What have we done? My mind reels. *By sending the Nigh-kutu to the shadow, we have given them ultimate power.*

The sky above darkens.

I hold my breath as tiny flecks of the approaching shadow touch Jychanumun. I feel his pain. I quickly push light energy into him, Mardoch and Dragun, to counter the effects, but the shadow grows closer and darker, overwhelming all else with the warriors' intent. As the shadow touches my barrier, I see tiny flecks like black dust settle like mould. The black dust starts to push out tiny vein-like lines that try to connect together and contaminate the barrier's energy. I push more energy into the barrier, repelling the specks of black, but still more descend. I push out more energy. More dust. More repelling.

Arrunn moves ahead of his warriors, swooping down in a dive towards us. He looks like a giant hunt-wing. I feel like a mouse.

From within the ranks behind Arrunn, I see one suddenly break away, moving faster towards Arrunn, swooping like an arrow. His broad black wings ripple, pulled taught as he gains momentum. His long black hair streams out behind him in tightly woven strands, like ropes beating the air. I can feel his intent; his intent to kill. He is formidable. He is almost as formidable as Arrunn.

The huge warrior pushes towards Arrunn. His mouth is pursed in determination. His brow is knitted into hatred. But his eyes are not focused on me, Jychanumun, Mardoch or Dragun. His eyes are fixed on Arrunn alone. I would not have recognised him if it were not for the eyes. It is Pall and Lyn, conjoined as one, full of power, fuming with hatred: fearless, fearful to all who behold them.

Pall and Lyn, as one singular being, propel themselves forward, using the momentum of the darkness behind them and the pull of the Earth in front of them. I do not think they will catch Arrunn up, but then I see a flash of grey energy, like a life crystal exploding. In one powerful leap, Pall and Lyn land on Arrunn with their feet on his shoulders and an arm around his neck. They lift a fist, shouting a loud guttural yell that sends shadow spitting in every direction, and then they drive it down hard on the back of Arrunn's neck.

Arrunn falters. It looks like his wings are about to buckle and fold. His step slows, but he does not stop flying. Pall and Lyn grasp the advantage, clasping Arrunn around his throat as they fly, pushing energy up through their fingers. Their silver grey energy weaves around Arrunn's throat like a tightening noose, moving up his neck and pushing into his mouth to choke him. Arrunn gags, grasping at the hand, trying to pull it away to release himself.

Pall and Lyn, as one being, look as if they are about to disable Arrunn. But then, in a swift move, still flying, Arrunn snatches their hair, quickly winding it around his wrist as he ducks, moving at an angle that allows him to twist in their grasp. He yanks hard. The energy withdraws from his throat. He wrenches Pall and Lyn around so that now he is flying with them held suspended in the air at arm's length. They twist and turn, kicking hard at Arrunn's side to get away, their face contorting as they shout noises of power, pounding against Arrunn's grip. Arrunn glances unflinchingly, pulling Pall and Lyn towards him, and then, fast as a predator, yet not slowing the momentum of his flight, he bites deep into their throat.

The instant seems to go in slow motion as I see Pall and Lyn's eyes bulge wide. Shadow blood streaks from their neck. Arrunn pulls them away, strands of energy caught between his teeth, Pall and Lyn bleeding from the gaping wound. And then, with one fast punch, Arrunn thrusts his unused fist, sending a ball of black energy into their torso. The energy drives straight through my two beautiful friends, pushing out the other side, leaving a large gaping hole and blood spewing out behind them.

Arrunn flies for a moment more, holding the two boys that I love so much by their hair. And then, with his sights fixed on Jychanumun, he throws them to one side, limp, lifeless; discarding them like an unloved rag doll.

Immediately, I push a surge of my energy forward, a line of multi-coloured light, sending it past Arrunn, towards Pall and Lyn. As Arrunn turns his head to glance at the flying energy, I wrap it around Pall and Lyn's broken form like a restorative bubble. But it is too late. Even as the bubble encompasses them, their energy is reducing, shrinking in on itself until it is nothing more than a black ball that would fit in my fist. In a breath, it is gone completely. Nothing is left of them.

My mind goes numb with the awfulness; the loss of my loved ones. Just gone, as if they were nothing more than an inconvenience.

Tachra, Jychanumun calls into my mind. *Do not crumple. Keep focused.*

I force myself out of myself. Neither Arrunn nor his army have reduced their haste. The burst of aggression from Pall and Lyn seems only to have increased their flight speed and fuelled their aggressive objectives.

I now re-direct my energy towards them, into the approaching shadow, to try to slow their advance, glancing towards the light.

The light, too, is almost upon us: a vivid shower of brilliance that sparks with jagged shards. Within the brightness, the light gradually peels away to reveal faces I know well. Peniva leads them. He is strong, rippling, his golden aura now visible, his body showing scars that have not fully healed. Full lines of golden auras fly behind him. All have faces. All are Anumi. Across the Anumi's bodies are straps made of light. I see weapons, but weapons also made of light: shields and spears and basic fastenings in the simple abstract shapes that pure power can be moulded to. Behind the golden light are hues of many colours, all with faces. They are kutu whose bright wings surge with purpose. I see my friends; Orion, Chia, Stanze, Kraniel, Gabriel and more. They see me. They do not smile.

Despite my efforts to repel them, Arrunn and his armies speed forward. Arrunn's sights are set on Jychanumun. Closer. So close I can make out the darkness in his eyes. Closer still and the shadow intent completely touches the barrier. As it does, I feel the change. The aggression and the intent create more contaminated patches within the barrier. There's no more time to mend it.

Closer.

Closer still.

I push my hands more firmly into the barrier above, ready to give my friends strength as I see and feel it, pushing my strength into the barrier too. I draw energy from below, letting it saturate my body. I brace.

Hold.

Hold.

Not now. Not now.

Now.

I suddenly push a wave of additional energy into Jychanumun.

Jychanumun's wings immediately expand to touch Mardoch and Dragun. Dragun and Mardoch, their heads bowed, their eyes directly ahead, expand their wings so all three Nigh-kutu are connected. Their energy heaves and undulates as their shadow is touched with hues of green, brown and white. They crouch. They build. They build. Stronger. Stronger. Potent power emanating from them, barely contained.

Suddenly, Jychanumun launches forward. Mardoch and Dragun go with him, conjoined by wings and energy. They move so fast that my vision can only see a blur of movement. Together, they propel directly towards the Nigh-kutu, rising up above them and then swooping down with force, hitting hard, hitting Arrunn with a power that should shatter worlds.

Arrunn deftly weaves away at the last moment, yet is still caught on the shoulder and one wing.

I see a fragment of Arrunn's wing shatter, exploding away, yet he merely tumbles and rolls as if he is no more than scratched. Jychanumun, Mardoch and Dragun continue, their wings forward, their edges like the sharpest razors, using the potency of both the shadow and light to impel them. Through the lines of Nigh-kutu they lunge, their razor sharp energy dismembering, slashing all the kutu that they move through. Shadow limbs fly in every direction. Shadow blood floods from the undulating blackness, streaking the air like ink in water.

As Nigh-kutu fall, the lines behind the wounded continue forward as if untouched by the loss of their comrades. In their trailing midst of shadow, the injured stand again, breathing in the shadow energy, becoming whole, driving forward to rejoin their ranks.

They're using the shadow not just as a weapon, but to heal. This is terrible.

Together, as one unit, Jychanumun, Mardoch and Dragun swiftly arc around, aiming for Arrunn alone. I push repelling energy up to Arrunn. It only slows his flight by the smallest amount, but it's just enough. The Shaa catch up. The Nigh catch up. Jychanumun Mardoch and Dragun swoop, dividing up as they fly. As Jychanumun aims for Arrunn, Mardoch and Dragun dive into the midst of the warriors.

A flash of pure shadow. Another flash of light.
The two forces clash.
An explosion pounds against the barrier, sending a wave around

the hemisphere, vibrating my essence with pain, making the barrier judder with such power assailing it.

Potent aggression against protective might, equal and deadly in conflict. Shouts of intent. Weaponless weapons being drawn or harnessed. Explosions and poundings and howling and yells and screams and guttural groans rage above and around. Shards of light and spears of shadow. Flurries of fingers that are blades and daggers and bolts thrown like arrows and spears. All universes feel like they're splitting.

I can just make out Arrunn and Jychanumun tumbling, caught in battle. Jychanumun winds his wings around Arrunn, squeezing, pushing his hand against Arrunn's face, pressing his fingers into his eyes. Arrunn has an arm free, driving black energy from his fingers and around Jychanumun's hand to loosen it. I feel the singe of pain as the shadow energy tightens around Jychanumun's wrist, cutting through both energy and matter. Jychanumun pulls his hands away before it's severed completely and breathes deeply, letting the roar of pain flow from his mouth, saturating Arrunn's essence to disable him. It should have crippled Arrunn, but Arrunn only smiles and then lets out a loud howl, loosening Jychanumun's wings. Jychanumun quickly fights against it, winding both arms around Arrunn's head, pushing his fingers deep into his face, sending shards of energy into him to cleave his head in two.

A fragment of light suddenly splits the shadow, aiming for Jychanumun. Shaa-kutu; dozens of them.

At first I think the Shaa-kutu are going to aid Jychanumun, but then shards of light flash forward, hitting Jychanumun in the back, sending him spiralling and Arrunn readying to attack again. Arrunn seizes the opportunity, swooping towards Jychanumun, pushing shadow against him.

Mardoch and Dragun fly towards Arrunn, launching directly

at him like shadow lasers. Their momentum directly hits Arrunn, sending all three tumbling with crumpled wings. A Nigh-kutu veers to one side, taking the opportunity to grab Dragun, and the two of them, arms pounding and fists beating, get lost to my vision in a whirl of shadow.

Arrunn quickly regathers, flying back into the midst of battle as the small group of Shaa-kutu launch towards Jychanumun, throwing spears of razor sharp light. I see a blaze of yellow in their midst, huge light-wings trailing yellow light stained by shadow; Shursa. Shursa has other Shaa with him attacking Jychanumun, turning to attack other Shaa.

The lines of light and shadow warriors keep pounding against the barrier, against each other. The heat is immense, as if from a thousand suns. I see kutu blood; so much blood. I see limbs tangled in powerful combat pressed against the barrier.

Beyond the pounding hordes, at the edges of the darkness, I see more glints of colour approaching within a smaller ball of shadow. The colours define. I see mainly hues of orange with a few flecks of others.

Orange energy. The Gatherers. The Nar beasts. The Nars are kutu. The kutu are Nar.

As that smaller ball of shadow surges forward, touching the mass of darkness, I see those hues of orange break forward and rise up, up from the masses within the shadow. As they move, the glimmer of orange tints the edges of their wings. Their form starts to morph. Like an anger of the ages seething with breath, I see their shapes change. Their bodies broaden, their necks elongate. Two legs become four. Their faces transform from kutu to wild, snarling creatures.

Around a dozen Nar beasts, their eyes glowing orange, their mouths open revealing glistening sharp teeth, have separated from the masses. They part-sprint, part-fly forward, their clawed feet finding substance within the shadow. One charges at Arrunn in the midst of conflict. Others turn on the outer rings of Nigh-kutu. I see Nigh-kutu fall. I see Nigh-kutu gather, attacking within as thrusting claws strike forward, ripping, slashing; as jaws clamp and teeth gouge, shredding and rupturing.

Floods of shadow bombard the Nar. The Nar seem to breathe it in, taking the strength, not the hit. Shursa and his team turn from Jychanumun, throwing shards of light at the creatures. The light sends them tumbling. It thrusts them back. It makes them fall, whelping in pain. Yet, despite their injuries and the orange blood flowing freely from their wounds, they still stand, muster energy, and surge towards the bulk of Arrunn's warriors once again.

My barrier is weakening. Quickly, too quickly. Nigh-kutu stand over it, above me, around me. Any moment that they are not under attack, each joins a rhythm of pounding the barrier with their fist. Each pounding makes the barrier vibrate like the shock of lightning, and I feel the pain of it. With each pounding and each contact, residual shadow energy remains, staining my barrier, eating away at it like a disease of the flesh.

It will have to hold. Too many need my help.

I see a surge of gold within the shadow as Shaa-kutu Anumi push forward. Within the shadow all around the barrier I feel Nigh-kutu pulled away, I feel the clashing of combat, the fierceness of intent. An Anumi swoops down, throwing aside a Nigh-kutu about to sound his weakening rhythm on the barrier. The golden-haired Stanze lands on the Nigh-kutu's back, between his wings, stabbing a long golden spear through his body and another through the back of his neck. Stanze then pulls out his spears, leans down, picks up the black-winged warrior before he can heal, and throws him beyond the shadow. As four Nigh-kutu turn to disable Stanze, Stanze leans down and, putting his hand on the barrier where my hand touches, holds my gaze just for a moment.

I push energy into Stanze, feeling his thoughts and sensing his intention, strength and conviction.

My friend, I think, *do not fall...* I thrust a surge of energy into Stanze as the black-winged ones descend upon him.

Stanze channels the extra energy through both his golden spears, stabbing and slicing with the purpose to protect. I see more Anumi directly above, fiercely battling the Nigh-kutu who try to destroy the barrier. I send those Anumi more energy, my focus pulled to flashes of bright red. The flashes are like sheets of red lightning, repelling and repelling again. I know this must be Orion.

Surrounded by hundreds of Nigh-kutu, all trying to get to him, Orion stands like one of Viir's statues. His red robe flows around him as if a great wind encircles him. A great wind does encircle him. Racing around him in a blur of violet, too fast for my eyes to perceive, is Chia. As Chia runs, slashing with knifes at any who draw close, Orion stands, head bowed, drawing in his energy, drawing more, and then stamping his foot. As he stamps his foot, a potent wave of red energy rolls outwards, touching all in a broad sphere except Chia; and all touched by it are filled with the dreams and phantoms of confusion. As the Nigh tumble forward, unsure as to what they are seeing, Chia slashes and then slashes again. But Chia is outnumbered. With each penetrating blast from Orion and with every Nigh cut down, double the amount of black-winged ones push forward, the shadow healing the wounded as they fall.

I see a single Shaa-kutu swoop down toward Chia. I feel his malicious intent. Shursa.

Shursa has an expression of hatred in his eyes. He lunges towards Chia, twisting away from Chia's blades, slicing at Chia's torso with his own knives. Shursa is not touched by Orion's waves of confusion. As Chia desperately regathers, holding a gaping wound in his chest, Shursa launches forward again, and the Nigh-kutu draw in.

Chia and Shursa thrash aggressively in a blur of violet and

yellow, and then Shursa throws Chia to the ground, slashing and gouging with his bare hands. His arms beat down, again and again, scratching and cutting and pulling at Chia's flesh and energy. While black-winged ones descend, assailing Orion, Orion stands, moving his hands as if weaving air. Suddenly, Orion stamps his foot again, sending out another flash of red light. The Nigh-kutu are flung back, but Shursa holds tight to Chia, punching his face, fuelled by the power of vicious hatred. Orion takes a step forward and pivots as if in a dance, redirecting his red energy so it points from his hand like his kathani blade.

In one fast move, Orion severs Shursa's head.

Shursa's body slumps, lifeless.

I want to cheer, but cannot, for just as Orion drags a badly wounded Chia behind him, dozens of black-winged warriors descend on them again. I push energy towards them, but can no longer see them. All I can see are the surges back and forth as Orion tries to hold firm and protect his friend.

I see Nigh-kutu against Nigh-kutu, Nigh-kutu against Shaa-kutu, Shaa against Shaa, creatures with claws and teeth charging. Bar the faces I know well, I can no longer tell who is attacking, who is defending; nor, even if they do attack, what side they are on. Some don't even know whose side they are on, apart from their own.

There are only the sounds and sights of bodies being ripped and sliced and imploded and exploded and melted and vaporised and burnt and compressed. And all that time, the shadow grows, slowly encompassing the light.

It is mayhem, chaos, fuelled by the will to bring death.

The Earth turns.

The battle does not abate.

It is barbaric. Never could I have imagined such strength wielded without any restraint. This truly is a fight for life itself.

Through exhaustion and pain the will drives on. I see my

friends charge and then charge again, almost spent, damaged, bleeding. Jychanumun is wounded with wounds upon wounds, but will never give up. Nar beasts gather, bleeding, ignoring their damage, turning to charge in unison again. They will never give up. Arrunn will never give up.

This war is to the end.

I see Kraniel pick up a fallen comrade, dragging him beyond the contamination of the shadow. His hair sticks to his face, slick with kutu blood. His shoulder is lacerated with so many cuts. His leg is broken so he cannot stand, relying instead on only the strength and perseverance of his wings.

Kraniel spots something: an Anumi in trouble, surrounded by black-winged ones. Golden light flows from within the midst of the Nigh-kutu as they rip the Anumi apart. Kraniel picks up a discarded sword made of light, a sword dropped by the fallen, and moves the sword in his hand, accustoming himself to its weight, and then flies up, swooping into the black-winged ones, slashing their wings and their arms.

The shortest moment of opportunity allows Kraniel to drag the Anumi free, but the Nigh-kutu rally, throwing themselves at Kraniel with vengeance. I push energy Kraniel's way, but as the energy moves, a huge Nigh-kutu, Deimom, swoops past, deflecting it with a shield made of shadow. I quickly send more energy to Kraniel. I send as much as I can. I too am growing spent.

Still the fight does not abate, despite the wounds, the blood, and the fallen. Attacking, defending, maimed and bleeding; those who can go on do not stop.

The Earth turns again.

I see that the beauty of the light is diminishing. I see Anumi, whose intentions I know, disabled and maimed, their bodies floating aimlessly beyond the shadow and light.

All the time, despite how many black-winged ones are pulled

from the barrier, more come, intent on penetrating the protective shield. Their fists beat a rhythm. The rhythm thumps through me. They raise their arms, gather shadow energy, direct their might, and with a guttural yell they thump.

Thump. Thump. Thump.

Each fist creates blackness within the purity of the shield.

There is so much potent power. Thousands upon thousands of kutu. All fighting for life and life itself. The intent is palpable. The ferociousness screams through all worlds. The screams of attacks and defence.

I push my energy into Jychanumun, willing him to get up, willing him not to give up.

The battle grows stronger, fiercer, with its drive to death and annihilation. Flashes, rips, the tearing of limbs. Bodies being thrown upon the barrier, attacked by dozens with bare hands, intense energy and malice.

I try to repair the darkening stains that eat away at the barrier's strength, but the faster I work, the faster it degrades. The barrier was strong. But now it is not holding. The fighting is too fierce. I see patches of the barrier almost degraded to nothing. Its strength has become thinness, blackened by so much dark will. It is becoming beyond repair. It shudders and shudders repeatedly. Its energy, like pale water, is stained by the intent of the attacks assailing it.

Now, here, sliding through, his wings unfurling, a Nigh-kutu is getting through the barrier.

I push energy out to counter the Nigh-kutu, trying to stop him. But then another comes, pushing through the hole. Another hole starts opening. There are now three areas that have been penetrated, contaminated by too much shadow. The shadow streams down, opening the way for more black-winged ones. I push energy into those gaps trying to seal them, but the contamination spreads faster than I can repel it.

I push more energy into the barrier, more into my kutu friends, and I look down as a black-winged one descends towards my planet. I connect to that Nigh-kutu, sensing his desire. He intends to kill everything. That was Arrunn's instruction. Kill everything: kutu, human, mammal, bird, reptile, fish, insect. Everything. The more they kill, the greater the victory. He isn't bothering with me, although destroying me is tempting. I have been singled out for Arrunn.

I see another Nigh squeeze through my degrading barrier. Soon all Nigh-kutu will be able to break through.

Suddenly, a flash of rose streaks my vision, lashing towards the descending Nigh-kutu. The line of energy winds around his torso, confining his wings, and then retracts, leaving a glowing band around him as he falls, tumbling, unable to navigate his fall. A streak of green then moves towards the falling Nigh-kutu, grasping him, changing direction and moving towards me. Catching up to that streak of green are two others in shades of gold, blue and sandy-brown.

From beyond the horizon on Earth, three beings move at an incredible speed. They approach using the power of shadow and light to propel them. They do not even need to use their wings. They are running on energy as if time means little to them.

I know them: Viir and Brune, with Iris in their midst.

Iris veers to one side, rolling as she gets close to the second descending Nigh-kutu. As she does so, she puts her hand on her hip, pulling away the belt of retribution. She lashes her arm, the belt turning into a whip, the end of the whip winding pink energy around the second Nigh-kutu. As she releases it, leaving the Nigh-kutu tethered, Brune runs to collect him, and all three draw closer.

Viir and Brune are clad in Nigh-kutu war-wear. Weapons of every size and type, both Shaa and Nigh, are strapped to their bodies. Vapour daggers, long swords, sonar rods, throwing discs, dart shards and shadow givers. Iris runs in the midst of the boys, her long hair blowing behind her, her short sword ready in her hand, her body clad in similar war-wear, the belt of retribution around her hips, her eyes fierce with concentration, a smile touching her lips as she has her sights upon me.

There is no time for words. As Viir and Brune wield their weapons upon the descending Nigh-kutu, Iris flies towards me, wingless, with speed. She comes to a sudden halt below me, pulls her belt from her hip and flicks it to one side where another black-winged one has climbed through the barrier and is about to attack. Another climbs through behind him. Iris works fast, tethering the captured kutu, casting him to Brune and Viir, ready to stop another.

I protect, too, Iris tells me, breathless.

I have no energy to direct my concerns about Pall and Lyn, but Iris senses my thoughts amidst the worries about so many.

They'll heal. . . she throws the thought into my mind as she captures another descending Nigh-kutu. *Are healing. I had their energies bound.*

I want to be joyful at this piece of knowledge, but a cloud of black within blackness suddenly pounds so hard against the barrier directly above my head that I lose my balance. Iris tumbles back. My hands release from the barrier as the surge of energy sends a shockwave throughout everything.

The shadow courses through the barrier, blackening its entirety as far as my eyes can see. I feel it. My energy feels it. I scream with the pain. The pain of my energy resonates with the destructive shadow and also the pain of something else, someone else.

Jychanumun.

Jychanumun is face down, directly above me. His face is pressed against the barrier. I quickly move my hands to give him energy.

A wound across his face bleeds shadow light. His torso is ripped; one arm is barely connected to his body. His wings are frayed, one limply crushed beneath a hundred feet. Dozens of Nigh-kutu and even some Shaa-kutu hold him down, pressing him against the barrier in an awkward, broken pose.

From nowhere I see a Nar beast charge. At first I am not sure who it is aiming for until it turns, ramming into the heaving mass of Nigh-kutu holding Jychanumun. Another Nar joins the charge, fighting the Nigh-kutu off Jychanumun. Suddenly, the Nars tumble in a flurry of blood and ripped flesh, with black-winged ones spinning in all directions, limbs ripped from their torsos, wings ripped from their backs, scales and razor-sharp teeth tumbling with them.

The hordes part. The battle melts away from Arrunn as he walks towards Jychanumun.

I see a lone Nar charge in Arrunn's direction. Without glancing at it, Arrunn's hand shoots out, just as the Nar is about to bite. He grabs its neck, digging his fingers deep into its orange energy, twisting and pulling, ripping tendons and energy strands away from its throat. The Nar drops, shuddering with spasms.

Arrunn stands on Jychanumun's back, coldly holding my gaze. Around him, several Nigh-kutu watch, guarding. Beyond that, the battle rages fiercely.

Staring at me, Arrunn thumps the air with his fist in the same repeating rhythm as those trying to penetrate the barrier. With each thump, a surge of energy bolts from Arrunn's fist and into Jychanumun's back, bleeding into him, contaminating his flesh and energy.

I feel Jychanumun's pain, although he tries not to let me. I see the effect of the contaminating energy. As it seeps through his back, it creates veins of black that thread through his entire body. I give him energy. I give him more energy, yet that shadow in his body will not abate. The shadow is contaminating him, killing his essence, making his own energy bleed, the conjoined specks of luminous black and white leaving his form, soaking into the barrier.

Jychanumun manages to move one arm, putting his palm against the barrier. I move my hand to be below his, trying to hear his thoughts.

I want to hear that Jychanumun has a greater plan. I want Jychanumun to tell me that he is merely getting something into position in order to act. But he does not. He just holds his hand in place above mine, his sights fixed upon me. I hold his gaze. I see only his eyes, as if connecting to the deepest part of his soul. For that moment, in that instant, it reminds me of the moment before Meah died. I do not think my heart can fracture again, but it is fracturing now, and even greater than before.

Jychanumun is incapacitated.

The barrier is breaking.

My friends are outnumbered.

Most of my friends are injured. Many are dead.

We are losing this war.

Again.

Close Elysium, Jychanumun tells me with his mind. He can still think, but his thoughts are muddied as if he can barely make them form.

Close Elysium – Those two simple words mean so much more than they seem.

Jychanumun knows we are losing.

I have no time to fret over those two simple words. This is as Jychanumun and I had discussed, and I know what I must do. We had contingencies in our many plans. Contingencies that, if we thought we would lose this war, we could at least protect others.

My task is now straightforward. I do not need to move anywhere. All I have to do is close the door to Elysium in my mind.

I hold one hand against the energy barrier beneath Jychanumun, feeding him my own dwindling strength, and let my mind open a door to Elysium.

* * *

Elysium. The home for the old souls. A moment of perfection caught in time. Timeless.

I reach forward to close the entrance to Elysium forever. But then one comes forward; an old soul.

"Iastha Tachra," he calls, with his essence blue and green.

I know that soul. It is my much loved flesh father, a firstborn on earth.

"I wish to take flight," he says. "I want to fight."

Then, from the distance, more walk forward, taking form. There are thousands of them: old souls; all the old souls. They are singing a warrior's song, showing me their essences. The entirety of their presence is united yet singular.

Realisation dawns on me.

Horror, love and respect consume me.

"Do you all wish to leave?" I ask.

"We wish to leave so we may fight," chorused their reply.

"But the war for life rages and we are not winning."

"Do not grieve. It is not about winning or losing, but making a stand for life. It is our choice."

Yes, it is their choice: Harsh, cruel, beautiful, pure choice. I cannot deny it, I recognise with honour.

I step aside as they leave, walking past the boundary of Elysium. In that moment, I see the world as if distanced from it. I see myself standing, one hand on the barrier, and the battle raging. And there, moving into formation, are the old souls. I hear commands of movement from them. I recognise voices: my father, Jin, Jan,

Ren and many more. They stand in position, stretching around the Earth, below my barrier, also reaching up to give it strength.

The moment of timelessness pulls me back to the same moment of war.

* * *

My thoughts are pounding and my essence is screaming as soon as my mind steps from Elysium. My hand is fused to the barrier. The barrier is now so weak that it draws directly from my essence. Jychanumun still holds my gaze, his hand directly above mine. Only a fraction of a moment has passed. Arrunn still thumps bursts of energy into Jychanumun, contaminating his essence, killing him, his gaze fixed firmly upon me.

I sense movement below me.

The Nigh-kutu who have climbed below the contaminated barrier are fighting. Iris whips and contains all immediately around us, moving at a speed beyond that of a kutu. I now see a group of old souls, like those that Mardoch and Dragun had fought with, taking their stance, charging bravely towards a Nigh-kutu as he swoops down to the planet's surface. I see Ren commanding soldiers, with faces I know and love, who are moving through the barrier to take a stand with the kutu. They are pulled into battle immediately, moving and defending the kutu way, as a group of black-winged ones launch towards them.

I feel Iris falter in her step. She is charging towards the planet surface. Below her, a Nigh descends. Iris shapes her body like a bullet, flashing past the Nigh-kutu, catching him with her belt of retribution. But the Nigh throws a spear of shadow which pierces her side. She reels in pain. Viir and Brune charge forward, picking Iris up; and, as Brune pulls her to safety, Viir goes in to attack.

I want to send Viir energy, but I have none left. Any morsel that I'm producing is keeping Jychanumun alive. But even that is waning. Soon I will be spent.

Soon Jychanumun will die.

Around me are the ones I know and love: Iris, the boys, the old souls, my beautiful kutu friends; and the being I love most with mind and heart. But they will die. He will die. Jychanumun *is* dying.

I might not have the ability to win this war. But Jychanumun does.

I can give Jychanumun my strength. I can give him my entirety. I can give him my soul. I *will* give him my soul.

I start pushing my essence through my body, up through my arm and then hand, and into Jychanumun.

Jychanumun realises what I am doing. He shakes his head, too weak to speak with his mind anymore. But I have made my decision. I am giving Jychanumun my life. All of it.

Despite his fading strength, Jychanumun pulls his hand away, breaking our energy link, yet holding my gaze.

No, he manages to say. *Live.*

But I don't want to live without you, I try to say. But Jychanumun cannot hear. He has closed his eyes as the remnants of his life seep away.

With the darkness overpowering all, and Arrunn holding my gaze as he kills my beloved kutu, I still have something: a last choice.

"Arrunn," I call.

I see Jychanumun muster the last of his life to try to turn and face me. He is trying to shake his head. His hand clasps and unclasps frantically, yet he is tethered by what look like thick black webs that blend through his body, and he cannot move.

"Arrunn," I call again, making my voice connect to my words.

The sounds around seem to melt, fading into the distance so that my voice is heard.

Arrunn pauses.

"I call you, Arrunn," I hold out my hand towards him. "You said that one day I would call you by choice. And I do. Today, now, I call you to me willingly."

Arrunn straightens and, without breaking my stare, walks around his warring kutu and kneels on the barrier above my head.

He puts his hand on the barrier. I put my hand up, pushing my fingers through the protective shield. I wrap my hand around his hand.

I allow you to pass. And with that thought, I pull Arrunn through.

I feel Iris charge forward. She flicks her belt, trying to enclose me and pull me away to safety. But the energy of her belt passes through me.

I must do this, I tell Iris. *It is the only chance left.*

Iris pauses for a moment, watching, analysing. But then another descending Nigh-kutu, and then another, draw her away.

"You call me by your choice." Arrunn says. He stands powerful, contained. "Do you stand down, or join with me?"

"Join with you," I reply.

I hold out my hand. There in my palm is the matte-grey crystal. "Your emotions. You need to take them back."

"No," Arrunn looks at me coldly.

"Without them, you will not be whole," I say. "If you are not whole, then together we will not be whole. If we are not whole, you will not have access to the Old One."

I hide my intent in the deepest part of my mind and energy, concealing it with thoughts of nothingness. Of course Arrunn needs to be whole in order to join the Old One. But once Arrunn has consumed that grey crystal he might be weakened, just as he was before his emotions had been removed. If he is weakened, and I move swiftly, I might be able to confine him. It is my final, desperate option.

Arrunn looks down at the grey crystal, his expression filled with distaste.

"I understand," he nods.

Arrunn takes a step forward, taking the crystal from my palm. He closes his eyes and sighs.

Suddenly, Arrunn lunges towards me, quicker than I have time to react, wrapping me with shadow. He has a hand at the back of my head, holding my energy, lifting me from the ground, his energy weaving out from him, holding me firm.

He holds the crystal against my forehead and pushes hard.

I feel it pass through the edge of my energy.

Deeper. Deeper still. The crystal reaches into the area where flesh and bone and brain would once have existed.

"We will join," Arrunn says, "but you will carry the crippling pain of suffering, not me."

Arrunn's palm presses hard against my forehead as he pushes the crystal deeper.

I feel the crystal bleed its knowledge into me. It saturates my head, my body, and then the entirety of me.

The crystal is inside my head, yet I feel it everywhere, as if every part of my essence has the knowledge of Arrunn's pain and suffering and grief from all the kutu's past. It bleeds into my essence like rot. The pain is excruciating, as every terrible, crippling emotion consumes me.

I see and feel the moment when the universal consciousness fragmented to become the kutu, as if I am there and it is happening to me. I feel that moment when wholeness changed to imperfection: acute, painful, agonising imperfection. I feel the disharmony. I feel the chaos. I feel the struggle to understand. I feel the inability to understand, the inner conflict, the hatred for all that I am and all that is beyond me: the dissatisfaction, the distaste for all others, the fear of the inevitable pains yet to come, the frustration to never be that which I once was. I feel it all, and it hurts beyond any hurt of the mind or energy.

It hurts my very soul.

I collapse to my knees. The pain and suffering are too much to bear.

I can hear shouts in the distance. Someone is calling to me. They are dislocated from me. They are only words, words from another incomplete, imperfect, suffering being. I cannot bear the pain. I cannot bear *their* pain. I feel their pain too, all of it: their angst, their fury, their fear. It is too much.

I must find a place within myself that is not saturated with this agonising existence. I push deeper into my energy, but the deeper I push, the more the horrors consume me.

I fall deeper into myself, trying to find a place of peace to retreat to. Deeper and deeper. Towards the Old One. But no matter how deeply I retreat, the suffering comes with me. It is mine. It is mine to bear.

As I fall deeper into the Old One, the Old One's energy reacts. He too feels those things as if they are his own. The Old One feels the pain as if it is his pain. He feels the suffering as if he himself is suffering. The fear is overriding, blending with the dissatisfaction and anger and sorrow. And he feels the split of the universal consciousness as if it is him splitting.

The Old One pulls inward too, looking for peace. But there is no peace, only greater suffering. Every morsel of negativity from Arrunn's knowledge of the moment the last universal consciousness collides, and then the split, consumes him. He feels the duality of the knowledge that caused that pain and suffering, yet it is he who is in pain, as if it is him splitting, as if the suffering is his. He is in anguish. His pain is immense. I feel his everything drawing in.

The Old One is enveloping himself. He is imploding.

The Old One folds in on himself, seeking his peace, his everything dreaming.

I fight against the agony that consumes me, aware of Arrunn's fingers around my throat, aware that he is waiting for me to give up.

Something in the deepest recesses of my mind finds a familiarity with the suffering.

I know that sorrow comes from love. I have felt love.

Suffering comes from joy. I have felt joy.

Pain comes from bliss. I know bliss.

Anguish from happiness. Tachra knows happiness.

I know all those things. I feel all those things. They are perfectly balanced. The focus is on the beauty, not the horror. It is the beauty of life. I embrace that within me – all of it. All the bad and the good, all the positive and the negative. It surges through me; not just feeling for the humans and kutu I have come to know and love, but all of them. I focus on Meah and Jychanumun and Iris and Soul and my flesh parents and my flesh siblings; on the four boys, Orion, Chia, Mardoch, Dragun, Kraniel, Stanze, Peniva, Jin, Jan, Ren, Coran, Pallyn, Una, and so many more kutu. I have been blessed to love so many. I focus on everything I love.

I hold onto that clarity, knowing that the pain and anguish are not for the Old One. He is perfect.

All this pain, my foggy thoughts call out to the Old One, *it is not yours. Let it go.*

The energy and knowledge pours out of me, saturating the Old One's consciousness.

Father of fathers, I call.

Father of fathers, hear me, I call again.

Still I cannot make him hear through his pain.

And then I speak the word that I had promised him I would never speak again. I call his name, his true name.

The sound of the Old One's name resonates though all things and all times.

The Old One hears.

The Old One has no choice but to hear, for I call his true name.

For a moment, the Old One is angry that I have spoken his true name. The anger tumbles around his everything along with the pain and anguish and suffering and fear.

Stop, I tell him.

STOP, I demand. *It is your name and you are my father of fathers; it is my right to speak it at such times.*

A moment. A pause. The Old One does not want to listen, but I am going to speak anyway, and if I feel him not listening I am prepared to call his true name again and again until he hears me.

You cannot invert because of the things I feel, I say. *This is not your choice; this is mine. These are not your feelings; they are mine. If you wish, choose to feel through me, but know those things are mine and feel the love as well as the hate and hope as well as despair. For that is my balance of greatness – not yours.*

He listens, held poised.

Just because you are more powerful than me, it does not give you the right to choose for me, I continue. I know this. It was a difficult lesson I had learnt. *I am whole. I have choice. And this is my choice, not yours.*

He hears, his all-encompassing consciousness held static by my words.

My imperfections are perfect to me, perfectly balanced. You want to understand imperfection and choice. Now you do. Together, we are as one, but our choices are our own. I will not allow you to take my choices away. And you know you cannot.

And that is what I had seen as the Old One and I had fallen deeper. My imperfection completed his perfection. Together, we were complete. Perfect and imperfect. Separate yet joined.

The Old One knows the truth of my words and choices. He accepts. I feel him rebalance, knowing that the pain he sees is mine and mine alone. A new calm fills me. The calmness is my own.

I feel the Old One push me away, gently letting me go, as if I am a leaf in his palm being blown by a breeze.

Jychanumun is above me. His gaze has never left mine. To one side, Chia's face pushes against the barrier, trying to shout at me. Orion stands over him, thrusting waves of red light into those assailing them. Iris moves in a blur of speed, cracking her whip, winding its coil around the swarms trying to descend towards the planet, the two boys aiding her, the souls joining the fight to protect the planet they love so much.

In front of me: Arrunn.

I look into Arrunn's empty, cold eyes. In many ways, Arrunn and I have become one, but not how he thought it would happen. I now have everything he never valued, and that which is most precious of all: his connection to all kutu. That which is his weakness is now my strength.

Old One, Father, I call. I brush against his dreaming. *Father, hold my hand, be my hand.*

I calmly peel Arrunn's fingers from around my throat. Arrunn cannot stop me.

Arrunn goes to grasp me again, his energy reaching out to consume me like a hungry beast.

"No," I hold up my hand.

I keep my hand poised, stopping Arrunn from drawing any closer. I bind him with my energy and the strength of the Old One.

"To be alive is to value life," I tell Arrunn. "And you are already dead."

I touch Arrunn on the forehead, and then, stepping close, I cup my hands around his ear. Quietly, I whisper a word into his mind. Just one word. The word that none can hear and none can speak; but the Old One speaks it through my mind. He is my father and I am his voice, just as he can be mine. The Old One whispers his name.

As that sacred word fills Arrunn, Arrunn stiffens, his every essence expelling and receiving, barely able to hold itself together.

I take Jeshuahn's black kutu knife from the folds in my gown. It has taken thousands of lives, all by Arrunn's doing. I bind that knife with the rose energy of retribution, feeling the lost essence of the thousands it would avenge and rebalance.

This is Jeshuahn's knife. This knife created Arrunn. Jeshuahn had loved Arrunn.

I lift the dagger and thrust it into Arrunn's inner core.

"I told you that I would kill you with love," I say.

As I remove the dagger, the energy of retribution floods through Arrunn's essence.

Arrunn's energy explodes from his body. Its multi-coloured shadow surges in every direction, splitting and then splitting again, shattering into a million pieces of nothingness, hovering in the air.

I think of Wirrel, the flame-dweller, calling his fire to me from realms unseen.

Immediately, the fire form of Wirrel stands before me. Within his flames is Soul, my eternal friend. They are as one, working together. They look glorious, with the fire curving around them and through them, symbolic of their passion and love.

"Fuel for your fire," I smile, "my friends."

I need not say any more. They both sense my intent. Wirrel and Soul's fire expand outwards, devouring every speck of what once was Arrunn, now non-life.

I stand amidst it, bathing in it like rain made of flames.

Arrunn is gone forever. He is nothing, nowhere. He is dead. He has been for a long time.

I reach up, touching Jychanumun's hand. My beloved is near

dead. The war still rages. Arrunn is gone, yet the battle continues. My work, our work, is not yet done.

With his last efforts in life, Jychanumun's hand pushes down. I thread my fingers through the barrier towards him. He clasps onto my hand. His black and white energy bleeds from his injuries, dripping down his hand and then my arm, falling like raindrops of beauty.

Dozens of black-winged ones are still on Jychanumun's back, their punishment and intent to kill relentless in their fury. And all because Arrunn had made them believe this version of ascendancy. They have been blinded to who they truly are: beings of beauty. They do not need to kill to show their power. There are many other glorious ways.

Do not let go, Jychanumun beseeches me. *Do not go.*

Jychanumun's dying thoughts to save me. How I love him.

I will never let go, I reply. *It is **you** who must let go.*

For a moment I am concerned that Jychanumun believes I have been overpowered by Arrunn's will. He saw what Arrunn did.

See the truth of me, I say.

And as I speak the words, I open not just my mind, but my heart to him too.

Instantly, Jychanumun sees the truth of me. No part of me is consumed by Arrunn's will.

Beloved, I tell him. *Let go of yourself. . . Come to me.*

Jychanumun relinquishes all that remains of him. His essence flows through his hand, through my arm, flooding my entirety. His form above me is now empty of his life. His life, his essence, now surges through me.

I can feel Jychanumun's thoughts. We think as one.

Now joined as one, I feel my wings, our wings, expand. We are shadow edged in light, light edged in shadow, colours of my colours, colours of the kutu through Arrunn's discarded awareness.

With the internal collisions of so many repelling and opposing forces, not just of mind, not just of emotion, but of essence too, our opposites grow in strength, increasing two-fold, and then ten-fold, one-hundred fold.

Life and death; these things are in my hands. Balanced. Tick. Tick. Tick.

A moment. To us, that moment stretches almost to infinity.

Together as one, our wings expand through the barrier, and greater still: through the battle. Shadow and light. Pure black and pure white. All colours. We spread our wings wider. Wider still. We stand over everything.

I breathe in the shadow. I breathe in the light. We breathe in the shadow and light. Stronger. Stronger still.

And we let that shadow and light blaze down upon all life. It touches them all. Nigh are touched by light. Shaa are touched by shadow. Humans and souls bathe in the enhanced awareness of both.

The Nigh-kutu know light. The Shaa-kutu know shadow.

And then we let out a cry; a cry from the heart and the mind and the soul. Colours of every colour blend with the shadow and light flowing from our mouths. They fill everything, flowing through the kutu – all the kutu. The sound is the sound of many things, wrapped in choral notes: many voices, one voice, singing the song of the Old One, singing the song of the kutu warriors, singing the song of souls, singing that song in the language of intent, directing that intent towards all kutu.

As we rain down shadow and light in this sound of intent, touching all life, I see the presence of more beings. Great creatures made of light, their double wings outstretched, carrying injured Shaa in their arms, walk forward. They stand, absorbing, bathing in the knowledge.

Though our breath has gone, the sound keeps resonating from

our lips. For this is our intention, and it will not stop until all life is touched.

Those songs of intent will be felt by all.

Weapons fade.

Shields fall.

Battles pause as awareness grows.

We stop.

Stop.

All is touched.

We hover above all, our wings outstretched. Jychanumun and I are as one, perfectly balanced. Below us all kutu, all life.

All kutu are poised, stopped in battle because they have heard, they have seen, they have felt, and they have become aware. Their stopping is not forced; it is their choice.

At last, after millennia, the kutu are connected once again. They are independent yet joined. Shadow is tinged with light and light is tinged with shadow. They feel intent. They see intent.

There is no true battle here.

"Orion, my friend, our friend." Our lips release more choral notes. "You are the one red kutu, the kutu who can embrace imaginations with possibilities and hope. Sing your song of awakening and let all feel their possibilities."

And sing Orion does.

With blood dripping from his face and his wings in tatters, Orion lifts his face and begins to sing.

It is more melodic than any bird, more rhythmic than my father's crop cutting, and full of the strangest, most wonderful sounds, enchanting and merging together to form something beautiful. It is the song of awakening, sung to all kutu. It is a song that they cannot help but hear.

And the Old One hears, yet he is not disturbed, for this is my choice to hear, and he can choose whether to listen through me or not.

Jychanumun and I separate our energies. The strength of our bond has healed and restored him and he is aglow with pure power.

We stand side by side, listening together.

All around is silence, bar the beauty of Orion's song.

This has been the time.

There is no immortal divide.

The war for life is won.

FORTY-EIGHT
The Choice

Tick. Tick. Tick.
    We all have choice.

Glossary

A

Ada – Human female. Slave at the Nigh-kutu camp.
Adan – Surname of a human family from Hollow.
Alean – Human male. One of the first councilors in Hollow.
Alnsehahn – Nigh-kutu. One of the monks of Ilstahrn. Grey energy.
Amaddon – Nigh-kutu. Forecaster for Arrunn.
Anumi – The warrior/defender trained section of the Shaa-kutu. Recognizable by golden armor.
Arrunn – Nigh-kutu. Leader of the Nigh-kutu Warrior clan.
Ah-rru-unn – Pronounced *Ach-ruu-unn*. Nigh-kutu. Original name of Arrunn when a monk of Ilstahrn.
Assendia – Home planet to the Walker clan of the Nigh-kutu.
Axiona – A stone planet. Original home to the Nigh-kutu Weaver clan.

B

Baala – Human female. Friend of Viir.
Belee – An ancient type of tree found on Earth.
Ben – Human male. Mate of Runs-with-sun.
Bios – A unit made by the Shaa-kutu to harvest energy.
Book of Fate – Prophetic book written by Jychanumun.
Brave – Shaa-kutu. Anumi warrior.
Brennal – Human male from Hollow. Friend of Shaul.
Brune – Half human, half Nigh-kutu. Biological son of Doe. Adopted son of Coran. Sandy-brown energy.

C

Cathunali – The Nigh-kutu word for broken beyond repair.
Charrsah – The Nigh-kutu word for infinity.

Chia – Shaa-kutu. Sensor and trailblazer. Friend to Orion. Violet energy.
Caniper – A long, brown, bitter vegetable cultivated on Earth.
Coran – Human female. Mother to Viir.
Corvidae – Ancient breed of large black bird found on Earth.
Cranun – Nigh-kutu. Leader of the Walker clan. Friend of Jychanumun.
Crystal – The kutu's commonly used storage medium.

D

Dana – Human female. Resides in an in-betweener hut.
Dannel – Human male. Mate of Ellen. Father of Tachra.
Deimom – Nigh-kutu. High-warrior to Arrunn.
Dhasmiel – Name for the Nigh-kutu prophecy of a lone red kutu.
Dih – Human female. Sister of Tachra.
Dimaru – Planet in the realm of shadow.
Doe – Human female. Mother of Brune. Sister of Doro.
Doro – Human male. Brother to Doe.
Dragun – Nigh-kutu. Weaver clan. Light-brown energy. Friend to Tachra.
Dral – Human male. One of the original councilors in Hollow.

E

Eden1 – Planet. Home-world to the Shaa-kutu.
Eden3 – Planet. Abandoned bio project by the Shaa-kutu.
Eifassi – A plant that the Shaa-kutu harvest Roa from.
Eliahn – Nigh-kutu. One of the original Walker clan. Killed by Arrunn. Grey and Brown energy.
Ellen – Human female. Mate of Dannel. Mother of Tachra.
Elysium – Tachra's valley. Subsequently also the name given to the place for dead souls.
Erek – Human male. A surviving prisoner of the Nigh-kutu.

Eskah – An exclamation term used by the kutu. Also a Shaa-kutu mythical being.

F

Factor X – The original name given to the unknown energy on Earth by the Shaa-kutu.

Findal – Human male. From Hollow. A teacher.

Fluchean – A kutu musical instrument.

G

Gabriel – Shaa-kutu. Pale gold and blue energy. Teacher.

Gale – Human female. Survivor of Nigh-kutu. Dies in childbirth.

Gattal – Shaa-kutu. Head of interpretations. Bright-blue energy.

Gatherer (clan) – Clan name for Nigh-kutu who gather and utilize energies.

Gem – Human female. Tachra's oldest sister.

Gera – A tall, evergreen tree found on Earth with a sweet, heady scent.

H

Harrtriel – Kutu beings made of pure light.

Heart-Of-All-Things – Nigh-kutu term to describe where the Old One sleeps.

Hiela – Human female. Niece to Tachra. Daughter of Dih.

Himsfields – A small desert-village near Hollow.

Herun – Nigh-kutu. Gatherer clan. Orange energy.

Hollow – Desert town. Place where Tachra meets Soul. First temple city.

Horsewind – Human male warrior. Dragun joins with him and fights alongside him.

Huru – Human male. First self-declared ruler of Hollow.

Hytach – Shaa-kutu. Councilor.

I

Iastha – The Shaa-kutu given title to Tachra. Means 'I am three'.
Ila – Human female. Tachra's favorite niece. Daughter of Marl.
Immorah – Planet. Nigh-kutu home-world for the Warrior clan.
In-betweener hut – Dwellings built between towns for travellers.
Iris – Human female. Soul and Wirrel's daughter. First born of love. Friend to Tachra.
Ish – Kutu word for the love bond of friendship.

J

Jamusk – A rich, aromatic scent enjoyed by the Shaa-kutu.
Jan – Human male. Younger brother of Jin. Friend of Tachra.
Jenev – Human female. Survivor of the Nigh-kutu slave camp.
Jeshuahn – Nigh-kutu. A monk of Ilstahrn. Grey and cream energy.
Jin – Human male. Older brother of Jan. Friend of Tachra.
Jychanumun – Pronounced *Jii-kan-nuu-mun*. Nigh-kutu. Pure black and white energy. The Death-path-walker.
Judia – Human male. Mate of Little-smile.
Junir – A wheat-like crop cultivated on Earth.

K

Kathi – A ground shrub with sweet red berries. A favorite of Tachra.
Kathani – A long kutu blade charged by the owner's energy.
King – Human male. Ruler of Nehol.
Kiyala – A kutu drink, both fizzy and creamy.
Kraniel – Shaa-kutu. Researcher and scientist. One of Orion's original team. Green energy.
Kutu – The race of beings derived from the fragmentation of the penultimate universal consciousness.

L

Leil – Human female. From Hollow. One of the first priestesses.

Lewey – Hardy, vine-like foliage that grows in forests.

Lia – Kutu word for love of the mind.

Life-crystal – Engineered crystals to contain the unlived life energy of another.

Light – A form of pure energy.

Lightcatcher – Human male. Mardoch joins with him and fights alongside him.

Linsi – Human female. A surviving prisoner of the Nigh-kutu.

Little-smile – Human female. Daughter of Runs-with-sun and Ben.

Longplain – Neighboring village to Threetops.

Longsdale – Offshoot village of Longplain.

Lyn – Half human, half Nigh-kutu. Son of Pallyn. Twin brother of Pall. No freckles. Grey and silver energy.

M

Mags – Human female. Mother of Ren.

Mah – Female wildcat. Sister of Meah.

Mane – Human woman. Formerly known as Tooth.

Mardoch – Nigh-kutu. Walker clan. Clan-brother to Jychanumun.

Marl – Human male. Tachra's favourite brother.

Materializer – A kutu device that transforms energy into substance and visa versa.

Mazium – A hard, transparent substance that emits its own force field.

Meadsins – Earth village. Birthplace of Ren.

Meah – Female wild cat. Bonded to Tachra.

Mele – Human female. From Threetops.

Memorite – A rare stone which holds memory, used by the Shaa-kutu.

Monks of Ilstahrn – Jychanumun and Arrunn's original clan.

Mosa – Human male. From Hollow.

Motion Dagger – Small kutu knives triggered by motion.

N

Nehol – Sister town of Hollow.

Nanos – Microscopic machines made by the Shaa-kutu.

Nar – A ferocious beast that Nigh-kutu of the Gatherer clan can transform into.

Nigh – Of the shadow.

Nigh-kutu – Kutu who use shadow energy as their foundation energy.

Nirrious – Shaa-kutu. Friend of Chia and Orion.

O

Ochrah – A staple food substance of the Shaa-kutu.

Old One – Commonly used name, on ancient Earth, for the last universal consciousness.

Orion – Shaa-kutu. Composer. Overseer of the original Earth mission. The only kutu with red energy.

P

Pall – Half human, half Nigh-kutu. Son of Pallyn. Twin brother of Lyn. Freckles. Grey and silver energy.

Pallyn – Human female. Originally from Meadsins. Survivor of the Nigh-kutu. Mother to Pall and Lyn.

Peniva – Shaa-kutu. Head of the Anumi warriors.

Pers – Human male. One of the original councilors of Hollow.

Pod – The smallest of the kutu flying crafts.

Psia – A living microscopic entity which can mend the broken. Used for healing.

Punni berries – Ancestor of the redcurrant.

Q

Quakemakers – A Nigh-kutu weapon that produces explosive energy bursts.

R

Ragbeast – Nigh-kutu slang for bios that stray and become independently sustaining.

Rapereals – Kutu word for the large desert hunting bird.

Ren – Human male. Son of Mags. Friend of Tachra.

Retuning disc – A Shaa-kutu device to aid their transformation from energy to matter and visa versa.

Rew – Human male. Orcharder from Threetops.

Rian – Human female. From Hollow. Later becomes mate to Huru.

Ros – Kutu word for the passion of love between humans.

Runi – A tall tree found on Earth with glue-like sap and tough bark.

Runs-with-sun – Human female. Mate of Ben.

S

Sail – Human male. Mate of Mane. Inventor of a type of sturdy raft.

Seeta – Human female. From Himsfields, near Meadsins.

Sensitive – A Shaa-kutu who can detect energy without enhancers.

Septa-sol-shirana – Kutu. A double winged kutu made entirely of light.

Shaa – Of the light.

Shaa-kutu – Kutu who use light energy as their foundation. Creators of humans.

Shadow – A form of pure energy.

Shadow giver – Nigh-kutu weapon.

Shaul – Human male. From Hollow. Sprinter. Son of Trell.

Shemya – Nigh-kutu. Formerly of the Gatherer clan and then Warrior-first to Arrunn. Orange energy.

Shilimar – A type of tree, ancestor of the oak variety.

Shursa – Shaa-kutu. Councilor to Una. Yellow energy.

Sonar rod – Shaa-kutu weapon.

Sonic reactor – Microscopic Nigh-kutu device, implanted in the throat to make the voice a weapon.

Sonic-shaft – Shaa-kutu weapon that gathers and expels energy through sound.
Soul – Human female. Mother to Iris. Friend of Tachra.
Stanze – Shaa-kutu. Anumi warrior. Golden energy.
Spicket doe – A timid creature. Also Nigh-kutu slang word for a coward.
Supreme – The title of the nominated leader of the Shaa-kutu.

T

Tachra – Human female. Daughter of Dannel and Ellen. Linked to the Old One.
Tarrian – Shaa-kutu. Anumi warrior.
Threetops – Tachra's birth village.
Temple of Learning – A building on Earth, constructed by the Shaa-kutu so that humans and kutu could teach and learn.
Tiahn – Nigh-kutu. Grey and brown energy. A monk of Ilstahrn.
Tooth – Human female. Later known as Mane.
Trailblazer – A Shaa-kutu who seeks new resources that can be harvested.
Trell – Human male. From Hollow. Father to Shaul.
True vision – An inner sight that sees more than physical matter.
Tumultus – The Shaa-kutu word for complete and ultimate war.

U

Uana – A conductive gold metal found on the planet Uan.
Una – Shaa-kutu. White energy. Voted Supreme.
Una-sol-shirana – Una's original name in full.
Urdan – Human family name, formerly from Hollow.
Urtia – Human female. Resides in in-betweener hut.

V

Valiant – Meah's male wildcat cub.

Vapour dagger – Kutu weapon; a small, sharp hand-blade.

Viir – Half human, half Nigh-kutu. Son of Coran. Maker of modern civilization. Green and gold energy.

W

Walker (clan) – Nigh-kutu who can move between realms.

Warrior (clan) – Nigh-kutu who thrive on combat. Last remaining shadow-clan.

Watersedge – Neighboring village to Threetops.

Weaver (clan) – Nigh-kutu who weave both energy and matter.

Whitehill – Neighboring village to Threetops.

Wirrel – Human male. Later the flame-dweller. Soul's lover. Father of Iris.

Woodnose – A small Earth mammal, now extinct, similar to the hedgehog.

X

XLS – A residential Shaa-kutu craft used as a sub-station in Earth's orbit.

Y

Yemmel – Human male. Mate of Dana. Resides in in-betweener hut.

Yem – Human male. Resides in in-betweener hut.

Yew – Human male. Mate of Ada. Killed by the Nigh-kutu.

Z, 0-9

7A – A Shaa-kutu biomechanical ship. Chia's favoured craft.

About the Author

KS Turner

Kate Sarah Turner was born in the suburbs of Norwich in the UK. She trained and worked as a designer and artist in London, and now lives and writes in Somerset. Kate's passions range from music to sculpture, math to art, and science to philosophy. The novels in the *Chronicles of Fate and Choice* series were inspired by a series of dreams.

Time: The Immortal Divide is the third and final book in the *Chronicles of Fate and Choice* trilogy.

To find out more about Kate, her novels, and projects, and to read reviews, visit www.ksturner.net